THE WICK AND THE FLAME

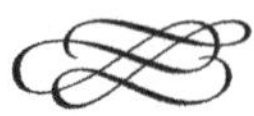

HILARI T. COHEN

Copyright © 2021 by Hilari T. Cohen

All rights reserved.

No part of this book may be reproduced in any form or by any electronic or mechanical means, including information storage and retrieval systems, without written permission from the author, except for the use of brief quotations in a book review.

Cover Art design by Books Covered

ISBN:979-8-985113-0-9

❀ Created with Vellum

For my father, and the promise to never forget; for my friend Danny and the promise to always return...

ne

Paris
August 1942

Albert Levin knew that he shouldn't stop on his way home for a drink of cold water. He didn't need to be reminded of just how dangerous one small mistake might be, or what it might cost him. But he was too hot not to be tempted by the elaborate wrought iron fountain which sat just inside the gates of the *Cimètiere du Père Lachaise* near his house in the 11th arrondissement of Paris. *Just one minute,* he told himself, was all he would need to feel that icy trickle of refreshment run down his throat. The sun was high overhead, scorching the pavement below the worn soles of his shoes, miserably heating his feet, causing him to crave the shade of the tall oak trees lining the winding walkways, the large leaves barely moving in the lackluster breeze that was whispering around the old stones that marked the graves. *I'll be quick,* he thought. *No one will see me.* He moved with care, making his way without a sound through the familiar surroundings, although he had to keep reminding himself that the city he'd called home for his entire eighteen years was no longer the friendly place it once was. Everything had changed.

The world was at war and for the time being, Albert was sure that Paris was at the center of it all. The Nazis had invaded two years earlier, taking control of the government, ransacking the museums, and now rounding up the Jews. It was only a matter of time before they would come for him and his father.

Of that, Albert was dead certain. The hope was that they would escape to the south through Vichy, avoiding arrest, and flee the country on their way to either Palestine or, if they were truly fortunate, Cuba, then America. Albert's father Henri had put a plan in place and each night would review the details with his son. As a merchant, Henri had more than one connection to the black market and the dealings that were made daily for essentials like bread and candles, a rare bit of meat or some eggs. Recently, he'd been bribing a few of the more corrupt Nazi soldiers for information about when they planned to put both Henri and Albert on a train to a work camp. Rumor had it that these camps were terrible places, but since none of their neighbors knew of anyone who had returned from one, the conditions were based on speculation at best.

As he approached the gates, Albert sprinted toward the fountain. No one else dared to be outside in this heat; he was able to make it into the shadows and take a long pull of the cool, metallic tasting water. He drank until he felt that he could not risk one more minute there, in case a few soldiers decided to rest in the shade as well. Splashing some precious chilled handfuls of the liquid down the back of his neck, he felt somewhat revived and ready to make the rest of the journey home. Quickly, he retraced his steps out of the *cimètiere* and walked briskly and with purpose on the Boulevard de Belleville toward the small street where he and his father lived.

Albert's mother had died when he was a young boy. She had suffered a sudden fever and within a few days, she was gone. He hadn't even thought of his mother for a long while, but just a few nights ago, as they sat together eating a sparse meal of bread and cheese, his father said, "It would have been too hard on her, you know. Seeing Paris this way." He shook his head and looked at his son. "Your mama. She loved this city."

Albert didn't know how to respond. He was sure that his mother had been happy living in the place where she, too, had been born. Yet now, he could barely remember the sound of her voice, the smell of her perfume. He had only the one photo of the three of them together in the garden outside their house to jog his memory of her. He couldn't have been more than two years old in the picture, wearing short pants and a stiffly starched shirt. His parents were formally dressed as well. It all seemed like a dream of another time, long past, when his father's leather goods business still flourished. Then they had nice clothing, not the scratchy, coarse cheap wool with its uneven patchwork to cover the holes in the worn material and the yellow star on the front of his jacket. Albert had grown but there was no money for new pants or shoes. He had to contend with old hand-me-downs from neighbors. But what he wore on his back was truly not a concern. The fear that he and his father would be taken at night before they could make their escape was what kept Albert on edge.

He rounded the corner of the boulevard and made his way down the block to the heavy brown wooden doors that marked the entry to the courtyard where they lived. A cluster of small homes sat right behind them, each with a scrap of a garden, separated by cobblestone pathways. When he saw the doors sprawled wide open, his heart slammed in his chest in a hurried, unnatural rhythm. There were soldiers everywhere, and among his neighbors he could make out his own father standing in a line of men. *They are being rounded up! All that money paid to the Nazi guards and still...*

Albert pushed himself up against the warm brick of the grocer's shop across the street behind a display of rotting onions, feeling the sweat pool in the small of his back and drip down to soak the band of his underwear. He knew what he had to do. This was something his father had told him again and again: *The plan is to escape together, of course. But if they take me first, go to Mrs. Moreau at the tabac shop. She has been very helpful with the Resistance. She will have an envelope for you. Take it and go south. I will find you. I will.* His father had told him this repeatedly over the past few weeks as they washed the dishes from their supper. With a glass of weak tea, a precious sugar cube, and an ashtray overflowing with the finished ends of his father's ever-present Gualoises cigarettes at his elbow, their bittersweet, distinctive scent always hovering in the air above their heads, Henri would repeat the instructions to his son over and over again. And Albert's reaction was always the same.

"I can't go without you, *Père*. I will go where you go."

"If it's possible, we will go together. But there are no guarantees. If they take me, run. Do you hear me, Albert? Do not think. Run."

Watching now, as he hid in between the shop's stalls, he saw the soldiers march the inhabitants of his little neighborhood toward a large black truck for transport. Albert tasted fear as it rose in his throat, a sickly combination of bile and the few slices of salty cheese he'd eaten for lunch. His father was pushed by the butt of a rifle into the vehicle and it was all Albert could do not to scream out, to run, to pull his father back out of harm's way. But there was no place safe for them. They were marked as Jews, to be dealt with in whatever manner Hitler dictated. His evil soldiers were there to carry out those orders. Before long the trucks began to move down the block, turning onto the boulevard and out of sight. It took less than five minutes for the men to take his father and his neighbors away, and Albert knew that once the Nazi commander checked his census, they'd realize that he was missing. They'd come looking for him. With every fiber of his being and clinging to the shadows, he forced himself forward toward the tabac shop. He would take whatever Mrs. Moreau had for him and he'd do what he'd been told. But once this war was over, he'd find his father. He swore an oath to himself. Albert took the briefest moment to look skyward, dark gray eyes wide open. He sealed his vow with God. Then he kicked up the gravel beneath his feet and ran as fast as he could.

Tel Aviv
November 1942

SIXTEEN-YEAR-OLD EVELYN ANN STERN sat stiffly on the overfilled and unyielding horsehair sofa, holding a cornflower-blue bone-china teacup. She concentrated for a moment on the tiny floral pattern etched onto it before returning it to its matching saucer. She had one wish in that moment, that she could remove the layers of fabric that rested against the back of her stockinged legs. It was unbearably hot, despite every door and window of the formal living room open to the courtyard and the servant boys fanning them with large palm leaves. Evelyn was overdressed for the weather. She longed to run upstairs and sit naked in a cool bath until nightfall, the only time they ever got any relief from the humid, dank air that surrounded her home at this time of year. But her mother would not hear of it. Despite being thousands of miles away from her beloved England, Sarah Rothchild Stern ran a strict British household. And she was determined to have her sole daughter introduced into society in the only way she knew how: at a debutante ball. As the offspring of a high-ranking government official, Evelyn was expected to follow a standard set long before she had even been born, one that had been in place for generations of women in her family, of privilege, wealth and service to the monarchy. Any thought of appealing to her father for a reprieve from this pomp and circumstance was hopeless, she knew. Aside from being busy with the work of keeping the British government in power on this small piece of disputed land in the Middle East, Evelyn understood that while her father's job was to manage Palestine with the mandates of the powerful hand of Britain, it was her mother who made the rules at home.

"Evelyn. Are you listening?" her mother asked, demanding her daughter's full attention.

"Yes Mother." She refocused her thoughts. "Although I don't understand why you insist on this antiquated farce. We're not in London, after all."

Sarah sighed. "I realize that, dear. We're in this godforsaken desert surrounded by heathens."

Evelyn's teacup clattered loudly as she set it down roughly on the highly polished wood table in front of her. "They are not heathens, Mother," she hissed with an embarrassed glance at the servants standing in every corner of the room awaiting her mother's next instructions. "I'll remind you that they were here way before we ever were!"

"Don't speak to me in that tone, Evelyn! It is unbecoming for women to argue in front of the help."

"That's ridiculous! This is 1942. Things have changed everywhere but here." Evelyn could feel her frustration mount. "For goodness' sake! American women are volunteering for the war effort, working in factories, collecting money for bonds. We should do something important to help people back home in England. Bombs are falling, Mother. People are dying. Can't you do more than plan a silly ball? Why put your efforts into such frivolity?"

Sarah brushed away a speck of lint from her ivory silk skirt before continuing. "Because if we don't preserve our way of life, dear, it will be lost forever. It's a tradition, like lighting candles at Hanukkah or reciting the ten plagues at the Passover Seder."

"Are you truly comparing religious ritual to a damned party?"

Sarah stood then. "Language, Evelyn, please! I am your mother. Watch your tongue."

Evelyn looked up at the ceiling in an attempt to squash her own anger before focusing her gaze on her mother, unclenching the balled-up fist she'd made, and finally saying, "So sorry. It's not my intention to be rude. I just don't see the reason to go through these silly machinations. I mean, please tell me that you don't expect me to marry one of the boys from school. That's who you'd have here. I know them all and don't find a single one of them appealing. What then, is the point of this entire charade?"

Sarah's pale blue eyes narrowed. "Evelyn," she began in a soft, even tone. "Make no mistake. You will marry a proper English gentleman, someone with a pedigree that your father and I approve of."

Evelyn stood up in a rage. "You can't be serious. I will choose a husband when I'm ready, which believe me, I am not. Besides, women don't need to have that decision made for them anymore."

Sarah fixed her gaze on her daughter's lovely face. "The women of this family do," she said firmly. "Now finish your tea. We have fabrics to look over and dress designs to choose."

Her mother's words were clear, her tone full of meaning, but Evelyn didn't care. Matching her mother's icy stare with her own deep blue one, she said, "No, thank you. Choose for me, if you insist. Just be prepared. I will most assuredly disappoint you. Do not plan on my attendance at your *soirée*." She stood, then turned on her heel and began to walk out of the room.

"Have it your way, dear. But know that whatever I pick, you will wear. And whomever we choose for you, you will marry. You will behave like the lady I know you've been raised to be. You may be angry with me, but you will not disappoint your papa."

Evelyn stopped and whirled back around to face her mother, her dark brown hair wet with sweat and clinging to the back of her neck. "We'll see about that!" But for all of her outrage, for all of her resolve, she knew just how difficult it would be for her to act in a way that would displease her beloved father. As she fled the parlor to seek out refuge in her own bedroom and the promise of that cool bath, she knew the truth. In the end she would have to attend her mother's ball, where she would most inevitably dance to her own demise.

New York City
April 1944

Naomi Rabinowitz stood against the railing of the old refurbished battleship watching the skyscrapers, the street traffic, and, finally, the Statue of Liberty disappear from view. As she and her fellow passengers floated farther away from the only home she'd ever known, she felt a slight, momentary pang of regret. She drew in a deep breath and let it all wash over her, knowing that she'd left everything that was familiar behind, acknowledging she had only herself to blame for being here in the first place. No one had forced her to head off into the great unknown that was Palestine, but rather it was her own sense of adventure that propelled her forward. While her family had not stopped her from leaving, she knew that they were worried for her well-being; after all, she was heading to a place fraught with danger, the threat of war with the Arabs an everyday reality since the riots nearly twenty years before. None of it mattered now. She was on her way and she would write it all down, chronicle the journey and whatever it was she'd find once she arrived in the Holy Land.

Only nineteen years old, Naomi had been a journalism major for the last two years at Columbia University before growing restless. *Why just study a topic? Why not jump in with both feet?* As ardent Zionists, her wealthy parents could hardly refuse her request to go to Palestine for a year, to study at Hebrew University in Jerusalem and write about whatever she saw there. They wanted their daughter to be fulfilled, to live a life of worth and meaning, so they booked her passage on the first ship they could find, packing her luggage full of canned goods and the types of things they knew she'd never find there -- a portable radio, a travel clock, an iron. While Naomi understood how difficult it was for them to allow their only child to journey so far from home, she was grateful for their love and support and for letting her go.

She pulled her heavy white wool coat closer around her body, securing her green silk scarf around her neck against the chill of the night air as they chugged along into open waters. Her red curls flew back from her face and she felt the spray of the cold ocean mist on her skin. The first of the night's stars was visible. In the gathering darkness, Naomi thought about all the travelers who'd come before her, all of her ancestors who had looked up at the same sky, and she felt a connection through time to the brave pioneers who ventured out of their safe spaces for unknown destinations, in search of something bigger than they were or could have ever possibly imagined. Were they frightened? Were they seeking something different than what they'd always known, like her, and did they feel as she did, that life was meant to be something more? Somehow, deep down within her, Naomi knew on the most unconscious level that she was not running away from her life in America. She was heading into uncharted territory, to something greater than herself. She knew this with certainty. Taking in one large gulp of salty air, she turned to go below to the bunkroom she was to share with twenty other women. It was her first step toward rewriting her life. And after a full night's sleep she knew that she'd be one day closer to the Promised Land.

It didn't get better, or more interesting as the journey went on. The days were tedious, the meals barely edible. But Naomi kept her resolve. She was heading off on a great adventure; she told herself repeatedly. Then finally, after two long weeks of churning seas, overcrowded quarters, and absolute boredom, Naomi watched as the port of Haifa grew larger now in front of her eyes. It was a warm day, as April had turned to May, cloudless with a welcoming, soft breeze gently lifting the hem of her skirt. She felt a growing sense of anticipation build in the pit of her stomach, extending outward to her fingers and toes. She was almost there and could barely contain the excitement she felt. She had tried to write a letter home earlier, knowing that she would be consumed with the details of getting herself around this strange country and to Jerusalem. She would need to settle into the university there over the next week or so, and she felt she owed her parents news of her safe arrival. She sat down on a rickety deck chair and began to write again, this time painting a picture with words of the frantic activity she observed from her vantage point:

. . .

Dear Mom and Dad,

I have arrived in Palestine, safely, I might add, although the trip was not without peril. We hit a storm crossing the Atlantic Ocean and it was very turbulent for a number of days in a row. I was one of the fortunate few with a strong enough constitution not to have to throw up over the rail of the ship nightly, although I did not have much of an appetite for the very uninteresting menu served on board. A lot of oatmeal and overcooked vegetables, over and over again. My clothing is looser on me now than when you saw me last, but I am just happy to have made it here at all!

I can see the workers on the dock unloading large crates from the ships already moored there. They don't look all that different than the men working at the pier back in New York. Now I can only hope that my language skills hold up–I tried speaking Hebrew to some of the passengers but none seemed to know it at all, so I resorted to both Yiddish and English for the most part. Oh, and occasionally some French that I'm sure I bungled somewhat, but at least I tried. I could hear Madame Balmain in my head the whole time. It was like being back in her classroom at Spence all over again, stuttering badly and making no sense at all, I'm sure!

I promise to write a longer letter as soon as I can. For now, I just want to gather my things and get off of this ship!

Your loving daughter,

Naomi

Naomi put down her fountain pen and the onionskin paper she'd been writing on to look toward the shoreline as they inched closer and closer to land. She could see the men working on the dock clearly as they approached. They were dressed in khaki shorts and neutral toned shirts, almost devoid of any bright colors at all. As she scanned the crowded pier, drinking it all in, her eye caught the figure of a tall, good-looking man who stood out from the rest. He wore dark slacks and carried what looked like a black woolen coat folded on one arm, a stuffed duffle bag slung over his shoulder. He moved gracefully as he climbed up the ramp of a large cargo ship and disappeared into its depths. There was something interesting about him, mysterious and exotic. Although it seemed that he was leaving the country just as she was arriving, Naomi had a preternatural feeling about the stranger. She had no idea who he was, but she had the craziest hunch that it was not the last time she was to see him. At least she hoped it was a premonition, not the musings of her overtired mind. She went below to gather up the rest of her belongings so that she would be ready, as soon as she was given permission, to disembark this ship and walk into her future.

Jerusalem
May 1944

NAOMI LIFTED her head off of the lumpy pillow and squeezed her eyes shut against the strong sunshine filling the room. The day before she had finally made her way from the ship to her dorm room at the Hebrew University in Jerusalem. It had been a hot and dusty trip consisting of two ancient buses grinding their way along dirt roads and a long walk through the mystical *shuk,* its hookah dealers and carpet merchants calling out to her in a variety of Arabic dialects as she walked along the narrow pathways of the ancient marketplace to find her way in this strange country. The vibrant colors of the hundreds of varieties of odd spices, their sharp and pungent fragrances hanging in the air, the dried fruits, piled in high display, the unfamiliar meats roasting on spits, it was all so foreign, so exotic to her. She could only imagine the interesting gifts she could buy here to bring home to her parents at the end of the semester. She could see in her mind's eye her mother's delight at receiving a sack of saffron, or her father wearing a Tallis, hand spun in the Holy Land. There was so much to see, so many experiences to be had. It was all she could do to tear herself away from the sights and sounds of the place to make it on time to check in at her dorm. Luckily, her luggage had been transported here separately on a truck from the dock. There was no way she could have handled the large suitcases on her own.

She now realized that the contents of her bags would be mostly useless here; the colorful patterns of her clothing would stand out way too much in this barren environment. And the white wool coat she'd worn as she left a chilly New York City? Totally useless in this hot and arid climate. *What a shame!,* she mused. *I did like the high fashion sense of the thing.*

When she opened her eyes once more, Naomi watched as dust motes gently drifted through the air and for a moment she wanted to pinch herself to prove that this wasn't a dream, that she was no longer at home in the room where she'd spent her childhood, but instead in the place she had longed to be. The thought propelled her up and out of bed, grabbing her bathrobe and small cosmetic bag with her shampoo, soap, and toothpaste on the way toward the strangely empty communal bathroom down the hall. It was so different here. There were sinks, of course, and toilets, but the shower stalls had no curtains or doors, just a series of faucets that offered a weak spray of water, mostly cold. It was primitive at best, but Naomi felt it just added to her sense of adventure.

She quickly learned that a short shower was the way to go,

shivering a bit as she stepped outside of the range of the icy water's reach while she soaped up her body and washed her hair, rinsing off as quickly as she could. As much as she realized that in a climate this hot she should appreciate the refreshing temperature of the shower, it was still a shock first thing in the morning. She made a note to herself to consider nighttime bathing instead.

Hair still wet, Naomi returned to her room to dress. She found the plainest brown skirt and coordinating taupe short sleeve cotton shirt from her still unpacked suitcase and threw on her clothing, running a brush through her dripping red curls. No sense in taking the time to dry her hair; the gathering heat outside her window would quickly do that for her. With a quick look in the mirror, which hung over the ancient wooden dresser in her bedroom, she swiped a slash of dark color over her lips and slipped the tube into her purse. Squaring her shoulders, she went off in search of breakfast. It didn't take long to find the small cafeteria in the basement of the building and Naomi made her way toward the chatter she heard from the other students already there.

Grabbing a tray on her way into the room, she looked at the choice of breakfast the school offered. Chopped cucumbers, sliced onions and tomatoes, some hard-boiled eggs, a rather lumpy looking yogurt, and cut-up pieces of some sort of green-fleshed melon were available, set in dishes on a long table. She quickly realized that there would be no bacon. Unlike her home in the United States, this kitchen was kosher. She grabbed an egg and some fruit along with a breadlike product that was round and unfamiliar. There was no brewed coffee, either, just some instant dried crystals or bags of tea. *This will definitely take some getting used to,* she thought to herself.

Meal in hand, Naomi made her way over to where some of

the other students were sitting, found an opening and asked the assembled group, "May I join you?"

A good-looking man smiled up at her. "Of course, please," he said, sliding over to offer her more room to maneuver her way onto the bench seat. "Where are you from?" he asked in a flat and clearly American accent.

"New York. And you?" She put her tray down on the worn table and sat.

"Cincinnati." He motioned to the assembled group with him. "We all are. Here on an exchange program with our university, looking to study archaeology on an actual dig. We have a number of sites set up. What's your area of interest?"

"I'm a journalist. Well, I'm studying journalism. But I plan on chronicling this whole trip, you know, writing about it."

"You hear that, boys? Be careful what you say. She's writing it all down," the man teased before extending his hand. "I'm Simon. Welcome."

"I'm Naomi. You're all Americans, too?"

"We are," one of the women chimed in. "But there are people here from all over. Last night I met a guy from Russia!"

"Are you sure, Sarah? You were two sheets to the wind, or do I need to remind you?" Simon added.

"No. I've got the headache to prove it. But he said he was from Russia. I'm pretty sure of that." She looked at Naomi's wet hair. "Please tell me that you didn't shower this morning. The water must have been freezing cold."

Just then Naomi glanced over to see that the other woman had a cup of tea in front of her, no food. She was nursing a hangover for sure. "It was. I'm guessing there's no hot water heater installed in this building."

"There is," Sarah answered, barely lifting her head. "But the government forbids heating water between 10 am and 6 pm because fuel is so scarce. That's why we all shower at night. We use what's in the tank in the evening and nothing's left by morning."

"Thanks," Naomi said sheepishly, feeling somewhat foolish in the moment.

"Do you know your way to the university?" Simon asked, seeming to sense her unease. "We're all walking over to orientation after breakfast. Feel free to join us."

"Thank you," she said, peeling the shell off of her hard-boiled egg. "I'll take you up on that. The last thing I need to do this morning is get lost and miss the program. Everything is so different here. I can certainly use the help!"

For the next twenty minutes, Naomi observed as the group ate and kidded with one another. They were clearly old friends who had chosen to make this trip together. She wondered if they thought her odd for coming on her own, but it really didn't matter. Before she knew it, they were all clearing their trays and stacking them up on one of the tables closest to the kitchen. In the next moment, they were outside in the heat of the day.

As they made their way through the streets of Jerusalem, dust rising up around them from the pounding of their shoes as they walked toward the university, she could see the Mount of Olives in the distance to the east. *It is stunning, really, to think about the antiquity of this place,* she thought to herself. *King David walked here. So did Jesus, for that matter, and so many other leaders of various religions.* It was daunting to think about the history, especially having come from her own country, which was less than two hundred years old.

"You're quiet," Simon remarked, keeping in step with her. "Or are you just making mental notes for your journal?"

"Hmm, no. I am just so taken with the image of all the thousands of people who lived here before us. Everything here is so, so…"

"Old?" he remarked with a laugh. "I know. That's the idea behind archaeology. Digging up the layers of the civilizations, the people who were here before us, finding out how they lived, how they fought for this land, how they died for this land. I can't wait to get started!"

Naomi nodded her head, drinking in Simon's enthusiasm, feeling her own excitement build as they reached the top of the hill. With the university in sight, they made their way toward the large auditorium where the orientation was to be held.

PRAGUE,
January 1945

THE RAIN WAS FALLING in thick sheets, covering the cobblestones of the city in a slick, icy bath that was sure to cause a maximum of discomfort to anyone who needed to be outside in the nasty winter weather. Feeling older than his twenty-five years, Judah Boulod walked swiftly through the empty streets seeking the warmth of the pub where he was to meet his team leader, Ariel Dahan, who had assembled the group of men they needed to inch closer to wrapping up their mission. They had been all over Eastern Europe over the last eight months, completing a dangerous and important assignment, the arranging and training his comrades with the arms they would need to fight the war against the Arabs. They all knew the coming conflict was inevitable. Ever since the Balfour Declaration in 1917, when the ruling British government announced their support of a Jewish homeland, it was assumed that it wouldn't be a peaceful transition when it happened, whenever that might be.

Judah kept moving, turning up the collar of his black wool coat against the cold rain; he wasn't used to these freezing temperatures. Much more accustomed to the warmth of Palestine, the miserable climate here was just another in growing list of reasons he longed to leave this place and never return. Aside from the overwhelming feelings of homesickness and loneliness, being a stranger in this godforsaken war zone was a different kind of danger than what he was used to. It was palpable and much more immediate. His olive skin and dark hair made him stand out in this city. Most of the Jews had already been transported to camps and not blending into his environment was a huge risk. He didn't need to get picked up in a random raid. Reflexively reaching into the deep pocket of his coat to find his forged identity papers, he felt only the tiniest bit of relief. Judah knew that if questioned by a Nazi officer he could probably get away with his disguise, or at least that was the hope and the reason he was chosen to be in this foreign city at all. His German was impeccable, his accent perfect, having spoken it, as well as Yiddish, with both his Sabra parents and immigrant grandparents since the time he could talk. With Hitler in power, German had become the official language of Prague. Shaking his head to clear the droplets of rain that had run down his face, he pushed his self-doubt away for the moment. Knowing the importance of his mission, he kept moving forward until the dim light from behind the pub's door came into view. Judah had arrived.

Once inside, he immediately spied the ragtag group of men he was there to meet. All mostly disreputable, they were the types to profit off of the misfortune of those caught up in this interminable war. They sat huddled together in one corner nursing their drinks. Shaking the rain off of his coat, he made his way over to them with the resolve to help negotiate a deal and then leave this place, vowing never to return again.

In the kitchen of the pub where he'd found work, Albert watched the heavy clouds drop a hard, freezing rain down into the growing puddles on the street outside of his perch near the back door as he dried dishes, thankful that he had made it this far, still alive, still looking for his father in every dark corner, at every turn. From that moment in Paris when he had picked up the envelope left for him in the tabac shop two and a half years earlier, he'd been on the run. Still not sure how his father had gathered a spare five hundred francs to leave him for his escape, Albert had hidden in forests and fields, empty barns and abandoned buildings, as he made his way through a war-torn Europe, often going days without something to eat or a safe place to steal a few hours of sleep. On the rare occasion when he'd need to bribe his way across a border, he'd find a private spot to peel a few notes from his precious envelope before slipping them into the open palm of an officer, one willing to look the other way for a cash reward. He'd worn his boots through to the sole within the first six months of leaving Paris and had replaced them with an ill-fitting pair he'd taken off of a dead body he'd happened upon as he walked as far away from his home as he could. He struggled to stay alive each and every day, the thought of the promise made by his father to find him propelling Albert forward when he thought he could not take one more step. Despite his struggle, he'd grown from a boy into a man in the intervening years, doing all he could to survive, even if it meant stealing a bit of food here and there or pinching a pair of pants or a threadbare shirt off of a laundry line when the mistress of a farmhouse had her back turned. If it wasn't for the widowed tavern owner who needed someone to haul heavy kegs of beer and wash the evening's dishes, Albert might have fallen into the hands of the Nazis in the waning days of their rule here in this majestic city. But Brigette had been good to him, asked him no questions, and made sure he had a hot meal at the end of the day. It was a brief respite, he knew. Albert's goal remained the same: to be reunited with his father at the end of this horrible war. On that one promise, he never wavered.

With the last dish neatly put in its place, he picked up a tray and went into the main room of the pub, hoping that any stragglers were finished drinking the watery brew that Brigette had to offer and that their empty glasses signaled the end of his work for the day. He was tired and longed to go up to the small garret at the top of the stairs that had been his home for these past months. As he entered the darkly paneled bar, lit only by the fat stubs of candles burned nearly to their ends at this time of night, he saw a small group of men lingering in one corner, cigarette smoke thick, swirling in the air above their heads. He knew better than to disturb them; although they were not dressed as soldiers, Albert didn't want to bring any unnecessary attention to himself. He trusted no one. He was moving as silently as he could, gently lifting discarded plates and overfilled ashtrays into the large black tray he carried, when he distinctly heard one of the men speak. He froze. Yiddish. He hadn't heard that familiar language since leaving home. *Who are these men?* he thought. *And how did they come to find themselves here, in Nazi-occupied Prague?*

Albert moved a bit closer, straining to hear pieces of the hushed conversation. *Ganz. Bulats.* And then, *kegnshtel!* Guns.

Bullets. Resistance! He felt a shiver run up his spine. He needed to know more. He stepped in even closer.

"We have the weapons, gentleman," the largest man said to the others at the table. "But we can't buy the ammunition. We'll need a way to make it for ourselves. We already have the machines for manufacture. That was smuggled piece by piece into Haifa from where we secretly stored it in Beruit. The next step is to gather a trustworthy team to train our soldiers. Will you come with us? Teach us how to make the bullets we need for the war that's coming?"

The men at the table seemed to move as one, heads all nodding in agreement. One spoke. "Of course, Ariel. For a price."

"Good," the first man said quietly, still speaking Yiddish. "You will be well paid, I can promise you that. We'll be leaving in two days. I'll send word with Judah of transport when it's all arranged." He stood, beer in hand, raising the glass to his mouth, finishing the contents in one large gulp before turning to leave.

Albert watched the rest of the men for a moment, trying to decide what to do. If he approached them and spoke in the language they shared, he'd mark himself as a Jew. Nothing could be more dangerous. But he was sure he heard the word Haifa. That must mean that they had some connection to the Holy Land, one of the places that his father told him to go if he had the chance. He hesitated. Then the one he'd heard call himself Judah stood and Albert knew what he must do. He gathered his courage to speak.

"Excuse me, please," he said in Yiddish. "Are you going to Palestine?"

Startled for a moment, Judah looked around, as if to check that there was no one else in the room with them.

"Were you listening in on us, tavern boy?" the man asked with a scowl.

"I'm sorry, but yes. I want to go to Palestine. Is there room for one more?"

"Hardly. And who are you to ask, anyway?"

Albert knew better than to show fear. He said in a rush of words, "My name is Albert Levin. I have been running from the Nazis since my father was rounded up in Paris over two years ago. The owner of this tavern has been kind to me, and I work hard in exchange for my board here, but I put her in danger with each day that I stay. I'm strong, I can do any job you need me to do. Please. Let me come with you."

Judah's expression barely softened. "Anything at all? Don't say that, tavern boy. There are jobs in war that no one wants to do."

"But the war is here, in Europe. If it ends with Hitler in power, my life will be over. I can't hide forever. Let me come with you to escape it, once and for all."

"Who said that there won't be war in Palestine?" Judah asked boldly, alluding to the fact that there would be one, and soon. "You will find all manner of discontent there, possibly even far worse than you'll find here."

"There is a chance, though, that my father has made it there already. I want to see for myself, to find him if there is the smallest possibility that he's searching for me."

Albert watched as awareness dawned on Judah's face and realized that this man must have known of the workcamps run by the Nazis and understood what happened in those horrible places. Judah picked his glass up off the table, paused to drain it, and said, "We're all leaving for Tel Aviv in two days' time. If you come with us, we will put you to work as a soldier. You may face the fight of your life there." He paused and looked directly at Albert. "Many will die. Is that what you want?"

Albert didn't hesitate this time, feeling no fear. Something deep within let him know that there was only one decision he had to make. He steadied himself, standing his ground. "I am already fighting for my life. Every day, so yes. Absolutely."

Judah then looked at the men gathered around the table one by one, securing their approval. He said, "I will send word of where and when to meet us. Take only what fits in your pockets. There is no room for anything more."

Albert felt relief flood through his body. "Thank you kind sir. I won't disappoint you."

"You'd better not, tavern boy. You'd better not."

Two

SEJERA, the lower Galilee
June 1945

EVELYN SHOOK the dirt from her hands and stood, lifting the canteen of water off her belt where it had sat secured by a piece of rope to a loop on her light cotton khaki skirt. The back of her shirt was soaked with sweat. Planting row after row of tomatoes in the hot sun was backbreaking work but she enjoyed every minute of it, knowing that it went a long way toward feeding the members of her adopted community. It had not been easy leaving the more modern comforts of her family home to join this kibbutz, Degania Alef, but it was important work, the very kind of mission she had been yearning to find. Even though Palestine was a small strip of land, being this far north at its tip, miles from Tel Aviv, made her feel like everything she'd ever known was on the other side of the world from the fields where she now toiled, day after day.

It hadn't been an easy transition. For all of her bravado, Evelyn had to admit that she missed her parents very much. It helped that the kibbutz was structured to be like a family; each person had set responsibilities, a job to do, and a role in the success of the collective. Meals were prepared by members on a rotating basis and shared in the dining hall, laundry was done together and distributed by size, not ownership and shelter was not anything like her room in her father's house. It was enough to have a bed to rest on after a long day's work and a roof overhead to shield against the rainy season. This particular kibbutz was the very first one ever established in Palestine at the turn of the century. It had grown quite a bit since that time, with more buildings going up as the population increased. Most recently, a large influx of young people began to arrive at the gates, many displaced by the ugliness of the war in Europe, members of the growing diaspora trickled into Palestine's borders. Even with the British clamping down on immigration, the most determined made it through. One day a week she worked in the Ulpan on the kibbutz, teaching both English and Hebrew to the new immigrants. There were random attacks against the kibbutz now and again from the Arabs who felt that the land had been rightfully theirs and unlawfully taken, but for the most part the members of Evelyn's adopted community lived a peaceful farmer's existence. Her skin had long since taken on a bronze tone from the sun, her wavy dark brown hair shimmered with auburn highlights that matched the ice blue specks of her eyes, and her body had developed muscles that she didn't know she had under the layers of the flouncy skirts she had once worn. Evelyn was strong now, in body and mind, with the life purpose she'd been searching for firmly set in every fiber of her being. She was a part of something larger than herself, bigger than anything that might have been possible in her former life. It was the triviality of what her parents had envisioned for her future that had cemented her resolve to change her own destiny.

As she walked down the hill toward the others for her lunch break, she reminded herself of the deep determination that she felt embedded within her soul. She was here to make a difference. On the night of her debutante ball, which as her mother predicted, she did attend, she set her mind on change. As the spaces on her dance card rapidly filled and the candy-colored dresses of her peers swirled round the ballroom of her ornate home in an odd sort of uniformity, she knew that she wasn't meant for this kind of life. She had a bigger role to play; she just had to go out and find it. Evelyn felt like a stranger that night as the partygoers sipped champagne, flirted with one another, and gossiped about nothing more important than their own social status and the current lack of new fashion coming from a war-torn Paris. They were an elite bunch: monied, powerful, with lineages that traced a path from where they stood now all the way back to the ancestral royal family of their beloved England. She knew her place there and what was expected of her--an arranged marriage to someone whose pedigree matched her own and to be the head of a household filled with servants and a calendar brimming with social engagements and parties. Eventually, she'd be expected to produce an heir or two, only to have her own children repeat the pattern once they came of age. As the music played and she was led from the arms of one suitable bachelor into another's, she knew she had to go. She had to leave this place, this gilded cage, and not look back. So she did.

Just over two and a half years prior, on that starless night a mere few hours after the ball ended but before dawn began to spread across the horizon, she stuffed the barest of necessities–one change of clothing, some soap, a toothbrush, plus a small, framed picture of her family--into a pillowcase. She tied the ends in a knot and dressed for travel: cotton pants, sturdy shoes, and a light sweater over a short-sleeved blouse, then she wrote a brief note to her parents, apologizing for leaving but going nonetheless. Evelyn knew how upset they would be but there was not much she could do about that. With a steely determination, she crept out of the stillness, careful not to wake any of the servants sleeping in their quarters as she slipped beyond the gates of their property. As she began to walk she felt her courage build, pushing her forward step after step until she reached the bus station. As the sun made its first appearance in the distance, Evelyn found a seat and settled in for the long ride north.

"Evie!" she heard someone call out to her, snapping her back into her day as she made her way toward the dining hall. "Evie, over here!" She was getting used to her new informal nickname. She could only imagine what her mother would have to say about it. When she looked up, Evie saw her friend Yossi, who was motioning for her to come join him and a few strangers. *Maybe they are new members of the kibbutz,* she thought to herself, wondering where they would be put to work.

"*Shalom,*" she said, reaching the assembled group.

"This is who I was telling you about," Yossi said to the men in an excited tone. "She can do anything!"

Evie looked at Yossi. "I don't know about that!" she exclaimed. "What needs to be done?"

One of the men put up a hand to shield his eyes from the bright sunlight. Evie couldn't help but notice that he seemed uncomfortable and overdressed for the occasion in wool slacks and a long-sleeved shirt. "Maybe we could go inside and talk?" the stranger asked.

"Of course," she replied, opening the door for the others and ushering them into the dimly lit space, taking a moment to allow their eyes to adjust. Then she walked them over to the communal table filled with fresh vegetables, platters of the ever-present hummus and tahina, and bowls filled with cut-up slices of juicy oranges, all home grown on the kibbutz. "Grab something to eat. We'll be right back." She pulled Yossi with her.

"Who are those men?" she asked him in a voice barely above

a whisper. She walked over to a sink to wash her hands, Yossi trailing behind.

"They came looking for some volunteers to start a new kibbutz in Rehovot. It's a big mystery. I don't have the details. But they asked for people who could work in strict confidence, who could do any job. I'm going and I thought of you." Yossi blushed, making it clear to Evie that aside from admiring her work, he had developed a quiet affection for her as well.

"I appreciate that, Yossi, I do. But I'm happy here. And I think Rehovot is a little too close to Tel Aviv for my liking." If Evie knew one thing, it was that she did not want to go back home again.

"Let's just listen to what they have to say. We could do some real good there, you never know. We need more kibbutzim in this country, right? Maybe our path is to forge a new one."

Evie sighed. She watched as the earnest look in her friend's eyes turned into something more, and it made her uneasy. She wasn't looking for that sort of connection; she didn't want to be part of a couple, attached to a man. She was still happiest being her own person, making her own rules without the worry of being linked to someone else. But, she knew she owed it to her countrymen to listen to what these visitors had to say.

"Okay, Yossi, but no promises. There's important work to be done here as well."

He smiled and took her hand, bringing her back over to the table where the new arrivals sat.

"How can I help you, gentlemen?" Evie asked brightly, accepting a scalding hot mug of tea from one of the others at the table.

One of the men hugged his own drink with both hands and said, "We're looking for a few brave volunteers to help us with a special mission. It is of the utmost importance that what we are about to discuss with you stays within this group." He looked at Evie and then nodded at Yossi. "Secrecy is paramount. This involves a certain amount of trust, I know. But I've been assured that you can be counted on." He then turned his gaze directly to Evie. "I hear that you're extremely resourceful. Is that so?"

"I guess that depends on what needs to be done. I'm pretty good at growing vegetables."

He kept his eyes on Evie as he pulled a cigarette out of a package in his shirt pocket, lit it and said, "This would be a completely different type of assignment. It involves what's coming next for this country."

"What exactly is that?"

"A war."

Evie sat back in her chair and asked, "with the Arabs?"

"With the British," the man solemnly replied.

"You do realize who I am?" she asked. "Who my father is? That he is a high-ranking British official?"

"Of course. That's why we're here."

Evie steadily looked into the eyes of the men before her, first the one who addressed her directly and then the other more quiet fellow.

"If you're looking for inside information on what the British government has in mind, you've arrived in the wrong place. I left home to come work here. I have little to do with my parents, and certainly no influence over my father at all."

"Yes. But once you hear what we came to ask you for, everything else will become crystal clear."

"Well then," she slowly replied. "Perhaps it would be best if you started at the beginning, with a proper introduction. I don't even know your names."

"My name is Yosef Avidar. I'm the manager of Ta'as. We're from the military."

"I know what Ta'as is, Mr. Avidar," Evie said softly. Her mind raced. Ta'as was charged with arming the underground army that she'd heard rumors about.

The man continued. "And my companion's name is Irwin Blau. He's an expert in the production of bullets." The man named Blau lifted his head and nodded without speaking.

"Ta'as?" Yossi interjected. "Don't you manufacture guns?"

"Yes, we do. But the guns aren't the problem. We can make them and we've acquired more via the underground network of arms dealers in Europe. No. Guns we have. It's the bullets we need."

"I'm not sure what you want from us. We're simple farmers," Evie said, sitting forward in her chair.

"Today you're farmers. If you come with us to Rehovot, we'll teach you how to make bullets. And from there we'll be ready to arm our soldiers for the war."

"What exactly is this war? When will it begin?" Yossi asked with excitement rising in his voice.

"It's the fight for our own independence from foreign oppression. We are a people in need of a sovereign nation, one not controlled by anyone other than ourselves. Throughout history, we've been tossed from country to country. The Jewish people need a home and with that, a free and democratic government. Hitler and his evil army will be the last to come for us if the world knows our strength. And as soon as we have enough ammunition, we will begin the fight. Can we count on you to join the revolution?"

By now Evie's heart was hammering away under her breast, and she could barely breathe. A free and democratic government? No more foreign oppression? Wasn't that the reason she left her parents' comfortable home in the first place? All the doubts she might have once had about running away, or a fleeting thought that she was betraying her family by making a move against the British government, quickly dissipated into the steam rising from her teacup. She cleared her throat in an effort to find her voice. "When do we get to work?" was all she asked.

hree

Haifa
November 1945

ALBERT BIT DEEPLY into the crunchy fried chickpea mixture. It was formed into a donutlike shape in the center of the fresh salad nestled deep inside the pocket bread that Judah told him was called a pita. He really didn't care what the name of this sandwich was, and his Hebrew, while improving, left some words still untranslatable in his mind. All Albert cared about was that his lunch was both filling and delicious.

As he chewed, Albert watched as Judah put a heavy teaspoon's worth of zhug onto his own sandwich. Despite the heat of the day, Judah still preferred his food to be as spicy as possible, and the Yemenite-born hot sauce was as fiery as the sun overhead. Albert had tried it once and still hadn't forgotten the burning he'd felt from the tip of his tongue to the base of his esophagus. He never found the need to use it again.

They had taken a short break from unloading the last of the cargo from the freighter tied up at the dock. After lunch they planned to inventory their bounty. From that fateful night at the tavern the January before until this very moment, Albert had been by Judah's side, aiding the cause, making sure that when the great war of independence came, the Jewish people of Palestine would be ready to fight. He'd proved himself a valuable student, growing stronger of mind and body, broad throughout his shoulders, skin bronzed from the sun as he helped move heavy crates of smuggled goods off a variety of ships that had made the long journey across the sea to this small country. It was dangerous work, especially since the British had officers patrolling the area constantly. They lived with the knowledge that if caught, they'd be sent to prison, or in Albert's case, somewhere worse--an internment camp in Cyprus. Having immigrated to Palestine illegally, Albert risked being transferred out of the country, so he was very careful. He didn't speak when there were British policemen around, keeping his head down, the same way he did as he fled the Nazis in Europe, ducking behind a tall stack of crates on the pier, or hiding in the shadows of one of the big ships tied up and anchored to the dock. He let Judah do all the talking if they were approached when together and he'd been lucky. He remained invisible. No one had questioned him or asked to see his papers. He planned on keeping it that way.

Albert liked being in this bustling port city. Each day he'd scan the faces of the lucky few immigrants who had made it across the sea from Europe. Thin, with bodies ravaged by both famine and fight, these refugees had a clear sense of why they were here, of what needed to happen. He longed to see his father walking down a gangplank toward him, but that only occurred in his dreams. He wanted to believe that his father had escaped from the Nazi truck on that horrible afternoon in Paris, that he'd been hiding somewhere and that now he was making his way to Palestine, as Albert had done. Just as they'd planned. He imagined his father searching tirelessly until they were reunited, until they found each other once again. He took the last bite of his sandwich and wiped his greasy hands on his already dirty pants leg. Then he lifted the canteen off of his belt loop and drank a large mouthful of the warm, tin-flavored water. Fortified, he was ready to go back to work.

"What should we do next?" he asked Judah, who had finished his own sandwich and had lit a cigarette, filling the air around them with an acrid smell.

Judah took a long drag and pulled a stray piece tobacco off of his tongue with his thumb and index finger before answering. "We'll inventory the goods we unpacked tonight once it's dark and send a message to headquarters. I think we've got just about everything we are supposed to have now. It's probably time to move on to join the others in Rehovot."

Albert sat up straight. "Leave Haifa?" He felt a momentary panic at the thought of missing the chance to see his father finally disembark from a ship.

"Yes. We need to start assembling all of the parts of these guns we've smuggled into the country. I've almost completed the transport arrangements and then we'll have to be ready to supervise their safe arrival."

"What's in Rehovot?"

Judah looked around before answering. "I don't want to talk about it now. It's not safe. Be back here tonight to complete the inventory. I have to go meet someone to finalize our arrangements. Be sure to return at dark and then be ready to leave here in the morning."

"But what--"

"Don't ask me questions, Albert," Judah admonished. "You were warned back in Prague. If you're here to be a part of the cause, then do just that. We leave at sunrise." He flicked the butt end of the cigarette into the water and stood, leaving Albert to his own devices for the rest of the day.

. . .

JUDAH WAS TIRED. Not just physically tired, either. He was emotionally spent. For the last two and a half years he'd been traveling back and forth from Palestine to Eastern Europe, buying arms for the cause, preparing for the battle to come. He had volunteered for the grueling assignment when he joined the resistance movement, right after all that had happened with his fiancée, Geula. The only thing he had wanted in that moment was to go somewhere else, somewhere dangerous and far away where he could immerse himself in another world. He really didn't care if he lived through the experience; he was numb, and looking for the kind of peace he knew he'd never have again was futile. That inner stillness would only be found in the arms of the woman he'd so desperately loved, and she had been taken from him with the kind of suddenness that left him in shock, even now when he thought about it. A bomb, lobbed over the border by an Arab who believed that the Jews farming the land had no right to be there. A brilliant blast of explosives that left no time to run, to hide, leaving in its wake a black hole of emptiness that Judah knew would never be filled again.

He reached in his pocket for yet another cigarette. Finding none left, he headed toward the small shop at the end of the pier where he knew he could buy mostly anything. Sundry items were displayed in plain sight; but if you knew what to ask for, a quick murmured conversation with the owner would gain you access to the back room where almost anything could be purchased at black market prices. This was a large port and travelers came from all over the world with a variety of legal and often illegal goods. There were times he had been tempted to try some of the more insidious mind-altering drugs for sale, thinking they might help to dull his pain. Hashish, cocaine, absinthe, or even heroin, it was all available in that back room. But not today. He needed a clear head in the morning; that was absolutely essential.

He walked into the shop, pausing at the counter long enough to buy his favorite brand of cigarettes, tucking the small, square package into the pocket of his shirt. Then he went back outside and found a spot at the café next to the market, sat down, and ordered a Turkish coffee. As Judah waited for his drink to arrive, he tore off the clear cello wrap and lifted out one of the thin, white tobacco-filled cylinders, then watched the bustling activity in front of him. Merchants selling rugs, hookahs, and spices. Beggars, looking for a generous soul to part with a coin. Prostitutes, trying to survive in the only way available to them. He watched as one woman tried to get the attention of a man sitting at a table not too far from his own. It had been a long time since he'd felt the touch of another; he'd been tempted once or twice on a cold night in Prague or Belgium when a perfumed lady would offer herself to him in a bar or from a dark street corner. But he knew that today was not the time to give into those baser desires. There was still too much work to be done.

Just then the waiter returned with his beverage and before Judah could take a sip, Ariel appeared and sat down next to him. It always amazed Judah that a man of his size could move with such ease and grace.

"Good to find you here, my friend," Ariel said. "Are you done working?"

"Almost. Just waiting for nightfall and then I'll finish."

"Ah, yes. Good. Then will you head south to Rehovot?"

"That's the plan. I hear they've already assembled a group to get started?"

"Yes. Mostly displaced youth, but all ready and anxious to go."

"Is the factory up and running?"

"I'm told so. Of course, I expect the worst. There will be kinks in the system. The equipment is old, mostly refurbished. I'm sure there will be problems along the way. My hope is that we can organize quickly and get things moving along."

Judah took a long drag of his cigarette. It burned low against his fingers. He leaned in to speak softly to the other man. "This has to work, Ariel. We need to be rid of the British and finally achieve sovereignty. It's time to stand on our own two feet. Do you see what is coming into this port each day? The refugees? The numbers keep growing."

The other man shook his head. "They need a place to be, Judah. They need a homeland too."

"I realize that, Ari. I'm only afraid that the British will shut the borders. I hear things on the docks. There is talk of turning ships away. Then what? These poor wretches have been through enough."

"True. But the British are not our only problem. There's always the Arabs who have a claim here as well. They hate us. And now there's talk that the underground movement of radical Jews have organized themselves as well. They are looking for a fight."

"The Irgun?"

"Yes, and the Stern gang. They will be trouble, believe me."

Judah just nodded and drained the dregs in his cup. Then, comfortable with the silence between them, the two men sat, each knowing that there were no further words to say. The time had come for action.

. . .

ALBERT KICKED a rock along the dirt path as he walked up the hill toward the boardinghouse where he and Judah had been sharing a room these past months. He had very little to take along with him to Rehovot. A toothbrush, a comb and one change of clothing, somewhat threadbare but still serviceable. It would all fit in the same canvas bag he'd picked up along the way after leaving Prague.

As he turned the corner toward the boardinghouse, he could smell a delicious sweet scent in the air. He hoped that his landlord, Mrs. Lobel, had been busy baking. To his delight, she had. It didn't take long for him to see the round, white honey cakes resting on the sill of the open window. He could feel his mouth begin to water at the thought of having a large slab of that delectable treat. He heard the oversized woman humming to herself while she hung freshly washed laundry on the line outside, just beyond the kitchen.

"*Shalom,* Mrs. Lobel," he shouted, hoping she'd offer him a slice.

She turned toward him. "Albert. Ach. Can you please to help me with these?" She pointed to a pile of clean, wet sheets in the basket at her feet as she rubbed her reddened, arthritic hands together. Even though she had lived in Haifa for over thirty years, having immigrated just before the outbreak of the first world war, she still had a heavy Romanian accent, making it difficult for him on occasion to grasp the meaning of what she said.

He ambled up the rest of the hill toward the large woman, nodding his head, reaching for the wooden clothespins that were piled high in a small bowl on top of the laundry. Together they lifted the sheets one by one, and by each corner attached them to the line, making fast work of their task. As the afternoon sun began its descent, the wind picked up a bit and the large squares of fabric swayed easily and dried quickly. He lifted the now empty basket and put the bowl inside of it, trailing behind Mrs. Lobel, carrying it all into the house for her. Just as he hoped, she motioned for him to sit at the worn wooden kitchen table. She pulled out a bottle of milk from the tiny ice chest and poured him a glass. Then she took one of the cakes from the sill and cut him a large slice, placing both the plate of cake and his drink in front of him. She patted his back and said, "*Ess*."

Albert began to eat, the soft, still-warm cake melting on his tongue. It was pure heaven. As he savored each bite, he wished he could tell the kind lady that he'd enjoyed his time in her home. His bed was comfortable, she washed his clothing for him, and the food that she prepared for both breakfast and dinner was hearty and filling. When she could get her hands on a chicken for Shabbat, Mrs. Lobel would roast the bird to perfection, rounding out the meal with something she called *kugel*, made with onions and potatoes. But he knew better than to tell her anything of their plans, for fear of Judah's wrath. He recognized that it was much safer for the kind woman not to know, so that if she was ever questioned she'd truly have no answers.

He finished his cake, drained the glass of milk, and brought his dishes to the large, dented sink. He smiled at the woman and said, "*Genza dank*, Mrs. Lobel," before turning to go to his room to pack his belongings. A good soldier, he would be ready to leave when Judah told him it was time to go.

Jerusalem

November 1945

LIFE HAD SETTLED into a routine for Naomi. She studied hard during the weekdays and explored different parts of this tough and rugged country over Shabbat. While she was busy with the rigorous curriculum at the university, she still made time to see a lot of her adopted home. There were bustling cities like Tel Aviv, religious centers like Jerusalem, and ancient haunts like Jaffa. With the small crew of friends she'd bonded with over the first semester, they traveled whenever they could, staying at a variety of kibbutzim along the way. Some of these places were primitive, an odd variety of tents with no running water or toilets. Group meetings were held around a campfire. Other farms had actual dining rooms or children's quarters, where the youngest members of each camp slept in neat rows. But all of these places had one mission in mind: to build a modern country from the harsh desert surroundings.

As she made her way toward the dormitory building, she saw Simon standing at the entrance wildly waving to her. She smiled and raised her hand to acknowledge him. As she got closer, he motioned for her to hurry, and she did.

"What's the rush?" she asked, grinning up at him.

"There's a group of people inside that want to meet us. They're from a kibbutz outside of Tel Aviv. I think we're invited there for Shabbat."

"I'm always up for a new experience." Naomi winked at him. "Besides, I love Tel Aviv. It's the closest thing this country has to a real city!"

As she stepped up next to him, Simon opened the door and they both walked through, heading to the dining room. Sarah and the others were already sitting at a table with cups of tea.

"Hey you two," Sarah called out. "Come join us."

They each grabbed a mug and filled it, then went to greet the already assembled group. Naomi couldn't help but notice one of the strangers was a woman who appeared to be about her own age. She looked fit and strong, her skin sun-kissed. She must be a member of the kibbutz Simon had mentioned. There was a man with her as well, his head bent in deep conversation with some of the others at the table.

"Is this everyone?" the visitor asked. Naomi was startled by the distinctly British accent the woman had. She had wrongly assumed that the stranger was a native-born Sabra.

"Yes," Sarah replied. "These are the other two I mentioned to you. We're all here now. What is it you wanted to ask us?"

All eyes turned toward their guests.

"My name is Evie and this is my friend Yossi. We're in need of a few more volunteers to help us with an important project in Rehovot. There's a new kibbutz there, and we're trying to get it off the ground. We need people who can work the fields, in a laundry, and in our bakery. It's right near a train station, walking distance, really. We need the best and the brightest among our countrymen to help with our cause. Any interest?"

"There's a semester of school to finish, and some of us are scheduled to be on an archaeological dig this summer. I don't know if I can commit to something like that," Simon answered. "As intriguing as it sounds," he added earnestly.

Naomi couldn't help but notice that Simon seemed interested in this stranger's good looks even though he and Sarah were clearly a couple and was surprised that he declined her invitation so readily. She, however, wanted to know more.

"I have some flexibility to my schedule," she heard herself say. "What exactly is entailed?"

Evie shifted in her seat to turn her attention to Naomi.

"Come for Shabbat. You'll understand it all better if you see it for yourself."

"I'd like that," Naomi replied.

"Actually, you're all welcome. We'd love to host you, even if you can't commit to stay with us this summer," Evie said to the group with a dazzling smile.

Naomi couldn't help but wonder if whoever was behind this new kibbutz used Evie as a recruiter because of her beauty and charm. She had the entire group hanging on her every word and she'd been there for less than an hour.

"Well, I am free this Shabbat," Simon replied. "Maybe you can convince me if I see exactly what you're talking about."

"Great!" Evie said, standing. "I look forward to hosting you. All of you," she said, smiling broadly at Simon. "For now, I've got to run. There's someone I need to meet while we're here in Jerusalem, and he only has a few minutes for me, so Yossi can fill you in on the details."

Naomi watched the other woman move with a quick, purposeful step and was struck by the thought that out of all the people she'd met on the various kibbutzim she'd visited so far, this was someone she'd like to get to know better.

Evie moved through the streets of Jerusalem with urgency. She had to be sure to meet up with Yossi and make the last bus back to Rehovot. Noting the sun's position in the sky, she knew that there was little time to complete her task before that. She walked swiftly into the market of the old city. Little had changed here over the course of centuries. She was familiar with the place and snaked her way around the colorful stalls until she found the one particular spice dealer she was looking for. She nodded at the old man as she walked through his space, pushed aside a tapestry hanging on the back wall, and stepped past it. In the dim light of the room, the first thing she noticed was the bitter smell of strong Turkish coffee; the aroma was so predominant that it practically overtook her senses, knocking out the array of heavily scented spices just a few feet away. There were two men huddled at a small table, each with a tiny cup in front of them filled with the dark brew.

"I'm here," Evie said once her eyes adjusted to the dimness of the space. "Do you have the envelope for me?" She felt her heart pounding rapidly in her chest. As she moved closer she could smell their unwashed skin and filthy clothing. She tried not to show her fear.

"Why would Ariel send a little girl to do his dirty work?" one of them asked the other. Turning to Evie, he asked, "Is he hiding behind your skirt? Why did he not come himself?"

"Ari is busy with other things. I was available to be here, so I am." She hoped her voice did not sound as shaky as she felt.

"So it's *Ari,* eh?" the second man asked. "You know him well, then, do you?"

She didn't like the lascivious wink he gave her. "We work together, that's all. The envelope?" she asked again, this time with a steady rising anger.

The first man reached into his stained shirt pocket and handed over a small white square. "This is what you need. Unless, of course, you want something more from me? Maybe something Ari isn't giving you?"

Both men burst into the kind of loud guffaws that made Evie's skin crawl. She would do almost anything for her homeland's fight for independence, risk her life if need be. But when it was over, she would make sure that men like this did not treat women in this way. She breathed in deeply and made that promise to herself, then she reached over and pinched one corner of the envelope with her index finger and thumb, careful not to touch the hand that held it for fear of being grabbed instead. The mere thought made her stomach churn uneasily. Once she had it in hand, she turned, walked past the tapestry on the wall, and ran directly to the bus station, all the while hearing the sound of the disgusting men's laughter ringing in her ears.

Four

Rehovot
November 1945

Merely a collection of canvas tents on a dusty piece of land in the distance. That's all it appeared to be to the unschooled eye, but Evie could not have been happier to see the familiar outlines of the kibbutz as the bus approached their destination. She recognized how important it was to travel around this small country to recruit new members and she did so without hesitation, visiting youth camps and universities, looking for volunteers. During the bumpy and dusty ride back on the bus from Jerusalem, all she could think about was the dirty men in the *shuk* and the little white envelope she carried for Ari. She could not imagine what was inside; it didn't even matter. All that she cared about was that Ari trusted her to complete this small mission.

It was important to Evie to prove to the others that she was more than the overindulged rich daughter of a high-ranking British diplomat. She realized early on that this would be her cross to bear unless she stepped up her level of involvement in the cause. For as significant as her original contribution was as a teacher, helping the new immigrants learn both English and Hebrew inside her classroom at Daginia Alef, this new assignment at Rehovot was her chance to make an impact, a real difference in the fight toward independence. She valued the trust that Ari placed on her shoulders with the utmost seriousness. Evie found herself wanting, above all else, to please him. There wasn't anything romantic about their relationship that made it special. What mattered most to her was their bond. He believed in her ability to lead others; she had accepted that responsibility and throughout it all they had become true friends.

The bus groaned and swerved around the last hill toward her adopted home, and Evie stood, shaking the sleeping Yossi awake and grabbing onto the seat in front of her for balance, signaling that she wanted to get off at the next stop. The sky was darkening quickly now, deepening into shades of murky violet and inky blues when finally, the driver slowed the large vehicle and she and Yossi eased themselves out into the encroaching sunset, the two of them making their way silently along the familiar trail alone. They walked past the railroad station, crossing over the tracks with care, then paused for a moment. "You go on ahead," she said to him. "I'll just be a minute."

He didn't argue. It had been a long day for them both and Evie was sure that her traveling companion was headed straight to his cot and sleep. As he disappeared down the path, Evie sent up a silent prayer toward the blackening horizon. If the students she'd met earlier that day from the university in Jerusalem agreed to join them, the team would be finalized and the real work could begin. There were two stone markers at the base of the camp across from the large building that housed the kibbutz's laundry and bakery. The mere sight of these solid structures was as comforting as two arms reaching out to pull her into an embrace. Shaking off her earlier unease from the events of the day, Evie moved forward into the kibbutz and toward her own tent amid the scattered makeshift structures strewn around the expansive fields. Once there, she lifted the flap and stepped inside, quickly undressing. Too tired to walk to the bathhouse to wash up, she dropped her clothes to the floor and slipped in between the sheets of her cot. As she allowed her mind to wander, she thought about the kibbutz. Everything about this place had been planned with the utmost of care, each component with a specific use and meaning. When she had come here for the first time, months before, Ari had explained it all to her.

"We chose this location," he said, "because we need a way to transport the bullets to the front lines when the time comes. Hence, the proximity to the rail station. And the laundry will be noisy. That will cover the sound of the bullet-making machines we've set up underground."

They walked toward the large cement building. It had two sides, each with its own entrance and a flat, tin roof.

"And the bakery? Is that meant to produce an income, or food for the survival of the workers?" she asked.

"All of that will help, of course. But what we really need is something to mask the heat that we'll generate when production of the ammunition is going full tilt. Maybe it's better if I show you," he said. "It's easier to understand if you actually see it."

She had followed him around the two large washing tubs in the laundry where he exposed a secret passageway that housed a narrow staircase.

"Be careful coming down," he remarked, dipping quickly into the dark depths beneath them.

As she concentrated on maintaining her footing on the steps under her feet in the dim light, she couldn't help but wonder how they engineered this entire project under the watchful eye of the British soldiers. But she didn't have much time to think about that feat, because once at the very bottom of the steps, she could not believe what she was seeing. A long and narrow room set up as a factory. There were multiple contraptions there, which made sense only after Ari explained it all to her.

"We bought this old bullet-making equipment in Prague. These sturdy workhorses date back to the first world war." He smiled then, patting one of the tarnished metal machines, as if sharing a secret. "Then we smuggled them in through Egypt in small pieces so as not to raise any attention at the docks in Haifa. They needed major refurbishing, believe me. We brought specialists in to get that work completed over the last few months and now we're just about ready to go. Once we are able to train our own people in the fine art of bullet production, we'll be set."

Evie found herself rendered speechless, taking in the factory and its machinery set out before her. But in the next minute she was filled with questions.

"Ari, how are we going to train everyone? How many bullets can we make? How do you know that they will be powerful enough to work? What if the British soldiers find out? What will happen then?"

Ari tilted his head back in laughter. "Take a breath, Evie, take a breath. We've got everything handled, don't worry. This is our mission now. We're going to take this country and make it ours. It will make some story to tell your children someday, eh?"

Snapping abruptly out of the memory of that conversation, Evie gasped as a chill ran up her spine. Her children? Would she even want to have a son or a daughter of her own someday when the world always seemed be at the boiling point of disaster? It was all too much to think about now. She reached down and lifted her pants off the floor, took the small white envelope out of the pocket, and slipped it beneath her pillow. For now, her mind reeling, she craved the blissful silence of sleep.

THE NEXT DAY, on the road to Rehovot

ALBERT TOOK in his surroundings as he sat backward, bumping along an uneven roadway in the flatbed of an old truck, headed toward his next home. He watched as the port of Haifa got smaller, shrinking into the distant horizon until he could not see it at all. He was jostled side to side on the hard metal floor of the vehicle, a few wooden crates filled with spare gun parts disguised as farm equipment his sole companions. The dust kicked up around the open truck on the dirt road, so much so that he had taken his shirt off and draped it around his head, pulling some of the fabric up over his nose and mouth. He imagined that he resembled some of the young Arab men he'd met, colorful keffiyehs whipping around them with each strong gust of wind.

The sun continued to track across the sky as they made their way south toward Tel Aviv. It was actually pleasant to feel the soft, warm breeze against his skin, his mind beginning to clear from the anxiety he'd felt after departing Mrs. Lobel's house. He didn't want to leave Haifa. He knew that there was always the chance that his father would step off one of the many ships that made its way there daily, but he had no choice. He was bound to Judah now, having promised to do a job in exchange for safe passage to Palestine. *Papa will understand,* Albert told himself. *He would want me to fight for this cause, for our freedom. Our long-awaited reunion will come, and I'll have some story to tell!*

The landscape rushing past him had been filled with olive and orange trees for miles, but now Albert began to notice that there were buildings scattered amid the groves. As they traveled on, it became apparent that they were driving through a modern city where clusters of short, squat nondescript structures abounded, but there were also buildings that reminded him of the more dramatic architectural designs he'd seen in photos of Germany. Here, there were actual sidewalks instead of dirt paths. In the bright sunlight, Albert could see shops and crowds of people carrying bags with their purchases as they rushed through the various activities of their day. He was grateful for the breeze that came from the truck's motion, as the afternoon heat was building and the air in this city felt both hot and heavy with humidity. He was hungry, realizing that he hadn't eaten anything since early that morning. He fished around in his shirt pocket and pulled out the boiled egg and slice of bread that Mrs. Lobel had pressed into his hands as they left her home; he quickly peeled off the shell and ate his snack in a mere two bites. Albert was still famished. Looking longingly at the cafés that lined the wide boulevard in this bustling city, he hoped against hope that Judah would tell the driver to stop for a refreshment. He knew better, though. They had to arrive at the new kibbutz before nightfall. There was work to be done. Albert closed his eyes against the rising heat of the day, and for the first time in months, thought of Paris. It was hard for him to believe that he'd run away from there over three years ago. He attempted to remember the details of the path to his family's home, the scent of lavender that lined the walkway to their front door. But as hard as he tried, he still only smelled the diesel fumes that surrounded the bed of the truck, sputtering black smoke in their wake, taking him even farther away from the place where he had been born, leaving his past a distant memory as he barreled ahead toward his future.

A LITTLE MORE THAN an hour later, the truck slowed as they came to the final curve in the road. Judah looked out from his seat, seeing the welcoming stones that stood in front of the kibbutz where he was to settle in for now. He couldn't think of it as home. After all, that was a place where your beloved lived. Geula was gone. Judah knew deep down that he'd never find his true home again. He flicked the remainder of his cigarette out the open window and banged on the glass that separated him from Albert, slumped over in the flatbed of the truck. They were finally here, in Rehovot.

He heard the younger man shuffling into an upright position and he motioned the driver to stop. He opened his door and stepped out. He had paid the man a good price to bring him and Albert this far, but he didn't really know him and couldn't risk having him see what Judah knew was already there. There were British spies everywhere and he had to be careful. They could walk the rest of the way. Besides, it felt good to stretch his legs after such a long journey.

"Albert!" he called out. "Help me take these crates out of the truck. We'll line them up and come back for them in a bit with some of the others."

Albert did as he was told. It had been a risk, bringing this survivor along with him all this way, but the tavern boy had proved himself a willing and eager companion. He was strong and he was able; Judah found him to be good company as well. He knew that Albert's father had been taken by the Nazis and that he was now alone in the world. He listened as Albert had repeated the story of the day his poor father was taken away, how he had somehow found his way to that tavern in Prague where fate had brought him to Judah. He also knew that Albert truly believed that his father was still alive and that they'd miraculously be reunited, but Judah was a realist. The odds of that happening were slim. But no matter. He wouldn't disabuse the young man of that notion. Not everyone needed to have their hopes and dreams shattered. Instead, he would deliver him to a new family on this kibbutz, one that was growing in number every day, one that was poised on the brink of forging a new nation that would be their own. He would be safe here, or at least as safe as one could be in a country on the verge of war.

They quickly emptied the crates from the bed of the truck underneath the shade of an olive tree, took their personal belongings and waved their driver off. As their ride sped away, into the distance, Judah turned to Albert and said, "Take your things and come with me. Let's see if we can find something to eat." They walked together up the rocky path, stopping at the concrete structure that was separated into two sections. "This side is the bakery," Judah remarked, walking out of the bright sunlight into the large building.

At first it was hard to discern where it was hotter. The oven was on, generating waves of hellish heat, that when combined with the sunshine pouring in from outside, was almost unbearable. But though oppressive, that blazing temperature bore fruit; there were freshly baked pitas in a basket on the counter. Judah smiled.

"Levi!" he shouted out over the noise from the laundry next door. "It's good to see you, my friend!"

"Judah! You're back!" The large man put down the wooden paddle he'd been holding and came around the counter to give Judah a bear hug. "Safe and sound. *Baruch Hashem*!"

"I am, here for now at least. No more traveling for a while. And meet Albert." He motioned to the younger man. "I picked him up along the way."

"Any friend of Judah's is a friend of mine!" Levi exclaimed, extending his beefy hand and embracing Albert with a sweaty hug. "Welcome."

"Where is everyone? We have some crates at the bottom of the hill that need to be put away. And we are famished!"

"Grab some bread for now," Levi said. "It's almost time for supper. We'll get you some help and then you can go wash up and settle in before we eat. Sound good?"

"Of course," Judah said before asking, "Is Ari here yet?"

"Yes," Levi responded, brushing flour off of his hands and then lifting a corner of apron to his brow to wipe away the sweat, which was running down his forehead and nearly dripping into his eye. "He's been in meetings all day. I'm sure he'll fill you in when we gather for our meal."

Judah nodded, grabbed two hot pitas, tossed one to Albert, and said to Levi, "See you in a bit." Then he turned to Albert. "Come with me. Let's get to work."

ALBERT LIFTED his hand to shade his eyes against the sun. He, Judah, and two other men had walked back to the entrance of the kibbutz to retrieve the crates full of spare gun parts and now had brought them back to the cement building next to the railway station. As they walked behind the bakery, Albert saw a large storage structure sitting adjacent to the building and off to one side. Judah went to open it. Behind the massive sacks of flour, there were more crates, similar to the ones they'd brought with them from Haifa, all of them stacked neatly against the wall. They had to remove the heavy burlap bags of baking ingredients before they could add the new contraband to the equipment that was already hidden there. It was hard work on a mostly empty stomach. All Albert seemed to think about was what kind of food would be offered for dinner in this place and when that meal might actually be served.

As they reloaded the last sack of flour, hiding the spare gun parts once more, they closed the door to the storage structure and Judah turned to Albert and said, "We have another hour before we eat. I'm going to take a shower. You might want to do the same." He walked along the path back to the front of the building where they had left their small bags with their possessions.

Albert knew that he had been sweating profusely but hadn't realized that a residue of the flour seeping from the burlap, combined with his efforts, had created a thick film that covered him from head to toe. He lifted his bag onto his shoulder and followed Judah deeper into the kibbutz. There were canvas tents in the center of the camp, all circling a large fire pit. Finally, Judah stopped.

"This is my tent. You can stay with me for now. The council will assign you a permanent spot as soon as they're able to find one for you. There is a shower on the edge of camp. We'll go there now. You can only use it if there are no women bathing. They have the right to privacy, as do you. We generally rotate, one hour at a time."

Albert nodded his head in understanding. He could follow the rules in exchange for a safe place to rest his head and a warm plate of food. Once at the bath house, they found it empty. As it was not the busy time of day for bathing, they were both able to wash the grime from their faces and bodies with the reasonably tepid water. Once dressed in clean clothing,

Albert had to admit that he felt refreshed and ready to face his next challenge.

He didn't have long to wait. Just as he finished picking up his dirty things, a young woman came into the communal dressing room holding a towel and a freshly laundered pile of clothes. She almost dropped what she was holding when she saw them.

"Judah!" she exclaimed. "When did you get here?"

Judah lifted her off the ground and twirled her in the air. "Evie! It's good to see you. We've just arrived. Let me introduce you to Albert. He's come from Paris."

She turned toward him and Albert felt all the breath leave his body. She was tanned from hours in the sun and her nose was sprayed with the tiniest freckles he'd ever seen. Her blue eyes seemed to sparkle as she smiled, and when she stepped toward him with an outstretched hand, he felt himself begin to tremble slightly. She was the most beautiful girl he had ever seen.

"*Shalom*," she began. "I'm Evie."

He found his voice. "You're British? Are you a spy?"

She laughed, placing her hand on his forearm. "No, not quite. I do the occasional bit of espionage, I guess, when Ari needs me for something, but no. I work here, on the kibbutz."

"That's being quite modest, Evie. You do more than simple farming and you know it."

Evie shot Judah an alarmed look. "This is a farm, after all, Judah. You know that."

"Albert is with me, Evie. He has seen the guns. We'll bring him fully up to speed later tonight, at the council meeting. For now, we'll let you bathe. See you later."

Albert watched as the young woman before him turned the

corner toward the shower and out of his line of sight. Then he turned to Judah, who was uncharacteristically smirking at him.

"Don't get any ideas, Albert. That one? She's all business. And besides that, she's like a little sister to me. You'll have to go through me to get to her."

Albert nodded his head, but was already plotting just how he would go about getting to know the enigmatic Evie better.

BACK IN HER TENT, Evie ran a comb through her hair and began to review a mental list of all the work she still had to accomplish this week before Shabbat arrived. Not religious herself, she truly did enjoy the enforced day of rest observed by the members of the group because it gave her a chance to recharge. This Shabbat, she was expecting the group she had met at Hebrew University in Jerusalem to come to the kibbutz. If she could convince them to stay on, to join their cause and to help get things going in the underground factory, then these final members would make her team complete. She had been charged with finding the best and brightest minds she could; these college students had the potential to fit the bill exactly.

She lifted the flap of the tent and was grateful for the breeze that accompanied the approaching sunset. At this time of year, the temperature was generally cool, but they'd been experiencing an unusual hot spell for the last few days. Now Evie sensed a shift in the wind, signaling a cooler night ahead. Her hair had begun to dry into its usual soft waves that lightly touched her collar. She'd left her hair down for a change, instead of pinning it into the familiar bun at the base of her neck. She was excited that Judah was back, and she had to admit to herself that she was intrigued by his companion, the handsome Frenchman that he'd brought along. There were people on this kibbutz from all over Europe, most having escaped the horrible conditions caused by the war there. The majority had come here alone, their families killed at the hand of the Nazis. She shuddered at the thought. It was an unthinkable atrocity, this genocide. And it made their cause here even more important. Jews needed a homeland; in this Evie was firm in her resolve. It was her responsibility to be a part of the revolution, to help make that dream into a reality. She tried to shake herself out of her thoughts as she continued walking toward the dining hall, but the newcomer's face kept flashing to the front of her mind. She abruptly stopped. *No!* she told herself. *No time for girlish romance. No involvements!* It had been her mantra all along, rebuffing admirers, shutting herself off to the flirting and advances of some of the men she had met in her work here. If she was to be taken seriously as a woman, she'd need to keep her focus, work harder than her male counterparts and do her best every day.

But there was something about this stranger, his soulful gray eyes, his broad shoulders, the gentle upturn of his lips. She was drawn to him and for some unknown reason, she wanted to get to know him better, to reach out and take his hand, to feel his touch on her skin. Evie looked at the sky from her position atop the hill where they'd placed the kibbutz and watched the sun as it continued to dip lower on the horizon. The first of the night stars had become visible now. She closed her eyes and made a silent wish. She needed to be strong and could not waiver in her intention to make a difference for her people. With all of her might, she wished for only one thing: not to fall in love.

Five

DINNER THAT NIGHT WAS A LOUD, raucous affair. The whole team was there: Ari, Judah, Levi, Yosef, and Irwin. Evie felt like her adopted family was finally reunited all together in one place, and for that she was grateful. They'd spent the last three years gathering both the people and the materials they would need to get to work. Ari and Judah had traveled throughout Europe, risking their lives in occupied countries; she'd been all over Palestine, tirelessly looking for volunteers. Now the day when they would begin their work in earnest was about to dawn.

To celebrate this special gathering, Ari brought out a bottle of fine Scotch whiskey that he'd picked up somewhere along his journeys. The assembled group had walked together from the dining hall to the pit that sat in the center of the circle of tents where they slept and a campfire had been built. The heat of the fire, combined with the warming effect of the whiskey in her stomach and the low murmur of conversations around her, had Evie feeling a rare, contented bliss. All of the problems of her daily life seemed to melt away, rising upward into the smoky air, small sparks from the dry wood cracking and shooting off like messages toward heaven. Someone was gently strumming a guitar. She swayed in her seat, eyes closed, feeling the music fill her with hope.

Then she sensed a shift in the night air. Evie felt his presence before she actually saw him. Albert had come to sit beside her. When she opened her eyes, there he was, silently waiting to be acknowledged.

She turned toward him and smiled, not sure of what to say, her mind racing.

"Did I disturb you?" he asked.

"Oh, no. I was just listening to the music." She felt herself blush.

"It's nice," he replied. "It's peaceful." He was holding two glasses of whiskey, one of which he handed to her.

Evie took the drink from him, sipping slowly and feeling the smoky liquid warm her stomach immediately. Feeling emboldened, she asked, "How did you meet Judah?"

With a matter-of-fact tone to his voice, Albert began to tell his story. "I was working in a tavern in Prague. I'd escaped from Paris on the day the soldiers came for my father, and for me as well. I wasn't home yet when they came, so I was able to avoid capture. My father had given me instructions on what to do if that were to ever happen, you know, if the Nazis came for him. I knew to run." His voice trailed off momentarily. Then he continued. "I hid as best as I could, living in forests and abandoned barns. I stole food, clothing. I'm not proud of that, but I knew that I had to survive the war by any means possible. Anyway, I convinced Judah to let me join him and now, here I am. I can only pray that my father finds his way here as well. He promised me." He paused, then emphatically added, "Someday, we will be reunited. I'm sure of it." He took a long sip of his drink.

"And your mother? The rest of your family?" she asked softly.

"My mother died when I was a boy, before the war ever started. As for the rest, I have to assume that they are either dead now or on the run as I was." He stared into the fire for a moment before turning to face her. "But I am alive. God must have a plan for me. I intend to figure out whatever that might be."

"His plan is for you to help us make our own country out of this desert. That's His plan for all of us," she replied with great certainty.

Albert nodded his head. "And you? How do you come to be in this place?"

"My father is a British official. I was born in England, but raised in Tel Aviv. I barely remember London at all, much to my mother's chagrin. But as I grew up in that over-privileged world of formal dinners and proper tea time rituals, I couldn't tolerate the idea that one type of Jew was above the rest, that any person was better than the next. I'm not a big believer in the class system that my mother country still clings to so fiercely. The British have no right to rule here. They were supposed to make a safe haven here for Jews, but instead, they've limited the number of displaced victims of Hitler's oppression. They've put a cap on how many are to be allowed to immigrate. This needs to be a Jewish homeland, a place for our people. It has to happen." She heard the passion in her own voice and looked into Albert's eyes. "And we will have a major hand in that movement by succeeding in our work here."

"It seems to me that you already do," he said sincerely. "I just need to catch up with you."

"You will," she said softly before catching herself from falling any more deeply into his piercingly dark gaze. "I mean, we need your help." She stood up abruptly, swaying a bit, the effects from the drink rolling in waves over her body. "I'm sorry. I think that I really need to get some sleep. Too much whiskey for me tonight." She handed him her now empty glass.

Albert jumped to his feet. "Let me walk you to your tent. Which one is it?"

"No, no. I'm fine." She dusted off her hands against the fabric of her pants leg. "I can make it."

She felt him watch her walk away. *Whiskey? Hardly!* Evie knew right then and there that she would need to guard herself more carefully when she was around this newcomer. There was something about this stranger that she found intriguing. And for the life of her, she didn't know what to do about it.

Albert watched Evie walk away, waiting for her to disappear into the depths of her own tent before making his way to the one he shared with Judah. His exposure to women was limited; a few of the prostitutes in Prague had shown him the basics of physical pleasure, but he knew nothing about how to woo a woman, especially one like Evie. From his brief exposure to her, Albert sensed that she was special and could barely contain his attraction to her. He would have to figure out how to let her know what he was feeling without scaring her away.

He downed the rest of his drink and brought the empty glasses back over to the table outside the dining hall. Then he walked the short distance to return to his tent. Pulling back the flap, he stepped inside and threw himself down onto the narrow cot sitting off to one side of the entry. Without thinking about what kind of work he'd be assigned the next morning, he fell into a deep, dreamless sleep.

Judah and Ari sat together as the last burning embers of the campfire glowed dimly against the night sky. All of the other members of the kibbutz had already gone to bed; they could hear the soft sounds of breathing from behind the canvas structures that surrounded the fire pit.

"What are your plans for the boy you brought along from Prague?" Ari asked.

Judah shrugged. "He's a good worker. He'll do anything I ask him to."

"Do you think he'd be good at smuggling, once we have the factory up and running?"

"If I scout out the roads with him in advance of any mission, I think so. He's unfamiliar with this part of the country."

"He knows the port at Haifa well enough, no? Can he be trusted to bring the ammunition we manufacture back there?"

"Of course. I would want to make sure he knows a few different ways to get between here and Jerusalem, though. He's not made that trip before."

"Right. Let's put him to use as a courier, to start. We'll have plenty of others to make the bullets and pack them up. If you trust this boy, I do, too. His job will require the utmost secrecy."

"He can be relied on. He's proven that to me already. And he's smart enough, and unattached. He has nothing–his family is gone, burned in the concentration camps, I'm pretty sure," Judah said matter-of-factly. "He really believes that his father will make it here to Palestine, but..." he shook his head.

"Say no more. Let him hope. We all need to believe in something," Ari replied, grounding the butt of his cigarette into the sand before tossing it into the dying fire, and standing up. As he stretched his arms into the air over his head, he remarked, "I'm turning in. See you in the morning."

"All right," Judah replied, reaching into his shirt pocket for one last cigarette before he headed into his tent. Sleep often eluded him, especially on nights when Geula haunted his thoughts. He replayed the day she died over and over again in his mind. If he had only been with her that morning, maybe they would have stayed in bed together long enough to delay her on her walk to work, keeping her out of harm's way. Or perhaps if he'd taken her with him, she would have still been here, warm and alive. That last image he had of her was of her beautiful brown hair fanned out against the white sheets of their bed, her soft, naked body curled softly around his own, her long eyelashes fluttering slightly in sleep; that memory had become his own personal circle of hell. He was locked away inside himself now, with no hope of escape. He could sacrifice everything for this cause simply because he had nothing left to lose. His life had been taken from him already.

Judah looked up at the inky, black sky studded with stars. *Geula, my love. I'll join you someday when this fight is done. We'll be together again.* And then with a sigh, he stood and made his way to the tent where Albert lay sleeping, knowing that he'd close his own eyes but still find no relief from the sorrow that sat dead center in his chest, having taken up permanent residence in the middle of his heart.

THE SHABBAT GATHERING, later that week

EVIE WAS A BUNDLE OF NERVES. The students she'd met at Hebrew University were on their way from Jerusalem to the kibbutz. If she could convince a few of them to stay and work in the factory, the entire team would be in place. She walked quickly through the dining hall, already set for dinner with crisply laundered white tablecloths, her hands full of colorful wildflowers. She wanted to put some on each table to brighten the room and make their Shabbat meal even more special. As she separated bunches of flowers into drinking glasses that would serve as makeshift vases, she couldn't help but think of her mother and the endless dinner parties that she hosted for other British officials and their wives back home in Tel Aviv. Maybe Evie had been paying more attention to the small details of her life there than she ever realized; her mother would never invite her guests into a dining room unadorned by floral arrangements, fine crystal, and her best china. Evie felt the need to do the same with the limited resources available to her.

They were fortunate to have both a dairy and a chicken coop here. Meals were not all that imaginative, but there were plenty of staples available for the kibbutz members to eat each day. They grew their own produce: lettuces, tomatoes, cucumbers, and onions; the dairy provided goat's milk and cheeses and yogurt, as well. They had chicken on Friday nights, but most other meals were meatless, which was fine as far as Evie was concerned. And of course, the bakery turned out delicious challah and rolls, breads and cakes. They ate well. Better, she was told, than most of their countrymen. But then again, their mission was incredibly important if they were going to make a country out of this desert. They needed fuel to get the work done.

She could smell the aroma of roasted chicken waft into the dining room and she realized that she hadn't eaten much that morning. She pushed through the door to the large kitchen to see if she could scavenge up a piece of bread to stave off her hunger until their guests arrived. She immediately saw Ari and Judah at the long steel counter, huddled over two steaming cups of tea, a plate of pound cake between them.

"Planning something?" she asked both men.

"You know better than to ask, Evie. We're always planning something," Ari replied with a smile.

"True. But it's almost Shabbat and we all could use a rest, right? Our guests should be here soon,"

"You have high hopes for them?" Judah asked.

"They are Americans, students at Hebrew University. Americans have money, or at least that's what I've been told."

"So I've heard," Ari said wryly.

"We're going to need to convince them to help us tap into that American pocketbook somehow. That's why this Shabbat has to be really special."

"Ah, Evie. Every Shabbat is special. You know that," Ari replied.

"I know, I know, but you know what I mean. I think this could be the final piece to our puzzle."

Judah got up and put an arm around Evie. "I know how much you'd like these people to fit in here. We'll do our best to make them feel welcome."

"Just let them ease into things, okay? No need to talk about war right away."

"It's inevitable. It might come up naturally," Ari said.

"Yes, but since half the people here are totally unaware of what our main goal is, I think we can keep the story of our factory quiet for this Shabbat. If these students commit to us and decide to stay, we'll show them what we have planned. But only after we can be sure that they will keep our secrets. Otherwise, we endanger both the operation and everyone here," Evie said.

Judah stood and squeezed her shoulders with his large hands. "Okay, Evie. We hear you. Everything will be fine. You worry too much."

Grabbing a still-warm slice of cake from the plate on the counter, she said, "I wish I didn't have to worry. These are the last of my recruits. It hasn't been easy to convince people to come here. Time is short and we need these people to stay."

Judah sighed. Then he said, "We know how hard you've

worked. It's out of your hands now. We'll work with the team we have in place, if need be. But I have a feeling that these Americans will help. Now, go. Get out of here and get ready for Shabbat. I'm sure the line at the shower is growing by the minute."

She took a bite of the delicious cake, allowing herself the pleasure of the sweet flavor to sit on her tongue for a moment before responding. "It wouldn't hurt for either of you to bathe as well. Let's all make a good impression on our guests."

"We're right behind you, Evie," Judah said. "And we promise to be on out best behavior."

She turned to leave, praying that they would be true to their word. Scaring these new recruits off might cost them the price of the upcoming conflict. And that, Evie knew, was too much of a risk to take.

ON THE ROAD to Rehovot

NAOMI COULD BARELY CONTAIN her excitement. One more semester and she'd have her bachelor's degree in journalism from Hebrew University and she would be returning home to New York City. Armed with the experience of living in the Middle East, she planned on applying for a foreign correspondent job with whichever large newspaper hired her. It was a dream come true. And now, with the two-week holiday break stretched out before her, she sat back on the bus with Simon and Sarah as it bumped along the rutted road toward the kibbutz they were to visit this Shabbat. She had been curious about the woman who had come to the school to speak with them about this new community on a hill right outside of Tel

Aviv. Evie had made the place sound so intriguing. Naomi had visited many different types of kibbutzim since arriving in Palestine. Some were as basic as could be, just a farm with no running water or amenities. Others were more established, with shower buildings, dining halls, and community centers where residents could watch theatrical performances or come together to celebrate a holiday. Naomi had the impression that the kibbutz that Evie represented landed somewhere in between.

She looked over at Simon and Sarah who sat very close together, heads touching. They had become an "item," as her mother would say, never spending a spare moment apart. It seemed to Naomi that their main objective in visiting the kibbutz for Shabbat was to find their way into a tent together for the weekend, only appearing at meal time. It didn't matter to her either way; she was truly curious to see the place that Evie had described in such vivid detail.

Thinking for a moment about her mother, Naomi reached into her small canvas travel bag and pulled out a few sheets of onionskin paper and a pen. Using the bag as a steady surface on her lap, she started to write.

Dear Mom and Dad,

Can you believe that I've been in the Holy Land for nineteen months already? It's been such an experience, one I'm sure I'll never be able to replicate. I've seen so much of this beautiful country, from the hills in the Golan to the mud of the Dead Sea down to the Gulf of Aqaba, each part of this land unique and full of history.

I have to admit, I like Jerusalem best of all. Not because it's my home while I'm here, but because of the wonderful cobblestoned streets and markets, the beautiful old buildings, and the magnificent Wailing Wall. This Shabbat, however, I'm headed to a kibbutz on the outskirts of Tel Aviv, which by the way, is as modern a city as one could expect to find in a desert! One of the members came to our school to invite us there, and if you can believe it, she's the daughter of a high-ranking British official. I can just imagine what the dinner conversation was like when she decided to tell her parents that she was leaving them to work the land! Oy!

I just love visiting these places, meeting the hardy souls who have made it their mission in life to build this country literally out of shifting sand. I find them inspiring in oh so many ways.

JUST THEN NAOMI felt the bus jolt to a stop and Simon called out to her.

"C'mon, this is us!" he said over his shoulder as he carried his and Sarah's bag high above his head so as not to hit anyone still seated with their luggage along the narrow aisle of the vehicle.

Naomi barely had time to shove the hastily composed letter into her bag, grab her red sweater off the seat back, and hurriedly jump down the three steep steps of the bus before the driver put his charge back in gear and steered it away. Looking around, she saw two stones set evenly apart on the ground and realized that this was the spot Evie had mentioned would be their meeting place. She lifted her hand to shade her eyes, squinting a bit against the sun, having made its way down from its zenith in the sky hours earlier. In the distance, she watched as two small figures ambled toward them, growing more life-sized as they approached. She recognized Evie right away, but she was with a man who, as they got closer, stole Naomi's breath right out of her.

He was tall and although he moved with a casual step, Naomi could sense that he was a leader. It was just the way he carried himself, his broad shoulders and long legs quickly eating up the distance between them. As he got even closer, she could see the square set to his jaw, the neatly cropped dark hair, and she wondered about the color of his eyes. He looked incredibly strong, the type of man that could conquer any obstacle in his way, and for the only time in her life, Naomi could imagine that there was some truth behind the saying "love at first sight." She was immediately drawn to this stranger and her only coherent thought was that she prayed he wasn't attached to Evie. Before she could compose herself, the two kibbutz residents were standing in front of them.

"Naomi, Simon, Sarah! We are delighted that you've come to join us for Shabbat! Welcome!" Evie said, one by one grabbing each of them by the shoulders and pulling them into her warm embrace.

"Happy to be here as well," Simon replied to Evie before stepping up to the other man with an extended hand in greeting. "Thank you for hosting us."

"Ain byah," was the man's answer in Hebrew. He quickly switched gears to speak in English. "Evie has spoken highly of all of you. You're students, right?" He barely smiled.

"Oh, so sorry. Let me introduce you," Evie interjected, putting her hand on the man's arm. "This is Judah. He's one of the head officials here in Rehovot. He had a lot to do with the formation of our kibbutz."

Judah, Naomi thought. *What a beautiful, biblical name. One of Jacob's sons,* she recalled, searching her memory for what she'd learned as a child in religious school. He shook hands with both Simon and Sarah, then turned to her. His eyes were a deep brown and gave away nothing when they locked with her own. As he reached out for her hand, Naomi knew what would happen next. His touch was electric, as she expected it would be, drawing her into the mystery of him. It was with every bit of her self-control that she let his long, tapered fingers drop away, realizing in that moment that she would do whatever it took to get to know him better. She was intrigued to uncover what lay behind the mask he clearly wore. Something told her that he was a keeper of secrets. All at once she knew that it would be her goal to try and figure out exactly what he was hiding.

ix

THE DINING HALL at Rehovot

SHABBAT DINNER WAS a huge success and Evie could not have been more pleased. Their guests seemed engaged and excited to be there. The roast chicken and salads had been delicious and now, as they sat around the table, wine glasses empty, drinking tea and eating cake, she knew the time was right to test the waters, to see if Naomi, Simon and Sarah would be interested in joining them permanently. Without a commitment, Evie would not tell them about the underground factory or the task the assembled group had been charged with; she'd allow them to believe that this was just another ordinary kibbutz. She had a good feeling about these Americans. With their involvement, perhaps at the very least she could open a pipeline of dollars to help support the cause. As the room began to empty, the other members of the kibbutz heading out to their tents, Evie realized that the moment had come. There was no one left in the dining hall without the high level of clearance needed to know the truth about their mission. She nodded across the room to Judah and Ari, making it clear that she wanted them to come over and join her as she spoke to the trio of students. Both men stood and walked across the room, pulling back chairs and making themselves comfortable.

"We're so delighted that you've come to stay with us for Shabbat," Evie began. "I'd like to tell you a bit more about what we intend to do here."

"Of course." Simon leaned in. "I'm fascinated by the kibbutz movement. How the devil you grow things in the middle of all of this sand is amazing."

"Yes, it is," Ari interjected. "But we're also involved with the movement to make Palestine a Jewish state. That's what we want to discuss with the three of you."

~

NAOMI COULD FEEL the hair stand up on the back of her neck. She looked around and for the first time realized that everyone who had been at dinner here was young. On other trips to kibbutzim, there was a mix of people of all ages. Yet here, she had only seen people around her own age. *That's strange,* she thought.

"We need your help. We're looking for a few more volunteers to complete our team."

"We're not farmers, we're students," Simon replied.

"We'll teach you everything you need to know," Evie said, then adding, "It's not hard to learn."

Simon just shook his head. "After the success of our first expedition last summer, Sarah and I have already committed to spending our entire next semester on a dig under the Western Wall in Jerusalem. It's important work as well."

"Ah, of course," Judah responded. He pulled his chair closer and focused his attention on Naomi. "And you?"

For a moment, all she could do was pray that the sound of her own blood coursing through her veins was not as loud to the others as it was to her. As he waited for her to respond, Judah's eyes were locked with her own.

"Um, I think I would like to hear more," she said with a measured tone, careful to keep her nerves out of her voice.

"What?" Simon interjected. "I thought you were gung ho to graduate and travel the world as a reporter for some newspaper. You want to stay here instead? On a farm?"

Naomi could feel her face flush. She wasn't sure what she truly would do at the moment, but she was sure that she wanted the opportunity to get to know this mysterious man a lot better.

"Wait a minute, Simon, don't be so quick to judge. This could make a great piece for a paper, open up a few doors for more work. And I'd like to learn what it's like to live full-time on a kibbutz." She heard herself say the words convincingly, even though she wasn't sure she believed them.

"What about school, your degree? Why not finish up the semester and then come be a farmer?" he asked.

Just then Evie jumped in. "Or take one semester off. We'll need help with the harvest, which will happen shortly. You can always go back to the university, right?"

Naomi's head was swimming. She knew that she should stick to her original path and just complete her degree. Simon was right, she had a plan in mind for herself. There was no real reason for her to deviate from her original intention, but on the other hand, there was no real reason for her not to. She was intrigued, not only by the kibbutz, but by the people. She wanted to get to know them better. She wanted to get to know Judah better.

"I'm going to take the night to consider my options," she heard herself say. "I'll decide in the morning."

"That's great," Evie said with an even tone. However, it was obvious she wanted them all to stay. "We can talk about it again tomorrow, after lunch."

"Yes," answered Naomi. She pushed back from the table and stood up. "I'm going to get some sleep. Thank you for a delicious dinner and a most interesting evening."

"I'll walk with you. It's dark on the path. I'll get you to your tent where you can rest," Judah said, standing as well.

Naomi blushed. "That's not necessary. I think I can find my own way there." She felt the need to dissuade him, even though she couldn't believe that he'd want to see her to her sleeping quarters. Her heart was pounding at the base of her throat.

"I insist," he said before turning to the group. "See you all in the morning."

When he casually put his hand on the small of her back, Naomi felt that jolt of electricity once again. She concentrated on putting one foot safely in front of the other. The last thing she wanted to do was be clumsy and trip. They made their way out of the dining room and onto the dirt path that led a short distance to the encampment. It was a moonless, starry night, inky darkness spilling out in every direction, magnifying the silence between them. Then Judah spoke.

"You have to forgive Evie. She is enthusiastic about our work here, very committed. She sees you as someone who could be a close ally, and she doesn't have much of that. We're a bunch of men, soldiers, really. I think she's looking for some female companionship, someone who she can truly talk to. It's lonely here for her."

His compassion for Evie made Naomi wonder if they were romantically involved, but she didn't want to ask. Instead, she said, "I can understand that. I left my sister back in New York and I miss her terribly. I can tell her anything."

"Right. And Evie has become very dear to me. I just want her to be happy. She works so hard. It would be nice for her to have someone to talk to."

Naomi couldn't help herself. The words just spilled out. "Is Evie your girlfriend?"

Judah abruptly stopped walking, pulled a cigarette out of the pocket of his shirt, held it to his mouth, and lit it. After what seemed to Naomi like an eternity, he answered, "No. I'm not looking for any sort of romantic attachment. I am here to fight for my fellow countrymen, to make this place a safe haven for Jews everywhere."

Naomi was grateful for the darkness. She felt the blush rise from her feet to her face. "Of course, of course. I understand," she said, even though she didn't. "You two just seem so close."

"We are. She's the sister I never had." He began to walk again, drawing them closer to her tent. Finally, they reached their destination.

"So, Naomi. You have some thinking to do. I'll leave you for now. Pleasant dreams." He turned sharply and walked down the path, disappearing into the night.

Naomi entered her tent and sat still on her cot for a moment, more confused about the choice she had to make than she was before Judah walked her back here. On the one hand, this opportunity could be something she'd take with her throughout her life, knowing that she played a part in making Palestine a Jewish state. On the other, that attractive man just told her that he had no interest in any sort of relationship that might interrupt his work here. Either way, she knew one thing: there would be no "pleasant dreams" for her this evening. With all she had on her mind, she doubted there would be much sleep for her at all.

AS HE APPROACHED the entrance to the dining hall, Judah could only hope that Ari was still inside and that there was some whiskey left in the bottle. He wanted to drink away the thoughts that kept rattling through his mind about the intriguing American woman he'd just left moments before. *Not since Geula died.* He hadn't noticed another woman since the love of his life had perished violently that awful morning. The truth was, he blamed himself for her unnecessary death. He didn't deserve to find another love, or to ever be happy again.

When Naomi had asked him if he was romantically linked to Evie, it startled him. He had stopped thinking of himself ever being involved with a woman in that way again, of allowing himself the delusion that he could give his heart to another. Besides, there was too much work ahead of him, most of which was extremely dangerous. He knew that Ari would assign him the most difficult tasks and he would take on whatever was required, no questions asked. It would be wrong to get involved with another now, to bring an innocent woman into the whirlwind that was his life. He might not survive the conflict that lay ahead of him, ahead of them all.

But that green-eyed American? The one who made him think about his future again? Like a lightning bolt, realization struck him where he stood, and Judah understood the truth. In one quick evening, she had gotten under his skin, and the mere thought that she might join them made him feel something he hadn't felt in a very long time. Hope.

NAOMI LAY restless in her tent deep into the night, not sure of what to do, so she began to make lists in her mind. She had one semester to go and then she'd have her degree. She could sort it all out after that, see the world if she so desired as a foreign correspondent, chronicling her travels as she went. Or, she could learn to be a farmer and help build a country out of the dust of this land. When she left home, she never expected to be confronted with a situation that would tie her down to any one place. She had a burning desire for new adventures; that's what drew her to Palestine. She turned the nearly flat pillow over seeking a bit of cooler cotton to soothe her overheated skin. It was not even that hot outside. She felt warmed from within and she knew that there was only one reason for that: Judah.

Sleepless, she tried to run her list over in her mind, but was having no luck, so she sat up and pulled the letter she'd started to her parents on the bus trip here out of her bag. Rummaging around, she found her pen and began to write.

I'M BACK to tell you more. I stopped writing earlier because we had arrived at the kibbutz. It's late at night now. We had a marvelous Shabbat dinner with the members of this kibbutz and now I'm in my cozy tent (well, maybe not cozy, but it is private!), working through an interesting proposition. What would you think if I stayed here, in Rehovot, for a few months? I can always go back to the university and finish up my degree, but there is important work to be done on this farm, and I think I might like to try my hand at it. I know this must sound so terribly foreign to you, as it would have to me as well before I left home. I mean, if we need tomatoes, the A&P is right on the corner and they deliver! But I'm being offered a rare opportunity--to farm the land and help feed my people. I hope you won't be too disappointed in me if I choose to try this out for a while.

NAOMI HELD her pen poised over the page for a moment and reread what she had put down on paper. It sounded to her like her decision was made. But was she doing the right thing? She still needed to convince herself that she wasn't making this choice because of a man she'd just met. That would be foolish. She continued her letter.

. . .

Besides, I feel like this work is important, equally so to my actual degree. There are certain things that you can't learn in a classroom, after all. Maybe I'm meant to write about this experience, to let the rest of the world know that Jews have a place to come live in and to find refuge from the oppression that has followed them for centuries now. We just have to build it with our own hands and hearts. That's exactly what I'll be doing.

I miss you all. You can still write to me at the university. I'll keep my mailbox there and pick up your letters when I visit Jerusalem. Besides, I'll be returning there in the fall to finish up my degree.

Love you,
Naomi

She reread what she had written, realizing that it was done. Her decision was made. It always helped her to work out a problem if she committed her thoughts to paper. She folded the thin sheets of onionskin and stuffed them into a matching envelope. She would ask Evie where she could post the letter in the morning. For now, she closed her eyes and willed herself to think of anything other than Judah's face. Finally, the events of the day caught up with her and she drifted off to sleep.

Late the next morning, after a brief religious service to commemorate the Sabbath, the group gathered back in the dining hall for a lunch of cold salads and endless cups of tea. No work was done on this one day a week, leaving most of the members of the kibbutz free to rest. Evie decided that this would be a great opportunity to show the American visitors the rest of the camp, leaving out, of course, the factory that sat underneath.

As they walked together in the bright sunshine, she pointed out various landmarks. "That small building over there, right before the orange grove? That's the children's house."

"Yes, we've seen that before on other kibbutzim. I still can't get used to the idea that children don't live with their parents," Sarah said.

"It actually works for us," Evie explained. "The children have professional child care and the parents can concentrate on whatever their task is on the kibbutz. Everyone benefits."

"But don't the children miss their mothers and fathers?" Sarah asked.

"They see them every morning, before school begins. We have great teachers here and the education is quite comprehensive. And they see their parents again at dinnertime and of course all day on Shabbat."

Sarah just shook her head. "I could never do that. If I have a child, I'd want it to be with me."

Evie nodded. "That's fine. I'm sure you'll make that decision for yourself someday." She had started walking down the path when Naomi stopped her and asked, "What if a child doesn't want to sleep in the children's house? Is it mandatory?"

"For now, it is. We have important work to do here. We need all of our workers to be able to do their job with no distractions." She heard herself say the words, but what she didn't divulge was even more important. *We are keeping a dark secret, one that no one can know. If we are exposed, we will not be ready when the war comes. Children can't be trusted to know what they can or can't say to a stranger. That's why we so desperately need them to be separate.* She turned to the visitors and said brightly, "Let me show you the chicken coop and the herb garden. They are truly remarkable."

SUNDAY MORNING AT DAWN, Simon and Sarah were ready to leave to catch the bus for Jerusalem.

"Are you absolutely sure about this?" Simon asked her one last time as they stood at the entrance to the kibbutz.

Naomi reached out and put her hand on his arm. "I am. But I'll be back at some point to pick up my things, so we'll see each other then. And I'll need to put in the forms for a leave of absence for the semester. You know how fast the time will go by. Besides, you're going on that dig. You and Sarah won't be around anyway."

"I do know that. Doesn't make me worry less, kiddo."

Naomi gave his arm a little squeeze. "I'll be fine. No need to stress over me. I'm looking forward to learning how to farm. I'm always up for a new experience!" Of course, what she didn't tell him was just how much her interest in the mysterious Judah played a role in her decision-making. Just then Sarah leaned in for a hug.

"We'll miss you! Promise to write?" she asked.

"Of course!" Naomi answered. "That's my job!"

They all heard the bus rumbling up the hill and turned toward it. Naomi felt a fluttering of butterfly nerves in the pit of her stomach. *If it doesn't work out, I can always go back,* she told herself. She deliberately kept the smile fixed on her face as her friends climbed into the rusty old vehicle and found seats within it. They both waved from behind a dirty window as the wheels kicked up sand and dust behind them, diesel fumes filling the air. Naomi waited until they were out of sight before she turned and walked alone down the path toward what was to be her new home. *Be brave!* she told herself as she went in search of Evie to find out what her assignment was. She was here to work, and right now was as good a time as any to get started.

Naomi found Evie sitting at a table in the dining hall, ever-present clipboard in her hand. She had a puzzled look on her face.

"Good morning. I'm here for my assignment. I can teach English to the children, you know. I'm a whiz at grammar."

Evie smiled. "Yes, I'm sure that you are. Americans always think they have a good grasp of the mother tongue. My own mother always reminded me that there is only one proper usage of our shared lexicon. The British way."

"Well, you did speak it first and all," Naomi teased. "But aside from making some minor adjustments, we Americans do well with it, don't you think?"

Evie peered over the clipboard and without a word made Naomi aware that she disagreed. No matter.

"If not as a teacher, what do you suggest for my particular set of skills? I've never farmed, but I'm a quick study," she said with enthusiasm. Rambling now, she added, "I think the only place you don't want me is in front of the oven. Cooking is not something I'm familiar with at all. My mother never let me in the kitchen. We always had a cook and a maid…" Realizing now how her words must sound, she stopped talking.

"Well, we're very much alike then," Evie responded. "My mother never let me inside of our kitchen, either. I'm not sure she even knew where it was located in our home." She shook her head. "I really had to get out of there."

"What about your dad? How does he feel about you being so involved with the kibbutz?"

"I don't think he fully understands it at all. I'm not even sure what he truly believes. I'm convinced that he has talked himself into the idea that I'm farming the land, nothing more."

"Of course!" Naomi responded. "Because that is what you are doing. Providing food for the workers, for the surrounding neighbors. It's an important effort."

Evie put her clipboard down on the table and looked directly at Naomi. "It's time I tell you something more about what we do here. We're not just farmers."

Naomi sat glued to her chair as she felt a chill travel up her spine from the tone of the other woman's voice. "What? What do you mean, exactly?"

"I think you'll understand it better if I show you. Let's go."

With that, Evie stood, picked up her clipboard and walked toward the door. She turned to look back at Naomi, who was still seated, a blank expression on her face. "Well, come along, then. We haven't got all day."

Naomi scrambled to her feet, following Evie out into the bright sunshine. They walked in silence over to the building that housed the laundry on one side and the bakery on the other. Once at the doorway, Evie said, "It's almost time for the first water break of the day. Come inside. We'll wait for that to happen before we go any farther."

Confused, Naomi did as she was told. They stepped into the dimness of the large, overheated space. It was sensory overload. The ovens were blasting, the smell of freshly baked bread almost as strong as the bleachy scent of laundry soap from the enormous tubs on the other side of the wall. It made for a strange but pleasant smell that overwhelmed the space. People worked behind both the washing tubs and ovens, doing their jobs in this inferno. And the noise! The industrial machines filled to capacity with dirty clothing made a terrible, clanging sound. It was all Naomi could do to stand her ground because the floor beneath her feet was actually vibrating. Sweat immediately began to pool between her breasts and drip from the nape of her neck and down her back. She tugged on the light blouse she'd put on this morning. It was already wet and they'd only been inside for a matter of minutes.

All at once, she heard a worker chant, *"Hafsaka, hafsaka!"* and everyone else put down what they were doing. One by one they filed out of the building and out to the large basin of cool water kept in the shade of an olive tree, each taking a turn at the ladle for a refreshing drink.

As the last person left and Naomi found herself alone with Evie, she asked, "What would you have me do? Laundry or baking?"

"Neither. I have something important to show you, and we only have twenty minutes to get it done. What you are about to see is highly classified. No one can know. I will explain more after our little tour. Just look, don't touch a thing. It will be clear when I fill in all the details afterward."

Fully intrigued, Naomi said, "All right. Lead the way."

With that, Evie stepped behind one of the laundry machines and pushed it to the side, revealing a steep staircase. "Watch your step," she advised as she quickly disappeared underground. A moment later, Naomi followed her newly found friend, deeply aware that whatever lay beneath the surface was important. She dipped her head down to navigate the winding staircase into the darkness below.

Seven

A SHIVER RAN down Naomi's spine as she descended into the dim underground space. She stood at the base of the staircase and waited a moment for her eyes to adjust. What she saw before her left her breathless. The room was narrow, with concrete walls that made her uncomfortable at first, imbuing her with the feeling that the oxygen was limited and that she'd suffocate if she stayed too long. As her vision cleared, she recognized that an entire line of machines stood silently, neatly lined up next to each other in a tight row in the windowless space. They looked old and somewhat beat-up, but she could tell that they were well cared for by whomever had brought them to this place. "What is all of this?" she asked, turning toward the other woman.

"This," Evie responded, spreading her arms wide to include everything Naomi was seeing, "is how we win our independence. It's bullet-making equipment, purchased by Ari and Judah in Europe and shipped here piece by piece. We've been working on this project for a number of years. Now we're ready to put our planning into practice."

"You know how to use this equipment?" Naomi asked with wonder, reaching out and putting her fingers on the cool metal of the closest piece of machinery, but quickly pulling her hand back as she remembered Evie's admonition not to touch anything.

"I've been shown how, yes, and I'd like to include you in the group that will begin training on its proper usage later this week. You can be part of something big here, Naomi. Really important."

"I'm not sure I understand. I thought I was going to help on the farm. You didn't mention anything about all of this..."

"That's because not everyone here will know about this factory. There will be people who work the land who will never be told the true purpose of this kibbutz. Secrecy is of the utmost importance. If the British get word of what we're doing here, well, let's just say we'd all be in big trouble. I shudder to think what they'd do to us."

"How can you possibly think that you can keep this a secret from the others? That will be impossible!" Naomi said.

"I can assure you that we've worked it all out," Evie replied, draping her hand casually on one of the silent machines and looking directly at Naomi. "Let me tell you a story. Many years ago, a group of giraffes were transported from Cairo to their new home in the Tel Aviv zoo. Have you seen them?"

"Of course. A bunch of us went there last year. They're elegant creatures."

"Yes, that's true. But what you don't think about when you see them is that special transportation was needed to accommodate the long necks of those animals. The tops of the train cars were cut away to allow the giraffes to make the journey. They could see everything as they rode along the rails, but the British soldiers who accompanied the giraffes were sitting inside the windowless compartments. They missed out on the scenery the whole way between Cairo and Tel Aviv."

"Okay, but..." Naomi began, not following exactly where Evie was going with her story of these animals. "I don't see a connection here."

"We will have people in the same position as those British

soldiers. They will make the journey without seeing the truth. The farmers, those who will work the land? That will be their purpose here, nothing more. We will call them 'giraffes'. Those of us, the small group who will be cleared at the highest level of security, we are the actual giraffes. However, we call ourselves soldiers. We will see everything, be in on every plan and movement. We will create enough ammunition so that we have a decent shot at winning this war that is bound to happen, and sooner rather than later." She paused, sensing that Naomi was ready to ask her a question.

"Don't you have the names reversed? Why call the farmers 'giraffes'? They are more like the British soldiers, not knowing what they are missing."

"Irony," Evie replied. "Or sick war humor, if you will. But that is how this will happen. There will be about forty people who will work down here and will know the actual facts about our mission. Everyone on the top, those farming the land? They will be left in the dark." She waited, letting the magnitude of what she'd just shared sink in before continuing. "Now is your moment of truth. Can I count you among us?"

Naomi stood still for a moment. She truly felt overwhelmed by what Evie had just described to her, but she knew instantly that she had only one choice. She might not have been born here, but this small country was already deeply embedded in her heart. She would do anything to make it free. As her eyes took in the enormity of the factory, all these strange machines just waiting to be put to use, she felt a courage she'd never experienced before, not even when she first stepped on the ship that brought her to this battlefield. This was a carefully thought out and highly technical plan for independence. And she knew exactly what she would say next. She drew in a breath.

"I have two questions," she began. "You plan on making the bullets. What about the guns? Will you have to manufacture those too?"

Evie smiled and said, "No. Ari and Judah were able to purchase the weapons. Second question?"

Naomi pulled herself up to her full height and asked, "How can I help?"

EVIE SMILED as relief flooded her body. She knew she had been right about Naomi, that this woman would say yes and stay. She had recognized that determined air about her new recruit from the first time they'd met and was thrilled that she was right about her own judgment. It was important to have people around her who she could trust. She hoped they would become even better friends as they joined forces in this fight. "There is a whole lot that you can do, Naomi. But first you must swear to keep our secret safe. No one can know. You can't tell Simon or Sarah, or any of the other students at the university. You can't write about this place for a newspaper or for anything else for that matter. Do I have your solemn word?"

"Yes," Naomi replied softly, immediately realizing that she'd need to keep this information from her parents, that her letters home would need to be carefully worded.

"Then let me start by explaining exactly how this factory works. Come with me." She walked them down the line, pointing out the use of each machine. At the last one at the end of the row, she stopped. "This is the final step in the production of the bullets. The tip of each bullet is cut and the final product is sent into the next room for packaging and shipping. We call this machine 'the *mohel*,'"

"*Mohel*? As in the rabbi who performs a bris?"

"Yes! Just as an eight-day-old infant boy is snipped in the age-old ceremony of declaring himself a faithful member of the tribe, so are these bullets. Fitting, don't you think?"

"Giraffes, *mohel*... I think someone in your group has a strange sense of humor."

Evie's tone grew serious. "It's war, Naomi. If you can't laugh, you'll find yourself crying all day long."

Naomi looked over at the other woman and could tell just how intent she was about her work, this cause. She reached out and put her hand on Evie's shoulder. "I guess that's true. I want to help. Show me how."

For the next rushed few minutes, Naomi asked what seemed to her like a hundred questions about the place where they stood and Evie answered each inquiry with patience and thought. Every contingency had been planned for. There was special ventilation to accommodate the workers in this underground space. The laundry would run all day above their heads, the rumbling of the washing machines covering the sound of the factory below. The bakery next door would generate enough warmth to mask the heat rising from the cavernous space where the bullets were to be made. Workers would show up early, the switch behind one of the washing tubs would be pulled, and they would descend down, only to come back up for lunch and sleep at night. There would be one person in charge of making sure that no one else could see them enter or exit the factory and to further maintain the illusion that these workers were farmers, a sunlamp and tanning bed were installed to give the bullet makers some color on their skin to cover up the fact that they remained indoors all day. There was even a shooting range so that the bullets could be randomly tested for quality control. Naomi firmly believed at the end of her conversation with Evie that no stone had been left unturned, no detail unattended.

"This is all so remarkable," she said to Evie. "It's a lot to take in all at once."

"Yes, it is. I've had time to digest it all slowly, having been a part of some of this as it happened. I know it's overwhelming, but then again, so is the problem with our Arab neighbors, not to mention the British soldiers."

"When do we start?" Naomi asked.

"Next Sunday."

Naomi's eyes widened. "That's so soon," she whispered.

"There's no time like the present. The war is almost here, and we need to be ready."

Naomi nodded, signaling her understanding and followed Evie as she began the climb back up the narrow stairs to the surface. She could feel her heart beating an unsteady rhythm in her chest and she tried to keep her breath even despite her fear at the reality of the situation she now found herself in. This would be a serious fight for survival and she somehow found herself placed squarely in the thick of it. She could only hope that she was up to the challenge.

AT THE SAME time that Evie was explaining the inner workings of the factory to Naomi, Judah decided that it was time to fill Albert in on the true purpose of this kibbutz. He would need to see the machines for himself, to get a sense of the importance of their mission if he was to become an essential part of the success they all hoped to secure. Even though he wouldn't be a factory worker, Albert's job as a courier depended on his knowledge and understanding of how important each aspect of the mission was. He needed to develop a true sense of the urgency of staying undetected as he scouted out safe routes for the soon-to-be manufactured bullets as they made their way into the hands of the members of the underground and then delivered to the newly formed army.

As they entered the building and made their way over to the washing tubs, Judah saw Evie and Naomi emerge from the hidden staircase. He turned to Albert and watched with a bit of amusement as the younger man's face clearly gave away the shock of seeing the two women ascend from what appeared to be a hole in the ground. They'd need to work on that. Albert must learn never to show surprise or give his true emotion away.

"Ladies," he said, "good morning to you both." He couldn't help but notice that Naomi's face wore a similar expression to Albert's.

"*Shalom,* Judah," Evie replied. She turned away quickly before allowing herself to be distracted by Albert's confused look. "Naomi has seen what's downstairs. Are you headed there now?"

"We are," he replied.

"Better hurry," Evie said, glancing at the large clock hanging on the wall over the tub. "The workers will be returning soon. You have ten minutes."

"We'll be quick," Judah replied.

As they passed one another, Judah brushed against Naomi's arm. He couldn't help but notice that she was shaking.

"Are you okay?" he asked, his concern genuine.

All she could do was nod her head.

"It's a lot to take in, I know." He dipped his mouth to her ear and said in a low and gentle tone, "Evie trusts you. I'm sure you'll be a splendid addition to the team." He moved in a step closer, their bodies briefly touching and it was all Naomi could do to continue to breathe with the warmth of him so close to her. "I knew we could count on you." She felt his eyes pierce her own in a manner that was so intimate that she had to force herself to look away. When she did, Judah turned to Albert and his whole tone changed to one of strictly business. "*Zues.* Let's go. It's your turn to see what we have planned."

ight

ALBERT HAD BEEN KEPT BUSY. There was constant work to be done, most of it back-breakingly physical. His biceps strained against the ever-tightening material of his shirt; since leaving Prague all those months ago, his waist had narrowed and his thighs thickened into sheer muscle. As he passed Evie in the laundry, he realized that all of the heavy lifting he'd done over the past few days had further strengthened his body but left little energy to ruminate about this beautiful woman who occupied his dreams. For the past few nights, when he closed his eyes she would appear, those piercing blue eyes seeing into the depths of his soul. He had no idea how to get to know her better, but he thought that if there was a way, he'd find it. He had to. Albert felt an unspoken connection to Evie and he fervently hoped she felt it as well. She was kind to him, he knew that, and she always seemed pleased to see him whenever their paths crossed. But how could he tell if she was feeling the same sort of attraction to him as he was to her? He really had no idea his inexperience hindering him, but he hoped that somehow he'd be able to recognize a sign if she gave him one.

As he continued to follow Judah, he shook his head. He had to clear his mind and focus on whatever task he was about to be asked to do. At the end of all of this, when he was reunited with his father, Albert wanted to be sure that he had done everything he could to make him proud. It was important to Albert to believe his father was alive, that the other man was fighting within an inch of his life to make his way to Palestine to find his only child. And it was Albert's responsibility to be sure that there was a Jewish homeland when all of this was over, so that families like his own had a safe place to escape to after surviving the unspeakable atrocities they'd endured in Europe. All of these thoughts, along with his confusion about Evie, swirled in his mind, jumbling his brain until he was sure he'd never have another clear thought. Instead of dwelling on what he could not control, Albert embraced the now and followed Judah down into the unknown recesses at the bottom of the staircase, unaware that what he was about to experience would make all else pale in comparison.

NAOMI WATCHED as the two men went down into the factory. She thought that she should feel numb from all that she'd just seen, but the truth was that she felt as though her entire body was on fire from Judah's brief touch. She felt her stomach churn and barely heard Evie call her name.

"Naomi." Then again with more urgency, *"Naomi."*

"Yes, yes, sorry Evie. I am just trying to process all of this."

"I wish we had the luxury of time, but we don't. I need to walk you through the way this is going to work." She stopped on the path and stood still for a moment, and could see that her new friend looked as harried as she felt. She drew in a deep breath. "I guess we can take a little break," she said gently. "Let's go get a cup of tea. It will settle your nerves for now."

They walked in silence toward the dining hall, and once there, each filled a mug with the hot liquid. Evie spilled a splash of milk and two sugars to hers, Naomi added nothing. Then they sat at an empty table and watched the steam rise from their drinks for a minute before Evie spoke again.

"Did I overwhelm you? I tend to forget that there are so many details to consider. I've just been living with this plan for so long now, it seems like a part of me." She paused. "I hope I didn't scare you off or anything."

Naomi took a moment to reply. It wasn't anything she'd learned from Evie that scared her. It was her immediate attraction to Judah and her confusion over the fact that she was pretty sure he felt it too. But she couldn't tell Evie that. "No, I want to help, I do. I just didn't expect all of this. It's dangerous, isn't it?"

"Very," was Evie's reply. "If anyone leaks the truth about what we are doing here, we'll all be doomed. We'll never have a homeland for our people and the good Lord above only knows what will happen to those of us who were involved here. The British won't tolerate our insurrection well."

Naomi listened to what her friend said, shook off the confused feelings she had for Judah and reached across the table to take one of the woman's hands in her own. "What about your family, Evie? What would they think if they knew about what you're truly doing here?"

"They'd sit shiva for me, Naomi, because I would be dead to them. It would be the worst type of betrayal, almost as bad as marrying outside of our religion."

Naomi sat back in her chair, feeling Evie's words envelop her. "That would be terrible," was all she could say.

"So, you see, the need for secrecy is multi-faceted. I would like to see my parents again, someday. I can only do that if they never know of my involvement here."

"What will they do if we win and the British are forced to leave Palestine?"

"You mean *when* we win? I'm sure they'd go back to their lives in London. My mother would be pleased, believe me."

"But you would stay?"

"Of course I would!" Evie replied, sipping her drink. "This is my home now. There is no place I'd rather be. And to have it be free? To call it our own? That's everything to me, Naomi. It is my life's truest mission." Then she squeezed Naomi's hand. "You'll see," she continued. "You'll feel the same way soon. There is something about this place that curls up around your heart, making it impossible to think of living anywhere else. This is our destiny." She sat back in her chair, pointed to her friend's mug, and said, "Now drink up. We have work to do."

Naomi nodded, realizing that she was about to embark on a journey far more risky than anything she'd ever considered might happen in her lifetime. She was going to play an important role in the war effort. That was truly remarkable. So then why did her thoughts keep drifting back to Judah? Did he plan on staying here after the war? Would he make Palestine his home as well? She didn't know him at all, yet she sensed that there was something preventing him from putting down true roots in any one place. *Perhaps if I stayed that would change,* she found herself thinking. Her body had long stopped tingling from his touch, but her mind? That was an entirely different matter.

AFTER JUDAH SHOWED Albert the factory, he took him back up the staircase and out of the building into the sunshine. He pulled a cigarette out of his pocket and lit it, giving the younger man a chance to digest what he had just seen. "See, tavern boy?" Judah smiled. "I told you we had something special to take care of. That factory is our way out of our indentured servitude to the British."

Albert nodded his head in affirmation. "But what about the Arabs on the borders? Aren't they the ones we need to truly worry about?"

"Of course. We have multiple enemies, including people from within. The Underground is growing every day. We both want the same thing, to be free in a homeland under our own rule, but some of their methods are questionable. They are bound to be trouble, but the truth? Our only way to freedom is through a show of our strength. We are all soldiers in this cause."

"You're worried about the members of the Underground? What they might do?"

"I'm worried about everything. But for today, let's focus on what your assignment is."

"Am I going to learn how to use those machines? I'm good with my hands and I am sure that –"

Judah put up his hand, stopping Albert from saying more. "We all have to train in the fine art of bullet-making. But we have something else in mind for you to do. Ari and I want you to serve as a courier. You'll help us plot out the routes to the front lines, to get the ammunition into the hands of those who can use it best."

Albert's eyes widened as he nodded. Maybe being on the road would afford him more of an opportunity to inquire about his father's whereabouts. He was bound to meet new immigrants when they traveled to any of the port cities. "Anything you need, of course," he responded evenly.

Judah smiled. "You're a good man, Albert. Now our real work begins. You need to learn the safe passageways between here and Jerusalem and between here and Haifa. Most of that will be on public buses, but some will be on foot. You'll need to be careful, and not let any of the British soldiers recognize you as you travel. Many of them have permanent posts. After you make multiple trips, they may start to question you. You'll need to learn to be as invisible as possible and use disguises when necessary. Now, let's get to work."

By the end of the day, Albert's head was swimming with the details shared by both Judah and Ari. He had spent the waning hours of daylight alone in his tent, maps spread across his cot, various roads highlighted in red ink. He was charged with memorizing those red lines, burning them into his brain, understanding the most direct roads and having a strong grasp of the circuitous routes if the main roadways were blocked in any way. He ran his finger along one of the lines between Rehovot and Haifa. It took him back to the port city, to thoughts of his father making the long journey across the ocean to finally reunite with him. *Père. Be proud of me. I am fighting for what is ours, this homeland. If you are out there, just know that I am waiting here for you...* He shook his head but the image of his father, sitting at their kitchen table in Paris, smoking one in an endless chain of cigarettes kept popping into his mind. He could almost smell the fragrant smoke of the Gaulouise that rested between his father's fingers, taste the tang of the buttery wedge of brie that he imagined sat on a plate between them. He closed his eyes for a moment. What he wouldn't give to go back there, to Paris, to his family, to a time before it all went bad, before Hitler and his minions had seized control of his beloved city. He knew, right then and there that one day he'd return and reclaim his childhood home. For now, he had nothing more than his memories to cling to and those he vowed to hold safely in his heart.

He went back to the maps, taking the time to sear the images into his brain. Albert quickly realized that he had the ability to close his eyes and still keep the picture of the map in his mind, almost like looking at a photograph, each detail preserved. He worked in silent devotion all afternoon and when he finally looked up, he could hear members of the kibbutz begin to walk down the path outside of his tent that led to the dining hall for dinner. He quickly gathered his papers into a neat pile and replaced them in the large tan envelope that Ari had left for him and tucked it under his blanket and out of sight. He then pushed open the tent's flap and joined the others in the gathering darkness, his lips sealed about his true mission. He would keep up his end of the bargain. He had made that promise to both Judah and God. Above all and having nothing else to offer, Albert's word was his solemn vow.

WITH THE THOUGHT that she might see Judah at dinner, Naomi took an extra minute to tie a pretty white ribbon in her thick red hair. She wasn't sure what to make of her reaction to this man; she only knew what she felt deep inside. She wanted to be close to him, to feel his touch on her skin, his lips on her own. He made her knees weak and her heart beat faster in her chest when he was near. But with the importance of their mutual mission, she had to be a realist. They were all here for the same reason and that left no room for romance. She swiped a slash of color on her lips before turning away from the mirror, depositing her lipstick back in the small cosmetic case she'd brought along for the weekend. She'd left the majority of her things in Jerusalem, so she sparingly used what she had here. Checking over her image one more time, she was satisfied with what she saw before leaving her tent. She met Evie on the path to the dining hall.

"Long day, no?" the other woman asked.

"Certainly not what I had in mind when I woke up this

morning," Naomi teased back. "Imagine. I thought you were going to teach me how to plant tomatoes!"

"Are you sad that you won't be learning that necessary skill?" Evie asked, a wide smile appearing on her face.

"Maybe. I'm just glad that you trusted me enough to reveal the truth about this kibbutz."

"We're going to have our first training session tomorrow right after breakfast. It will be great to test out the equipment with everyone all together. I'm excited to get started."

"I imagine you are. You've known about this plan longer than most." Naomi linked her arm with her new friend. "What other secrets can you share?"

Evie laughed. "Haven't I told you enough?"

Naomi hesitated a brief moment, then gathered her courage and asked, "What can you tell me about Judah?"

Evie stopped in her tracks and turned to her friend. "What do you mean?"

"Is he attached to anyone? Is there a girlfriend I haven't met yet?"

"Now you're entering some dangerous territory. Judah is off limits."

"What's that about, Evie?"

"He's not going to be interested, so save yourself a whole lot of grief."

"And what exactly does that mean?"

"Just that he had his heart broken and isn't on the market. That's all I'm going to say."

"Broken? By someone here?"

"She's not here anymore. But I really can't talk about it, Naomi. It wouldn't be right. If Judah wants to tell you himself, if you find yourself that close to him at some point, I guess he'll let you know. I'm not at liberty to say anything."

“Well that sounds kind of mysterious. No wonder why he trusted you with all of this classified information about the factory. You’re good at this!”

“Leave it alone, Naomi.” Evie linked their arms again and pulled Naomi down the path, stopping outside the dining hall. “Besides, we have serious work to do. I for one plan to keep my head down and my mind on the outcome we all need. That’s the only way to succeed.”

“Okay, okay, I hear you. I will try to keep my head clear of anything other than making bullets,” Naomi whispered back.

“Good. I knew I could count on you to do what’s important. Now let’s eat. I’m starving.” Evie pushed open the doors to the dining hall and pulled Naomi inside with her. “I hope there’s something good for dessert, too. I’m craving sweets.”

Naomi looked at Evie with amazement. The other woman always had a pocketful of candy, put sugar in her tea, and remained stick thin. “I’m just hoping that whatever dinner is, it’s something other than tomatoes and onions. I can’t believe that you can eat that combination at every meal.”

“Get used to it. If we grow it, we eat it!” Evie said with a laugh.

With that, the two women picked up their trays and went off to find their dinner.

Nine

Rehovot right before midnight

Judah stretched his legs out on the narrow cot. Albert was snoring lightly in his own bed and the other members of the kibbutz were asleep as well. For Judah, rest did not come easily. Aside from the work that lay ahead of him, his past haunted him and kept him awake, especially when Geula appeared in his dreams. There were nights, like this one, when he felt her presence nearby in the close confines of his tent, where he had a sense that she was there, sitting right beyond the rim of his consciousness. He could imagine that if he were able to reach out through time, he would be able to touch her again. Had he conjured her to his tent tonight from the guilt of admitting to himself that he was attracted to Naomi? These feelings left him both overheated and agitated, knowing that there would be no peace for him anytime soon.

Accepting that sleep would elude him, he decided to sit outside instead. He pulled his pants back on and grabbed his shirt, slipping his arms into the sleeves without even buttoning it up. Grabbing his cigarettes and tucking them into his front pocket, he stepped into the cool night air and for a brief moment, he thought he was seeing a ghost. She sat in the dim light of the dying campfire, her white nightgown more sheer than she must have realized. Her naked, slim form was silhouetted, the curve of her breasts and roundness of her hips clearly visible. Her red hair was tied back away from her face and she was holding a pen in one hand, a stack of papers in the other. For a moment he stood stock-still, not wanting to alarm her or make her aware that he saw her there. He silently stepped back into his tent and then with a deliberate motion, loudly cleared his throat to signal his presence. It gave her just enough time to lift her head and acknowledge that she was no longer alone. She immediately clutched the papers she held to her chest, quickly crossed her legs, and nodded at him.

That small movement of her head gave him the permission he needed to cross over to where she sat, the glowing tip of the cigarette he had just lit and low embers of the remaining campfire the only light between them.

"Can't sleep either?" he asked.

Naomi barely moved. "No," she replied in a voice hardly above a whisper.

"What are you writing?"

"A letter. Home to my family."

"It must be hard for you not to tell them the truth of why you are here, no?"

He watched her eyes soften as she grew a bit less wary of him.

"You know that Evie told me everything?" she asked. He nodded his answer and she continued. "It is. I'm trying to fill in the spaces with descriptions of the planting fields and the people instead. I would never betray our true mission."

He nodded. "I know. Evie trusts you and so do I."

She smiled then and for the first time in what seemed like an eternity, he felt his heart slightly shift in his chest. The small movement, almost like an expanding sensation, surprised him.

"Tell me something about you, Naomi. All I know is that you're a student. What made you cross the ocean from glamorous New York City to this empty desert? Why would you do such a thing?"

He watched her compose herself further and his instincts told him that she was carefully crafting her response. Then she replied, "I wanted to find an adventure. Something more than the routine type of life I was living there."

"More?"

"Yes. To make a difference somehow. I thought I'd do that with my words, you know, write about my experiences and share them. Not too many people can travel around the world as freely as I can. I thought that was my mission, to document exotic places and the people who live in them. But now instead, I'll test the theory of actions being louder than words, I suppose." She lifted her chin and looked directly at him. "And you?"

"What do you mean? I'm fighting for my country." He ground out the butt of his cigarette in the sand beneath his feet. His hands, now empty, felt strange, almost with no purpose. He rested them on his knees.

"There must have been a time when you didn't have to fight. Tell me about what you did before you were a soldier."

He had to look away from her to answer. "I honestly don't remember. My family lived on the border and there was always one conflict or another with our Arab neighbors. We'd live peacefully for a while and then a bomb would fly into a field or a home, either killing our crops or our friends. This is a part of the world that has been at war forever. I don't know anything else."

She shifted the papers onto her lap and reached across to touch his arm. He could not help but notice the swell of her breasts beneath her thin shift as she moved. For the briefest moment he longed to reach out and touch them and that desire surprised him. He'd not craved that sort of intimacy since Geula died. He looked away, into the fire pit, to the last of the glowing embers instead of into her warm, emerald eyes.

"I'm sorry for that," was all she said. "It must have been a very hard way to grow up."

"No, I don't think it truly was," Judah replied as he tried to bring his mind back to their conversation, away from the unexpected desire beginning to build between his legs. "I became strong. Resolved. This project of ours? It has to succeed. This is our homeland, and we must claim it once and for all."

He knew that he should pull away from her now, stand up and walk back to his tent and let her finish her letter home, but he could not. The light touch of her hand on his arm was a magnet, a pull that he could not deny. There was something between them, something deeply sensual that he wanted to explore, but knew he should not. This sort of distraction was dangerous to their mission. He shook his head to clear his mind. "But promise me something, Naomi from New York." She looked up and he was almost certain that he saw her own longing staring back at him. "Listen to whatever Evie says. Be careful. Be safe. This is a dangerous undertaking and a precarious time for all of us."

"I know," she whispered. "I promise."

"Good. Good." He stood then, and her papers scattered to the ground between them. They both bent to pick them up, her shift dipping even lower until he could see one of her rose-colored nipples peeking out from beneath it. Judah needed to leave before he did something he might very well regret. Knees bent, he handed her the pages of the letter she'd written, then straightened to his full height and said, "Try to get some rest." With those words he turned and walked back to his own tent, very much aware that sleep would without a doubt elude him now. He needn't bother to try.

NAOMI SAT BACK and reorganized her papers, all the while trying to catch her breath. He had been here. Talking to her. In the dark, at night, as she sat in her nightgown. She felt a soft breeze brush against her overheated skin and lifted her head, allowing the cool air to bring her temperature and pulse back to a more normal level. She could not deny the attraction she felt toward this mysterious man. Knowing that she shouldn't get involved with him made the whole situation all the more intriguing. He was definitely forbidden fruit.

Naomi was not unaccustomed to the attention of men. At home, she had her pick of a stable full of them. She was also not an innocent. She had been in two relationships, one of them a very passionate affair with a fellow student at Columbia that had lasted over a year. While he had been kind and gentle with her, he had left her craving more, something either unknowable or unobtainable, or so she'd thought. Until she met Judah.

He was smoldering beneath the surface; she could tell that from the way he looked at her. When he made his way around the fire pit and walked toward her, his shirt wide open, baring his chest to her view, she knew. He was strength, he was power, and she wanted to make him her own. She wondered, then, what it was that stopped him from kissing her just now. What had held him back? Naomi recounted Evie's words earlier that day. He was off limits, in love with someone else, perhaps someone who had left the kibbutz? Her curiosity was beginning to run away with her, her journalistic skills about to kick in with full force. She'd get to the bottom of his reluctance; she would. One way or another, he was meant to be hers.

. . .

On the road to Jerusalem

On Monday morning, Evie appeared at the entrance of Naomi's tent. The sun had barely crested over the horizon, but Naomi could tell that her friend had a firm purpose.

"Naomi," she whispered. "Can I come in?"

"Of course," Naomi replied, kicking the thin sheet off and sitting up, all in one motion. She rubbed the sleep from her eyes.

"Get dressed. Ari needs me to go to Jerusalem and run an errand there. Didn't you say that you needed to return to the university to gather your things? Now's your chance. Pack a small bag with what you will need for the next couple of days and we'll go."

"Give me a few minutes. I'll just wash up. I'll be ready."

"Meet me in the dining hall. The next bus is scheduled to arrive in a half an hour." With those words still hanging in the air, Evie was gone, leaving Naomi alone and curious as to what kind of errand her friend had been tasked with in Jerusalem. But Evie had made a good point. Naomi did need to empty her room at the University, and knowing that she may not get another chance to do both that and fill out the appropriate forms for a school-approved leave of absence from classes, she propelled herself out of bed and down the path to the shower, washing away all doubts about her decision to stay in Rehovot. She was more determined now than ever that a formal education could wait for her return and that some time spent with Evie in Jerusalem would be priceless.

A short time later, as they sat on the bumpy ride to the holy city, Naomi finally gathered the courage to ask Evie what Ari wanted her to do. Evie looked out the window for a moment, but then turned back and said, "I sometimes act as a courier. Ari gives me an envelope and I take it to a man in the *shuk*. Then I wait a day or so to see if the man sends for me with something to take back to Ari."

Naomi looked around at the other passengers on the bus before whispering her reply. "What's in the envelope?"

"First rule of thumb. Speak in a normal tone. No one notices a conversation that seems ordinary. Understand?"

Eyes wide, Naomi nodded.

"Now, to answer your question, and if I had to guess, I think it's money," Evie said softly. "But I'm not sure. It's not my job to look at the contents. It's my responsibility to pick up and deliver the goods."

"Oh," Naomi replied, her mind racing. "But how do you know where to go?"

"I've done this before. The first time was tricky, but I've learned a few things since then."

"This man you mentioned. Does he ever come to the kibbutz? Do you know his name?"

"Why the interrogation, Naomi?" Evie smiled. "I'm a soldier, in an army. And I'm carrying out the orders of my commander!"

Naomi was taken aback by Evie's easy tone. "Am I pressing you for answers? If so, it's just my journalist's training," she replied, trying to lighten her own tone.

Evie's mouth turned up at the corners as she let out a sigh. "Understood."

Naomi put her hand on Evie's arm. "It's okay. We're all under the same stress."

Evie looked up then and changed the subject. "I think it's

amazing that you've chosen this path, you know, to be a reporter. Was that encouraged in the States?"

"Yes. It was," Naomi replied.

"You're lucky. For as long as I can remember, I wasn't taken seriously at home. My parents just assumed that I would follow in the path they chose for me, that I would marry and have children and do as my own mother did. But I never wanted that. I want to make a difference in this world, not throw dinner parties and sit in the background while the men go off to smoke cigars and make all the important decisions. I don't think you can understand that."

"Yes, I can," Naomi replied, nodding her head up and down. "As supportive as my parents are of my choice, I came here alone. You won't find many women who would brave an ocean and leave their family behind all in the name of adventure."

Evie considered Naomi's words while she formulated her response. "That's true. You Americans view life differently than we British do. For me, it was an uphill battle with my mother. I come from generations of women who did as they were told. I couldn't bear to be another meek little sheep dictated to by a husband of my parent's choosing. When I met Ari and Judah, everything changed. They see me for the person I am. Ari trusts me to do this errand for him. It means the world to me that I've earned that trust."

Naomi sat back in her seat for a minute, mulling over what Evie had said. She had a different experience at home. Her parents might not have been thrilled at her choice to come to Palestine, but they had stood by her decision. They could have stopped her, but they didn't.

"You're right, Evie. Up to this point my life has been very different than yours. But now we're both in this fight together. I won't question you again."

Her friend smiled. "Oh, you can question me. Just don't be surprised if I don't give you the answer you want to hear."

"That's a deal."

They rode the rest of the distance in companionable silence, each lost in her own thoughts. The bus bumped along the road until the city came into view and Naomi shifted in her seat to get a better look. She had not been gone that long, but she felt like everything had changed for her since she'd last been in Jerusalem.

"Are we headed straight to the *shuk*?" she asked Evie.

"No. We'll go to your room first. I have to wait for my signal that the meeting is set."

"Okay. I know where we can find a cot for you to sleep on. We'll bring it to my room. At least I can show you around the university. I think you'll find it interesting."

"I'd like that. And my favorite café is near where we are headed. We can grab something to eat."

Naomi hesitated before asking her next question. "How do you receive the signal for your meeting?"

Evie stood and indicated to the bus driver that she wanted to get off at the next stop. "All in good time, Naomi. For now, let's get ourselves to your dorm room."

A SHORT TIME LATER, they were in Naomi's closet, sorting through her clothing. There were two piles, a small one of articles they would take back with them on Evie's cot and a much larger one that would be boxed and left in a storage locker in the building's basement resting for now on Naomi's bed.

Naomi held up a filmy red camisole of a whisper-thin silky material. "Take?"

She passed it to Evie, who was folding the clothing into the tiniest bundle she could.

"Well, it's light enough. But where would you wear it?"

Naomi's eyes narrowed in thought. Then she said, "I don't think I'd use it all that often. But it would be appropriate sleepwear, don't you think?"

Evie laughed. "I don't think you'd get much sleep wearing this. Unless, of course, you were alone. Which would be a waste!" Evie put it in the pile that Naomi intended to take back with her. "Just promise me that you will enjoy wearing it, is all."

"I have to admit, Evie, that despite what you told me about Judah, I am attracted to him," Naomi confessed. Then she added, "And I think the feeling is mutual."

"Well, that would be something," Evie replied. "He's been shut down emotionally for so long. It's part of what makes him such a good soldier, I think."

"And you still won't tell me why he's this way?"

"No. It's not for me to tell you. It's for Judah to share, if indeed he feels you need to know." She stood up and walked over to the window that overlooked the Mount of Olives. "Everyone on the kibbutz has a story, Naomi. You understand that, right? We've come from all over the world, each person with their own reason for joining the fight. Some people want to talk about their past, and others just don't."

Naomi listened and took a chance, asking her friend a personal question. "What about Albert? It's clear that he's interested in you. Has he told you about Paris, and his father?"

"Yes, he has. In fact, the thing I find most intriguing about Albert is his faith that he will see his father again. Odds are that his father never made it out of Paris. We've all heard the stories of the Nazi brutality, and he was an older man, not as useful to them. But Albert truly believes that his father is alive. I admire him for that."

"Admire him? Is that what you feel for him? Admiration?" Naomi tried to keep the smirk off her face. She watched as Evie's ever-present mask of seriousness melted for the briefest moment.

"If I am being honest, I am attracted to him. But I made a promise to myself, Naomi. I have a mission one that I must see through. When this is over, truly over and we are a free nation, I'll make the time to fall in love. But for now, I'm going to stay focused on accomplishing our goal."

Naomi heard her friend's words, but she knew better than to believe them. She also knew that love eventually overruled reason, each and every time. For as much as Evie believed in what she said, Naomi knew that the other woman would not be able to avoid the inevitable. She might lose her heart to Albert, and if she did, it would be unwillingly. As a matter of fact, Naomi was fairly certain that it had already happened.

The women continued to work in companionable silence until the last of the items had been sorted and boxed. The only thing still hanging in the closet was the white wool coat Naomi had worn on the boat ride from New York City to Haifa. It looked forlorn and out of place now; it almost seemed like it belonged to someone else living in a completely different time. While it would be useless to her on the kibbutz, Naomi decided to take it with her anyway. She carefully folded it and lay it on top of the other clothes in her bag. She wanted it to serve as a reminder of who she once was, and a symbol of who she wanted to be. In every Hollywood movie she'd ever seen, the good guys always wore white, and for today, she considered herself a member of that very elite club.

. . .

The Shuk, Jerusalem

Their work in Naomi's room was finished. For now, they were able to leave what they couldn't carry back with them in a storage closet in the basement of the dorm building. Then, after heading to the registrar's office so that she could submit the forms for her academic leave, the two women made their way, Naomi playing tour guide and pointing out different sites on campus, then leading them through the narrow streets toward the *shuk*. Right outside of the marketplace Evie stopped at a café and motioned for Naomi to sit down at one of the many outside tables.

"Let's get a tea and some lunch," she said, pulling out her own chair and gracefully folding herself into it.

Naomi did as she was told. Immediately, her journalistic senses were heightened. She watched as old women dressed in black, long skirts and headscarves walked in and out of the stalls at the entrance to the marketplace, filling their net bags with a variety of produce from the colorful selections. She listened to the exchange between the buyers and sellers; it was a game of give and take, a negotiation over each ripe plum and apricot before a few coins changed hands. She could smell the exotic mix of spices each time the breeze blew their way and she was eager to see the rest of the *shuk*, to explore what lay beyond the first few stands of the various goods that were in her immediate sight line.

"Will you take me with you when you run your errand?"

Evie, who had been looking over her shoulder, turned back to Naomi. "No. I don't think so. It wouldn't be wise."

"Why not? Is it dangerous?"

"It's not so much that it's dangerous, but rather that the men

I meet with don't want to be identified by a wider circle of people. They tend to lurk in the darker corners of society."

"Well, I'll do as you wish, but don't rule it out. We'd be safer together."

"I'll take your offer under advisement. Now, let's order. I'm starving!"

THE NEXT DAY and the day after that they returned to the same café at noon. They sat in the open air, drinking tea and chatting until Evie felt that it was time for them to leave. By Thursday, Naomi was certain that today was the day her friend would receive the sign from their spot at the café that the meeting was on. Naomi watched as Evie prepared her tea, first adding milk and two spoonfuls of sugar into her cup before pouring the brew over the mixture, then asked, "Is today the day? Have you received the signal yet?"

Evie carefully rested her spoon on the cup's saucer. She lifted the tea to her mouth and took a sip before responding. "Not yet."

"But this is the place, right? This is where they somehow reach out to you? I mean, the falafel is good here, but we've come every day, we sit in the same location." She leaned in and pressed her friend for an answer. "This is how they find you, right? C'mon, Evie. It's almost Shabbat. We have to head back soon. They have to reach out today."

"Patience, Naomi. That's the key. If it's meant to happen, it will. If not, we take the bus to Rehovot at noon tomorrow to be back before sundown." She lifted her teacup again. "Are you hungry?"

"How can you be so calm? Don't you want to know if they will contact you?"

"I can only do so much. I'm here and willing to comply. Ari knows that I'll do my best."

She looked at Evie's face. Outwardly, she appeared serene--until Naomi noticed that her friend's leg was bouncing up and down under the table. She breathed a sigh of relief. The other woman was human after all.

WHEN IT HAPPENED, the signal was so subtle that Naomi almost missed it altogether. They had just finished eating lunch. The waiter dropped the check on the table and with it, a small note tucked underneath. Evie quickly read the message and stuffed the tiny piece of paper into the pocket of her skirt. Pulling some money out of her wallet, she quickly settled their tab and stood.

"I have to go," was all she said.

"Can I come with you?" Naomi asked.

"No."

Naomi reached out and put her hand on the other woman's arm. "If anything happens to you in there alone, I'll never forgive myself. Please. Let me come with you."

Naomi watched a shadow cross Evie's face. *Was it fear?*

"If I let you come, you must do what I say. You must stay quiet."

"I will. I promise," Naomi agreed. She watched as Evie wrestled with her conscience before making a quick decision.

"Alright then. Come along. Just keep your eyes down. Don't engage with the people you're about to meet."

"Right. Okay."

"The idea is to do what is necessary and go home in one piece." Naomi watched as Evie adjusted her shoulders back in an effort to steel herself for whatever it was that lay ahead. Observing her friend's small movement made Naomi pause.

Something made Evie's body tense up in anticipation, and Naomi realized immediately that it was out of character for the other woman to react in this way. "Follow closely behind me and whatever you do, keep up!" Evie commanded as she stepped inside the *shuk.*

Naomi did her best to stay with Evie as she wound her way past the vibrantly hued headscarves and fragrant stalls of the coffee vendors. They ducked in and out of the aisles, heading toward the center of the exotic marketplace until finally they stopped at one stall, a spice vendor, his brightly colored wares piled high on the various tables that surrounded his space. Naomi stayed closely behind Evie as her friend nodded to the man out front and continued on past him to the back, pushing away a large tapestry and stepping into a small, dimly lit room. Two men sat there, a table between them, each smoking a cigarette. The room smelled of old tobacco and sweat, causing Naomi to wrinkle her nose in distaste. One of the men leaned forward in his chair and leered in her direction.

"Brought a partner with you, Evie?" Then facing Naomi, he said, "Step closer, young lady, let me get a good look at you."

"No," Evie said with a stern tone to her voice. "She's not a part of this transaction. Let's just complete our business and we'll move on."

"Easy there, Evie. You know we like the ladies," the other man said as he sat up straighter in the rickety wooden seat beneath him. "She's pretty. Look at that red hair!" He leaned in closer and from the short distance between them, Naomi could smell the alcohol on his breath. "What's your name, *motek*?"

Naomi felt her heart race. She was frozen to the spot on the floor. This man was looking at her in a way that made her feel naked and vulnerable.

"Don't say anything," Evie directed her before turning to the men. "Do you have something for Ari or not?"

The man turned away from Naomi and said shortly, "That depends on what you've brought us today, Evie."

She stepped forward and dropped an envelope on the table. "Here. Now give me what I came for and we'll leave you in peace."

"Oh, I see. That's how you think this works." The man smirked, revealing two gold teeth at the front of his mouth. He pounded his fist on the table hard enough to make his coffee cup shake, the thick liquid inside almost spilling over the edge and onto the oily cloth. "You're not in charge here, I am. I determine how this goes," he shouted.

It was then that Naomi saw the gun tucked into the waistband of his pants. She shuddered and stood still, rooted to the spot. He moved quickly and grabbed the envelope, rummaging through it with his back turned so that they could not see the mysterious contents. When he finished, he pivoted around to face them again. "You're lucky it's all here this time." He fished around in the pocket of his stained trousers and pulled out a worn map. "Give this to Ari. But tell him that next time he'd better show up himself. Tell him to stop sending women to do a man's work!"

Naomi watched as Evie took the limp piece of paper gingerly from the stranger. She folded it carefully and put it in her own pocket. Then she grabbed Naomi's hand. "We'll be going now. I'll tell Ari what you said." She began to pull Naomi along with her toward the exit of the room.

"Wait!" the second man barked. He stood up and walked closer to Naomi. "So pretty," he said, putting one dirty hand on her soft curls. "I've never seen someone so lovely before. . . your hair is remarkable. So soft . . ."

Quickly, Evie inserted her body between the man and her friend. "She's not here for your pleasure. Keep your hands to yourself. We're leaving!" She yanked Naomi hard, causing her to nearly loose her balance as they hurriedly made their way out of the stuffy room, hearing the men's raucous laughter echo in their wake.

The two women flew through the *shuk* and didn't speak until they were back in Naomi's room with the door closed firmly behind them.

"Who were those awful men, Evie? Please tell me that you haven't been going there all alone. What did he give you for Ari?"

Evie just held her hand up, the simple gesture imploring Naomi to stop asking questions. "Listen to me. I didn't want you to come with me or to see that. I should have known it would unnerve you." She crossed her arms over her chest. "Besides. I'm fine on my own. It's not for us to question Ari's decisions. You know that. We're just soldiers in this war, Naomi. We follow orders."

"But, Evie," Naomi began.

"No!" the other woman responded sharply. "Don't say or ask me anything else." She picked up the towel she had been using since they arrived in Jerusalem and grabbed the toiletries they'd been sharing. "Seeing those men always leaves me feeling dirty. I'm going to shower. I suggest you do the same." Then she turned on her heel and left the room.

Naomi was still trembling, but after a bit she began to feel her breathing return to normal. She stood there in thought. Through it all, the discovery of the secret factory at Rehovot, the revelation that their mission was to make bullets, the wait to find out what they were meant to do in Jerusalem, war had always been a distant, hazy concept. When she lived in New

York City, she'd attended USO dances and raised money for war bonds, had performed what she thought was her patriotic duty for her country and the troops. She had listened to Ari and Judah discuss the likelihood of war coming to Palestine, the very one that she'd vowed to support with her work on the kibbutz. But today, in the center of the *shuk* in Jerusalem, of all places, it became real. Those two men. Their lascivious stares, making both she and Evie feel unclean. One of the men with a gun dipped into his waistband. She shuddered. The potential for violence was evident in the men's menacing looks, their posture, their voices. It brought it all home for Naomi. And to think...she had begged Evie to let her come. She put her head in her hands. What on earth had she gotten herself into?

en

Rehovot
November, 1945

JUDAH STOOD outside his tent and ground the butt of his cigarette under the heel of his boot. He and Albert had made it back to the kibbutz after completing a very successful scouting mission. They'd been able to shorten the trip between Haifa and Jerusalem significantly by changing the route, cutting across the country instead of hugging the coastline as they'd previously done. It was not as great a distance between the kibbutz and the hub of Tel Aviv; that trip could be made in a day. But to travel the miles to the port of Haifa took longer, especially if they were to be transporting contraband. They'd need to make that trek under cover of darkness, through small towns and villages with the potential for running into bands of Arabs, who would not appreciate their unwanted company. Many of these men had joined forces with the rebel Al-Jawrashi, who was famous for his dexterity in building and planting land mines. Al-Jawrashi was quickly assembling his own army of soldiers. They buried these bombs underneath roadways and dirt paths, leaving death and destruction in their wake. Judah understood the truth--danger accompanied them on each and every mile they traveled. True peril came with each footstep they took.

Judah was immune to the fear of the unknown. He had bought and sold guns all over Europe during the war and had negotiated with nefarious types who would have killed him over an ill word if they had the chance. For a long time, since Geula's death, he hadn't truly cared for his own safety or well-being. It was only recently that he'd begun to care again, and he realized that his new-found feelings for Naomi were to blame for that sentiment. He silently shook his head. Unwittingly, he'd become intrigued by the American beauty and now she occupied his thoughts all too often. He needed to regain control of himself, to deny the primal urge to bury himself deep inside her for some level of comfort, but he could not. He thought back to the bus ride to the kibbutz from Jerusalem the day before yesterday. He actually had to physically restrain himself from stroking Naomi's hair when he sensed somehow that she was anxious. He knew that he would be overstepping his boundaries entirely by pulling her into his arms, so he resisted the impulse. Instead, he just whispered a calming message, leaning in close enough to feel the soft shell of her ear against his lips. That small point of contact was enough to send both his body and mind reeling, that brief connection the thing that now remained foremost in his thoughts. For as much as he knew that he needed to keep his emotions at bay, he was relieved to realize that, in fact, he could still feel anything at all. Drawing in a deep breath of the clean morning air, he turned and headed off down the dirt path from his tent to find some breakfast, and, if he was lucky, a glimpse of the object of his sudden affection.

NAOMI SAT in the dining hall wishing that the tea in front of her was as strong as the coffee she was used to drinking at home. She was tired, despite the enforced rest she had gotten the day before on Shabbat. Whenever she closed her eyes, she saw those two dirty men in the *shuk*, their leering expressions burned into her brain. Their blatant intention to make both her and Evie feel like objects, not people, was something she'd not soon forget.

To complicate matters even more, Judah and Albert had joined them for the return trip to the kibbutz. The two men had been out together on a scouting mission, the target of which remained unclear to Naomi, making her extremely aware of all she did not know about the war effort she'd gotten tangled up in. Sitting with Evie on the bus ride back with Judah and Albert in the seat directly behind them, should have made her feel more comfortable, but it gave Naomi a greater sense of unease. As much as she wanted to be a part of this cause and to make a difference, an unexpectedly big piece of her wished that she was back in Manhattan, safely tucked away with her family. Just as they rounded the last bend of the bumpy road back to the kibbutz, when the homesickness was starting to overwhelm her, Judah had leaned in from his seat behind her and whispered into her ear, his warm breath caressing her skin. "It will be okay, Naomi. You'll be fine. We're almost home now."

She didn't know how it was that he sensed her anxiety because she didn't think that he knew her well enough for that. But when he said "home," the sound of the word warmed her soul. It confirmed for her what she already knew: that there was a definite connection between them. She had to decide what exactly she wanted to do about that, but for the moment, the reassuring tone of his voice had made her homesickness recede a bit. Naomi returned alone to her tent after dinner that night to rest. She knew that the next day, when they started work in the factory, would be a challenge. Try as she might to dismiss her thoughts, she could not. Instead, she spent hours tossing and turning on her cot, unable to find a comfortable position that would allow her to sleep. She couldn't turn off her mind, which had shifted to the questions she had about Judah. What had happened in his past that kept him at arm's length? Could she take the chance and try to break down the wall between them, or would the looming war, the very thing that brought them together, be the thing that kept them apart? After hours of relentless uncertainty, she stepped outside, where she was surrounded by the inky blackness of the night sky. The air was still and she was alone. It was so peaceful, the literal calm before the storm. She stood in the quiet for a long time, watching the sky begin to lighten. In the dawn of the new day, Naomi finally went back inside her tent to put on her clothing. It was time to get to work.

ON SUNDAY MORNING, as the dining hall began to fill with the other members of the team, she found herself scouring the room for Judah, but he was nowhere to be found. After a short while, Evie joined her, dropping a sheaf of paperwork and what looked like maps on the table with a loud thud.

"Good morning," Naomi said quietly.

"It is a good morning. Today's the day we begin our work in earnest," her friend said, eyes shining brightly.

"I still don't understand how you plan on keeping all of this," Naomi spread her hand over the materials Evelyn had placed down between them, "from all of them," she said, pointing to the group of farmers on the far end of the room.

"You'll soon understand how this works. After breakfast is done, each person goes off to their morning assignment. We've got this timed out perfectly. The factory workers will start to make their way to the laundry in small groups, pretty much under the radar. The farmers know that there are people who work here in the dining hall, in the laundry, or in the bakery.

They don't expect us to be in the fields with them. It's very well orchestrated."

"If you say so," Naomi said, shifting in her seat.

"Anyway, for today," Evie said, "just follow my lead. You'll get the hang of it very soon."

"Where have I heard that before?" Naomi could barely keep the sarcasm out of her voice. "Hmm. Let me think. Oh yes. The *shuk*."

Evie stood, ignoring her friend's last comment. "Eat something, Naomi. It will make you feel better. Besides, lunch is a long time from now and you'll be standing on your feet all morning. Once we're downstairs, there's no coming back to the surface before the all clear sounds at noon."

"Yes, Mother."

"Not funny," Evie replied, but the small upturn of her lips made Naomi smile.

"Do you want me to bring you anything?" Naomi asked as she stood up.

"A boiled egg and a pita, if you please. I'll get my own tea."

"Sure thing," Naomi said turning toward the kitchen. Just then she saw Albert approach, carrying a tray laden with food, heading toward them.

"I think someone else beat me to the punch," she said as she winked at Evie. "I'll sit over at Ari's table. Meet me after breakfast?"

Naomi started to move away, but not before she noticed her friend's confused expression. Then Evie saw that Albert was headed directly for her and her face softened. Naomi made a hasty retreat when she recognized that universal look. Evie was smitten.

Walking toward the kitchen, she picked up a metal tray from the table at the door and began to walk past the counter laden with food. She still couldn't get excited about eating onions, tomatoes, and cucumbers for breakfast, but she did like the thick, tart yogurt. She put some on a plate and added a few pieces of a light green fleshed fruit, grabbed a warm pita, and returned to the main dining room. She made her way over to where Ari was sitting alone.

"Mind if I join you?" she asked through the smoky haze of the cigarette burning low between his fingers.

"Of course, of course. Please sit." He smiled but then became serious. "I heard about your experience in Jerusalem. I know it wasn't pleasant, but war makes for some complicated alliances."

"Is that what you'd call those men? Allies?"

"Yes, as a matter of fact, I would. As unappealing as they are to have to deal with, they are a necessary part of our operation. They keep a line of communication open that we need to have available to us."

"I understand, but–"

"Let me stop you. There are no 'buts' in this scenario. We all must be willing to do whatever it takes to win this war."

Naomi looked at the man, her green eyes narrowing. "I'm looking forward to doing the important work we have ahead of us and I'm willing to accept the risks." She paused, choosing her next words carefully. "Those men were not as dangerous as they were lecherous. There's a difference."

"Of course," Ari said, walking back his original statement. "I don't mean to offend you, or devalue your contribution to the cause. As you know, we feel that the women on our kibbutz are as vitally important to our success here as the men. Not everyone on the outside sees it that way. You need to know that there will be many offensive circumstances in the days ahead. It's best to be prepared for anything."

"No offense taken," Naomi replied, knowing that Ari meant

what he said and that he could not control the actions of others. As she lifted a spoonful of yogurt to her mouth, she watched Ari's face as he looked up. Turning quickly, she saw that Judah was behind her.

"Good morning, Ari. Naomi." He sat down on the chair next to hers, close enough that she could smell his shaving soap and see the small nick he'd made on his chin from his razor. She put the spoon down so that the men she shared the table with wouldn't see her hand shaking.

"Today's the day, eh?" Ari said. "What we've worked toward."

"It is," Judah replied. "I just hope we're truly ready."

"We are. Look, we built the damned thing in less than a month. It can't take more than that time to get it up and running," Ari replied.

Naomi felt her own eyes widen. How could they have excavated and built that entire factory in such a short time? It didn't seem possible!

"Building it and getting it running are two entirely different things, my friend," Judah said, taking a sip of his tea. "Let's wait and see what today brings." Then he turned his body to face Naomi, his knee grazing her own.

"Will you walk over to the laundry with me?" he asked.

She couldn't find her voice for a moment, so she nodded yes instead.

"Well then, Ari, here we go. We'll make our way now. See you there."

He stood and pulled Naomi's chair back for her to stand as well. Her thoughts felt jumbled in her mind and she willed herself to take in a deep breath so that she'd be able to speak.

Once outside, she said, "Ari mentioned that it took less than a month to build the bullet factory. How could that happen so quickly?"

"The plans were first sketched in 1938."

She raised her eyebrows in surprise. "Wow. That's a while ago."

He nodded. "Yes. We've had this factory in mind for a very long time. We excavated one side, began building walls, and then dug out the other side. Yosef Avidar's Ta'as workers from all over the country helped with the casting. As soon as we had the roof in place and the work was dry, we insulated everything in asphalt. Then that asphalt was covered with four meters of earth. You've been downstairs. You know that it's long and narrow, but what you might not have realized is how sturdy the structure is. We made the walls and ceiling from thick concrete. It took twenty-two days, exactly, from start to finish."

"And there's only one entrance?"

"No. There are two. That was the toughest part of the project. Because of the explosives we are manufacturing, we needed an emergency exit in case of fire, or some sort of uncontrolled blast. But the way we set it up was for one to be used by the workers, coming up and going down. The other is for lowering machines, supplies, and in the worst case, a safety measure to get our people out if disaster strikes."

Naomi visualized the factory in her mind, getting a clear picture of what Judah was describing in her head. "What about the air? When we are all downstairs? I mean, when I was down there with Evie I did have a moment when I felt like I couldn't breathe."

"We thought of that as well. There are two chimneys. One for clean air to enter the space, the other for dirty air to be expelled. There are special compressors and tin pipes built especially for this purpose. Fresh air will be supplied to the factory eight times an hour. You'll be fine. There's plenty of air for everyone to breathe down there."

His words were reassuring and Naomi let her mind wander a bit as they walked toward the laundry. She wondered if she would be working with him, side by side, each day, and if that happened, would she be able to keep her mind on her tasks? Once at their destination, Judah held the door open and Naomi walked through into the dimly lit building where they joined the others already assembled there. Moments later, a few more people appeared, including Albert and Evie, who brought up the rear. Then, as if by magic, someone pulled a switch behind the large laundry tub and it moved to the side, exposing the entrance to the factory. One by one, the workers descended the staircase, and all Naomi could think was, *And so it begins.*

Eleven

The Bullet Factory
November, 1945

Naomi had to remind herself of Judah's promise that there was enough air for everyone to safely breathe as the group assembled underground for the very first time. It was crowded in the confined space as they all stood, shoulder to shoulder, surrounding the machinery. The overhead lamps provided enough light, but it still seemed to Naomi that each corner was cast in shadow. There was an anxious excitement that she could feel, radiating off of each body as Yosef Avidar cleared his throat in an attempt to get everyone's attention.

"Good morning, one and all," he began. "And welcome to your new workspace." He placed his hands on the machine closest to him. "You will begin your training today. This equipment," he spread his arms wide to include everything in the confined area, "is our ticket to winning our independence. Treat it with respect and guard it with your lives. I know that you all understand the importance of this mission. We are counting on each of you to get this job done."

Naomi felt Judah slip in to stand behind her, so close that she could feel his breath on the back of her neck. She strained to concentrate on what Yosef was saying as he ran through the use of each component on the assembly line.

The group listened in rapt attention as he explained the bullet-making process. He held up two separate pieces of metal. “This strip is copper. This one is brass. They make up the cartridges that hold the lead which houses the gun powder. That’s what makes the bullets effective once they’ve found their target. Some of you will be responsible for loading these metals onto these machines.” Two other members of Ta’as offered to demonstrate, making the intricate task appear simple. Yosef waited until the strips were firmly in place before continuing down the line. “Others will be carefully measuring out the lead to fill the cylinders, once they are stretched to the correct size.” A different man stepped forward and operated the machine, showing the group the end result–a perfectly formed bullet--before handing it back to Yosef. He held it up for all to see and moved on. “There will be a group responsible for making space in each bullet for a cap, and a hole for ignition. After that’s done, a group of *mohels* will snip off the ends of each piece of ammunition. Before a bullet leaves our factory, it is to be engraved with an A for Ayalon, the name of our factory, and E for Eretz Yisrael, and the year of manufacture.” He waited as those tasks were completed by a few more Ta’as members. “Finally, there will be packers, those who will load fifty bullets each into cardboard boxes,” he paused to hold up an example, “and then those who will load those boxes into cartons of one thousand bullets each. Once that job is complete, we’ll get those supplies to the people who can use them best. Any questions?”

Multiple hands shot up in the air. Naomi looked around at the eager faces and realized that she had better learn the names of the people she’d be working with. They were going to be together for many long days and nights, functioning in very close quarters. Already she felt overheated, sweat beginning to trickle down her back and between her breasts.

“What happens if the British soldiers get suspicious? What is the plan to keep them from finding us?" someone from the back row shouted out.

"Actually, we want them to feel comfortable in the laundry and bakery. We've invited the soldiers to drop off their dirty uniforms and to buy cake and bread from us. The idea is to make ourselves obvious and aboveboard, to hide in plain sight. They'll never come down here, we'll make sure of it. But you need to be careful. The only time you can enter and exit is set in stone. Once you're down here, there will be no going upstairs until the assigned time. Plan accordingly."

A soft murmur went through the group as people processed this information.

"What if the British are around when we are supposed to come down or go back up?"

"We will be closed for business during those times. You needn't worry about that," Yosef responded.

"What if we get stuck down here for one reason or another? What then?"

Judah stepped forward, moving around Naomi and nudging himself through the crowd to stand next to Yosef. "We've planned for that as well. There's a restroom for you to use and we have food and water stockpiled here, just in case. We'll make the best of it. We always do!"

"If that's so, make sure to leave a bottle or two of schnapps!" someone else shouted.

"Good idea," Judah said with a laugh. "I'll see what I can do to accommodate your request!"

Just then it seemed that everyone in the small space began talking at once. Yosef raised his hand to recapture the group's attention.

"I know that we will succeed here. We have all seen the worst of war. Many of you have suffered the loss of a loved one." His somber words hung in the air for a moment before he continued. "Countless numbers of us have been slaughtered in Europe just for the crime of being a Jew. That cannot continue. We are here to ensure our future, for our right to live freely and without prejudice in a country that we can claim as our own. And you? Together, my friends, you will make that dream a reality."

A loud cheer went up from the assembly of workers.

"Are you ready to begin?" Yosef called over the voices.

"Yes!" they cried, almost in unison.

"Good, good!" Yosef shouted back. "Ari and Judah have your assignments. There are members of Ta'as ready to train you in your tasks. Now is the time to get to work!"

The room filled with the energy of those ready to get started. Naomi waited patiently for Judah to come and give her a job to do. She watched him make his way through the crowd, doling out assignments until almost everyone had a specific duty. When it was just her and two other younger women, Rebecca and Tamar, left waiting to be told what they'd be responsible for, he finally turned to them. "Ladies, follow me, please."

He led them down a narrow corridor to a long table with large wooden crates piled on the floor underneath. He pulled out the first one and opened it, lifting out a small, flat piece of cardboard.

"These are the boxes the completed product will be packed in. You need to assemble them and then place exactly fifty bullets inside each one. At the end of the work day, we'll collect the filled boxes and prepare them for shipping. You're to inspect each piece before packing them. They should look like this." He held up a single bullet. "Smooth metal. No flaws. No imperfections." He put the bullet in Tamar's hand for closer inspection. Once she was done, she passed it to Rebecca and it eventually ended up in Naomi's palm. It was smaller than she would have imagined, and lighter, too. It was a dull copper color and shaped like the lipstick tube she carried in her pocket, pointy on the top, flat on the bottom. When she had finished turning it over and then over again, she handed it back to Judah, her fingers brushing against his once more. This time she forced herself to concentrate on her task instead of the way his roughly calloused fingers felt against her own skin. *You're here to work,* she told herself. *Keep your mind on the task.* But when she looked up, she saw that he was staring at her. There it was. His obvious desire reflected back at her and she hoped that the other two women didn't recognize it. She looked down quickly, willing her heart to stop pounding rapidly in her chest.

"Do you understand what is expected of you?" she heard him ask.

"Yes, sir," both Tamar and Rebecca said at once.

Naomi just nodded. She wasn't exactly sure what he was asking of her. Of course she could assemble and pack a box with the bullets. That was easy. She just wasn't clear about the heat in his eyes when he looked at her. It was as if he could see inside her very being. What did that mean and what did he expect her to do now? More importantly. What did she want to do?

Judah broke his gaze with Naomi and turned his attention to the other two women. "Good. Now let's begin." He left them standing around the table. As her workmates began to pull the flat pieces of cardboard from the crate, she shook her head to clear her mind. Forcing herself to smile, she did what she knew best. Interview.

"So, Tamar, Rebecca. Tell me. How did you end up coming to Rehovot?"

"I come from Poland," Rebecca said, a haunted look in her deep brown eyes. She was thin, but sturdy. "I escaped a camp and walked my way through the coldest winter of my life. I promised myself that if I survived I'd come to Palestine and never be that cold ever again."

"Were you alone?" Tamar asked.

"Yes," Rebecca replied, barely above a whisper. "My parents and my little sister? I never saw them after we arrived at Treblinka. I was sent to one line, my mother and sister to another. My father was taken away with the men. I don't think they survived a week there."

"How. . ." Tamar began to ask, but Rebecca cut her off.

"You don't want to know, believe me. I did what I needed to do to make it through." A tear ran down the young woman's cheek.

Naomi put down the box she was assembling and went around the table to embrace her.

"Of course. No one can know your pain. And we have no right to judge. Whatever you did, whatever it took to make it here, it doesn't matter now. We are your family. We are right here with you."

Rebecca nodded, regaining her composure. "I do this work for them. For my parents. For my sister."

"May their memory be for a blessing," Tamar said.

"Amen," Naomi replied, walking back to her spot at the work station, lowering her head and attending to the task at hand. They had boxes to make and no time to waste on what was. This was the time for action, to take charge of their future. She got to work.

. . .

THE WOMEN WERE ENGROSSED in the process of making of boxes when a loud alarm bell went off. All activity around them ceased and Naomi realized that it was lunchtime. She stretched her arms up over her head, feeling for the first time that she was using shoulder and back muscles that she hadn't exercised before. She felt a bit sore from having been huddled over the table with her new friends all morning and was happy to take a break. Judah stepped in front of the staircase to the laundry.

"One more rule. Before leaving the factory, please clean off the bottom of your shoes and check your pockets for metal filings. We don't want to have to explain these artifacts aboveground. You'll do this each time you leave this place."

Quickly, the workers from the underground factory formed a line, doing as instructed, then headed up the snaking staircase into the laundry. They made their way out into the sunshine of the day toward the dining hall. Mere moments later, the workers from the fields did the same thing. Naomi grabbed a tray and walked toward the kitchen. More than anything, she wanted a cup of tea. She walked over to one of the large urns filled with the hot liquid and lifted a blue mug from the shelf beside it. The aroma of the strong, dark brew was calming. Placing the tea on her tray, she took a bowl of yogurt and an orange and went into the main room to find a place to sit. Evie was already there, a large stack of papers on the table beside her.

"Are you going to work through lunch?" Naomi asked her friend.

Evie looked up from her task. "There's just so much to do. I'm making sure that everyone's assignment is the best use of our resources. We think we have it right, but every good plan needs adjustment."

Naomi's voice took on a teasing tone as she asked, "Interesting that you thought I'd be good at packing and assembling. I guess you didn't want me snipping the tips of those bullets, huh?"

"Are you kidding? You've got one of the most important jobs. Quality control. We expect not to send any duds out with you on the case!"

"Maybe you can teach me to shoot straight. Then I can really test the product."

"What are you saying? You want to handle a gun? Go out onto the battlefield? No, I don't think so. . . You don't know what you're saying," Evie remarked as she shook her head back and forth. "Besides. You're needed here."

"Well, maybe not the battlefield. But the target range? The one I know is at the back of the factory? What do you think? Will you teach me?"

Evie put down the paper she held in her hand and calmly asked, "Naomi, what makes you think I'm the one to teach you that particular skill?"

Naomi sat back in her chair. "C'mon, Evie. We both know that you can shoot straight. I have absolutely no doubt."

Evie looked away for a minute, then locked on to her friend's gaze. "Okay. I might not be able to deny that allegation. But we'd need Yosef's permission. And we'd have to find a way to do it in secret. No one else can know."

Naomi smiled broadly. "Great. I look forward to learning. Just tell me when." She dipped her spoon into her yogurt. "Aren't you going to eat something?"

"I'm not hungry."

"Evie, you've got to eat. You can't work at this pace without fuel."

Just then, and as if by magic, Albert walked over to where they sat, a tray in hand with a plate piled with salad, cheese, and a warm pita. There was a steaming mug of tea on it as well. He placed it in front of Evie. "I thought you might like some lunch. Two sugars, a splash of milk, right?"

Naomi watched as Evie's eyes widened at the sight of the food, a blush spreading across her cheeks. "Yes, that's right. Thank you, Albert."

"*Mon plaisir*," he said as he walked away.

Both women looked at each other for a moment.

"Is there something you want to tell me?" Naomi asked.

"Not that I can think of," Evie replied.

"Well, I think that boy's got it bad for you," Naomi said knowingly.

Evie waved her hand in the air between them. "Don't be silly. He's just being kind."

"Look around, Evie. I don't see him serving lunch to anyone else but you."

In a rare moment, Naomi watched as Evie let down her guard and said, "I do think he's pretty special."

Naomi winked at her friend. "Of course he is," was her only reply.

ALBERT HAD a job but then he also had a mission. His job was as a scout, working with Judah to find the fastest and safest ways to get the bullets to the front lines. His mission? To keep Evie safe. He had been watching her, picked up on her habits and preferences. He knew exactly how she drank her tea, which foods she seemed to favor, and which ones she never chose. He was drawn to her and he wanted to do all that he possibly could to keep the beautiful woman happy. He didn't really think that he had a chance to be more than her good friend, but that didn't stop him from fantasizing about what it would be like to hold her in his arms. Bringing her a tray of food was the very least he could do for Evie. He longed for the opportunity to do even more.

After leaving the meal in front of her, Albert went back onto the line and put together his own lunch. A pita, stuffed with salad and falafel, and drenched in creamy tahina sauce had become his favorite food. He assembled his sandwich, poured himself a large glass of cold water, and went over to the spot where Judah sat, wondering if he had further instructions to share. Albert folded his legs under the table and took a place on the bench seat across from his mentor. Not a word passed between them until Albert was almost finished eating.

"I have another assignment for you," Judah said quietly.

"Yes?"

"Tonight, I want you to make the trip between here and Tel Aviv."

"And do what once I'm there?"

"You will receive a package. Then you'll turn around and return."

"A package? From whom?" Albert asked as he chewed the spicy falafel, his curiosity peaked.

"You'll recognize the courier when the time comes. I can't hold your hand, tavern boy, and I want to be sure you can do this alone, without me as your guide."

"I know the way. I am sure that---"

Judah held up one hand, signaling Albert to stop talking. "You probably do, but this is a test to be sure. It's one thing for you to get lost on your own, or miss the drop-off from the courier. It's another thing to have you get lost with a shipment of bullets in the back of your truck, or get captured by the British. That would be worse."

Albert looked directly at the other man and without a word, accepted the challenge. "What time do I leave?"

"Ten minutes to midnight. Right before the guards by the railroad change shifts. It's better to find those bastards with tired eyes on the road rather than guards with fresh ones."

"I understand," Albert responded with a nod of his head.

"That goes for you, too. Head back and rest, try to sleep. You'll be up all night. We don't need for you to doze off behind the wheel and expose us."

Albert took the final bite of his sandwich, swallowing carefully before speaking. "Yes, of course." He wiped his lap clean of any remaining crumbs.

"I won't be here at dinner but will meet you back in our tent before it's time for you to go. We'll review the route one last time," Judah said, then pushed back from the table and stood. With a nod in Albert's direction, he left the dining hall without another word.

Albert took a long drink from his glass just as the people at other tables started to move. The bullet factory workers began to trickle out and back to the laundry so that they could return to their jobs ahead of the clothes washing crew and the bakers. Albert watched as the carefully choreographed scene unfolded before him. In groups of twos or threes they left and swiftly made their way to their assigned posts. Once they were gone, the farmers went back out toward the fields, leaving just Ari, Albert, and Evie in the vast space. With one last glance in her direction, Albert made his way outside and walked toward his tent. As much as he would have liked to spend the afternoon with Evie, he knew she had work to do. He'd have to settle for hoping that when he closed his eyes, he'd dream of her instead.

Twelve

By the end of the day Evie's head ached, her insides were churning with anxiety, and she desperately needed a shower. Aside from the mountain of paperwork that just seemed to grow each time she looked over at it piled high on the floor next to her cot, she had to keep an eye on the workers in the factory. She felt responsible for each and every one of them; most were her recruits and all of them were vitally important to the success of their mission. She wanted to be certain by the end of that first day of full operation that each and every person felt secure in their role on the assembly line. For Evie, the worst possible outcome was to have a disgruntled worker. There was the issue of secrecy, of course, and a person with a gripe might express that unhappiness to someone on the outside. Plus, the group had to gel quickly and produce the bullets rapidly without any conflict or disagreements among its members; efficiency was fundamental to their expected outcome. She knew that was a lot to ask of virtual strangers crammed together in a small space, but the stakes were enormous. This plan of theirs had to work. She made a mental note to catch up with the majority of them in the dining hall during the evening meal. She could casually check in as they all ate together, ask a few questions and take their comments back to Ari and Judah.

Evie gathered her towel closely around her body, grabbed her clean clothing and toiletries, and headed back out into the late afternoon sunshine to walk down the dusty path. It was nearing the end of the time when the women generally bathed, a brief moment of sisterhood, a time to swap gossip and trade advice, to shore each other up after a long day of work. As she approached the low, squat, gray cement building that housed the showers, she could hear the clamor of voices as the women spoke loudly to one another over the sound of drumming of the water. It was interesting to hear them speaking a mix of Yiddish and Hebrew, most with accents from a variety of different European countries. It was a wonder that they could all communicate with one another, despite their varied backgrounds. Smiling to herself, Evie realized that the combined strength of this group of women was, most assuredly, an immeasurable force.

Once she stepped inside the communal bath, she was hit with a wall of steam rising from the showers and she was more eager than ever to wash off both the grime and the stress of her day. She put her fresh clothing on a hook in the changing area and went to find a vacant stall. It was all so different than the well-appointed bathrooms in the home where she was raised; here they didn't even bother with shower curtains. Modesty among these women was not a consideration and Evie smiled at the thought that her mother would be appalled. Her own nakedness, or even the bare bodies of the other women around her, didn't bother Evie at all.

She stepped into the warm water and soon began to feel her muscles relax. As she lifted her arms to wash her face, she realized just how anxious she'd been all day. Her neck had been so stiff with tension that it actually ached as she massaged shampoo into her scalp. She let the spray soothe her for a bit longer than she should have, especially knowing that the men of the kibbutz still needed to bathe as well, and that hot water was a commodity that they all valued equally. Sighing, she finished by washing the rest of her body with the one true luxury she allowed herself–a bar of lavender scented soap. She had purchased some when she and Naomi were in the *shuk* in Jerusalem and she savored its relaxing perfume as it filled the air around her. She drew in a deep breath, calming her thoughts with the gentle fragrance of the delicate flowers. A few moments later, she turned off the water and pulled her towel from the hook, wrapping it tightly around her body. Then she went into the outer room to find clusters of women finishing up, checking their faces one last time in the small mirrors that hung over the sinks. That's where she found Naomi slipping into one of the pretty cotton shirtdresses she'd helped her friend pack to bring to the kibbutz. This one was a light blue and white checked gingham pattern, cinched tightly at the waist, the top buttoned discreetly to avoid revealing too much cleavage.

"Enjoy your shower?" Naomi asked, as though they'd already been in mid-conversation. The lack of formality was one of the traits about the other woman that Evie had decided was very American. She smiled at the no-nonsense approach of it.

"It felt pretty wonderful," she replied, pulling her own clean white blouse over her shoulders, feeling a bit more limber now. "So does being in the sunshine after a day underground." She toweled off her lower body and then slipped into her panties, adjusting her plain, khaki skirt on over them. Looking up at Naomi, she said, "I like your dress."

"Thanks! Feel free to borrow it anytime!"

Evie smiled. "I think the top would be too big on me. But it looks good on you."

Naomi laughed, straightened her collar, and then replied, "We can make it work, if you're interested!"

"Not today, but maybe another time," she replied as she

watched her friend reach into a small embroidered bag and pull out a tube of lipstick. She marveled at how quickly the splash of vivid red color made Naomi's whole complexion look brighter.

"Suit yourself!" her friend teased. "Should I wait for you? Are you heading down to dinner?"

"I think so, but you should go on ahead. I need a minute to collect my thoughts. It was a busy day."

"Okay. I'll see you there. I'm starving!"

Evie nodded, then watched as Naomi turned to leave. "Oh, one more thing," she called after her. Then she lowered her voice as the last few women passed on their way out. "How was your first shift at the factory?"

"It was fascinating, actually. You were right to put me at the packing station. It seems that I have a true talent for quickly fitting those pesky bullets into the boxes. Who knew?"

"I guess I did," Evie answered, feeling herself relax just a bit.

"I'm glad someone has a handle on what needs to be done." Naomi winked and walked out of the room, leaving Evie alone in the now vacant space to sit in silence for the first time all day. But not for long. She heard a familiar man's voice call out, checking to see if it was safe for him to enter, not wanting to disturb the women if they were not yet finished. It was Judah, and Evie knew that it was her cue to leave.

"It's just me, Judah," she called out. "And I'll be out in a minute."

She quickly gathered her things, ran a comb through her hair and pulled it back into a wet bun that sat on her collar, soaking through the material there. She slipped into her sandals and stepped back outside into the sunshine, shading her eyes with one hand. She found Judah leaning against the building.

"Your turn," she said, smiling up at him.

He threw the remains of his cigarette down and ground it out under his boot before asking, "How was it today?"

"Some kinks, but that's to be expected, right? I'm going to find out how everyone else feels when I see them at dinner. Did you find any glaring problems?"

"At the factory? Not really. I'm more concerned about tonight's mission."

"Why?" Evie asked.

"It's Albert's first solo run. I just want it to go off without a hitch. He's an important part of this process and I'm trusting him with a huge responsibility. He'll end up being one of the primary couriers of the bullets once we get this up and running fully. It's a lot to handle."

Evie felt a shudder run up her spine. She knew that Albert was to have a job outside of the factory, she hadn't known what that was until just now.

"Will he be transporting bullets tonight?"

"No. It's a practice trip, really. He'll deliver a small package to a couple of our men in the field, but it's a true test. He can't get lost and he can't be seen along the way. Those are two big pieces to our ultimate success."

"Wait," Evie began. "I thought we were shipping the bullets both by train and by lorry. Isn't that why we built this kibbutz so close to the station? Didn't you hire a team of drivers for the trucks?"

"Yes, we're using a three-pronged approach. The bullets we send by railroad are to be stockpiled in a variety of places and distributed as needed. The lorry drivers will eventually get the bullets through to the front lines. But Albert needs to be able to get ammunition directly to our couriers when the war begins. He'll plug any holes and distribute the goods with pinpoint precision, so they can be delivered exactly where needed when the battle starts. This method will insure that our soldiers have the tools required to win this war."

Evie steadily held Judah's gaze. She didn't want to give away the truth, that her insides were shaking at the mere thought of Albert risking his life in this way. She had barely admitted to herself just how she felt about him. She certainly didn't want to tip Judah off and signal that she had a soft spot for their French comrade.

"When does he go?"

"Around midnight, after the camp is asleep, right before the soldiers at the station change guard. I told him to get some rest now so that he stays awake on the ride back and forth."

"Good plan," she replied, hoping that her voice sounded normal, that she didn't give anything away. Then, starting off in the direction of the dining hall, she turned back and asked, "Will you be at dinner?"

"I'll stop in to grab something, but Ari and I have a lot to review. I'm meeting him in his tent."

"Right. I'll catch up with you tomorrow, then."

"Goodnight, Evie," he replied as he disappeared into the bathhouse.

She stood still for a brief moment, watching a few other men begin to trickle down the path, wanting to shower before they ate their evening meal. So many thoughts swirled in her mind, but the one at the forefront was about Albert and the job he was tasked with tonight. Squaring her shoulders, she set off down the path, making her mind up as she went. She wanted to see him before he left the kibbutz and she needed a plan to make it seem as casual as possible. But what to do? That's when inspiration struck. She'd ask Naomi. For some reason, Evie knew the other woman would have the answer.

. . .

When Evie pushed open the door to the dining hall, she was struck by the loud chatter rising up from the vast space. People who had been mostly strangers until today were now animated in conversation; bonds were being formed by coworkers, friendships cemented by a common cause. It was everything that Judah and Ari told her would happen if they got the kibbutz up and running, and Evie felt a warm rush of pleasure travel up her spine. She had played a major role in what she now saw in front of her and for the briefest, strangest moment she wished she could tell her father about it. She wanted him to know that she was more than a pretty debutante, that she wasn't interested in her mother's fancy social circle of wealthy, overindulged women, that she had the ability to make a real change in the world. She wished that her own family could see her for who she truly was, the way that Ari and Judah viewed her. But then she remembered that they were on opposite sides of this war, really, and it was like a splash of cold water to her face. Shaking off the melancholy that began to descend over her like a rain cloud, she went off in search of Naomi, scanning the room until she located her friend at a large table full of laughing people in one corner. As Evie approached, the group quieted, recognizing that one of their leaders was about to crash their raucous party. It was then that Naomi, sensing the group's unease, turned and joked, "You sure know how to make an entrance, Evie!"

"Oh, no. I'm so sorry. I just need to speak to you for a moment, Naomi," Evie said quickly. "But I didn't mean to interrupt your dinner." She motioned to the crowd around the table. "It can wait." She turned on her heel to walk away.

"Don't be silly," Naomi replied, reaching out to grab Evie's hand. "What do you need?"

"I just had a question. Can I see you in private?"

Naomi stood. "Of course." Then turning to her dinner mates, she winked then added, "Don't have too much fun without me." She linked arms with Evie and walked with her over to a corner of the room. "Is there something I can help you with? Something in the factory?"

"Oh, no. Nothing like that. It's personal."

"I see," Naomi responded, her brows lifting. "Let's step outside then."

The two women left the dining hall and went to sit on one of the benches at the far end of the building. Once settled, Naomi turned to Evie. "What is it? Are you okay?"

"Yes, yes. It's silly, actually," Evie replied, now nervous to admit to Naomi the depth of her feelings for Albert.

"Just tell me."

"Okay." Evie gathered her thoughts. "Albert is going on his first mission tonight. I want to do something nice for him, to let him know that I'm here for him and am waiting to see that he returns safely."

Naomi broke out into a big grin. "I knew it. I knew you had feelings for him."

Evie blushed and twisted her hands together in her lap. "I do care about him, but I am concerned for all of the members of the kibbutz."

"No," her friend replied. "It's different between the two of you."

All Evie could do was nod her head up and down. "That's true," was all she said, then added, "Any ideas? How can I let him know that I am interested in him?"

"Let me think," Naomi replied.

Evie waited silently for a few tense moments. She was startled when Naomi jumped out of her seat.

"I know. Bring him a thermos of hot tea for the ride. Maybe

a piece of cake as well. Meet him before he goes. Be at the truck when he's supposed to leave. And wish him good luck on his mission."

"Should I tell him how I feel?"

"I think your actions will make him aware that you're attracted to him. And," she added with a wink, "we know that it's mutual. I mean, he's always looking out for you!"

"Do you really think so?"

Naomi sat back down and grabbed one of Evie's hands. "I don't know how to tell you this, but the whole kibbutz sees it. That boy is crazy for you."

"How can you tell that he's just not being kind? That seems to be his nature anyway."

Naomi laughed out loud. "You haven't done this before, have you, Evie?"

"Done what?"

"Been involved with a man."

"Well, um, I'm not sure. . ."

"If you're not sure, you're telling me all I need to know."

"I've been busy with our mission, Naomi. I've had no time for any, any–what did you call it? Involvement?"

"Oh, honey. It's more than that. It's the feeling that your heart is racing out of your chest whenever you see him, that if you can't get close to him you might just die. That you want the moment when his lips touch your own so badly that if he doesn't kiss you, you might faint!"

Evie laughed out loud herself then. "That sounds like one of your American movies! That's not real life."

"Oh, my dear. It most certainly is the truth. I have fallen in and out of love before. Actually, I've experienced it all," Naomi smugly replied.

"All?" Evie turned her full attention to her friend. "Really?"

"Are you scandalized now?" Naomi inquired. "I've had my fair share of experience, if that's what you're asking."

Comprehension dawned on Evie's face and she did her best to remain unfazed, although she desperately wanted to know the details. She wanted to know everything.

"How many… how many men have you 'fallen' for?" she asked, trying to sound unaffected by the turn in the conversation. She realized that Naomi was referring to more than just mere attraction. In Evie's mind, that made the American woman all the more exotic.

"A few. Let's leave it at that," Naomi replied.

Evie could sense that her friend didn't want to divulge too much, but she knew that if she could be patient, she'd get the full story out of Naomi bit by bit.

"So you think that if I put together a care package for the road, Albert will know I'm interested in him? Could it be that easy?"

"It's a start and you're a novice. Let's take it slowly, let this relationship unfold at its natural pace."

Evie listened intently, knowing that having a friend like Naomi was going to be invaluable. She needed this kind of guidance from another woman; it was something she'd never experienced before.

"Okay. I need to find a thermos, then."

"I have one. I brought it from home. It's in my tent."

"Can I borrow it!"

"Of course you can, silly! I love that you're involving me in your romance with Albert. It's just so exciting!"

"Now who's getting ahead of herself? I'm just going to bring him tea and cake. Didn't you just tell me to take it slowly?"

Naomi stood and pulled Evie up with her. "I see why Ari and Judah trust you, Evie. You're a quick learner!" she teased. "Now let's go get that thermos and decide exactly what you're going to wear when you go see Albert later."

And just like that, Evie was thrown into the unknown world of the type of intrigue she'd only read about in dime novels. It almost made the work she'd put into the mission of building a kibbutz and devising a war plan pale in comparison. . .

Thirteen

BEFORE SHE COULD GIVE it further thought, Evie found herself carrying a mesh bag with a full thermos of hot tea and a thick piece of marble cake wrapped in wax paper tucked inside. She gathered her courage and headed through the dark kibbutz toward the garage where the trucks were parked. Feeling a little bit uncomfortable in Naomi's borrowed clothing--a tan silk blouse and beige linen pencil skirt--she stepped carefully on the rocky path in her friend's strappy wedge sandals. Wearing the very feminine apparel made Evie even more aware of her attraction to Albert. She had finally admitted to herself that despite their different backgrounds, they were very much alike in one way: they each longed for their father's approval for their current mission, but they would probably never have that desire fulfilled. Knowing that they shared that one wish made her feel close to him in a way that she'd not felt about anyone else before. It was thrilling and frightening at the same time.

Evie cursed softly under her breath. Unaccustomed to wearing a high heel, she nearly turned her ankle on a small stone on the path. Once she made her way around a large olive tree, she saw Albert talking to Judah, most likely going over the last of the details for tonight's trip. She could barely make out their hushed words to one another as she waited in the shadows to remain unseen; she did not want to reveal herself to Judah. When he grabbed Albert by the shoulders and pointed him toward the truck he was to drive that night, Evie felt her heart pick up speed. She could only hope that she'd have a moment to see Albert alone before he drove off. Luckily, the men parted ways and Judah walked in the direction of the dining hall, quickly disappearing out of her line of sight in the darkness. She willed her feet to move toward Albert, making her way to the lighted garage and she watched as his body tensed for a moment, sensing her presence. He turned then, recognizing her, his face clearly surprised to see her walking toward him.

"Evie? Is that you?" he whispered.

"Um, yes, Albert. It's me."

"It's late. You shouldn't be here," he admonished.

She searched her mind for the words she'd practiced with Naomi. They had worked hard to come up with exactly what she'd wanted to say, her friend coaching her on the precise phrasing. "I've brought you a little something for your trip. I thought you might need a small snack to help keep you awake." She hoped her words sounded casual, yet concerned. That was the approach she and Naomi—well, mostly Naomi--decided was best.

He smiled then, stepping in closer to her, reaching for her outstretched hand still holding tightly to the bag. "How kind of you," he said, looking directly into her eyes.

"Of course. You have an important job to do tonight."

"Yes, but you should be fast asleep, Evie. I'll be okay. I know the way. And you have another long day tomorrow."

"I just wanted you to know…"

"Shhh," was all he said. His fingers lingered on her own as he took the bag from her and she felt a flash of energy course through her body. It was unlike anything she'd experienced before and from the expression on his face, she knew he felt it, too.

"What? What did you want me to know?" he asked in a whisper, stepping even closer.

She drew a deep breath and could smell the spicy scent of his soap that lingered on his skin. "Just that I am thinking of you tonight."

His face changed, his eyes searching her own before he pulled her in close to him and softly kissed her lips.

Evie realized that she should be more careful than this, that the vow she'd made to herself not to fall in love until her mission was complete must remain intact; however, in that moment, nothing else mattered. His lips were warm and so inviting. She wanted to remain in his embrace forever and will the rest of the world to fade away, to allow her this man, this moment. Her first kiss. It was magical.

When he pulled back, away from her, he seemed as breathless as she felt. "Evie." He searched her face as if he was memorizing its every detail. "You make it hard for me to leave you."

"I'll be here when you return, Albert. So please, be careful and come back home safely."

"I have all the more reason to do that now," he replied, placing his hand on her chin and tilting it upward, searching her eyes with his own. He quickly gave her one more brief kiss, then turned away and walked toward the lone truck. Once at the door, he turned toward her, winked and stepped up into the seat. When he twisted the key in the ignition, Evie heard the engine roar to life and watched as he carefully steered the vehicle onto the road. She waited until she saw the last of the truck's red tail lights disappear around the bend, placing Albert firmly on his mission. Sighing, she slipped off the wedged shoes and walked barefoot all the way back to her own tent, feeling somewhat off-balance from her encounter with Albert. She knew that sleep would be elusive, because when she closed her eyes all she would see was her own worst imaginings of what he might encounter on his trip. Evie knew that she would hold her breath until morning, until the time when she might see him again, praying for his safe return, longing for the warmth of his embrace, and cursing herself for feeling this way at all.

ALBERT HAD MEMORIZED THE TWISTY, dark turns in the road that would take him toward the bustling city of Tel Aviv. He had not seen another vehicle on the quiet road, but it was late at night, not a time for the residents of the sleepy towns between Rehovet and Tel Aviv to be out. Luckily for him, he did not spot any soldiers or any other travelers for that matter, and even more importantly, he knew the way cold. The fact that he did not have to fully concentrate on the direction he needed to take was a blessing, because all he could think about as he kept the truck on the main road was the kiss he'd shared with Evie. He knew how he felt about her, but it was thrilling to discover that the unrequited longing he'd experienced was actually shared by her as well. *Evie!* His mind raced again when he thought back to the kiss they'd shared. The softness of her lips lingered on his own. He had no idea how he'd garnered the courage to reach for her when he did, but it was as if a primal instinct took over and he could not do anything other than pull her into his embrace. *And that kiss!* It was all he could have ever imagined and more. To know that she was feeling for him the same way he was feeling for her was exhilarating and he knew that he wanted more. It was somewhat undefined in his mind as to what that meant exactly, but he was eager to explore that unknown territory with Evie. She was his soul mate. That sudden realization made him smile as he sat alone in the darkness of the truck's driver's seat.

As he rounded the last bend in the two-lane road before the twinkling lights of the city came into view, he forced his mind back to his mission. He was to travel to the outskirts of the business district and check in with two of Ari's foot soldiers there before he could turn around and head back home. At least on this paved road, he didn't need to worry about land mines. That was a relief. He had a small package, wrapped in plain brown paper and twine on the seat next to him that he was to pass along. In his mind's eye, he could see the exact route he was to take; he kept his hands steady on the large steering wheel as he cruised along the smooth pavement and made his way to the arranged location. When he was close, he turned off his headlights as instructed and pulled into a lush orange grove under the cover of the majestic fruit trees. Cutting off his engine, he hopped out of the truck and glanced back at the package still sitting safely on the passenger seat, knowing that he was to wait until Ari's courier made contact. It was dark and silent in the fragrant orchard, but he wasn't afraid. Albert had faced worse, hiding out from the Nazis as he worked his way through war-torn Europe; he knew how to disappear into the shadows if need be. He waited patiently, thinking about the hot tea and cake that Evie had packed for him and he decided that he would wait to eat and drink until he was safely on the way back to the kibbutz.

As he reached up to grab a ripe orange from a low branch, he thought he saw a shadowy movement in the distance. *Someone is out there!* he thought to himself, standing taller, forgetting the fruit for the moment. As the form inched closer, Albert relaxed. He realized what he saw were two Bedouin women, each of their long burqas scraping the dirt path, small stones scattering with their steps. The first thought that crossed his mind was that it was late at night, and perhaps the women were lost. Why else would they be in the grove at this hour? Were they hiding from something, or someone? Albert remembered all too well what that felt like and decided that he might ask them if they were hungry; he could share his cake if need be. Then he noticed that they were covering the ground between where he stood and themselves at a very rapid pace and were almost upon him. He stepped onto the path to greet them.

"*Shalom, mttim,*" he called out in a steady voice, hoping that they spoke some Hebrew, his newly acquired language of choice. When they said nothing in reply at first, he wondered if they understood him. Then, trepidation crawled up his spine. Maybe these Arab women meant to do him harm. Perhaps they hid a weapon of some sort under their long robes. He could not make out their faces because the only feature left uncovered by the niqab each wore was their eyes. Before he could move back to the safety of the truck, they were in front of him. One nodded at the other then turned toward Albert and asked him in a surprisingly deep voice, "Do you have the package?"

Men? They are men? Albert's mind raced. *Why are they dressed like women? And how can they possibly know of the package?*

"Who are you?" he demanded.

"You are Albert, aren't you?" one of the disguised men questioned in perfect Hebrew.

All Albert could do was nod in assent.

"Then no matter who we are. Ari sent us to pick something up from you. Now hand it to me and we'll be on our way. The sun won't wait for you or for me, now, will it?" The stranger pointed eastward, up toward the star-filled sky.

At the mention of Ari's name, Albert realized that these men, whoever they were, knew his commander. They expected the package to be delivered and that he'd better hand it over. He scrambled back to his large vehicle and grabbed it off the seat. "Here it is," he said, extending the offering with a swift movement. In a flash, it was taken from him and the stranger tucked it into the large sleeve of his costume.

"Alaykumu s-salam" the man murmured and then nodding to his accomplice, began to walk slowly away from where Albert still stood. The entire transaction took less than five minutes, but it took much longer than that for Albert's heart to slow back down to its normal pace. *Men disguised as women? To what lengths would Ari's troops go to deceive the British army?* So much for this being a simple reconnaissance trip.

Albert shook his head as if to clear his thoughts. It was then that awareness dawned. He had been granted admission inside the veil of secrecy that surrounded so much of what Ari and Judah did. First the bullet factory and now these strange couriers. It was a much bigger evaluation of his ability than he could have possibly realized when he left the kibbutz earlier that night. It wasn't his driving and navigation skill put to the test; it was that Ari and Judah both knew that he would never speak of this to anyone else. Not ever. He continued to watch as the two figures made their way across the grove, becoming small specks in his line of vision until they disappeared into the inky darkness between the large orange trees. When he could finally see nothing moving in the distance, Albert climbed back into the truck and turned the engine on. It was then that he realized his hands were shaking. He willed himself to be calm, wrapped his fingers around the cool metal of the steering wheel, and closed his eyes, visualizing the route back to the kibbutz, pulling a mental map up behind his lids. Once the picture crystallized in his mind, he drew in a deep breath and allowed it to reach his hands in an effort to calm himself. He took a moment and flexed his fingers. In the next minute he depressed the gas pedal and steered the vehicle back onto the road, the promise of a cup of tea and a bite of cake his only companions on the way home.

. . .

THE PALE-YELLOW LIGHT of daybreak was just beginning to brighten the sky as Albert made his way up the last steep hill of his trip. The engine of the truck groaned at the incline, so he downshifted to give the vehicle one final burst of power. He was rewarded with his first glimpse of the entrance to the kibbutz and he smiled. Just a little more to do before he could head off to his bed and sleep. He wondered if Evie was awake yet and thought about the kiss they'd shared the night before, still tasting her lips on his own and the sweetness of the last bite of cake she'd so thoughtfully packed for him. He also wondered when he could be alone with her again.

He had so many questions swirling around in his head: Who were those men dressed as women? What was in that small package he'd carried? When was his next mission? He maneuvered the truck past the laundry and bakery and into the nearby garage. Once he cut off the engine, he grabbed the thermos and wadded-up wax paper from the seat, jumped out of the truck and walked over to the pegboard where he hung the keychain back in its proper place. He stepped outside and saw a few people walking into the dining hall for an early breakfast and wondered if he'd find Evie inside as well. He made his way there and pushed through the doors to look around for himself.

It was still early enough so that the space was nearly empty, and he could see right away that she wasn't there yet. Disappointed, he turned to leave, knowing that he needed to get a few hours of sleep so he'd be ready to get back on the road later that night if Ari had another assignment for him. Just as he got to the exit, Judah walked in, nearly knocking Albert over.

"So, you made it back in one piece?" Judah asked with a mocking tone.

"Yes, of course I did," Albert responded in a hushed voice. "Were you aware of who Ari sent to meet me? That they were two men dressed as Bedouin women?"

"No, but that isn't surprising. We have men in various disguises enlisted in our fight. It's just one way to stay ahead of British Intelligence. We need to be smarter than our enemy, Albert."

"That may be true, but I wish I'd had some warning," Albert replied, watching Judah's eyes narrow and regretting the words that had just left his tongue.

Sternly, Judah replied, "You had no true need to know. Must I remind you that you're a soldier in this army now? You get an order and you carry it out. That's all!"

Not wanting to be reprimanded in such a public place or jeopardize the trusted status he thought he had achieved by being sent on the mission at all, Albert replied, "I understand. If you'll excuse me, I'm going to my tent to catch up on some sleep." He waited for Judah to dismiss him, even though he wanted to get as far away from the other man as he possibly could, then he saw Judah's face soften.

"It's for your own protection, too, you know. We've placed a lot of trust and faith in you, Albert," he said softly. "I know you'll carry on with complete compliance. Sometimes it's better not to know, but rather just to do what's asked of you, no questions asked. You'll have to believe me on this one."

"You're right, Judah. It won't happen again."

"Go. Get some rest. I'm sure Ari has questions for you once you've gotten a few hours of sleep." Judah turned to go but then turned back and said, "And, Albert, one more thing. Thanks for completing your mission. Good job for a novice!"

Albert couldn't help but grin at the praise. *"Todah raba."*

"B'seder," was Judah's reply as he continued into the dining

hall and out of Albert's sight. Still smiling, Albert tightened his grip on the empty thermos and made his way to his tent for a few hours of much deserved sleep.

SWAMPED by the amount of work sitting in front of her on the table in the dining hall, Evie had no ability to concentrate. She couldn't help but wonder if Albert had returned to camp as of yet. She hadn't seen him this morning and the worry for his safety was gnawing at her stomach, tying it in knots and making it impossible for her to swallow anything other than some weak tea. Staring into space, she didn't realize that Naomi had come up behind her.

"May I sit here?" her friend asked with a wink, "Or are you waiting for someone else?"

Evie reached over and swept some of her work into an even larger pile to make room for the other woman. "Please do," she replied.

Naomi picked up a spoon and began to eat some yogurt. In between bites, she asked, "Do I need to ask or are you going to fill me in on what happened last night?"

"It was perfect," Evie answered with her head down, immediately shuffling her papers to avoid having to fill in the details.

"Oh no. You don't get to keep this to yourself. I spent two hours with you choosing just the right thing for you to wear. Spill it, sister."

Evie looked at Naomi's wide-eyed stare and knew that she'd have to tell her about what had transpired. "Well, I took the thermos of tea and a piece of cake to him, just like we discussed. It all went well. He was very appreciative." She pulled an imaginary thread off of her simple khaki colored blouse.

"How appreciative?" Naomi asked.

"Um, very, as it turns out. He kissed me."

Naomi's spoon clattered on the table. "I knew it!" she exclaimed. "I knew it the minute I saw you."

"Really? How is that possible?" Evie asked with alarm. She didn't want to reveal to anyone exactly what she was feeling.

"I think that I've gotten to know you pretty well and I can sense that something happened. Now I want to hear it. Tell me everything!" she said as she leaned in closer.

Evie sat back in her chair, remembering each detail of the prior night's interaction. Then she replied, "It was beautiful. I gave him the tea and the cake and he kissed me!"

"I'm assuming that you liked it, right?"

"Seriously? It's all I can think about this morning. I mean, look at this." She gestured with her hand to the pile of papers stacked in front of her. "I can't concentrate on anything else!"

"I'm so happy for you, Evie. In the midst of a war, you find someone to love. Amazing!"

"Whoa, Naomi, not so fast. I never said that I was in love with him. I barely know him."

"Sure, but I see the two of you as the perfect match." She nodded her head up and down. "Yes. A match. Absolutely. This is so exciting! What a great angle to the piece I will write about after the war."

"Hold on, Naomi. I'm not sure this was anything more than a kiss. He was leaving on a mission and maybe felt a little vulnerable. Let's see if it happens again."

"Who are you kidding, Evie? You want it to happen again, right?"

Evie bent her head to avoid her friend's direct gaze. "Yes," she replied softly.

"Good! Then it will."

"It seems so crazy to wonder about where this will go

considering our mission here. Who knows what will happen tomorrow?"

"That might be true," Naomi answered with a bit of authority in her voice. "But isn't it wonderful to think that in the midst of all this subterfuge and danger, you've found the person that was meant to be by your side? Your one true love?"

Evie's eyes widened. "Who said anything about 'one true love'? It was just a kiss."

"Okay, Evie. If that's what you think. But I know that it was more. Albert is crazy about you and you have a soft spot for him, too. The sooner you admit it, the better off you'll be."

"No. The quicker I get through my work, the better off I'll be. Aren't you expected somewhere else now?" She motioned to the large clock on the far wall.

Naomi glanced up and registering the time, jumped to her feet. "Yes, you're right. My shift starts in less than a minute. I've got to go." She reached to take her dirty tray to the kitchen when Evie stopped her.

"Go. Don't be late or you might be seen going down to the factory. I'll clean this up for you."

"Thanks, Evie," she said, scurrying away toward the laundry building. Then she turned back and shouted, "I'll see you later and we'll finish this discussion."

"Not sure there's anything left to say," Evie replied to no one. Naomi was already gone.

Fourteen

JUDAH STEPPED out of the dining hall and ground out another one of his ever-present cigarettes in the dirt. The sun was beginning to sink down toward the horizon, casting a pale orange tint on the sparse cloud cover. The air was starting to cool. He put his hand on the back of his neck and tried to ease some of the tension out of the muscles there, but it was useless. He felt like he would never be able to release the kinks that had formed after a day bent over maps and tactical plans with Ari. Now that the factory was running, they had to find a way to disguise the boxes packed with the newly made bullets. They knew where to start sending the ammunition, and they had a means to transport it. All they needed now was the proper subterfuge to protect their mission. He began to walk down the path to his tent. He was tired. Maybe if he closed his eyes briefly, inspiration would hit. Or more likely, he'd lie down and struggle with the racing of his overactive brain, which never allowed him to rest. If he wasn't thinking about the mission, he'd see Geula's face drift across his consciousness. And more recently, he couldn't get Naomi out of his thoughts, either.

She was uniquely exotic, endlessly fascinating, and she truly fit the image of what he'd imagined an American woman would be like: bold, forward-thinking, and beautiful. He wasn't easily challenged by the lure of the opposite sex, but something about Naomi made him want to get to know everything there was to know about her. Intimately, in fact. He was undeniably attracted to her and it was getting more and more difficult to deny that truth to himself. He had finally covered the distance to his tent and reached out to pull back the flap when Naomi stepped out of her own canvas shelter. She was wearing a simple blouse in what looked like a soft fabric, the buttons barely closing over the swell of her breasts. He wished that he could lean over to touch what he knew would be the softest of skin, to feel her heart flutter beneath it. Instead, he knew that he had to look away or give himself up; he didn't want her to recognize the effect she had on him. He watched a subtle shift in her expression as she noticed him and knew that it really didn't matter what he did. When he saw the reflection of his own longing in her eyes as he drew in a bit closer, he knew where this would lead. He had to find a way to take this woman as his own. Gathering whatever calm he could, Judah stepped in even closer and said simply, "*Erev tov…*"

Her green eyes flashing at him as she smiled, she replied, "Good evening to you, as well. Long day?"

The small fidgeting motion of her hands, almost not knowing where to place them, gave her away, and Judah felt himself smile. Years of spy training told him that she was as shaken to be in his presence as he was to be in hers. When Naomi shifted from one foot to the other, the floral scent of her perfume caught on the breeze and reached his nose. He allowed himself a moment to inhale deeply. He then had to work hard to concentrate on his response. "All days are long when you're preparing for war, I suppose. How about you?"

"I must have packed a few hundred bullets today, so I'd say it was worth the hours we all put in." She shifted once more on her feet and the small handbag hanging from a silver chain that had been perched on her shoulder slipped to the ground, spilling its contents. They both bent down to pick up her belongings.

"Oh, no, please, Judah. It's okay. I can do this," she said as she scrambled to retrieve the coins that began to roll away from her.

"Let me help," he answered, grabbing a stray package of tissues and two gold cylinders with the ornately carved initials "EA" on the side of each one. He stared at them for a moment before standing up with his hand outstretched, offering her things, which were resting on his palm. As she reached over to take them from him, her fingers grazed his open hand and he felt a warmth flood his entire body at her brief touch. It was as if she had ignited a sensory memory and all he could think about was that he wanted even more. "Is that everything?" he asked, his voice more husky now.

"I think so," she said, looking around for any stray items, not meeting his gaze, concentrating on stuffing her possessions back into the bag.

"Are you heading down for dinner?" he found himself asking, not wanting to let her leave yet.

"I am," she replied in a soft hush. She looked up at him. "Are you?"

"No, no. I need to do something first. But go now. Enjoy your meal." He didn't want to reveal that if he didn't rest his head for a bit, he would not be able to focus on much of anything important.

"Right," she said. She moved to go around him and he realized that he was blocking her way.

"So sorry." He shuffled to one side. "There you go."

Naomi quickly nodded and continued down the path, her errant purse now secured once more on her narrow shoulder. He couldn't help but watch her walk away, and once she was out of his line of vision, he pushed the canvas flap out of the way and entered his tent.

The air inside was stagnant, still hot from the day's earlier heat. He kicked off his heavy boots and stretched out on his cot, closing his eyes and longing for sleep, for the kind of rest that he was sure would escape him now. Breathing deeply, Judah conjured up an image of Naomi, replaying their recent encounter over again in his mind. She was nervous around him, so much so that she'd dropped her shoulder bag. And suddenly inspiration reared its head. He shot out of bed.

Those cylinders. The ones that fell out of her purse, the ones with the ornate carvings. What were they? The shape of them, he realized, was very similar to the bullets they were making in the factory. Maybe Naomi had handed him the last piece of the puzzle they were trying to solve. Stumbling around his tent barefoot, he realized that he needed to find her and hold those objects in his hand. He needed to see them up close. He hastily shoved his boots on and quickly laced them. Within seconds, he was back on the path in pursuit of the one person who may have unlocked the secret to how they were going to actually win this damned war.

MOMENTS LATER, Judah stepped into the crowded dining hall and quickly scanned the space, looking for Naomi. Just as he was about to go table to table in search of her, he caught a glimpse of her distinctive red curls in the far corner of the room. She was seated with some of the women who worked alongside her in the factory. He drew in a deep breath. Even though everyone at Naomi's table knew about the secret underground business conducted at the kibbutz, the slightest whisper overheard by those at the other tables about the truth of their work could put them all in jeopardy. He would need to get her attention and ask her to step outside with him for a private talk. Most importantly, he had to make his request seem both casual and personal to avoid any speculation from those seated at the tables around her. Stopping at the long counter set with large pots of steaming tea, he poured some into a cup and slowly made his way through the diners and found himself standing behind her. The women were done eating, their plates empty and the dirty silverware stacked all together on a spare tray. Most had a cup like his own, filled with tea, in front of them. One of the women looked up from the animated conversation in and stared at him. Naomi, seeing that her friend's attention had shifted, looked up as well, her eyes widening.

"Judah!" she remarked. "I thought you weren't coming down for dinner just yet."

"Actually, I hadn't planned on it. But then I remembered that there was something I needed to show you in the laundry," he said. "It's important that you know about it before your shift tomorrow." He took a hasty sip of his tea, trying to maintain his composure.

"Go, Naomi," one of the women said with a wink. "You heard Judah. He has something important to show you. You can tell us all about it in detail after you see whatever it is!"

At that, the other women burst out into peals of laughter.

"Now, now, Rifka," Naomi said with a coy smile, grabbing her handbag and gently placing the chain strap on her shoulder. "Take your mind out of the gutter and finish your tea. Tomorrow will be another long day and you'll need to be ready." She stood up and pushed away from the table. She turned to Judah and said, "Okay. This must be important if you came all the way down here to find me. Lead on."

He stepped back and once she was at his side, he put his cup down on the table before turning and leading her through the room and out into the approaching evening. "Walk with me," he said, starting to head down the path toward his tent.

"Wait," she said, pointing to a cluster of buildings. "The laundry is in the other direction."

"I realize that, Naomi," he replied. "But I don't want to go there. I just wanted to get you out of the dining hall and go somewhere quiet where we can talk." He watched as apprehension clouded her face. "Trust me. I think you may have the answer to the problem that's been plaguing me right inside your purse. I just don't want to share this with anyone else yet. Not until I'm sure."

He looked directly into her eyes. They were more green than he remembered them to be. "I wouldn't ask if I didn't really believe that you might hold the key to the war in that small handbag of yours."

Thankfully, she chose to believe him and said, "Okay. I can't imagine what you mean, but let's go."

He put his hand gently on the small of her back to help guide her on the uneven path through the lengthening shadows of the evening. The sun was barely visible over the horizon and the first of the night's stars appeared low down in the sky. He barely allowed his fingers to touch her, yet it was enough of a connection to make him wish he could have more. Judah had to remind himself that there was a time and place for everything and that this was not either.

When they reached his tent he held the flap open for her and she slipped inside. He lit the small kerosene lamp on the one tiny table he kept at his bedside and then turned and held out his hand. "May I have that, please?" he asked, motioning for her purse. She slipped it off of her shoulder and handed it to him. He quickly flipped it over and dumped the contents onto his cot, relieved to see those two gold cylinders once again. He lifted one of them up to the light, turning it in his hand before pulling the top from the base. "Lipstick?" he asked.

"Yes, of course, silly," she remarked before adding sarcastically, "although I really don't think it's your shade."

He let out a breath, and for the first time in a long while felt like he'd finally come up with a way to transport all those bullets they planned on manufacturing. "I agree. Besides, it suits you perfectly." In his excitement, he drew her in for a hug. As he held her, he said, "Well, well. I think you just solved my biggest problem with your fancy American cosmetics. Imagine that!"

"I'm not sure I know what you mean, but I bet Elizabeth Arden would be happy to hear it," she said, her voice somewhat shaky.

He let her go and noticed that she had a little trouble finding her balance, so he took her by the shoulders and sat her down on the edge of his cot. Then he pulled his rucksack out from underneath it and rummaged around to find two loose bullets that had been made in the factory underneath the laundry. "Look, Naomi. Look at the shape of the lipstick and the shape of the bullets. They are almost identical. If we make cases for the bullets to resemble lipstick, we can fill the tops of the cartons with them and then label and ship the boxes as such. We can fool the British this way!"

He watched as understanding dawned on her face which in turn resulted in a broad smile. "Oh, I see. The boxes will be safe if the soldiers think you're shipping makeup. But wait. Won't they think that odd? I mean, there will be hundreds of boxes. Isn't that a lot of lipstick? And women's makeup isn't an essential item of war."

"First of all, the majority of bullets will be transported by lorry. We have drivers for those routes, and that ammunition will be smuggled in the bottom of milk cartons. But for the smaller deliveries, the ones that are meant to be pinpointed to certain spots, the lipstick idea works. And if the British think it's lipstick, that's fine. They won't open all the cases. Besides, I'm not sure that those soldiers are doing too much thinking about it at all. They are there to inspect shipments, not decide if the goods within them are necessary or not."

"I hope you're right about that. It would be terrible if we did all this work and the product never made it to the front lines."

"This will work, Naomi. It has to work." He lowered himself to sit on the cot next to her, running his fingers over the lipstick case. "So simple, really. Just a diversion. That's all we need." When Judah looked up at Naomi, she was smiling. "What? What are you thinking?"

"I'm pretty sure that you would have come up with something eventually. Nothing is going to stop you from turning this desert into a country, is it?"

Judah put down the lipstick and grabbed on to both of Naomi's hands. "No. Nothing will stop us, but you just made my life a lot easier by showing me the way." Then, without thinking, he leaned in and touched his lips to hers and felt a searing heat shoot through his body when she eagerly returned the kiss. Slowly, he teased her mouth open with his tongue, feeling the kind of desire he hadn't experienced in a very long time, and he knew. He knew right then that he had to make this woman his own.

He gently laid her down on the cot, pushing the spilled contents of her purse to the floor and continued to explore her slowly, allowing himself this one moment of pleasure. As she responded to him with the same sort of passion that he himself felt, his body reacted in the most primal of ways. She wanted him, too, and recognizing that made his blood heat even hotter. But then his mind began to churn. Increasingly aware that there was too much at stake for this sort of romantic diversion, he tried as best he could to pull away from her. It took more will than he thought he possessed, but he forced himself to sit up and compose himself.

"Naomi," he whispered. "I'm sorry. That should never have happened."

She lifted her torso up to rest on her elbows and said huskily, "I want you, too, Judah."

He was shaken by her bold words. "I know, Naomi. I'm sorry for what I just did, but now isn't the moment for anything like this."

"You can't choose the precise time in a war, Judah. We don't know what will happen tomorrow."

He knew that she was right; he knew that she was willing. But he also knew that the work they had in front of them left no time for romantic involvement. They needed to be single-minded in the focus on their mission.

"I realize that, Naomi, but I think we should slow down. If this is meant to be," he motioned to himself and then to her, "then it will happen anyway. For now, I think I should walk you home." He stood up and put his hand out to her.

She hesitated for a brief moment. "If you say so," she replied, shaking her head.

Judah pulled her up quickly and they stood for a moment, cheek to cheek and chest to chest. He could feel her nipples pebble under her thin blouse. He bent down and whispered in her ear, "Something tells me, Naomi from New York, that this won't be our only opportunity to be together. You need to know that I am using the last ounce of my self-control not to strip us out of our clothing. I want to touch every inch of you, to have you for myself. But now is not the time." He stepped back.

She looked directly into his eyes and took his hand. "Until then," she said and allowed him to walk her the short distance to her own tent. Once there, he lifted the flap and directed her inside. "*Laila tov* and pleasant dreams." Then he turned and walked away as quickly as he could. The temptation to return to her immediately was so strong that Judah knew one thing for sure: when this war was over, he would make that woman his own. No question about it.

NAOMI STOOD ALONE in the darkness of her tent. She didn't even have the strength to light her lamp. Instead, she wrapped her arms around her body for a moment and thought about all that had just transpired between her and Judah. She fought the urge to go and find Evie, to tell her friend what had happened, that Judah had kissed her, but decided against it. She recognized that this moment was special, best kept between them, their own private encounter.

The lipstick that she'd accidentally spilled out of her purse earlier in the evening triggering his brainstorm about concealing the bullets, was brilliant but overwhelming at the same time. *He's smart, he's savvy, he's strong. He's a major figure in this war.* Naomi's thoughts about Judah swirled through her mind. While all of that was true, she couldn't help but focus on the kiss they shared. She hadn't expected it and now that she knew how he tasted, she wanted more. She knew that he did, too. But how could she keep her heart safe when this country was about to go to war? More importantly, how could she keep him safe? Was that even possible?

Naomi absentmindedly began to undress, tossing her clothing onto the only chair in the space. *Is this what Evie feels each time Albert goes on a mission? This fear of the unknown? The idea that he won't return, that some harm will come to him?* She slipped into her nightgown and lay down between the cool sheets on her cot. This attraction to Judah was not something she'd planned on, if one could ever actually plan to fall for someone. *But it happened so fast!* she thought to herself. She willed her heart to slow down, to stop racing with each new thought about Judah, about what might happen next. And for as much as she knew she should sleep, Naomi realized that rest was not going to come easily that night. She was left with a longing that had no resolution.

She thought about getting up to peek outside and see if he was once again seated at the entrance of his own tent, but she thought better of it. When she finally closed her eyes, all Naomi saw was the image of Judah's dark eyes reflecting back at her, the desire they both shared and his promise that they would someday rest satisfied in one another's arms. She swore to herself that if he wasn't brave enough to make that happen, she was. They were meant to be together and nothing would stop that. Naomi was sure that she was intended to know everything there was to discover about Judah. Sooner or later, he'd be her own.

ifteen

Rehovot
December, 1945

EVIE COULD NOT HELP but notice that the factory, now up and running for over two weeks, had a rhythm all its own. The workers had bonded, coalescing into a tight unit, each one aware of how important their task was to the success of the war effort. The bullet production had become seamless. Box after box was filled and packed with the precious ammunition, made ready for shipment to the front lines when necessary. The plan, which had seemed like an elusive dream when it all began, was now a reality and Evie was hopeful that all of their combined hard work would lead them to both freedom and independence.

Naomi had been persistent in her request to have Evie teach her how to handle a gun, and after that day's work was complete, Evie finally relented, even though she knew that staying underground after the last shift of the day was against the rules. A small target range had been built into the factory itself, set aside in a far corner, away from the heavy machinery. It was important to randomly test the bullets for quality; it would do them no good to be up and running, yet producing duds. Evie had told Naomi at their lunch break to hang back and not to leave with the others at the end of her shift. She watched as her friend told her coworkers to go up the steps to the laundry without her, assuring them that she would clean up the debris from their day's efforts on her own. Once they were alone in the factory, Evie nodded to Naomi and the two women walked silently toward the range.

There was a large target hanging from the far wall. It always reminded Evie of the overstuffed down pillows on her bed in her parents' home in Tel Aviv. A big, white fluffy affair, the cushion was designed to muffle the sound of a bullet's impact. She stopped and turned to Naomi. "Are you ready to learn about this gun?"

"Of course. I've been ready for a while, now. Don't you think it's important for me to be able to defend this place," she said while spreading her arms wide, "if ever the need were to arise?"

Evie smiled. "That's not your job, Naomi. We just need you to package those precious bullets. Leave the defense planning to Judah and Ari. They've got it covered."

"But, Evie, I think I need my own weapon. I know I'll be good at handling one."

"Baby steps, Naomi. You'll need a lot more education before you are issued your own gun. Let's review." She carefully pulled her small pistol out of the holster that sat on her hip. "This is a CZ-27. It's compact, but it's powerful." She passed the dull black firearm over to Naomi. "It holds eight bullets, and be aware. It is currently loaded."

Naomi's eyes widened. "Don't worry," Evie quickly added, noting the surprise that she saw in her friend's gaze. "There's a safety mechanism and it's enabled."

"It's not going to go off without warning, is it?" Naomi asked. "I don't want to shoot my own toe!"

"No. But safety is the most important part of this first lesson. Never be cavalier around a gun. You'll learn to shoot straight, I'm sure of that. But this," she pointed to the pistol, "can kill. We always are serious when we handle a weapon."

Naomi's smile had vanished. "Of course. What's next?"

Evie took the gun back and stood shoulder to shoulder with her friend. "Here are the sights. One in front, one in back. You use them to take aim." She raised the pistol and showed Naomi the proper stance, legs spread slightly and knees bent, both hands on the butt of the gun with her right pointer finger on the trigger. "Even though this is a small weapon, there will be some kickback when you shoot."

"Kickback?" Naomi asked.

"Yes. The force of the bullet when it's propelled out of the chamber can knock you off your feet if you're not prepared for it. That's part of why you practice shooting. It's not all about aim, although clearly that's important, too. You don't want to be compromised after you discharge it. If you miss and the gun knocks you on your behind, your attacker will gain the advantage."

"Gee whiz! There's a whole lot more to think about than I realized," Naomi said.

Evie smiled. "That's right. But that's why we're here. As I told you, there's a lot to learn."

For the first hour, the two women went over each part of the body of the gun, its purpose, and the proper usage and maintenance involved. When Evie felt that Naomi understood the basic information, she said, "That's a lot to take in for your first session. We can do this again tomorrow and practice your stance and the proper way to aim."

"You mean I don't get to shoot today?" Naomi asked in a disappointed tone.

"You're not ready yet."

"It looks so easy in all the John Wayne movies I've seen!"

"This isn't Hollywood. This is Palestine. We're much more of what you Americans call 'the Wild West' than your precious cinema could ever depict!"

Naomi laughed, then said, "That's the truth. I guess I just wanted to try out some of those bullets I've been packing away."

Evie shook her head. "Those are too big for this gun. We're making 9mm bullets here, for the Sten machine guns used on the front lines. My pistol takes 7.65mm ammunition. Look." She quickly opened the chamber of her own weapon and shook out a bullet. She motioned for Naomi to follow and they walked back over to the table laden with the day's filled cargo and pulled out one piece from a random box. "Do you see the difference?"

Naomi took both bullets and rotated each between the thumb and forefinger of each hand, carefully inspecting them. "Yes. The ones we make are larger."

"Bigger gun, bigger bullets. But then, a machine gun will propel the ammunition a farther distance as well."

"How far can your gun shoot at a target?"

"It's meant for close-up use. I'd have to be pretty near what I'm aiming at to hit it. But once in my range, this gun is as accurate as the person who pulls the trigger."

"Accurate when *you're* shooting, then," Naomi replied. "We'll see what happens when I get up to that point in my tutorial. Despite my talking a good game, I'm not sure that I have as steady a hand as you."

"That's what practice is for, my dear. It takes time to get used to just holding a gun, let alone shooting it straight."

Naomi sighed. "So much to learn," she said.

"Well, it seems to me as if you've got Judah to protect you right now anyway!"

"*Evie!*" Naomi said with mock indignation. "I don't know what you mean."

"Come now, Naomi. I've known Judah for a long time. I don't ever remember him being as distracted in someone else's company as he is with you."

Naomi felt herself blush. "Do you really think so? Because if I'm being truthful, I am absolutely terrified at how attracted I am to him. I think about him day and night."

Evie smiled. "I think that's what's been happening to him as well." She paused. "It's nice to see. It's been a long time since I've seen him with that old spark."

"I still don't know what happened in his past to make him so closed off."

"And I'm still not going to disclose what I know. But something tells me that he will tell you himself when he's ready."

"I sure hope it happens soon. I don't know how much longer I can hold out."

"Patience, Naomi. All things unfold in their own time. Back to our lesson now. You need to know that shooting a gun is like falling in love. It takes some time to get it right. Just like it will take some time for Judah to reveal himself to you."

"Teacher. Philosopher. Best friend. I count on you for so much, Evie!" Naomi teased.

And there is so much more I need to learn from you, Evie thought to herself. *Like what to do the next time I find myself alone with Albert.* Leaving her innermost thoughts unsaid, Evie simply replied, "Hungry? Let's go find something to eat!"

A FEW WEEKS later Evie brought Naomi out into one of the fields for her first real target practice. While Evie realized that it was probably better to start out in the factory before coming outdoors, the confined space of the underground bunker where they spent their days had begun to wear on the inhabitants. By the last hour of the work day, the only thing the brave volunteers wanted was to spend some time in the fresh air and sunshine outdoors on the kibbutz, and that included Naomi. On this bright January afternoon, Evie knew that she'd have an hour or so before the light waned and the sun shifted too low on the horizon for proper visibility. There, on the tip of the kibbutz's border with its Arab neighbors, and in between the tall grasses and the olive trees, was another target ready for their use. She had secured a weapon for the other woman to practice with without mentioning to either Ari or Judah that she'd borrowed it. She knew that she'd need to tell them, but wanted Naomi to have a chance to practice first. It was the only reckless thing she'd done since stealing away from her parents' home in the middle of the night, but she felt as though she had this all under control. Evie also felt like Naomi was her first true friend here and she valued their relationship. She wanted to help her in any way possible.

"Okay, Naomi, let's review," Evie began.

"I know, I know," her friend replied impatiently. "Set my stance, line the target up in my sights and slowly squeeze the trigger."

"You left out 'prepare for kickback', Evie smiled.

Naomi looked directly at her friend and mentor. "How can I prepare for something I've never experienced? I've not shot this thing yet, remember?" She wildly gesticulated with her free hand, careful to keep the gun steady with her other one.

"I know, I know. But just be cautious. Dig into your stance. Fire when ready."

Naomi set herself up, her legs slightly spread and knees bent. She pressed her soles down into her boots to try to root herself to the earth. Drawing in a breath, she depressed the trigger on her exhale, just as she'd been instructed. The sound of the pistol firing was deafening. Worse, she felt her entire body vibrate, her feet becoming unmoored as her balance shifted. It was all she could do to remain standing.

"You weren't kidding, Evie," she said as she tried to clear the shock from her brain. "This gun does pack a punch!"

"Why do you think I kept repeating myself over and over with all of those safety instructions. That is a weapon, not a toy."

"I absolutely get it now," Naomi replied, shaking her head in an effort to relieve the ringing in her ears. "Did I hit the target?"

"Let me get a closer look," Evie replied. "But first, put the safety on that thing."

Naomi did as she was told while Evie walked over to the large, stuffed scarecrow on a post across the field. She looked at it for a bit, then shook her head.

"No. No bullet holes. But wait for me. You can try again."

When Evie returned to Naomi's side, she smiled and said, "It's harder than it looks, eh?"

"It is," Naomi agreed. "But I'm persistent. I'll get the hang of it." Just as she was about to lift her arm and take aim, she thought she saw a slight movement out in the field. Evie saw it, too.

Evie spoke in a soft, even tone. "Lower your gun, Naomi. Someone is out there."

"Someone friend or someone foe?" Naomi asked, a trace of fear in her voice.

"I'm not sure. I can't really see them, but we're okay," Evie said calmly. "Either way, we'll be fine."

Naomi watched as Evie pulled her own weapon from its holster.

"Don't say a word. Just be still," Evie whispered.

Naomi could feel the blood rush to her head, pounding a rhythm all its own. Her mouth felt dry and her fingers tingled as she held her gun silently at her side.

"Wait for them to move closer. Then we'll know what we're dealing with," Evie murmured. She very quietly removed the safety from her gun.

Naomi stood stock still as instructed, hoping that the shadowy figures she'd seen in the distance were just two kibbutz workers, perhaps coming back late after their shift, or even better, lovers returning from a tryst. She blinked and in the next moment let out a huge sigh of relief. She knew who it was walking toward them: Judah and Albert!

Evie recognized them in the same moment and cried out, "*Mi zeh?* What are you doing out here?"

As Judah quickly covered the ground between them, he said, "I could ask the same of you! You know better than to come out this far alone right before dark! And why is Naomi holding a gun?"

Naomi pulled herself up to her full height and replied, "We were taking target practice. Is that a crime?"

"Target practice?" Judah looked back over at Evie. "Really?"

"Yes, of course. Naomi wanted to learn to shoot and I saw no harm in--"

"You know the harm, Evie. She's not a trained soldier. Nor should she have to be."

"I disagree," Evie began. "Besides. She wants to learn."

Judah shook his head. "No. Guns are serious business. Naomi doesn't need to shoot one. Ever."

Naomi watched as awareness dawned on Evie's face. Her friend broke into a wide smile. "Oh I see. You don't want

Naomi to have the ability to defend herself? Do you think you'll always be there to protect her?"

"No, no, of course not," Judah insisted. "That's not it at all. It's just that it puts her at risk to handle a weapon with no training."

"Who said I've had no training?" Naomi abruptly replied. "Evie is a great teacher. I've learned everything I need to know about this gun. I can strip it down, clean it and load it back up all in a matter of minutes. I've worked on my aim without ever having fired it and today was my first real chance to try and hit that target. So if you don't mind, we have a lesson to complete." She kept her eyes sharply focused on Judah's. Surprisingly, he blinked first and came to stand at her side.

"If you are going to shoot that gun, you'll do it with me here as well," he said in a way that sounded like a command.

"That won't be necessary. We were doing fine out here on our own," Naomi countered.

Without taking his eyes off Naomi's face, Judah said, "Albert. Will you please walk Evie back to her tent? I'll finish Naomi's lesson and bring her back when we are done."

"Of course, Judah."

Naomi turned away from Judah and watched as Albert put his arm out for Evie. Her friend hesitated. "It's okay, Evie," Naomi assured the other woman. "I'll come find you when we get back."

"You're being ridiculous, Judah, you know that, right?" Evie asked indignantly, moving closer to him to make her point.

"Well, that's one opinion. Let's hear what Ari thinks about this whole affair later, then. Or maybe we should just take up the matter with Yosef?"

With that, Evie threw her hands up in an exasperated gesture, turned on her heel and began to walk past Albert, away from where Naomi and Judah stood. Albert hurried to catch up to Evie and they began to walk back toward the center of the kibbutz together.

Naomi watched them go, then turned around to Judah. "This isn't such a big deal. Don't be angry with Evie. I asked her to teach me to shoot. She never offered. And I had to convince her, which believe me, wasn't easy. So don't blame her. Blame me."

"You both are at fault, but something tells me that you'll go a long way to get what you want, Naomi."

His words sent a shiver up her spine. They both knew that he wasn't talking about target practice anymore. She realized that she had to get control of the situation before it turned into something else entirely.

"Are you going to teach me to shoot straight or not? Because if you are, the time is now." She motioned to the sky. The first star would be visible soon.

The corners of his mouth turned slightly upward, almost as if he wanted to smile but was doing his best to remain serious. "Americans." He sighed. "Very bossy. Well, I'm here and you're the one holding the gun. Let's see if you can learn something before it's too dark to see." He stepped back and waited for her to take her shot.

ALBERT KEPT pace with Evie in silence. He realized that she was angry at Judah; he didn't want her to feel that same hostility toward him. She had started off walking quickly but now had slowed her steps considerably, keeping pace with his own. He was hoping that the rage she had felt in the field had worn off, or at least enough for him to be able to have a reasonable conversation with her. *You won't know until you try,* he told himself.

"Evie," he said as he pulled her to a halt by stepping deftly in front of her. "Don't worry about Judah. He didn't mean what he said. He just doesn't want anyone to get hurt, that's all. He's very protective of everyone here on the kibbutz."

"I'm not sure you're right, Albert. I did break protocol. I should have asked both Judah and Ari for permission before agreeing to teach Naomi how to shoot."

"You did what you thought was right. I'm sure of it." He reached out for her hand and held it in his own. She didn't pull away. "You only meant to help your friend." Just then he thought about the moment they had shared outside of his truck when she came to see him off before his first mission and how it had ended in a tender kiss. Could he take the chance and kiss her again? He moved his fingers lightly against her palm and stepped in closer to her, softly brushing his lips against hers. "Evie. It will all be okay," he said before deepening the kiss as he drew her body flush against his. He gently parted her lips and let his tongue explore her mouth, then dared to trace the outline of her breast through the material of her blouse. The contact seemed to sear the skin of his fingers. He wanted more.

Together in the open field, halfway between the cluster of tents that made up the living quarters of the kibbutz and the border of the hostile country that lay beyond, Albert and Evie remained locked in an embrace that stripped both of them of any pretense. In that moment of intimacy, tongues searching, their breath coming quickly, aching for more than they could have there in that place, they both knew. There was no one else for either of them. They were meant to be together.

"Evie," he whispered in her ear. "I want you. All of you."

"I want you, too, Albert," she replied, her blue eyes searching his deep gray ones. "But we're here to prepare for war. We can't do this. We can't be distracted."

He pulled her in even closer, weaving his hands through the dark brown hair of her ponytail, pulling off the rubber band and letting the hair cascade down her back. "Too late. Besides, if not now, Evie, when? We don't know what tomorrow holds for any of us. Let's see where these feelings take us."

As if she had been drenched with ice water, she abruptly pulled back from him. Albert could see that she was clearly struggling for control. Her voice thick with emotion, she said, "That sounds very much like what I would imagine a Frenchman would say." She took another step away, increasing the distance between them, wrapping her arms around herself to try and stop her body from shaking. "I, on the other hand," she continued stiffly now, "still retain some of my mother's proper British behavior. I won't do anything to compromise myself or our mission."

Even though her words seemed stern, Albert saw something else entirely: the subtle tremor of her hands, the slight stammer in her voice, the flush to her skin. He smiled. "You need not be afraid, Evie. I would never do anything to hurt you. No worries, *ma chèrie*. I will walk you safely home."

He watched for a sign, a signal that she might change her mind, and for the briefest moment he thought she'd relent. She softened her posture and with tears in her eyes allowed him to kiss her again. Afterward, she simply said, "I think we should go."

He leaned in and whispered in her ear, "Fine, for now. But I think we both know where we are headed."

"Home," she said quietly. "We're headed home."

And in Albert's mind, he couldn't help but agree. Even if Evie hadn't realized it yet, she was his home now. He had been unmoored for so long, searching for his father in every new face he saw yet rapidly realizing deep in his heart that he was alone in the world. He wanted to make her understand that together, they could build a beautiful future. Together, they could be unstoppable. Together, they could create a family of their very own. He was sure of it. All they needed was time.

WHEN ALBERT LEFT her at the entrance to her tent, Evie felt spent. She had been on her feet since dawn and the last few hours of the day had been an emotional rollercoaster from which she was not sure she could easily recover. She'd been called out by Judah and kissed by Albert all in one afternoon. She was confident that she could make Judah understand why she wanted to train Naomi how to shoot a gun–it made total sense that some of the workers in the factory should be armed in case the secret bunker was ever breached by the enemy while they were all captive underground. What she didn't know, what remained a conundrum, was how to deal with her feelings for Albert.

She was attracted to him; of that there was no doubt. What was she to do with her feelings? It was hard for Evie to erase everything she had been brought up to believe, that a man and a woman should wait until marriage before being intimate, but she lived in a time of great uncertainty. Albert would be going off on mission after mission, each time risking his life for the cause they all fought for. What if he didn't come back? What would she do then?

Evie paced around the small space. She wanted to talk to Naomi, to ask her advice, but when Evie peeked out beyond the flap of her tent, she searched for a sign that her friend was safely inside of her own. There was no light seeping out from the seams of the canvas; the tent was dark. Could she still be out in the field with Judah? Were the two of them doing the very thing Evie couldn't do with Albert? So many questions, so few answers. But Albert was right about one thing: in a time of war, the promise of tomorrow was never guaranteed.

Sixteen

Judah stood behind Naomi in the last moments of twilight, the purple sky alive with twinkling stars. He had wrapped his arms around hers as they extended the pistol in the rapidly cooling air and aimed at the target.

"On my count," he said softly, close to her ear. "One, two, three..."

She squeezed the trigger and he felt the force of the shot run through her body as she was pushed back against him. He couldn't help but savor the contact between them.

"I think I hit it this time," she said gleefully, rushing ahead of him to see for herself if her bullet had found its mark.

He laughed. "I hope so," he replied, and meant it. She was a novice shot but an enthusiastic student. He followed her to the target where she was eagerly searching for a bullet hole to claim as her own. He found it first. "Here!" he said, pointing to the indentation. "This one was yours!" It was near the center of the canvas, but just a little shy of it.

"Not bad," she said, placing her free hand on her hip, still grasping her gun with the other one. "I can do better, though. Shall we try again?"

"Another day, Naomi. It's too dark to shoot again now."

She looked up at the sky. So intent on her task, she had apparently been unaware that the sun had fully set. "Oh," she said with a surprised tone.

Judah reached out and put his hand on her shoulder. "We'll do this again. I promise."

"What should I do with this?" she asked, keeping the pistol at arm's length. "Can I hold on to it?"

"Not like that," he replied. "Empty the chamber and set the safety. Then put your weapon back properly in its holster." He watched as she did as she was told. He asked, "Do you have a safe place to store it?"

"Nothing that locks," she answered.

"Then I'll take it and put it in the foot locker under my cot. Let's head back now and put that gun safely away."

They began to walk together silently. Naomi wrapped her arms around her torso against the cool night air. "I didn't even realize how much the temperature has dropped. It's quite chilly now," she said.

"That's typical for the desert, especially at this time of year. Here. Take my sweater." Judah pulled the old knit garment up over his head and handed it to her. As it was, he felt overheated by his proximity to her. It was a relief to remove it. She quickly slipped it on. "Thank you. Are you sure that you're not too cold now?" she asked.

"No, I'm fine," he replied, hoping that he didn't give himself away. He knew that he had to change the subject. "Tell me about your work in the factory, Naomi. How's that going?"

"So far so good, I think," she replied, turning her face up to look at him.

Even in the darkness he felt himself falling into the emerald green depths of her eyes. *Concentrate,* he told himself. *You may need to answer a question or respond to something she says.* He forced himself to listen as Naomi continued.

"It's been a whirlwind, learning everything and then getting those pesky bullets into the boxes. They're slippery devils," she teased.

"Right. I imagine they are," he replied with a small smile.

"But more than the basics of the everyday details, I find my coworkers so interesting."

"How so?"

"Well, when I came here from the States, the war in Europe seemed like something happening at a great distance. I mean, we knew about it, our soldiers went overseas to fight, after all." She lifted a hand absentmindedly to tuck a stray curl behind one ear. "But aside from the bond drives and the USO dances, my life was barely touched by it." She looked up at him, her eyes turning serious. "The women I'm working with in the factory struggled and suffered so. They had no shelter. They were literally starving. Even worse, they lost their families, and they can't return to their native countries. It's overwhelming when you start to think about it."

"That's why we're fighting, Naomi. To give all Jews a permanent home. And we'll protect it against our enemies for as long as need be, once it's ours."

"It's astonishing, really. Everything you've done here is nothing short of miraculous," she said with emotion in her voice.

He stopped walking and reached across to touch her face. With one thumb, he wiped away a stray tear that had made its way down her cheek. "Miracles have often happened in this desert, Naomi. Think back throughout our history. The plagues we recall at the Passover Seder. The Red Sea parting. The oil which kept the lamps lit for the Macabees for eight days when it should have only lasted for one. Should I go on?"

"No, Judah. I understand." She paused for a moment, then asked, "Do you really think that we can make our own miracles happen, too?"

"I hope so. I really do," he replied. He knew that through his work, he had the opportunity to do just that. As she turned to him, her eyes shining with tears, his immediate thought was that he desperately wanted to kiss her. Instead, he restrained himself and reached for her hand, grasped it tightly and together they walked into the center of the kibbutz.

NAOMI STOOD inside Judah's tent, waiting for him to light the kerosene lamp, not sure what would happen next, but suddenly aware that the sweater he'd given her to wear on the walk back felt heavy on her shoulders. Once he ignited the wick, she looked around and realized that he had a larger space than she had. It was actually much more homey as well. There was a small bookcase on one side of his cot, as well as two chairs and a table in the center, the surface covered with maps and papers. He quickly cleared the mess off of the table and placed a bottle of a clear liquid and two glasses on it from the lowest shelf of the bookcase, motioning for her to sit down.

"Here," she said, unbuckling the strap to her holster and handing him her gun.

He held out his hand and took it from her.

"Evie was holding on to that before this. I just don't want you to think that I was cavalier about where it was kept. She had it safely locked away when we weren't having a lesson."

"I don't doubt that, Naomi," he said, sitting down next to her and pouring each of them some of the contents of the bottle on the table. "Vodka. This should warm you up some." He offered her one of the glasses.

"I thought that Albert shared this tent with you. Did he finally get one of his own?

"Yes. Once he started going out on missions, the council granted him his own space," he answered matter-of-factly.

Would she have consented to come inside had she known that important piece of information? she questioned quickly in her own mind, knowing the answer to be yes, then asked aloud, "What should we drink to?"

He looked directly at her. "Us," he replied. "And to winning this war," he added.

"Winning the war. Of course," she replied, hoping the clear spirit would calm her suddenly raging nerves. She tipped her glass on her lips and took a deep swallow. The drink tasted astringent and she had to stifle the urge to cough. She shook her head. "Is that really vodka? Or is it some sort of grain alcohol you think is vodka?"

He laughed out loud. "It's the best I can do for now. Our supplier is busy with other goods, as you know. Every now and then I can get my hands on the good stuff, but currently?" He winked at her. "This works in a pinch."

She smiled and whether it was the quick drink of the high-proof liquid or not, she felt bold. "It's nice to hear you laugh, Judah. I'm guessing that it doesn't happen often."

He sat back in his chair. "We've been at this war for so long now, Naomi. The planning, the preparation. There hasn't been much reason to laugh, I guess."

"But we're making headway, right? The first shipment of bullets is ready to go."

"Yes. Albert will be taking them to some of our troops very soon. And thanks to you, they will be disguised as lipstick. Pretty damned brilliant, I may add."

"I just dropped my bag. You came up with the rest." She took another sip, this time steeling herself for the taste. Feeling more comfortable, and with a bit more courage from the contents of her glass, she couldn't help herself. She switched topics and asked, "Will you tell me about her, Judah?"

"About who?"

"The woman who broke your heart."

She looked directly at him, expecting him to shy away or refuse to answer, but he never broke her gaze.

"It was a long time ago, Naomi," he said quietly. "And she didn't just break my heart. I'm responsible for her death."

Naomi felt her own heart beating faster at his words. "Will you tell me what happened?" she asked. She watched as he lifted his drink to his lips and downed what was left in one long gulp.

"We have always lived on the edge of violence here, Naomi. I realize that this might be difficult for you to understand coming from America. The war you fight is on far distant lands, not at your border, not in your backyard. But here the threat is everywhere. The enemy can be your neighbor." He reached over to the bottle on the table and refilled both of their glasses. "I guess you could say that's what happened."

Naomi sat as still as she could, hoping that Judah would continue, would tell her more, but he sat silently with his drink for what seemed like an eternity. Finally, she spoke. "How were you responsible for something your neighbor did?"

He looked directly at her but Naomi felt as if Judah saw someone else sitting in her seat. "I wasn't there when it happened. I couldn't save her," he replied quietly. "When the bomb was thrown into our house, I wasn't there and she was killed."

"Where were you?" she asked, more boldly now.

"On another mission, not that it matters. I should have been killed with her. She should not have died alone."

"How can you blame yourself for doing what you were supposed to be doing, Judah? You could not have known--"

He cut her off. "It no longer matters. I can't change the past, Naomi. Geula was my childhood sweetheart. She was very special to me. I loved her deeply. But I can't bring her back to life. I know that." He drained his glass again.

"Geula. That's a beautiful name," Naomi murmured. "I'm sure she knew how much you cared for her."

"Yes. Yes, she did. Or at least that's what I tell myself whenever I'm held hostage by my memories." He filled his glass one more time.

Naomi got up out of her chair and kneeled in front of Judah, placing her hands on top of his. "This work you do, you do for her, for all of us. You will make us free, I just know it. We'll have a Jewish homeland because of everything you've sacrificed."

"And you, Naomi." He intertwined his fingers with hers. "When the bullets are done being made, will you go back to New York? Will you leave this place, too? Or is this now your home?" He squeezed her hands and in one motion pulled her up onto his lap, their faces so close that they were almost touching.

The sudden proximity to him made her heart hammer away uncomfortably as his breath taunted her cheek. She forced out her words, trying to concentrate. "I don't know, Judah. I can only think about today. So much still needs to be done."

"Stay," was all he said right before he drew her in for an urgent kiss. She felt all of his anguish pour from his body into hers as his lips made contact with her own, his tongue teasing the inside of her mouth, leaving her quivering with need. She wanted to comfort him but was afraid of the desire his kiss had stoked. She felt an immediate connection to him that went much deeper than the surface attraction she had been feeling since they met, and she wasn't sure what to do next. He shifted her weight on his lap and she knew that he felt the same. She pulled back. "Judah?" she questioned.

"If you can't promise to stay here forever, can we at least have tonight?" he asked, his eyes ablaze with longing.

She simply nodded and then kissed him back with an intensity that left her both breathless and wanting more.

Judah stood up, setting her on her feet and pulling her in against his broad chest, his tongue tracing small circles down her neck before walking them both over to his cot. He slowly pulled his sweater, which she still wore, off over her head and tossed it into a corner. Despite the rapidly cooling air around her, Naomi no longer felt the cold. Instead, she was keenly aware of every sensation; his fingers, rough from work, against her softer skin as he unbuttoned her blouse, the sound of her skirt's zipper being lowered, the whooshing sound it made as it fell to the floor. She watched in the dim light of the lamp as he stood back and took off his own clothing, then stepped toward her, reaching to pull her close once again. With a swift motion, he lowered them both onto his cot. The scratchy wool of the blanket chafed against her bare skin as Judah unfastened the hooks to her bra and pulled her panties down past her toes, but she did not care. Once she felt the length of him pressed against her thigh, she was lost. As he gently explored every inch of her body, searching for the places that would bring her the greatest pleasure, Naomi felt alive. When he finally entered her, she gasped, not at the exact fit that she knew to expect, but at the sudden sensory overload of housing every inch of him within her. It was the most extraordinary thing she'd ever experienced. Wave after wave of her body's response reverberated through them both, causing him to explode within her in a warm rush. She could not have imagined anything quite like this moment; she only hoped that they would repeat it over and over again. For that brief time, until the stars disappeared in the softly lit sky and the sun fully rose the next morning, that is exactly what they did.

DAYS PASSED and Naomi was still reliving the memories of the night she'd spent with Judah. He'd left on a mission the very next morning and hadn't returned to the kibbutz yet. She was worried for his safety, but even more than that, she longed for his touch. The connection they had unsettled her; she'd never felt this way before. Lost in thought, she was absentmindedly filling boxes of bullets for transport, almost missing the sound of the all-clear siren that signaled the end of her day's shift.

"Are you coming?" Tamar asked.

"What's going on with you, Naomi? You've been daydreaming all afternoon!" Rebecca added.

Naomi looked at her coworkers and forced herself to return to the present moment.

"I'm fine, really. I've just been thinking about...home," she lied, trying to cover up for her lack of attentiveness. She could not share the events of the one night she had spent with Judah.

"Ah," Rebecca replied, nodding her head. "I know. It's so hard to remember what you've left behind. There are times I feel haunted by the ghosts as well."

"I think we're all feeling sad at times," Tamar said, walking around the table to give Naomi a hug. "I may have left no one at home, but I still imagine my family is there, waiting until the time when we will see each other again. But we have each other now, right? *Mishpucha*."

Naomi forced a smile. "Of course, family." She looked down at their day's work, stack after stack of boxes filled with the precious bullets. "And we're making a difference here. Go ahead of me tonight. Have a hot shower. I'll be there soon. I'll just tidy up and prepare for tomorrow."

"Are you sure?" Tamar asked "If we all work together, it will go faster."

"No, no," Naomi insisted. "You go on. I just need a minute." She reached for her red sweater and put it on to indicate her plan to come outside soon.

The other two women linked arms and climbed up the staircase toward the main floor of the building. Naomi gathered her thoughts and had begun to straighten the flat boxes that they would fill the next morning when Evie rounded the corner.

"I'm just checking to make sure everyone is out of here," she remarked. "You should be upstairs as well."

"I just needed a little more time to finish," Naomi replied. "I'll be leaving soon."

"Now, Naomi. You know the rules. We need to–"

Just then they were plunged into darkness as they both heard the sound of the laundry tub scraping against the floorboards above them. Someone had closed them inside the factory!

"What just happened?" Naomi asked nervously.

"I'm not sure," Evie replied, "but Ari knows that if I'm not at dinner, it means that something is wrong down here. Let's not panic."

"Please tell me that the air filtration system remains on all night," Naomi said to her friend. "My biggest fear is that we'll somehow suffocate in this space."

"First of all, just breathe. We're fine. Even if the filtration system was off, it's just the two of us down here."

Naomi could feel her body begin to shake uncontrollably, tears running freely down her face.

"Hey," Evie said, coming over to wrap her arms around

Naomi. "Calm down. We'll be fine." She took Naomi's hand. "Come with me." She led Naomi over to a wall of shelves filled with food and water in metal containers. "Look. We are prepared for this." She moved a few of the cans of beans to one side and removed a hidden bottle of whiskey. Smiling now, Evie added, "Very prepared!" Rummaging around further, Evie found a tin container of salted crackers and another of dried fruits. "It's cocktail time, don't you know? Let's have a party." She sat down cross-legged on the floor and motioned for Naomi to do the same.

Sniffing back any further tears, Naomi said, "I'm sorry. I'm just emotional, that's all. It's my claustrophobia kicking in. I know we'll be okay, even if we need to sleep here tonight."

"Don't be silly. Ari will come for us once the coast is clear. But what's wrong? Is there something you want to talk about?" Evie asked, prying open the tin of crackers.

Naomi hesitated. While she knew that she could trust her friend with any piece of information, she wasn't sure that she was willing to let slip the fact that she and Judah had slept together. She looked at Evie and simply asked, "Has Ari heard from Judah? Is his mission almost complete?"

"I haven't any idea. You know that each trip Judah takes off of the kibbutz is top secret. Ari doesn't fill me in on that sort of thing."

"Oh," Naomi replied, trying to keep the disappointment out of her voice. She just wished for the smallest bit of reassurance that he would be returning soon, but still did not want to give herself away. "I was just wondering if he was in Haifa or somewhere else."

"Missing him?" Evie asked with a wry smile, opening the bottle of whiskey and pouring some into two of the small metal cups that lined the bottom-most shelf.

"Well, you know..." Naomi replied.

"No, I don't know a thing. You're like a vault. You tell me nothing!"

Naomi accepted a cup of the dark brown liquid and some crackers from her friend. She bit into a corner of one and felt the salt melt on her tongue as she formulated her response. "I don't have much to say," she remarked. "I'm not well versed in war-time romance. I just don't know what to expect."

"Is that what you think this is?" Evie asked, her eyes widening. "Just a brief relationship? Is that what you assume about Albert and me as well?"

Naomi had heard the talk around the camp about her friend and the handsome Frenchman. She had seen them sit together at meals, heads bowed toward one another in deep conversation and had spied them walking hand in hand around the kibbutz. "No, of course not! I think that you and Albert are very sweet together. I just don't expect Judah to allow himself to fall in love during a war. He's been through so much, you know, with Geula's death and all."

Evie sat up straight. "Wait. He told you about her? When? Why didn't you share that with me earlier?"

Naomi took a bracing swallow of the whiskey. "Yes. He did tell me about her and how much they were in love. I just didn't think it was something that I could talk openly about. He told me in a...in a... private moment."

"What does that mean, exactly? I don't understand."

"It means that he told me when we were alone, together in his tent," Naomi said softly.

"Hold on," Evie said, clearly thinking about Naomi's words. "Did you spend the night with him?" Evie asked, eyes glued to Naomi's face in search of a response.

Naomi nodded her head and rushed to say, "I did spend the

night with him, Evie, but that doesn't mean that we are together. He left on his mission the next morning and I haven't heard from him since. For all I know, it was just a one-time thing."

Evie thoughtfully bit down on a cracker, chewed and swallowed before responding. "I don't think it was a one-time thing, Naomi. For the entire time we've worked together, I've never seen Judah look at another woman. Or at least not the way he looks at you. I think you've captured his heart."

Naomi sighed. "That's a very romantic view you've got there. I'm not sure that I agree, but for now, I'd like to believe you." She reached over and patted Evie's knee. "And thanks, by the way. I feel much calmer now."

"Ha! You only think you're calm now, but I want details. I'm a skilled interrogator and I need to learn what you know about men and relationships. You can repay me now for teaching you how to shoot a gun. Spare not one detail, Naomi. Tell me everything!"

Seventeen

Hours flew by as Evie sat listening quietly while Naomi filled her in on the details of the night she'd spent with Judah. It all sounded very exciting and romantic, but it still didn't answer some of her questions about her own blossoming relationship with Albert. She was attracted to him and wanted more than the sweet kisses they'd stolen in the shadows of the kibbutz, but she wasn't ready. At least not yet. And while she wasn't shocked by the story she had just heard from her more experienced friend, Evie could not shake off the formal British upbringing that had formed so much of her core values. Naomi's progressive American attitude was something that Evie admired. However, she still could not wrap her brain around the idea that one might actually have sex before marriage.

"Would you say, then, that Judah is a good lover?" she asked, crunching down on a cracker.

"You make it sound like I have a huge basis for comparison!" Naomi teased. The alcohol had loosened her up some and Evie realized that her friend, having unburdened herself of the secret she'd been keeping, became even more relaxed.

"It might seem that way to you, but any number of men greater than zero is a large amount in my world," Evie responded.

"Look, Evie. While my family might have something to say about me not saving myself for my husband if they ever knew, my friends back home all decided that with the war, nothing was guaranteed. We knew that it was time to try and experience everything we could, to live life to the fullest, just in case Hitler won. I don't regret a thing!"

Evie felt her eyes widen. "What else have you done?"

"Nothing all that extreme, really, unless you count me coming here alone, to Palestine, in wartime. I mean, this adventure I'm on certainly qualifies as taking a huge leap of faith and stepping outside my comfortable life at home."

"Well that's true," Evie replied. "And no one truly knows how this will all turn out."

Naomi lifted her near empty glass and said, "I'll drink to that!" She tipped her drink back toward her mouth.

"Are you in love with Judah?" Evie asked her friend. The words spilled out before she could stop them. The question was so direct, so unexpected, that Evie couldn't help but feel bad when Naomi almost choked as she swallowed the smoky liquid already in her mouth.

She coughed and countered, "Are you in love with Albert?"

Evie smiled. "I believe I am. That's why I'm asking you about Judah. If you love him, I can more easily understand giving into your feelings and sleeping with him. If you don't--"

Naomi interrupted her. "Listen, Evie. I'm not here to tell you what to do about your feelings for Albert. I don't want this conversation to convince you to have sex with him if you don't feel ready."

"But, Naomi, how will I know? How did you know for that matter?"

"That's probably impossible to answer. I think we have to follow our instincts and in the end, follow our hearts."

"But like you said, it's war. No one knows what tomorrow will bring. What if I never get the chance to be with Albert? That would be horrible!"

Evie waited for an answer as Naomi shimmied over the cement floor to sit next to her.

"You'll just know. When the time is right, that is. I'm sure of it."

"How can you be so positive?"

"Listen, Evie. I don't pretend to know as much about shooting a gun or fighting a war as you do, but maybe I've learned a little bit more about life and love than you have. When I tell you that there will be a time when you feel that if you have to live one more minute without Albert's touch, that if you can't be with him your own life will end, believe me. It's in that moment that you will give yourself to him and he to you. You'll see."

Evie shrugged her shoulders. "If you say so. I just hope that it happens soon. Every time he leaves the kibbutz for another mission with a truckload of bullets, I die a little bit inside."

"Well, that tells me that you're close to making your decision. But don't rush it. Wait until you are one hundred percent sure."

Just then both women heard the scraping noise of the laundry tub being pushed away from the exit at the top of the stairs. The sound of hurried feet descending the stairs filled the room. In a matter of moments, Judah and Ari were in the factory. Evie watched as Judah quickly made his way over to where they sat, reached down and pulled Naomi up close to him, and asked, "Are you okay?"

"You're here? How are you here? When did you get back?" She felt her words tumble from her mouth.

"Have you been drinking?" He turned to Evie, who was still seated on the floor. "What happened?"

"The alarm sounded and the next thing I knew, we were stuck down here," Evie replied.

Ari offered to help Evie up and she stood, brushing off the back of her pants with both hands. "Was there a problem in the laundry?" she asked the men.

Ari nodded. "Two British soldiers came in to inquire about having their uniforms washed. We had to quickly seal the doorway down to the factory to keep its existence a secret. Luckily, everyone else was already on the surface, except for you two. You should know that we were able to replace the tub before the soldiers saw anything," he huffed, and then with a scolding tone to his voice said, "This is why it is so important to stick to our schedule. The British switch shifts at the railway station ten minutes after our work day is done. What the hell was so important that you two were not upstairs on time?"

"Naomi was just trying to set up and be ready for tomorrow," Evie said.

Her friend interrupted. "Please, Ari. Don't yell at Evie. It was truly my fault. I was just trying--"

"I'm not interested." Ari raised his hands up in the air and replied sternly to them both. "First the incident with the gun and now this? Together, you two are trouble." He sighed, then continued. "Ladies, please. Rules are there for a reason, to keep our workers safe. Remember that." Then he turned to Evie, "You know better than this. Any breakdown in protocol could expose us all."

"Yes, Ari," she said quietly before adding, "It won't happen again." She looked down toward the putty-colored floor.

"It had better not," he replied gruffly. But then his demeanor softened. "Are you sure that you are both alright?"

"We're fine. We had a nice chat and a bit of whiskey. Good as gold, right Naomi?" She turned toward the other woman and as she looked up, Evie could feel the obvious attraction between her friend and Judah while they all shared the same small space.

Shaking her head, Evie was amazed that she hadn't felt it before. Realizing that Judah was there, back from his mission, she recognized that Naomi must feel nothing but relief. Before the other woman had a chance to respond, Evie said, "Let's go on up, Ari. I still want a proper dinner. This was a long day and I'm hungry."

"After you, Evie," the older man replied, his tone indicating that all was forgiven as they made their way toward the staircase.

"Coming, Judah?" Ari asked over his shoulder.

"Shortly," was Judah's reply.

Evie shuddered at the sound of Judah's voice as awareness rushed through her. This was exactly what Naomi had been trying to explain earlier; she heard it for herself in the way Judah answered Ari. There was a distinct tone, undeniable in its meaning. Judah needed to be sure that Naomi was okay because he was in love with her. The sound of his voice gave Evie everything she needed to understand what was between her friends. How had she missed it? Their attraction was electric. All at once Evie knew that Judah must have been afraid to think about what might have happened if the British soldiers found had them alone in the factory. *Isn't that what I feel each time Albert leaves the kibbutz? It is! And now perhaps it is time to do something about it...*

NAOMI STOOD stock-still until she no longer heard Evie and Ari's footsteps echoing through the factory. Then she turned to look at Judah. The expression on his face mirrored exactly what she was feeling herself. It was a heat, a longing, a sensual attraction that could not be ignored. She took one step toward him and reached out to put her hand on his face, running her fingers over his lips before leaning up to kiss him. What started off as a gentle caress quickly became something more as he returned her ardor with a deepening passion of his own.

"Naomi," he whispered. "Not here. Come with me."

She nodded and he took her hand, silently leading her up the stairs and out of the building with an urgency that she could feel as it radiated from his fingers to her own. In what felt like mere seconds, they were on the path heading toward the camp's living quarters. Once inside his tent, he pulled her into his arms and just held her against his body for a long minute before saying, "When I got back and found Ari pacing outside the laundry, I could never have imagined that it was you stuck down there. Do you have any idea of the danger you put yourself in?" He shuddered.

"Judah, please!" she implored, feeling fully sober now. "You face more peril than that every time you leave the kibbutz! Evie and I were fine. We were more than fine, actually. We drank some whiskey to pass the time and had a moment to catch up with each other." She deliberately didn't tell him how frightened she really was once they were sealed in the factory. Between the feeling of claustrophobia and not knowing what was happening above them, she had to keep drinking whiskey just to stay calm.

"I am totally in control when I leave here, Naomi. I know what I'm doing. You, on the other hand, might have been an unknowing victim of exposure had the British found you there. And had they, not even your American passport would have been enough to save you from execution. They would have charged you as being a terrorist." He took a step over to the shelf where he kept his liquor and poured them each a drink, handing over a glass to her.

"Really, Judah, we were fine. Nothing happened."

"You were lucky, Naomi," he said sharply. "Next time you might not have the same outcome. You have to follow the rules. We set them in stone for this very reason."

She nodded. "I know. I'm sorry to have worried you so."

He downed the contents of his glass in one gulp and placed it on the table. Then he reached out and pulled her back into his arms. It was all Naomi could do not to spill her drink as he ran his fingers up her neck and then down toward the swell of her breasts.

"Don't scare me like that again, Naomi. My heart can't take it. I can't lose you, too." He unbuttoned her blouse and leaned down to kiss the soft skin there. With abandon, Naomi slammed her glass down on the table and undid the snap at the waistband of his pants, lowering the zipper and slipping her hand inside to grasp the length of him. He moaned. Between the sound he made and the feel of his overheated skin, Naomi was lost. In seconds, he discarded the rest of her clothing and tossed the various pieces to a corner of the tent; she wrestled his shirt off and was rewarded with his strong body wrapped around hers. Once they were both naked, he gently laid her down on his cot, covering her body with his own. The remainder of the night was a jumble of legs and arms, an undoing of two individuals and the merging of two hearts as they soared together in blissful, heightened sensations and the solemn recognition that they were only here for this moment. Tomorrow, Naomi acknowledged, was always both a threat and the one thing that she knew not to count on, because the future came with no guarantee. The war outside of the tent's thin canvas walls was real, growing closer each day. She remained keenly aware of that not-so-small detail, yet for this brief moment she felt as though they had both silently agreed to ignore everything else but the comfort their bodies could bring one another. In spite of knowing all of that, as Naomi finally closed her eyes to sleep, she allowed herself to picture the two of them years from now, old, gray and living peacefully in what she'd just decided would be her adopted homeland. She knew now she could never leave him. With a sigh, she drifted off for some much needed rest.

EVIE SAT in the dining hall long after everyone else had gone to bed, the cup of tea on the table in front of her now cold. She replayed over and over again all of the bad scenarios that could have happened when she and Naomi lingered too long in the factory that afternoon. Even though she knew that Ari's gruff manner was mostly bluster, she had worked too hard to prove herself and her abilities to him to do something so careless. Luckily for all of them, the two British soldiers who had come to inquire about laundry service were apparently clueless to the real purpose of the place; their secret was still safe.

And then there was the matter of the entire conversation she'd had with Naomi about Judah and the physical relationship they shared. Evie longed for the freedom to give herself over to Albert in the same way, but something deep inside her held her back. As Naomi advised, until that changed, she knew she wasn't ready to move forward and explore what exactly that sort of intimacy with him would mean. *What will it take,* she wondered, *for me to change my mind?*

She pushed herself back from the table, the chair loudly scraping against the wood floor, and gathered her things. She lifted her tea cup up and downed the last sip of the cold liquid before walking across the large space and dropping the cup off in the deep stainless steel sink in the kitchen. Then she went outside and began to walk toward her tent. Once on the path, she began yet another internal conversation with herself. She knew that Albert was on the kibbutz at the moment; there was no mission that would have taken him away that night. Maybe she would just check in to see if he was awake, maybe they could just talk for a bit. Despite the late hour and the long day she'd had, Evie felt very energized. Besides, Albert had moved into his own tent a while ago and she still hadn't paid him a visit to see how he was getting along. *Yes,* she decided. *If there was a light coming from the inside of his tent, I'll see if he feels like spending some time with me.*

Evie could feel her heartbeat begin to accelerate as she neared the tight loop of canvas structures. There had been a bit of reshuffling to accommodate a space for Albert's tent leaving the stakes that held the shelters firmly in the ground very close together. She had to concentrate in order not to trip over any of the ropes or metal rods that kept the tents rooted in the sandy soil. The fire they kept lit at night within a circle of large stones was low, but the embers glowed just enough to allow Evie to see her way in the inky darkness. Once at the flap of Albert's tent, she could see a dim light seep through the thin khaki material. She gathered her courage and whispered, "Albert? Are you awake?"

She could immediately heard him shuffle to his feet and in the next minute, he was standing outside next to her, his shirt rumpled as he finished tucking the tails into his pants. "Is everything alright, Evie? Do you need something?" He smoothed down his hair with one hand.

All at once she felt foolish. "No. I mean yes. Everything is fine. I just thought that I would check in on you and see how you like your new accommodations."

He smiled. "This late at night?"

"Is it that late? I must have lost track of the time. I'm sorry to have disturbed you." She turned to leave, but felt his hand as he firmly rested it on her shoulder, holding her in place.

"Bit of a rough day?" he asked, then added, "Want to talk about it?"

Evie felt the breath leave her body. She nodded her head.

"Come on, Evie. Tell me what happened." He pulled back the canvas flap and took her hand, leading her inside. There wasn't much to see, just an unmade cot and an open duffle bag of clothing. He gently sat her down on the edge of his bed and then dropped down to sit on the ground in front of her.

"What did you hear?" she asked.

"Just that you and Naomi were stuck down in the factory. I'm not sure of the details."

She sighed. "Two British soldiers wandered into the laundry a few minutes after the shift was done for today. Luckily they didn't see the secret staircase. They dropped off some uniforms to be washed and left."

"Evie!" he said with alarm. "You could have been discovered. What made you not come up with the others?"

"Nothing that important to have risked everything," she replied, putting her head in her hands, feeling the tears begin to well in her eyes. The stress of the day had finally caught up with her. "But to make matters worse, I feel as though I've let Ari down. I've worked so hard to gain his trust. Our mission means everything to me, Albert. I gave up my whole family to be here." As the words left her mouth, she realized the gravity of what she'd said, the fact that Albert hadn't given up his family, but rather had them taken from him. She reached for him then. "I'm so sorry, Albert. How that must have sounded to you. This day just keeps getting worse!"

He rose to his knees and wiped the tears from her face. "Oh, no, Evie, no. Don't worry about me. I know what you meant. It's okay."

"No, Albert, it's not okay. Nothing is okay right now!" She could feel the torrent of tears escape uncontrollably, an unstoppable force streaming from her eyes, wetting them both. Before she realized what was happening, he was sitting next to her, pulling her into his embrace and running a soothing hand through her hair. They rocked together gently until she gained control over her emotions. When she cleared the last of the tears from her vision, she could see his intent gaze and she knew that he wanted to kiss her. In that moment, Evie decided to strike first. She tipped her face up to his and leaned into him, bringing her lips to rest against his, feeling the heat there and allowing his response to further embolden her. From that moment, Evie knew, there was no turning back. She wanted to feel his skin against her own and to know that he wanted the same; she wanted to give herself fully to him and then stay in his arms forever. She felt his response–the deepening of the kiss, the hitch in his breath when her fingers lightly caressed his neck. But then he pulled back.

"Evie, wait. We shouldn't. I mean we can't. We shouldn't do this."

"You don't want to make love to me?" She could feel her stomach turn at his rejection of her advances.

He stood and paced around his cot for a moment. She watched him closely as he tried to calm his own breath.

"Of course I do. But we should wait."

She heard Naomi's words rattle around her brain. Their future sat on shifting sand. The fight with their enemies would be upon them soon and then whatever might happen could separate them forever. She lifted her gaze to his and said, "Wait for what, Albert? War could break out at any moment."

"Wait until we marry."

"Marry?" She echoed his word. "What are you talking about?" She watched the worry cross his sweet face and then heard the apprehension in his voice.

"From the first time I saw you, Evie, I knew. I knew you were the one for me. I want to be by your side forever and always. I can only hope you feel the same way."

It took her a moment to process what he had just said. "Are you proposing to me, Albert?"

"I most certainly didn't picture a proposal to happen this way, Evie. I thought I'd ask you under the stars in a much more romantic way."

She smiled shyly. "Well," she replied, the fog lifting from her mind. Sitting up straighter now, her decision clear, she said, "We can marry under a canopy of stars. That would be very romantic, don't you agree?"

"Is that a yes?" he tentatively asked.

She nodded her head and stood up. "As crazy as it is, Albert, yes! With all that we have ahead of us, I see no reason not to grab whatever happiness we can. So yes. Yes. Yes."

He drew her into the circle of his arms. "*Merci, ma chèrie*. I promise to do my best to make you happy, always. *Je t'aime*."

"I know, Albert. I love you, too."

"Are you tired?" he asked. "It's been a long day, no?"

"Yes."

"We can lie down and rest. The sun will be up soon."

She followed him to his cot and they lay down, and in the warmth of his embrace felt herself begin to drift off, knowing that aside from breaking the promise to herself not to fall in love, a wartime romance was a risk. Anything might happen, but in the last moment before sleep claimed her, she realized that for Albert, she was willing to take the leap.

Eighteen

Rehovot

January 17, 1946

THE MORNING of the wedding dawned with bright sunshine and a crisp chill in the air. Evie was awakened by Naomi, who burst into her tent with Tamar and Rebecca trailing right behind her in an excited rush of female chatter.

"Get up, sleepyhead! We have serious work to do before you meet your intended under the *chuppah!*" Naomi said cheerfully.

As she opened her eyes to focus on the women surrounding her cot, she saw Tamar holding out a mug to her, steam rising into the chilly air.

"Here, Evie. No eating for you, but I thought that one cup of tea from the dining hall wouldn't count." Evie knew that Tamar was referring to the ancient Jewish custom of both the bride and groom fasting on their wedding day. Even though she didn't feel it necessary to keep up the old tradition, she didn't want to argue. Or tempt the fates, for that matter.

As the woman offered the fragrant brew, Evie knew that she should rise from the warmth of her bed to join in the excitement that the others shared, but she had begun to think about her parents the night before and felt sorry that they wouldn't be here with her at this most special event. She reached for the tea.

"What's wrong, Evie? You don't look like a woman excited for her wedding day," Naomi said.

"Or her wedding night!" Rebecca added with a giggle.

"No, it's not that." She swung her legs off the cot and placed them firmly on the floor, her toes curling at the sudden chill she felt run up her legs. "I was just thinking about home, that's all."

"Oh," Naomi replied. "I understand. Your father. You miss him."

"And if I'm being honest, my mother, too. Despite everything, I know how much she would have liked to be a part of today." Evie shook her head before continuing. "But then I remembered that if she were involved, everything would be different. She could never accept that her only daughter was to marry under the stars with no formal reception to follow."

"It might not be what your mother would have had in mind, but we're planning on one heck of a party!" Naomi said.

"You should see how busy it is at the bakery this morning, Evie. Levi has been working all night. So much cake!" Tamar's eyes glowed with excitement.

Naomi stepped closer to her friend. "Wait, Evie. Do your parents even know about Albert? That you're to marry today?"

Evie looked up and softly answered, "No. No they don't. What would be the point? I've never told them what we really do here. It's bad enough that they think I'm a farmer! Besides, Papa is a British official and my mother would lose her mind if she knew the truth."

"So you don't expect them to ever meet Albert? Even after we win the war? Will you tell them then?"

"When this conflict is over, Naomi, and our side proves victorious, my father will be sent home to London, probably in disgrace. My mother will hide in our house, afraid to be seen by her so-called socialite friends. Their life will be over."

Naomi's eyes widened. "Maybe you should have told them. Don't you think they'll need some joy in their life if that happens?"

"I'm not sure that this would bring them any happiness, Naomi. You don't understand my parents. My father would be devastated if he knew that I was part of a plan to rid this country of the British. And my mother, well, as I've said, she will never be able to accept my choice, my lifestyle. Marrying a foreigner? Someone not of British ancestry? Oh no. This news might push them over the edge entirely." She stood up then and walked over to the simple white linen shift with its long lace train that two of the women on the kibbutz had sewn for her to wear today, running her fingers gently over the fragile fabric. It had a high neck and sheer sleeves. Small flowers were embroidered in blue and yellow on the bodice and at the hem. They'd scoured the *shuk* to find the material for the dress, the train, and a veil of fine tulle, to which they secured colorful anemones intertwined with baby's breath as a crown for her head. While it all seemed perfect to Evie, she knew without a doubt that her mother would never approve. She closed her eyes and pictured her parents' faces. This was her day, a time to be happy, to commit herself to the man she adored and as much as she loved her father and her mother, she would not be deterred. She drew in a deep breath, took a moment, and sent up a private, silent prayer for them both. When she opened her eyes again, she looked at the eager women in her tent and said, "Okay. Do your best to make me look presentable. I'm getting married today!"

EVIE HAD ACTUALLY ENJOYED her time with these women more than she thought she would. There was no talk of bullets or war. Instead, they laughed and told stories to one another, taking the time to paint her fingernails and toenails, wash every inch of her body, then carefully apply eye shadow and mascara, finally brushing and curling her hair into a shining mass of perfection. She felt pampered and loved and she knew that they did all of it because they wanted her to have this moment for herself. Evie was sad to see them go and get ready for the night's festivities themselves. Only Naomi remained in the tent with her, having brought her maid of honor attire along earlier that day.

"This is such a big step, Evie. I'm so happy for you," Naomi said as she stepped into her dress. It was one of the only pieces of extravagant clothing she'd brought with her from Jerusalem. It was made of the finest silk in a deep, emerald green, which accentuated her eye color. It had a plunging neckline and a sweeping skirt with multi-layered crinoline beneath it, rendering it useless for kibbutz life but perfect for this rare and joyous occasion. The wide belt that cinched her small waist had tiny crystals dotting the buckle that reflected warmly in the candle-lit tent. She slipped on a pair of matching pumps and turned toward Evie. "I'll just fix my hair and then we can go," she said, reaching for her tortoise shell brush.

"Naomi," Evie said, grabbing her friend's hand before she could lift it. "Please assure me that I'm doing the right thing. I mean, not telling my parents."

The other woman took a moment to reply. "Well, Evie, you know them best. I've never met them and I'm not sure--"

Evie interrupted. "I guess it doesn't matter now." She turned away.

"Listen to me," Naomi said, commanding Evie's attention by coming around to stand in front of her, looking directly into Evie's eyes. "Everything that's important is waiting for you under the *chuppah*. You've made your mark here. You've done so much good for all of us. And I know that we'll prevail and win this war. When it's over, when we're victorious, you'll tell your parents and you'll bring Albert to meet them in London. You'll see. This will all be okay."

Evie felt the firm squeeze of her friend's hands on her own. "Promise me something, Naomi."

Evie watched the concern spread across Naomi's face. "Of course. What is it?"

"Promise me that no matter what happens, we'll always be friends. That we'll know each other forever."

"Of course we will! Nothing between us will ever change. You're just being silly now. Those bridal jitters are getting the best of you!"

"No, Naomi. I'm just a realist. Aside from today being a happy occasion, we're still fighting a war. Anything can happen. And if you follow the story of our people, you know that we must remember the hardships of our shared history."

"That's why Albert will break that glass under the *chuppah,* to remember and honor those who came before us. But for now, for this moment? Evie, I know that the odds are in our favor. We are doing the impossible, making a permanent place for all of us to simply live together in peace." She carefully drew Evie into a hug. "So," Naomi continued, "just for today, can we please concentrate on the joy that you've found with Albert?

Evie did her best to center herself and remain in the moment. She loved Albert with all of her heart; that wasn't the problem. She was just terrified that this feeling of true happiness was not meant to last. She took in one large, deep breath and nodded her head up and down.

"Good, it's settled then. Today is all about you and that good-looking soon-to-be husband of yours. Now," Naomi said, linking arms with Evie before lifting the flap of the tent. "Let's go get you married!"

. . .

NAOMI WAITED under the *chuppah* and felt nothing but joy. The night was magical and chock full of stars in the inky black sky. Albert stood tall, his face beaming brightly. She could see the love this man had for her friend, and his raw emotion made her acutely aware of her own feelings for Judah, which she knew were much more than just physical. When she glanced over at him, dressed in his best shirt and slacks as Albert's best man, she saw that he was looking directly at her. She had to avert her eyes, because she could see the desire in his; it mirrored exactly what she felt churning inside of her. He was handsome, but more than that, he exuded strength, and she found that to be overwhelmingly attractive. She felt herself begin to sway, a bit light-headed, and willed herself to breathe deeply and not ruin this moment. It belonged not to her, but to Evie.

At that thought, and almost on cue, Evie appeared at the *chuppah*. As she began to walk toward Albert, there was a palpable excitement that vibrated through the assembled members of the kibbutz. This was a group of people, Naomi realized, that while united in a shared goal, had separately known hardship, loss, grief and in some cases, unspeakable horror. Yet they were here, now, in this moment, to celebrate the gift of love. As Evie drew closer, Naomi watched as Albert's smile grew wider, his eyes shining, never looking away from his beloved as she made her way to his side. The man who served as their rabbi cleared his throat loudly before he began to chant the first of the multiple blessings that comprised the wedding ceremony. Naomi focused on her maid-of-honor duties, keeping an eye on the train of her friend's dress, careful to keep it out from underfoot so that Evie didn't trip as she circled her groom seven times in the age-old custom of their religion.

It what seemed like a moment later, Naomi watched Albert stamp down forcefully on the napkin-covered glass placed under his shoe, and heard the glass within shatter, signifying the end of the ritual. Raucous shouts of *mazel tov* rang out from the crowd and loud bursts of song filled the air when Albert reached for Evie and leaned her backward, giving her a long and passion-filled kiss. Once she regained her footing, the newlyweds ran off together back up the aisle for a few moments alone before they would join the party that the members of the kibbutz had planned in their honor. Naomi waited for the newly married couple to be out of sight before she stepped out from under the *chuppah*. She had begun to walk toward the area set up earlier that day outside of the dining hall, when she felt Judah's presence behind her.

"Beautiful," was all he said.

She turned around quickly. "Yes. It was a very special ceremony."

"That, too," he replied, his eyes bright. "But look at you..."

She felt herself blush and raised her hand to her head, smoothing her hair in a nervous gesture.

"You look handsome, too," she said quietly.

He smiled. "Come. Have a drink with me?"

"At the party?"

"Unless you have somewhere else in mind," he said softly as he leaned in toward her ear.

"No. We should join the others. We would be remiss to our best-man and maid-of-honor duties if we didn't show up," she replied before she could change her mind and allow him to take her somewhere more private.

"For now, I suppose you're right." He pulled back, the intimate moment between them dissolving into the cool night air. "Besides," he added, "Ari has culled from his private stash the best of the bottles of wine he's been hoarding, in Evie and Albert's honor, of course. The right thing to do would be to go raise a glass to the newlyweds." He winked at her, then held out his hand before adding, "That is if you're so sure that we need to do the right thing."

She slipped her fingers through his and he lifted them gently to his lips, softly kissing each one. Naomi could feel her resolve begin to weaken. "Judah...we really need to do what we both know we should."

He shrugged his shoulders and smiled, never letting go of her hand. "If you say so, Naomi. But I do hope that we can continue this conversation later."

She saw the promise in his eyes and immediately realized that if she didn't think she was lost before, Naomi now knew the truth. She was hopelessly in love with this man; he held her spellbound in the depth of his gaze and the promise of whatever he had in mind for later.

THE SKY BEGAN to lighten over the fields when the last of the wine was consumed at Evie and Albert's wedding celebration. The empty bottles and the crumbs of the cakes that Levi had baked were the only evidence of the loud and happy party that they'd all enjoyed: it was finally time for the newlyweds to retire to the tent that had once been just Evie's, but would now be the dwelling that they'd share as husband and wife. She was nervous. For all of Naomi's instructions, for all of the stories the other women had revealed to her about their own first sexual encounter, she was afraid that she would not be enough to please her new husband.

They walked back to the tent in silence and Evie couldn't help but wonder if Albert felt as she did; excited to be with the person she loved but worried that she'd let him down in some way. Once at the tent, he stepped in front of her and lifted her off of her feet.

"What is this, Albert? What are you doing?"

"I saw this in an American movie once, when I was a boy. It's all I really know about weddings, for that matter. The groom carried the bride over the threshold of their home. It seemed important, or at least in the film it did."

"No, Albert, put me down, it's okay. I am fine to walk."

He gently placed her back on her feet.

"That old tradition, the one you attempted to honor? It has to do with the bride not willingly wanting to go into her husband's home." She shook her head. "I don't want our marriage to begin that way. I am here because I love you. I want us to share our lives together."

"That's what I want, too, Evie. I'm sorry. It seemed so romantic in the movie."

She reached for his arm, placing her hand lightly on the fine fabric of his jacket, made especially for this occasion. "I don't need any of that, Albert. I love you and I know that you love me, too. That's all that matters."

He responded with a line from their vows, "I am my beloved's, and my beloved is mine," before he pulled her inside the tent.

"Oh my," she said once her eyes adjusted to the dimness of the space. Someone had been there before them, placing flowers in small pots around their cot, and lighting a variety of candles, which had now burned down low, casting warm shadows on the canvas walls. "How lovely," she remarked as she turned toward Albert. He was staring at her. Evie rubbed her cheeks, sure that she must have something there, something that had caught his attention. "What is it?" she asked.

"Nothing. It's just that you look so beautiful, Evie. I can't believe that we are truly husband and wife."

"We are," she said softly.

He stepped closer to her then, his breath sweet as he leaned in for a kiss.

Evie felt warm immediately, flush with the emotion of the day and her feelings for him. She reached up and put her arms around his neck, pulling him in close, longing to feel his touch. Her small movement ignited his desire as he began to undo the tiny pearl buttons that ran down the back of her dress, the fabric slowly falling aside and gathering around her feet. He slowly pulled down the straps of her bra, his fingers tracing soft circles on the sensitive skin right where the lace met the cotton, stoking the fire that had been long building inside of her. He unclasped the back and her breasts sprung free. She heard a soft moan escape his throat and when he caressed one of her nipples, she matched him sound for sound. Standing in just her panties, she kicked off her shoes and then with one stroke, removed the scrap of fabric, baring herself entirely to his gaze. She felt brazen and alive when she saw his clear desire for her straining against his trousers. She could wait no longer. Evie stepped back far enough to undo his shirt, pushing it over his shoulders to reveal his naked chest, strong and muscled, almost exactly as she had imagined it would be. In response, he reached down and removed his pants, stepping out of them, leaving only the thin material of his boxers between them, his arousal apparent. He quickly pulled them off and walked her backward to the cot where they fell together, a mad jumble of legs and arms, both of them fevered and anxious, their inexperience the only barrier left between them. Then, tentatively and gently with a careful motion, he was inside of her.

"Evie!" he gasped in a burst of utter passion.

She felt a sharp, piercing jolt and then a rush of warmth before he relaxed in her arms. A minute went by, the two of them motionless, his body still covering her own.

Then he pushed himself up on his elbows and asked, "Are you okay?"

At first, she wasn't sure. It all happened so quickly, it took her a moment to recover her senses. "Um, yes, I believe so."

"Judah told me to expect that our first time together would not be perfect. He told me that it takes some practice to get this right."

She smiled and felt herself take a breath for the first time since they'd entered the tent. "Is that right?"

"So he said," Albert replied, rolling off of her now and resting on his side.

"Well then," she murmured. "When do you think we can try that again?"

He smiled. "Any time you'd like," he answered before he slowly kissed her once more.

NAOMI WAS up with the dawn, despite having not truly slept the night before. As the wedding party had continued around them, she and Judah could barely control the impulse to touch one another. There was always a light caress or an excuse to stand close to one another as those around them continued to eat, drink and laugh. When they could stand it no longer, they made their way between the other members of the kibbutz, all enjoying the free flowing wine and sweet cakes as they celebrated well into the night. They headed to Judah's tent, where they surrendered fully, to one another, body and soul. Their connection was undeniable now. Naomi was head over heels in love with this man and she was sure that he felt the same way about her. They made love over and over again, finally slipping off to sleep as the sun began crest over the horizon.

She quietly dressed in yesterday's clothing and picked up her shoes, careful not to wake him. She wanted to return to her own tent before the others began to stir. Even though they had a rare day off in honor of Evie and Albert's wedding, Naomi didn't want anyone to see her leave Judah's tent. Gossip, she knew, was inevitable on the kibbutz. She just didn't want to be the subject of the idle chatter. Once outside, she realized that she had no reason to worry. All was quiet, no one was milling about, and the cool morning air helped her think more clearly. So much had happened since she'd left New York. Her life had changed in ways she could have never imagined. Her original plan of writing of her travels had been shelved for now, and her purpose was clear. She would take part in the birth of this country, standing shoulder to shoulder with the brave people she'd met here. They were forging a new frontier, together as one, insuring that those displaced by war and religion would finally have a home that no one would take from them ever again. And she had met the man she was sure that she would spend the rest of her life with, doing good work for the land she'd come to love. With hope in her heart, Naomi sent up a silent prayer for the future that she knew shined brightly ahead for them all.

Part Two

ineteen

Rehovot
October 31, 1946

EVIE HEARD the news first and was waiting for Naomi as the factory workers' shift was about to break for lunch. Both Ari and Judah had decided that the climb up and down the steep steps was too arduous for her now in what she hoped were the final days of her pregnancy. Evie felt fine enough, but even she had to admit that her expanding girth made it difficult for her to move with any grace at all. The last thing she needed to be was a liability to those making the bullets; she didn't want to jeopardize their safety if there was an emergency and the crew needed to get aboveground quickly. The truth, which she admitted only to herself, was that she went nowhere fast these days. She felt as though she was dragging her swollen body through quicksand most of the time. Albert always tried to make her feel better, telling her that she was doing the most important job of her life, growing a new member of the tribe inside of her belly, but all Evie felt was useless. Having grown so accustomed to being at the helm of the workers in the factory, these last few weeks she'd felt utterly lost. Sitting in the dining hall long after it emptied was depressing, so she'd gotten into the habit of listening to the radio to deaden the silence around her. That's when she'd heard the announcement and realized that Naomi needed to know. Perhaps there was something she could do to further help the cause.

Evie watched as precisely at noon the laundry staff left the building to head off to lunch. Minutes later, the large metal tub was pushed to the side, revealing the entrance to the factory as the first of the workers emerged from underground, all shading their eyes at the bright sunlight streaming into the room. She nodded her greeting to them as they drifted by her, then paced somewhat impatiently, scanning the crowd for her friend's face.

Finally, Naomi appeared. When she saw Evie, she gasped. "What are you doing on your feet? Shouldn't you be resting?"

"All I do is rest, Naomi. I have something important to tell you."

"Well, hold that thought until we get to the dining hall and you sit down. I don't want anything to happen to that godchild of mine!"

"Ugh. I am so tired of being babied like this. I'm fine. Women have been having children forever, Naomi. I'm no exception."

"You know what the doctor said. It's best if you take it easy now. Let us do our job. You do yours by saving your strength for what's important." Naomi walked close enough to Evie to link arms. "Now, if you really can't wait, just share your news. What's so vital that you had to drag yourself over here and tell me?" she asked as they began walking.

"Well, I heard an important announcement on the radio. It seems that your President Truman has just declared his support for the creation of a Jewish state!"

"It's about time. I mean, we knew he was headed in that direction last May, after he recommended that one hundred thousand displaced people should be admitted into Palestine. We need the protection afforded a sovereign country."

"Exactly, Naomi. So that's where I had the thought that you

might have a better line on raising more American dollars. Who do you know who can help us?"

They had reached the dining hall and Naomi opened the door for her friend. "That's tricky, Evie. I've asked my parents and I know that they've been generous, but I've never told them the truth about our mission. Maybe it's time that I do."

"Is there no other way? I mean, can they try to raise funds without knowing everything? Just on the basis of the importance of our independence?"

Naomi led Evie over to the table where they normally sat and motioned for her friend to get off of her swollen feet. Evie watched as the other woman swung her own legs over the bench and moved in close. Naomi whispered, "How much do we need?"

"As much as we can get."

"I'll write home tonight. But just so that we're clear. Don't tell them anything? Just ask in general for funds to help us become an independent nation?"

"I think that would be best, don't you?"

"I don't know, Evie. Americans like a cause but they also like a fight. I do think we could rally a small group of wealthy patrons with the truth more easily than a generic war bond rally."

"While that may be right, if news leaks out about what we're doing here, we might risk the whole operation. If I ask Ari, I doubt he'd agree to divulge the real reason we're here."

"Okay, okay. I understand. I'll figure out a way to ask for more money, one way or another."

"I know you will," Evie said, feeling some of the pressure of living in such a precarious time lift for a moment. Now let's eat. I'm starving all of a sudden!"

"Well, we can't have that, now, can we?" Naomi teased. "You sit. I'll go get some lunch for us both."

Evie turned her body with the intent to stand and was met by her friend's green stare.

"Do us both a favor and stay here. I don't need to face Albert's wrath if I let you do this for yourself! Please!"

"Oh, brother!" Evie replied. "I'm more than capable…"

"Save it, sister. I'll be right back." Naomi scurried off before Evie could protest again.

Just then she felt the baby kick, as if to reprimand her for even thinking of getting her own food. "Wow," she said aloud to her midsection as she shook her head. "You already have an opinion? Great." Evie realized that she had no further option but to sit and wait for her lunch to be served.

Naomi thought long and hard about what Evie had asked her to do and by nightfall she'd formulated the letter she wanted to write home. As she entered the tent that she now shared informally with Judah, she searched for her pen and paper, which she kept in the small leather case under his large cot. Then she took it over to the table and chairs that served as their desk, put her head down and began to write.

Dear Mom and Dad,

I hope all is well in NYC! It's Halloween today. I miss seeing all the colorful decorations in the store windows at home. Are you starting to think about your Thanksgiving plans? Are you having the whole gang gather at home, as usual?

We are fine here in Rehovot. The land is bursting with tomatoes and cucumbers--they are everywhere I look, in the fields and at breakfast, lunch, and dinner! I am turning into quite the farmer...

She stopped writing for a moment, hating the lie, but knowing it was the right thing to do. She placed her pen back on the page and continued:

We heard the good news today on the radio that President Truman has recommended that Palestine should be declared a Jewish state. That is just fantastic, but it takes more than his words to make that a reality. We need funds. Desperately. I know that you've done so much already and sent money, but do you think you can rally your friends to do even more? Anything at all is so appreciated. We can make a difference here but quite frankly, we need the American dollars to do it. So, if you can, please host a fundraiser! I'm counting on you to help...

She lifted her head in time to see the flap of the tent move aside. Judah stepped in.

"*Motek*," he said. "What are you doing?"

She put the pen on the table and stretched her arms up over her head. "Writing a letter to my parents, asking them to step up their fundraising efforts for our cause. Evie made it clear to me that we need the money now and I want to help. It would be better if I could tell them about our mission, but I won't. It's too risky."

He pulled out the vacant chair and dragged it close to her so that their knees were touching. Then he sat down. "Of course," he said thoughtfully. "But we do need the help. Maybe they will understand the urgency without you needing to explain all of the gritty details. After all, they know about the thousands of displaced souls arriving here daily. They can probably well imagine that it will take a whole lot of money to feed and care for these refugees. The matter seems clear to me."

"That's because you live it every day. You see what is happening here," she replied. "They could have no true idea what it is like to live as we do. Other than wanting to give money to the cause that will establish a Jewish state, they remain blissfully ignorant. From what I hear, America is welcoming back its soldiers with ticker-tape parades and dancing in the streets. So much has changed there since I've been here. My mother wrote all about it in the last letter I received from her. And she said that plenty of people are moving out to the suburbs, buying homes and raising families on large tracts of land. She wanted to know just how much longer I planned on being here, in Palestine, unmarried and farming. I think she wants some grandchildren. She made it clear that a good portion of her friends were grandparents already!" Naomi paused, realizing what she had said and not wanting Judah to think that having a child was the path she wanted to take. She quickly blurted, "Now, when I think of a large piece of land, my mind immediately starts to calculate how many tomatoes I could plant for a successful harvest." He smiled at her and Naomi instantly knew that he saw past her bravado.

Judah softly replied, "It's nice for your mother to dream about grandchildren, Naomi. It implies that she has trust in the future."

She watched as he fished a cigarette out of the pocket of his shirt, but he just held it unlit between his fingers before replacing it. "We are not as lucky as the optimistic Americans are," he said. "We don't know what tomorrow has in store for us."

"I understand that, Judah. I don't even know what I want to do with my life when this war is done. I had always thought that I would be a journalist. Now, I'm not so sure. I want to stay here. I want to make a difference, to do something meaningful."

He leaned in and kissed her cheek. "Whatever it is that you choose, Naomi, I know that you will be successful and make your mark on the world. You are smart, you are beautiful, and for right now," he murmured as he pulled her onto his lap, "you are mine."

With those words, their discussion abruptly ended. Clothing quickly shed, they took comfort in each other's bodies until way past the time when dinner was served in the dining hall and the moon was high in the star-laden sky. But as she drifted off to sleep, Naomi still questioned what her true destiny was. Did it include this man next to her, whose very embrace was the one thing that gave her strength, courage, and the belief that if tomorrow came, they would share it together?

THE NEXT DAY DAWNED BRIGHTLY. When Naomi woke up, Judah was already gone. He and Albert needed to prepare for their current mission and she thought she might find him in the dining hall poring over maps and charts with his protégé. She put her hand on his pillow, tracing the indentation he'd left there, remembering their lovemaking from the night before and wishing that he were still there, in bed with her. But for as much as she'd like to explore that fantasy further, she knew that it was time for her to get up and go to work, too. She quickly gathered her things and headed down to the bathhouse to wash up before the day got away from her. Besides, she had wanted to catch Judah to say goodbye. She knew that wherever it was that he was going, he was to be away from the kibbutz for a number of days this time. That's all he'd told her about the secret mission he had been charged with by Ari. She knew that he'd have Albert along with him, although that seemed risky to her at this stage of Evie's pregnancy. Albert stood the chance of missing meeting his new child right after her friend gave birth, but, she reasoned, it was to be expected. Each day she felt the war draw even nearer to where they were. Producing, packing and moving the bullets to where they could do the most good seemed more important than ever.

FOUR MORNINGS LATER, when Naomi entered the dining hall for breakfast, she found Evie sitting at a long table alone, ripping a stack of papers into shreds.

"Destroying the evidence?" she asked with a wink.

"No. Just getting rid of the excess. I can't seem to stop cleaning. Our tent is spotless, so I've decided to rid myself of any extraneous paperwork."

"Hmm. I've read about this nesting syndrome. Late in pregnancy some women tend to tidy up, making ready for their new arrival."

"Really?" Evie asked. "Is that what I'm doing? And why the sudden interest in my condition? Anything you want to tell me?"

Naomi shook her head, laughing. "No. Absolutely no. It's just the journalist in me coming out. I find so many things interesting, and quite honestly, you're my first friend to be pregnant. None of my classmates have jumped into the parenting pool yet. Not that I'm there to witness any of it, anyway."

"Well, you've gotten a pretty firsthand view of these last nine months with me! Not too appealing, eh?"

It was true. In her first trimester, Evie had spent an awful amount of time vomiting up anything she ate. Her persistent nausea had kept her out of the factory and confined to her bed, a bucket her constant companion. Then, just as she was feeling better, the warm weather hit. It was hot and sticky each day from sunrise to sunset and Evie's feet and hands would swell so much that it was all she could do to comfortably sit in front of one of the large fans in the dining hall, water in the glass that Albert made sure was always filled. Getting Evie to the bathhouse was an event as well. The kibbutz's doctor did not want her to be alone, so Naomi would time her own showers to coincide with her friend's, keeping an eye on her, insuring that she remained balanced and upright throughout. At the end of September, Naomi realized that the best course of action was to have a chair in the stall so that Evie could sit and let the coldest water she could tolerate pour over her body, allowing her a chance to cool off. Then finally, once dried and dressed, they would slowly make their way to the dining hall where Albert would be waiting with her dinner in hand. On the occasions when he had a mission outside of their camp, Naomi would make sure that Evie ate before walking her back to her tent and the comfort of her bed. Her friend was ready to give birth; now it was up to that baby in her belly to decide to finally make an appearance.

"What will you do once you're done cleaning up your paperwork?" Naomi asked as she peeled an orange.

"Not much. I'm supposed to be on bedrest anyway. I just

needed a change of scenery. I really don't think it matters if I'm sitting here or sitting in my bed."

"Yes, yes it does," Naomi responded, concern in her voice. "Maybe you aren't meant to be up and walking about." She looked down at her friend's feet. "Evie! Your ankles look huge! Maybe we should go see Dr. Weissbaum. I don't think that they are supposed to be that big!"

Evie looked at her legs and sighed. "I'll be fine. I just need to elevate them."

"In your bed. You need to elevate those ankles while lying down in your bed." She pushed the half-peeled orange aside and said, "C'mon. I'll walk you to your tent and then I'll go find the doctor."

"I'm almost done here, Evie, and you have to get ready for work. I'll be fine. I promise to go back to bed as soon as I finish."

Naomi felt torn. Whenever Albert left the kibbutz, he always found Naomi before departing and asked her to watch over Evie until his return. He didn't like having to be away from her at all, but now more than ever Naomi understood that he worried about his wife and their unborn child. Although she knew she was needed in the factory, she could miss her morning shift and return after lunch. Right now, she felt that her friend needed her more.

"No. You're done here. I'll tear the rest of these papers up for you after I settle you into bed and find Dr. Weissbaum. He needs to have a look at you."

"You're making a mountain out of a molehill, Naomi. I'm okay, truly."

"That's for the good doctor to decide. Right now, let's go back to bed, shall we?"

"I guess this is nonnegotiable?"

"I made a promise to your husband to keep my eye on you while he's gone. Don't give him a reason to be angry with me. Besides, if Dr. Weissbaum clears you to sit in the dining hall and work, then I'll leave you alone. Sound fair to you?"

Evie shifted in her seat for a bit before putting both hands on the table to brace herself so that she could stand. "None of this seems fair, Naomi. I feel useless and of no good to anyone. We need those bullets. We need to get them into the guns of our soldiers right now."

"That's what we are doing, Evie. You set the plan in motion. Now you have to allow the rest of us to follow through." She watched as her friend gained her balance before turning away from the table. Naomi linked her arm through Evie's and carefully guided her out of the building.

They made it halfway down the path toward the tent when Evie suddenly stopped and put one hand on the bottom of her belly. "That was weird," she said.

"What? What was weird?"

"A quick sharp pain. It's gone now."

"What do you mean by 'it's gone now.' Has it happened before?"

"A couple of times this morning. It's nothing, I'm sure."

"How can you be sure? Maybe it's the beginning of labor!"

"Oh, a little research and now you're the expert? It's not time yet. Besides, Albert isn't here. He promised to be back before the baby is born."

"I don't think that Albert gets to choose. I mean, no one gets a say here, unless, of course, you're that baby in there trying to get out."

"Now, who's being silly?" Evie began. "I'm not feeling any--" With those words, she turned to Evie, wide-eyed. "Oh no. I think my water just broke!"

Naomi looked down and saw an ever-widening puddle growing around the other woman's feet. "We have to get you to the infirmary. And then I have to find Dr. Weissbaum."

"No. Don't leave me alone. Please, Naomi. Please. Stay with me."

For the first time since they'd met, Naomi recognized what looked like fear in Evie's eyes.

"Okay, okay. One thing at a time. Change of plan. We're near your tent. Someone will be around. I'll send for the doctor and I'll stay with you. Does that sound like a good plan?"

Evie could barely nod her head in agreement before she doubled over in pain. This was all happening so quickly, Naomi realized, and she had to do her best to keep her wits about her. Feeling pretty useless otherwise, she decided that staying calm was the only thing in her power to do. That, and pray that Albert returned quickly if he wanted to see his child come into the world.

Twenty

DAY TURNED into night and still no baby. The doctor had come to check on his patient and ordered that Evie be brought to the infirmary. Almost immediately four large men, all farmers, turned up outside her tent and quickly carried her to the makeshift hospital. But to Naomi, that now felt like it had happened ages ago. It seemed like Evie's labor had slowed to a crawl. Despite it all, Naomi kept her word and stayed with her friend. She had heard a rumor buzzing through the halls of the infirmary that Albert was on his way back to the kibbutz, but no one really knew if that bit of news could be trusted. She was exhausted from the events of the last long hours. Shaking her head, she could only imagine how Evie felt.

"Naomi," her friend called out weakly from her hospital bed. "Is Albert coming? This baby won't wait much longer."

"I can't promise, Evie. Just let nature take its course, please. You must be so tired."

"I am, but I don't want him to miss this."

"I don't think that any of this is in your control, Evie." Naomi shuffled over to the other woman and attempted to soothe her with a cool washcloth, gently dabbing away the sweat on Evie's forehead.

"I know. I just want to go to sleep."

"Soon. Soon you'll hold your sweet baby in your arms and then the two of you can rest. I promise."

"If you say so," Evie said through a clenched jaw, closing her eyes as another contraction forced a spasm of pain through her body. She grasped on to Naomi's hand, leaving deep grooves from her nails in Naomi's palm. It was all Naomi could do not to snatch her hand back; instead, she hung on until her friend's body relaxed once more.

Just as Evie was regaining her breath, Dr. Weissbaum and a nurse entered the room. He was an older gentleman who had an easy way about him. He exuded confidence. Tall and thin, Naomi had heard that he was an early arrival to the kibbutz from Germany. He and his wife had escaped shortly before Hitler's rise to power, only to land in a country where another war was imminent. *So much struggle for one lifetime,* Naomi thought to herself. *Yet here he is, smiling and ready to guide Evie's baby into the world.* The sound of Dr. Weissbaum's voice as he spoke to her friend brought Naomi back into the moment.

"Listen, Evie. I've let you labor for a long while. I think it's time to consider a Cesarean section.

Evie struggled to sit up. "No! No surgery. It's too dangerous. I'll push harder..."

"It's not a matter of you working any more diligently than you have up to this point. I just don't think that your baby should continue to struggle. For that matter, neither should you."

"Can we just wait for Albert? He should be here soon, right, Naomi?"

Naomi could feel all the eyes in the room turn toward her. "I wish I could tell you yes, Evie. The truth is that I just don't know. I don't think you can wait for him any longer. Do what the doctor says. He knows what's best." She reached out and took her friend's hand and lightly squeezed it. "Maybe he'll be here by the time you wake up."

Evie's tired eyes filled with tears and she swallowed hard before softly agreeing. "Okay," she acquiesced, collapsing back onto the pillows in a sign of surrender.

The doctor looked at the nurse and gave her a nod of the head, signaling her to unlock the wheels of the hospital bed and move their patient to the surgery. Naomi walked alongside Evie until she was allowed to go no farther. The nurse pushed open the double doors to the restricted area and said in a thick middle European accent, "You can wait out here." She motioned toward two worn plastic chairs leaning against the wall of the hallway.

"One more thing, Naomi," Evie said anxiously as the nurse prepared to wheel her away. "When he finally arrives, make sure to tell Albert that I love him."

Naomi felt a pang of fear. She knew that her friend was scared and steeled herself not to show her own emotion. "Don't be silly, you'll tell him yourself. And you'll introduce him to your brand new son or daughter. You'll see. Everything will be fine, and I'll be here when you wake up."

With that, the nurse moved farther away with her patient and finally out of sight. Naomi felt all of the energy drain from her body. She barely made it to the chair before her knees gave way in pure exhaustion. She put her head in her hands and wept. She couldn't imagine where Albert was, or for that matter, where Judah was either. If Albert knew that Evie was actually having their baby right now, Naomi was sure that this was the only place he'd want to be and if it was within his power at all, he'd be here soon. She felt her own breathing slow as she gathered her wits about her, not wanting anyone who might pass by to see her cry. This would be okay. Evie would be fine and so would the baby. Dr. Weissbaum would make sure of that. Now, if only Albert and Judah would return before her friend woke from the anesthesia. That's all she could ask for as she sent that small, silent prayer toward heaven.

. . .

NAOMI HADN'T EVEN REALIZED that she'd closed her eyes and drifted off to sleep, but all at once she heard Judah whispering softly in her ear.

"Naomi." He gently shook her. "Wake up, *motek*."

"Judah?" she questioned as she slowly regained herself. "When did you get here?"

"Just a moment ago. Albert went to try and find out what's happening with Evie, if the baby is here yet."

"She struggled all day and into the night. She tried so hard to wait for him to be here. It was heartbreaking when the doctor told her it he thought it best that she have a Caesarean section right away and you weren't back yet."

"I know. I can imagine how it must have been so scary for you both." He sat down on the chair next to her and took her hands in his. He turned them over and saw the deep grooves left by Evie's nails. "What happened here?" he asked.

"That's nothing, just the end result of Evie's labor. She is a warrior, that's for sure."

"From the looks of these, so are you," he replied, kissing her palms gently.

Right then the doors to the surgical area opened, and Albert appeared, holding a tiny bundle wrapped tightly in a white blanket. Naomi and Judah both jumped up to greet him.

"I have someone for you both to meet. This is Deborah, our daughter!" He was grinning from ear to ear.

Naomi looked at the miniature version of her best friend, now comfortably asleep in her father's arms. She had long eyelashes, a button nose, and deep rose colored, perfectly formed lips. "She's the spitting image of Evie!" Naomi exclaimed.

"Isn't she? She's beautiful!" Albert replied, his eyes lovingly fixed on his daughter's face.

"*Mazel tov*, Albert. Or should we call you *Abba* now that you're a father?" Judah teased.

"I'm still not sure what I'd like her to call me, but I do know that I'm overwhelmed by my love for this little girl, and for her mother as well."

"That's right! How is Evie?" Naomi asked anxiously.

"She's fine. A bit groggy from the medicine, but other than that, she came through this like a true soldier."

"Of course she did!" Naomi said with pride and a little wobble in her voice. "That was never in doubt!" She sent up a private, silent prayer to heaven in thanks for both Deborah's safe passage into the world and Evie surviving the surgery.

"Listen, I'd like to go back inside and sit with her for a bit. Can I ask you to hold the baby for a little while? You two are her godparents, *n'est-ce pas*? I think you can manage for a few moments, right?"

"Yes, please!" Naomi said, extending her arms to receive the baby.

Albert gently placed the child in Naomi's embrace and she and Judah sat back down in the chairs. Albert kissed his daughter's head and then made his way back through the doors to find his wife.

"Judah! Isn't she lovely?" Naomi cooed.

"Yes. And her name. It's perfect. Do you know who Deborah was?"

Naomi tried to remember her bible studies, but the combination of exhaustion and the thrill of actually holding Evie's baby made her memory lapse. "I know it's Hebrew for 'bee,' but by all means, tell me," she said, now gently rocking the sleeping child in her arms.

"She was a prophetess. She lead her people to safety by

forming an army when they were threatened by the Canaanites. This little one was born to power."

"That's a whole lot of responsibility for one so small," Naomi remarked.

"She is the future, Naomi. We all rely on her strength to bring us forward. She is the new beginning that we've dreamt about." He extended his hand and softly touched the little girl's fingers. Even in sleep, little Deborah wrapped her small hand around his index finger. He drew in a breath and said, "This is exactly what we work so hard for."

Naomi looked down at the peaceful face of the sleeping baby and felt the connection between the three of them. "Indeed she is, Judah." She leaned over and kissed his cheek. "And may she be the first of many, many more."

NAOMI AND JUDAH SAT THERE, taking turns holding the baby, until Albert brought his daughter back to the nursery. Evie, he told them, was sleeping and he was going to sit with her some more before heading back to their tent to rest. Naomi could almost feel the adrenaline that coursed through his body seep into her own. She knew that Albert would remain awake for what was left of that night and was happy to know that he and Judah were home safe and sound once again. On the way back to their tent, she asked Judah why he and Albert had been so greatly delayed.

"I guess you were so busy with the events of your day that you were not able to listen to the news on the radio at all."

"The radio? No. Why?"

"There was a bombing in Italy. Two suitcases were left on the steps of the British Embassy and did a lot of damage when they detonated. The Irgun reportedly is behind the attack."

Naomi knew that the Irgun, an underground splinter group of soldiers fighting for the establishment of the Jewish state, had claimed responsibility for the bombing of the King David Hotel in Jerusalem the previous summer. The British administrative headquarters had offices there and ninety-one people were killed in the attack. It had been a tense time for all of them, but especially for Evie. Until she found out that her father hadn't been there, that he was safe and sound at home in Tel Aviv during that incident, she had been a nervous wreck. Naomi shook her head in disbelief.

"The Irgun? Again? Did you know this was going to happen?"

"We got wind of it and tried to get back here sooner, but once the news hit, the British soldiers shut down the main roads. We had to take back channels to get home, and believe me, it wasn't the easiest ride. Neither of us wanted Albert to miss being here when his child was born, but we did our best. We're here now." He looked at her reassuringly. "All is well."

"But, Judah, wait," Naomi began, her head suddenly filled with questions. She stood still on the path for a moment. "Go back to the bombing. Was anyone killed?"

He reached for her arm and linked it through his own, gently guiding her toward their tent. "I'm not sure. I know that the residential part of the building was destroyed. I heard that the British ambassador was the target, but he wasn't there."

"And so the British soldiers will be on high alert going forward?"

"Of course. We will need to be particularly careful over the next few weeks. No mistakes."

"What about you? When will you be going back out again?" She looked up at him with apprehension. She almost didn't want to know the answer to her question.

"I'm not entirely sure yet," he said as they approached their tent. He opened the flap and waited for her to step inside before he did. "But for the next week, I'm here, on the kibbutz."

Naomi felt a small part of her heart lift. This was a tiny reprieve, a chance not to worry about Judah's safety when he stepped outside the confines of the kibbutz. "Well then." She winked at him. "Let's not waste a moment." She reached for his hand and unbuttoned her blouse, determined to make every second of this gift of time together count.

As a chilly dawn crept over the horizon outside their tent, Naomi was grateful for the warmth of the man beside her. She burrowed even more deeply under the blanket and against the strength of his chest, careful not to wake him. She hadn't slept very much, but she didn't care. She would trade a night of lovemaking with Judah for a full eight hours of rest any day.

She thought back to their tender kisses, the gentle sweep of his fingers over her overheated and sensitive skin, his lips and tongue tasting each and every part of her. It was a moment of such overwhelming happiness that she almost wished that they could spend the rest of their lives in this very spot. Knowing better, she gently maneuvered herself out of the cot and quietly began to gather her toiletries to head off and prepare for her day.

She slipped into the worn khaki pants that she favored now. They were soft and very practical, with deep pockets where she often stored defective bullets during her day. It was crazy to think that she actually knew how to spot a dud immediately. It was a far cry from her life in New York City, or even her student days in Jerusalem. But she wouldn't trade her current job for any other opportunity. She'd finally found a true calling, a home.

Grabbing her red sweater, she left the tent and made her way toward the bathhouse, all the while wondering if she would have enough time to visit with Evie and Deborah before her shift began. *If I grab a quick cup of tea and a pita to go, perhaps,* she thought. She hurried to see if she could make all that happen. She couldn't wait to see her friend and her goddaughter again. Smiling to herself, she moved as quickly through her morning routine as she could.

AN HOUR LATER, Naomi sat by Evie's bedside as her friend drank a cup of hot tea and repeatedly thanked her for seeing her safely through the previous day.

"I could not have done it without you, Naomi. I mean that."

"Don't be silly, Evie. You did the work. I just held your hand." She absentmindedly rubbed the marks on her palms, leftover reminders of just that very thing.

"With Albert away, you were my rock. I'll never forget that."

"Did he tell you why it took so long for Judah and him to get back here last night?"

"Yes. Any further news from Italy?"

"I haven't heard anything yet, but if I do, I'll let you know." She glanced up at the clock on the wall over Evie's bed. "I have to get to the factory. But I'll be back tonight. Hopefully, I'll get a chance to hold my goddaughter again!" She smiled.

"Of course you will! I'll be here, feeling quite useless, I may add!"

"Don't be ridiculous! Savor the rest. You deserve it. Besides, we still have so much more to do. I know you'll be back on your feet soon." Naomi stood and then bent over to give the top of Evie's head a kiss. "Take a nap! You need to save your strength."

"I'll try, I promise."

"Good. I'll see you later," Naomi said as she stepped outside into the hallway. She wanted to catch a glimpse of Deborah, so she walked past the nursery where she saw a row of small isolettes lined up, tiny babies sleeping inside of them. She couldn't help but marvel at the thought that even as they manufactured implements of war, new life sprung up around them. All of these small children represented exactly what they were fighting so hard to protect.

Naomi had to drag herself away from the peaceful sight and rushed outside toward the laundry so that she'd be there before the large tubs closed back over the opening to the factory. She could see the last of the stragglers filing into the building and knew that she had a minute or two to get herself to her post. That's when the strangest thought crossed her mind and made her nearly stop in her tracks: Would there be children of her own in the future? Would their father be Judah? Was it even possible for her to allow herself this wonderful dream? With renewed determination, she pushed herself even more quickly to make it on time for the work day ahead.

Twenty-One

Rehovot
December 17, 1946

JUDAH SAT in the dining hall and looked at the table strewn with maps. It was time to open extra delivery lines to bring ammunition to the troops more quickly. He absentmindedly rubbed his hand across the back of his neck, reviewing the route he'd planned to take with Albert later that night. They would need to stay in the shadows. The British had been everywhere lately, even making a surprise inspection of the laundry and bakery the week before. Luckily, once again they had not discovered the secret that lay beneath the very ground they searched. And if one enemy wasn't enough, their Arab neighbors had been tossing bombs into the far fields of the kibbutz, sometimes wiping out entire crops of tomatoes in their wake. They had been fortunate not to have had any fatal injuries among their farm crew, but he realized that it was only a matter of time before there was an unspeakable tragedy where lives were lost.

Judah closed his eyes. He had the mission, its path and pitfalls, burned into his memory. He trusted Albert to do whatever it took to help bring the bullets to the soldiers waiting for them and then find his way back to Rehovot safely. But for the first time in a very long while, he doubted his own commitment to the cause. Lately he'd found himself thinking about the future, *his* future with Naomi, and he knew that allowing himself those types of thoughts left him vulnerable for the kind of disaster he'd already lived with Geula. It was very dangerous, he realized, to take his eyes off the prize of his homeland's ultimate independence and plan ahead. The future was not guaranteed for any of them. But the thought of the soft curves and warmth of Naomi's body curled around him at night made the lines that he'd held so steady for so long in his mind blur. He wanted her as much if not more than he wanted to win this war. If he could take Naomi and run to a safe place, somewhere just the two of them could live out their days together, he would do it. And he also knew that thinking these exact kinds of thoughts made him a liability to the team. He could not place his own desires ahead of the goal. He had to hope that when this war was all over, he'd be able to claim his rightful place next to the woman who brought him more joy than he felt he deserved.

Just then Ari appeared before him, a mug of steaming hot tea in his hand.

"You look like you could use this more than me," he said, passing the beverage over the papers to Judah.

"I appreciate that. I really do need to take a break." With the mug in his grasp, he rubbed his eyes with his free hand.

Ari looked down at the papers strewn all over the table. "Ready for tonight?"

"Of course. It's not going to be easy. Ever since the underground has been ramping up their attacks on the British, we've had to navigate around the checkpoints and guard posts."

"It will get worse before it gets better, Judah. The bombing last week killed six British soldiers. You know that they are just looking to take their revenge. Stay out of sight."

"It's going to be tough. Those narrow dirt roads were not built for trucks. Donkeys might be a better solution."

"Then get on it."

Judah grimaced with a swallow of hot tea. "It will take longer."

"But it will be safer in the long run. Think about it. The truck might not be your best bet right now. Tensions are high and if you are detained... Well, you and I both know that you're no good from the inside of a prison cell, or worse."

Judah nodded. "I suppose we could dress as Bedouins and caravan with donkeys to Tel Aviv." He took a moment to mull over Ari's suggestion then said, "You're right. It's the better move."

"Good, good. I'll secure the beasts. You brief Albert." Ari abruptly turned and walked toward the exit with clear purpose.

Judah waited for the other man to leave the building before he began to gather the papers from the table, straightening them into a pile and putting them into a large accordion file, securing the whole thing with a piece of ribbon. He sat for a moment, his fingers rubbing against the soft brown trim. He looked at the length of fabric for a moment, then had a sudden thought. He wanted desperately to give Naomi something, a token of his deep feelings for her, something for her to have while he was away. *But what?* And then it struck him. Lifting the file off of the table and tucking it under his arm, he checked the time. He had twenty minutes before Naomi's lunch break would bring her back up from the underground factory. He had to hurry if he was to complete his task before he saw her again.

NAOMI BLINKED as she stepped outside into the bright sunshine. She had a date to meet Evie in the children's house for a brief visit with Deborah before lunch and was looking forward to holding her goddaughter for a bit. The baby had begun to smile and coo when she was spoken to, trying to hold up her head and take in all that was happening around her.

As she hurried to her destination, Naomi took the time to stretch her arms out in front of her and then lift them over her head, flexing them as she walked. She found that the hours spent packing bullets may have strengthened her muscles, but no matter how much Judah massaged her tired limbs, at the end of a shift she was often sore. The only other thing that helped was holding the baby–Deborah was like a soothing balm; Naomi couldn't wait to get there. She finally stepped inside, let her eyes adjust for a moment, and went to find her friend in the nursery.

Evie was sitting in a rocking chair, Deborah at her breast. When she got closer, Naomi noticed that the little girl had her eyes wide open as she nursed, taking in her surroundings.

"*Shalom*, Evie," Naomi said.

"Ah, Naomi," Evie replied, lifting her eyes from her daughter's face. "How is it going?"

"Well, thanks. How about you and your gorgeous baby?"

"We're both good. She is a treasure."

Naomi couldn't help but notice the love in her friend's gaze when she looked down at her baby. It was beautiful. "Of course she is!"

"Do you want to hold her?" Evie asked. "She's almost done here."

"Can I?"

"Of course." A minute later the baby released Evie's nipple and looked up at both women, a toothless milky smile on her face. "Take her," Evie said, passing the baby to Naomi. Once Naomi had the child firmly in her arms, Evie tucked her breast back into her bra and rebuttoned her shirt.

Naomi held her goddaughter tightly, all the while rubbing

her back, gratified to hear a large burp escape the tiny body. "I'm getting quite good at this," she teased her friend.

"Well, apparently this one is as good a burper as she is an eater," Evie replied. "She makes us all look like naturals at this game!"

"I think she knows more than she lets on, don't you think? Look at the intelligence in those eyes!" Naomi exclaimed.

"You're just as prejudiced as Albert and me." Evie laughed. "We think she's brilliant."

"We all agree on that." Naomi nodded. "Can we take her with us to the dining hall? Can she have lunch with the girls?"

"No. She's due for a nap and I need a little time off. I'll set her down in her crib and then we can go."

"Okay," Naomi said as she reluctantly handed the baby back to her mother.

"Give me a minute. I'll be right back," Evie said as she walked back to the row of cribs set off in a corner of the room. Naomi watched as her friend settled the baby safely before she returned, leaving her daughter in the trusted care of the women who worked in the nursery.

Linking her arm through Naomi's, Evie said, "Let's go eat. I'm famished and I need some adult company. Fill me in on everything I've missed."

WHILE NAOMI and Evie were in deep conversation over a shared plate of hummus and pita in the dining hall, Judah was inside their tent, busily crafting a crude necklace from the ribbon he'd removed from the file folder. Rummaging through his pants pockets, he ran a finger over the two dog tags that he always carried with him. They were small squares, silver in color and lightweight. Each had a perforation in the middle.

One was meant to stay together at all times, the other to be split in two, with each segment tucked into the wearer's boots, just in case he was killed in battle and needed further identification. Judah took one of the tags and slipped the ribbon through the hole on the top, tying a knot at one end to secure it. Then he put it in his pants pocket for safekeeping before separating the remaining tag and tucking each end into his boots. He could always have a new tag made to replace the one he was giving away; for now it was the only thing of his to have any value that he could give to Naomi. He wanted to show her how much he cared for her, how much he wanted her to be a part of his future. He would ask her to wear his tag as a promise that they would stay together, that she would not return to New York but rather make this new country they were forging together her home, with him at her side.

Satisfied with his handiwork, Judah lit a cigarette and took a minute for himself. After tonight's mission, there would be new challenges to face, all increasing in danger as they found themselves deeper and deeper into this war. After Geula died, he'd longed for some refuge, some peace. He took the most dangerous and difficult assignments because he had no real desire to live. But now? Everything had changed. He had more and more reason to be on alert and return in one piece. He had finally found salvation in the arms of the American redhead, and he planned on spending the rest of his life in the warmth of her embrace. A rare smile crossed his lips. He lifted his head to the sun as he stepped out of the tent, took one last drag of the cigarette, and started down the path to find Albert. They had work to do. The sooner they completed this ammunition run, the closer they were to winning this war. And the closer they were to winning this war, the closer he was to finally finding the one thing he'd found most elusive in life: true happiness.

. . .

ONCE THE AFTERNOON shift at the factory was over, Naomi wanted nothing more than a long, hot shower. It had been humid underground for most of the day, and she felt the dust and grime covering every inch of her like a second skin. She quickly made her way to their tent, hoping to wash before Judah came to find her to walk to the dining hall for their evening meal. Once there she hurried to gather her things and head off to the bathhouse, happy to find it relatively empty. She chose a stall and turned the water on full blast. Even though it wasn't truly hot, the combination of soap and clean water made her feel much better. She rinsed the last of the shampoo from her hair and could feel herself get a second wind, the day's exhaustion running down the drain with the last of the soapy suds. Naomi put on her clean undergarments and then reached for her white cotton button-down blouse, absentmindedly wondering about what she wanted to eat that night. Sometimes she dreamed about the one thing that was never available on the kibbutz: a juicy cheeseburger, dripping in ketchup, a side order of well-done fries, and a black and white ice cream soda. Shaking her head to rid herself of the excess water that clung to her curls, she smiled. *How far I've come. No burgers, but some shakshuka would do the trick tonight,* she thought. *Those runny eggs and tomato sauce would be equally delicious.*

She slipped into a clean pair of pants and went to drop her dirty clothes and toiletries back in the tent before she could go find Judah. To her surprise, he was already there, waiting for her when she arrived.

"Hi," she said softly. "I didn't expect to see you here. I thought you'd be somewhere in deep discussion with Albert about tonight."

He straightened his back on the chair where he sat, looking imposing, broad, and tall. "Discussions are done. I'm here to spend time with you."

Naomi felt a familiar shiver run up her spine.

"Hmm. I like the sound of that," she said. "What did you have in mind?"

"Come here. Sit with me." He motioned to the other chair at the small table.

"This sounds serious. Is everything okay?" she asked.

"It is. I just have something for you. And there's something I want to say."

She pulled out the chair and sat down across from him. "I'm listening."

She watched him shift in his seat uneasily for a brief moment. He cleared his throat.

"Naomi, I find myself thinking about you, about us, all of the time. You know I love you, right?"

She looked directly at him. "Yes, of course. I love you as well."

"I didn't think this could happen to me again in this lifetime. I thought I'd spend the rest of my days alone. You've been such a gift to me, Naomi. I want to give you something as well."

"Judah. You don't have to..."

"No. I'm not a wealthy man, Naomi. I don't have material things. I've never had the need for possessions. So I only have this one thing," he said as she watched him reach into his pocket, "that I can give you. But it's a token of my love and deep devotion. I hope you'll wear it. Always."

And then she saw, that resting in his hand, was his dog tag on a ribbon.

"No. You need that, Judah. If anything were to happen and you couldn't speak for yourself, that is how I'll find you."

"Naomi, I have the other two tags. I will keep them in my boots. But never worry. It won't be a problem. I have every intention of returning to you." He stood and circled the table to where she sat. "May I?" he asked, holding the necklace over her head.

Too emotional, all Naomi could do was nod her head. He placed the tag around her neck and tied the ribbon at the back. She lifted her hand to feel the raised lettering of his name on the metal. "I will wear this always, with pride," she whispered.

He led her to their shared cot. All thoughts of dinner abandoned, they made love until the time he had to leave to meet Albert. In his wake, she realized that both men had good reason to move with care so they would safely return to the women they loved. She would take him at his word. She had no other choice.

After Judah left that night for his mission, Naomi felt fidgety. She decided that instead of tossing and turning alone in their cot, she'd write home. She had been too busy to answer her mother's last letter, which had been filled with news of her family and friends. Her mother was always sure to list which of Naomi's classmates had married since she'd left the States and let her know how her many cousins had new babies or had moved from New York City to the Westchester suburbs. It wasn't that her mother wanted her to do any of what some of the other women her own age were doing, but more that she felt the need to make sure that Naomi knew what was happening with her peers. Sometimes Naomi wondered if she were to return to the States if her mother just expected her to pick up where she left off, which was something Naomi was pretty sure she could never do. She had been restless enough to leave and she was convinced that she would stay here, in her new home with Judah, for the foreseeable future. She found her sheets of onionskin stationery and her pen and began to write:

Dear Mom,

Thanks for all the updates on what's been happening there. We've had a bumper crop of tomatoes here which has kept me very busy.

She stopped for a moment. She continued to hate lying to her mother but knew better than to expose their true purpose in Rehovot. However, she did think that it was time to share that she'd met someone special at the kibbutz.

And also, I have some interesting news to share. I've met the most wonderful man. We've been seeing each other for a while now. His name is Judah and if I'm being really honest, Mom, I'm in love! I hope that when this war is over you'll come here and meet him. Wouldn't that be grand? Imagine taking a trip here with Dad. I would so love that and I know that you would, too! I can just picture Dad's face when he sees the fields of produce we grow. It's simply remarkable...

She stopped writing to think about how she wanted to phrase the next part of her letter. A moment later she put her pen to the page again:

. . .

I'm starting to see this place differently. I feel very much at home here. I think that if you come over and see it for yourself, you'll understand exactly what I mean. I can't wait for you to meet Judah as well as my good friends Evie and Albert. They have the most adorable daughter. Deborah is six weeks old and just gorgeous! Promise me you'll think about taking the trip, alright?

Again, thanks for the check you sent. We can always use the help. If you and Dad could host another cocktail reception for the fight for independence here, we'd all appreciate it. Every dollar pushes us closer to the reality of a free nation for Jews everywhere. There is just so much more to be done and everything comes at a great cost. But you know that–I mean, how many war bonds did you and Dad buy, after all?

Well, it's getting late now, so I'll put this letter down. I'll try and add some more in the morning before I go to work. Love you, Mom.

Naomi put her pen on top of the sheet of paper and went to lie down on the cot. She would finish tomorrow. For now, she wanted to get some rest. She buried her nose in his pillow and drew in deep breaths to capture the spicy scent Judah left behind on the soft muslin case. The lingering trace of him soothed her enough for her eyes to become heavy and allow her some much needed rest in a dreamless, silent sleep.

Twenty-Two

THE NIGHT WAS full of stars.

That was the first thought Judah had as he and Albert made their way dressed as Bedouins with a caravan of donkeys loaded with their most precious cargo. A starry night, Judah noted, was good for two reasons. There was no moon blocking the constellations from putting on a show of twinkling light and there were no low clouds obscuring the view. No clouds meant no rain, another plus. *It is one thing,* Judah thought to himself, *to be dressed in this unlikely costume. It would be truly awful to be dressed in these robes if we were wet and the dirt path was muddy. At least, for now, the disguise will keep us warm.*

They made their way in companionable silence for the first hour of the trip, until Albert asked, "Did you bring the coffee pot?"

Judah smiled. Ever since becoming a parent, Albert had developed a taste for the strong, bitter coffee that Judah drank regularly. Perhaps it was his lack of sleep. Evie had chosen to keep Deborah with them at night instead of in the nursery of the children's building. "Of course. We'll travel a bit farther before we take a break. We're almost a third of the way there. Let's wait for the midpoint."

"Just trying to keep us both awake," Albert replied, his straight white teeth giving away the fact that he wasn't Bedouin at all.

"Don't worry about me," Judah quipped. "I'm fine."

"Of course you are, old man. I'm fine as well—not that you asked."

Judah smiled at the easy banter between them. They'd come a long way together since that first meeting in the tavern in Prague.

"What's the latest information on Al-Jawrashi?" Albert asked as he turned his head to look at their surroundings. "I know that he's had his men plant more than one land mine on this road."

"According to Ari, he's been laying low ever since the Stern gang and the Irgun's activity have picked up. And why not? He's letting them do the dirty work for him."

"I don't know, Judah. The man is still a threat. I don't understand why the underground doesn't just deal with him. I mean, we know the bastard would like to see us all dead."

"That may be true, Albert. But we're not going to kill the man just because he's buried a few mines. It's not our mission. Our job is to get these cases of bullets safely through to the men who are doing the real fighting. It's that simple."

"But he has such a deep hatred of us Jews. He wants to block us from ever having a true home to call our own."

"It doesn't matter, Albert. We will succeed. I know we will." Judah turned back to look at the line of donkeys, tethered together with rope, large wooden crates piled on their backs. "Let's keep moving," was all he said. But Albert's words resonated with him. They had a job to do, and it was dangerous. There were plenty of people who wanted them to fail, throwing all sorts of obstacles in their way. Missions like this one, where they did not have the illusion of protection by driving to the front lines in a heavy metal truck, were particularly harrowing. Even disguised, the open air, the narrow dirt path, the slow and deliberate pace they kept because of the animals they used, all of it seemed to heighten the level of danger for the two men. And the Arab leader was only one of their enemies. If the

British found them with this cargo, it would be very tough to convince those soldiers of the story they were to tell: that they were bringing a stolen shipment of women's lipstick to the *shuk* for a quick profit.

There was a time when Judah wouldn't have cared what might happen to him out on a night run like this one, but now, everything had changed. He had Naomi waiting for him at home and the thought of being captured took on new meaning for him. All he wanted was to return to the woman who had stolen his heart. Add to that the responsibility of insuring that Albert return in one piece to his wife and young daughter left Judah on high alert with all of his senses sharp and aware.

A few hours later, and with the confidence that they had completed half the trip, Judah pulled the rag-tag caravan off to one side of the road under the heavy branches of a large olive tree. He stretched his arms overhead in an attempt to force some feeling into his limbs. Bumping along on the back of a donkey left the rider both stiff and uncomfortable; he was looking forward to a little bit of rest before completing the mission. He started a small fire to heat some water for their coffee while Albert attended to getting water for the animals from the wooden cask they carried. They worked together in silence and caution. They both understood the danger of an unseen land mine and neither one wanted to unwittingly step on one. When the coffee was prepared, the two men drank slowly, knowing that an empty cup meant it was time to move once again. Finally Judah said, "We need to go. We only have about four hours before the sun rises. We have to be hidden from sight by then."

Albert nodded and dumped the dregs from the coffeepot on the fire as Judah smothered what was left of it, a wet heap of ashes and a trail of smoke drifting up toward the sky the only sign that they'd been there. In a matter of moments, they were on their way, precious cargo intact. It was all Judah could do not to allow himself to imagine getting back to Rehovot when this job was successfully done. He knew better than to think that far ahead. He had to stay focused. He had to stay alive. Despite the official reason for this trip, his personal mission was to return to his true love's bed, and he was living for that very thing.

When the sun rose over Rehovot that morning, Evie went to lift her daughter out of the tiny crib in a corner of their tent. She loved this time of day, when she could savor the moments she had to spend with her child. Since going back to work full-time, Evie missed seeing the baby whenever she wanted to—she was busy with the mission at hand. She knew that Deborah was well cared for, she trusted the women who worked in the children's building, and her daughter was thriving. No matter how many times she reminded herself that her work with the factory was vitally important to the nation they were collectively trying to build, she couldn't help but wonder what effect this would all have on her young child. Shaking off the self-doubt, she kissed the top of the baby's head before sitting down to feed her. It was the most peaceful time of her day. She vowed not to let anything get in the way of this shared bonding experience.

Once Deborah was fed, burped, and changed into clean clothing, Evie got herself dressed and ready as well. Holding her daughter, she walked down to the children's building where she dropped off the baby and then headed to the dining hall for a quick breakfast before getting involved in the details of her day. The hours passed quickly. She had requests for changes of shift from factory workers to deal with as well as a schedule to write for those who needed a little time in the tanning room that they'd built underground. Evie marveled at how every small detail had been thought out when this project was birthed. The team had realized that by staying out of the sun for days on end, the workers would begin to look paler than the farmers who worked the land. It was important to protect the secrecy of the work done down below, so the bullet makers rotated through the tanning chamber to insure that no one noticed anything amiss. She worked steadily until it was time for the underground workers to emerge for lunch and then gathered her paperwork, putting the new schedule on top to distribute as the team exited the building for their afternoon meal.

The sun was shining brightly at its zenith. Evie shaded her eyes with one hand as she quickly made her way to the laundry building. As she entered, she smelled the fresh scent of washing soap and waited a moment for her eyes to adjust to the dim light. Once her vision cleared, she knew that she had a problem on her hands. One of the laundry workers was still there. She should have left for lunch ten minutes prior, but Evie could see that she was trying to wring out a very heavy load of towels by herself.

"Malka," Evie cried out. "What are you still doing here? You should be at lunch!" She tried to keep the panic out of her voice, but she knew that in a matter of moments, the tub would move seemingly on its own and the workers would begin to surface from their morning shift in the factory.

"Oh, Evie. It's no problem, really. I just wanted to finish one last task before going to eat. I should be done shortly."

"No. You must go now!"

"But, Evie," the other woman began, wiping her wet, sudsy hands on her apron. "It won't take much longer..."

With those words, both women froze in place at the sound of scraping metal against cement. Then the tub shifted left. The next thing Evie knew, Malka had fainted dead away right in front of her. Dropping her papers in a pool around her feet, Evie ran over to where Malka lay motionless on the floor. The others, who had come up from underground, were standing around helpless as Evie tried to run damage control.

"Go. Go to lunch," she emphasized to the factory workers. "I'll take care of her. It will be easier to explain things without a crowd around. Just go."

"But, Evie," one of the women implored. "Let us help you carry her to the infirmary. Let the doctor look at her."

Naomi stepped in. "I'll stay. Do what Evie says." She quickly walked to a pile of towels and grabbed one, then dipped it into the jug of ammonia used to wash the clothing. She looked around. "You heard what Evie said, trying to rouse some of the workers who seemed glued to their spots on the floor. "We will handle Malka."

The crowd finally dispersed. When they were alone, Naomi knelt down, put Malka's head in her lap, and passed the towel to Evie. "Put this under her nose. She'll come around."

Evie did and Malka's eyes jerked open with a start. She struggled to sit up.

"Rest a minute. Wait until you gather your wits about you, Malka. You hit your head pretty hard."

"Did you see? There were ghosts in here. They came out of the ground," the shaken woman said.

"Just take a minute. We'll explain."

Evie knew she had no other choice but to tell this woman the truth. If she didn't, she risked a rumor sweeping through the kibbutz, one that might make the laundry crew not want to come back to work. She looked up at Naomi and said, "I have to let her know what just happened."

Naomi stared at Evie and said, "I agree." Then she turned back to the other woman. "Malka. Do you feel ready to sit?"

The woman shifted and pushed herself up and sat with Naomi and Evie on the floor of the laundry.

"Let me get you a glass of water," Naomi said, quickly going outside to the well and returning with a metal cup filled with the cool liquid. "Sip slowly."

The woman did as she was told. Finally, Evie said, "We've been keeping a secret, Malka, one that I will share with you now. But it is of the greatest importance that you never reveal what you are about to hear to anyone. Do you understand?"

Malka, wide-eyed, just nodded.

Evie proceeded to tell her about the factory below and the kibbutz's true mission.

"So you see," she said at the end of her explanation, "why you cannot whisper a word of this to the others?"

Malka sat quietly for a moment, then responded, "Can I see what is downstairs? Can you show me?"

Naomi looked directly at Evie. "I think we should."

Evie replied, "I guess we have to." She began to pick up her papers, which were still scattered all over the floor. Once she had them in a neat pile, she turned back to Malka. "Are you dizzy? Can you stand?"

"I'm okay now. I want to see what you are talking about."

"One minute," Evie said. She stood and placed her papers down on the steel table used for folding laundry. Then she turned back to the other woman. "Let us help you get up slowly," she said, motioning for Naomi to grab hold of Malka's arm. Together they brought the shaken woman to her feet.

"Are you sure you can do this? The staircase is steep."

"I'll be careful," Malka said.

"Let me go first. I'll walk in front of you in case you feel woozy again," Naomi said. She walked over to the opening in the floor. "But if we're doing this, we should go now. It's getting late."

"Agreed," Evie replied.

The three women moved slowly, one small step at a time, descending into the factory. Once there, Malka looked around. There were metal shavings all over the floor and half-filled cups of water left at various stations, the only sign that people had been there as recently as thirty minutes ago.

Can you tell me how this all works?" Malka asked.

Evie went into a brief description of exactly how the bullets were made, with Naomi filling in some of the details. When they finished, Evie glanced at her watch and asked, "Any other questions?"

"Only one," Malka said softly. "Can I be reassigned? I'd like to work here instead of the laundry."

Evie took the woman's arm and began to lead her back up the stairs. "I'll speak to Ari on your behalf. It it's possible, we'll arrange to make it happen. But until then, we don't mention any of this to anyone, right?

"Of course," Malka replied.

"Good. Now that this is all settled, let's grab a quick bite before it's time to get back to work," Naomi added.

The women made their way to the surface and Evie pushed the tub back into its rightful place over the opening to the factory. As they made their way to the dining hall, she tried hard not to worry over Ari's reaction to what had happened. She was not in the mood for a confrontation with her commander. It was all she could do to hold herself together waiting for

Albert to safely return. She did not want to face Ari's wrath in the interim.

JUDAH WOKE WITH A START. They'd successfully gotten the bullets to the distribution checkpoint right before sunrise and had slowly made their way back to a safe resting spot near a small stream, shaded and secure. The donkeys were fed and watered and Albert was soundly asleep after their night's journey. The ride home should not take as long without the heavy cargo they'd carried and a big part of him just wanted to go, to travel back along the road toward Rehovot. He knew better, however. It wasn't safe to move in broad daylight. There were too many rogue bands of Arab militia hidden away in the many caves that lined the dirt path and he didn't want to engage with them. They'd have to wait. He sighed. He just wanted to go back to the warmth of Naomi's arms. The depths of his feelings for the American redhead still surprised him. It had been so long since Geula's death, so long since he'd felt any emotion at all. He silently shook his head. They had been so young, childhood friends who had turned into lovers. He and Geula never really considered what life might be like for them as they aged, or if they'd even still be together. For as much as she was a part of him, and always would be, the feelings he had for Naomi felt deeper and certainly more immediate. Perhaps in losing Geula he had come to understand how rare it truly was to find someone who penetrated the tough exterior of his heart. It was if he felt all the blood in his body pump through his veins when he thought of Naomi; even now, his fingers longed to touch her smooth skin, to have them tangled in her hair, to have his lips explore every inch of her perfect body.

Since sleep eluded him, Judah allowed himself to daydream

about a life with his true love after this mission was over. He had to convince her to stay on the kibbutz in Rehovot, or perhaps they'd get a flat in Tel Aviv. He truly didn't care, because he knew that wherever Naomi was would be the place he'd call home. Smiling, Judah wondered if she would be happy being a farmer's wife. That was how he imagined living out their lives, surrounded by chickens and cows, a house full of children, laughter and peace. But if she wanted to live in the city, he'd do that as well. It truly didn't matter to him. Just knowing that she would be at his side would be enough.

Judah watched as the sun began to dip lower in the sky. He stood up, wanting to untether the donkeys and to pack his few things into the leather saddlebags on the back of one of the beasts before waking Albert for the journey home. As he finished his task, he glanced over to the younger man, eyes closed, napping on the braided mat he'd brought along for this purpose. That's when he saw it. Glinting sharply against the dying sun: a land mine. And if Albert made one wrong move in his sleep, he would detonate it, erasing the future for them both.

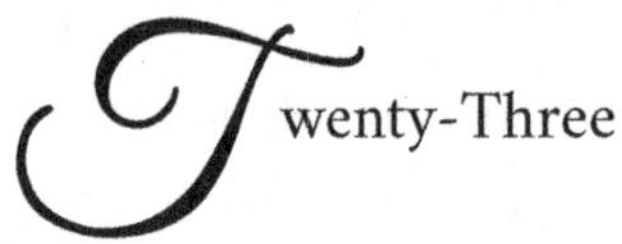

Twenty-Three

JUDAH STOOD FROZEN to the spot, trying to clear his mind to decide what to do next. He wanted to shake Albert awake, but that sort of quick motion might cause the younger man to roll over onto the bomb. Instead, he took a moment to strategize. Once Judah had accessed the situation fully, he knew exactly what to do. He slowly led the donkeys onto the dirt road, away from where they'd spent the day resting. He was able to see a clear path and safely steer the animals away from the danger. Once they were secured, he carefully retraced his steps back over to his friend and placed one booted foot on each side of his sleeping body, effectively pinning him in place. Then he bent down and gently shook Albert's shoulders. Albert mumbled something unintelligible in French and tried to roll over. Judah's boots kept him rooted to his spot.

"Whatever you do, don't move!" Judah said firmly.

Albert's eyes widened, and Judah recognized the fear there. "Land mine? Am I on it?"

"No," Judah answered. "If you were on it, you wouldn't still be here, now would you? It's just a bit off to your right. One wrong move and it will detonate."

"I guess that's the good news," Albert said glumly. "But how am I going to get up without setting it off?"

"I'm going to slowly back up. You'll grab onto my forearms and stand in one motion. Don't step left or right, just move straight ahead."

"But wait, Judah. If there's one land mine here, there may be more. How can we be sure that it's safe to move in any direction at all?"

"If we know anything about the way Al-Jawrashi works, we know that he plants his bombs in a circle, hoping to hit as many of us as possible in clusters. He expects us to travel in packs, like wolves. I don't see any other mines right here, but you're right. We need to step carefully to get away from this place."

Albert squeezed his eyes shut, made a slight nodding motion and said, "Okay. I'm ready."

"Then here we go. One. Two." Judah tightened his grip on his friend. "Three!" He stepped back and pulled Albert up and on his own feet in one smooth motion. "Don't make another move. Just wait a moment."

The two men stood still, arms still intertwined, the sky now fully dark, the sound of their breathing and the pounding of their hearts in their ears the only thing either of them could hear. As soon as Judah felt that they were both steady and balanced, he released Albert's arms and said, "Walk slowly and follow me." He took the first of a series of small steps toward the clearing that would put them by the donkeys and back on the path to the kibbutz.

"Are you okay, Albert?" he asked once they made it to the dirt roadway.

"I think so. That was close," came the anxious reply.

"Well, take a moment. Then we'll be on our way," Judah said, a reassuring tone to his voice. Then, after a few tense minutes of standing together digesting the fate they had just narrowly escaped, they began the last leg of their journey home.

By the time they reached the two stones that marked the entrance to the kibbutz, Albert felt like he'd been granted a new life. It was truly the second time that Judah had saved him; the first time was that night in the tavern in Prague. Tonight the older man had protected him from certain death from that land mine. While Albert knew that there was no way to repay Judah for these actions, he vowed instead to find a way to work even harder to help the cause.

"Albert," Judah said. "After we get these donkeys back to the stable, we'll need to find Ari and tell him to mark that grove on the map. It's full of land mines and must be avoided."

"Of course," Albert replied. Despite that the meeting with Ari would delay his reunion with Evie, he knew how important it was to fill in their commander on the task they'd just completed. "I'll get the beasts fed and watered. You find Ari and I'll meet you in the dining hall."

With a nod, Judah disappeared from sight.

Albert led the donkeys to their stalls. He made sure that they had what they needed before securing the door of the stable on his way out. In the small shed next to the stalls, full of the different costumes they used on their missions, he discarded his Bedouin robes next to the dusty ones that Judah had worn and made his way toward the meeting with Ari and Judah. He desperately wanted to find Evie as well, but knew that he'd have to wait.

Because of the late hour, the dining hall was deserted, the only two people in there were the men he was looking for. He grabbed a mug, filled it with tea, and went to sit down at the table with the others.

"Good job, Albert," Ari said as he sat down on the bench.

"Thank you, but it was Judah who did the heroic thing today, Ari. Did he tell you about the land mine?"

"Yes. I've marked it on the map," Ari said pointing to the stack of papers at his elbow. Al-Jawrashi won't be happy until he's killed as many of us as possible. As if it's not enough that we need to worry about the British soldiers." The older man shook his head.

"It's foolish to think that we won't have our Arab neighbors to deal with, Ari. We've been faced with this conflict for centuries," Judah remarked.

"I know, I know. But if we could all learn to live together, everyone would benefit."

"It won't happen," Judah said matter-of-factly.

"How do you know that to be true, Judah?" Albert asked. "We need to try."

"If they would be interested in making peace, maybe. But they're not. They want the same thing as us. This land. And we're not giving it to them."

"But if we could work out an arrangement, maybe…" Albert began.

"Judah's right," Ari interjected. "There will be no way to make that happen. We can only hope to fight one war at a time. We'll deal with Al-Jawrashi when we're done with the British. That's our best hope." He took a large gulp of his now cold tea before saying, "Now fill me in on what you saw near the transfer point. Did everything go smoothly with the bullets?"

"Of course, no problem," Judah replied. "But the next shipment will be directly to the lines, right? The lorries will be filled with milk cans, I assume?"

"Yes. This last mission was just to shore up the supply. The main delivery will be done by truck. The driver should be here by the end of the week."

"Good, good," Judah said. "These smaller trips are becoming very difficult."

"I know," Ari remarked. "I hope there won't be too many

more of them. I don't think I'll need to send you out again for a while."

Albert was relieved to hear Ari say those words. It meant that he could stay put on the kibbutz with Evie and Deborah.

"What can I do to help out in the meantime?" asked Albert.

"There's plenty of packing and loading of the bullets to be done. We've got dozens of empty milk crates that need to be filled so that when the lorry gets here we're ready and can have a quick turnaround time. But for tonight, go see your wife. I know she's anxious to know of your safe return home."

"Okay, I'm going! See you both tomorrow." Albert quickly stood to leave.

"Meet here in the morning and we'll work out a schedule for loading those bullets," Judah said.

"I'll be ready," Albert called over his shoulder. He was already on his way out the door to reunite with Evie and Deborah, all thoughts focused on taking his two girls in his arms and holding them tightly through the night.

EVIE HAD JUST FINISHED NURSING the now sleeping baby when Albert silently stepped into their tent.

"Albert! You're back!" she exclaimed with relief in her voice. The baby stirred for a moment and then settled back down.

"Yes, just now. I'm so happy to be home, Evie. This was a tough trip."

"I can imagine!" she replied. "Did those donkeys behave?"

"Oh yes, they did. Very reliable animals. But we did have a bit of trouble at the end." He held his arms open, inviting her to come closer to him.

Evie stood with Deborah in her arms and moved into her husband's embrace. Then she shifted her weight and passed their daughter to him. He brought the child in closer to his chest. "Sit down, Evie. I'll tell you what happened."

They rested in the lone two chairs they kept in their tent and he proceeded to explain how Judah had saved him from a land mine in the olive grove and how they had to carefully navigate their way out of the dangerous situation.

"And you must believe me when I tell you, Evie," he said, "the only thing I could think of was staying alive to see you and the baby. After everything I've lived through, running from the Nazis, starving, stealing food to survive, freezing in the cold of winter in war-ravaged Europe as I tried to make my way here, praying for a reunion with my father, all of it…nothing else compared to my fear of not making it back home to you."

Evie came over to where he sat with their daughter in his arms and knelt in front of him. "Of course you made it. You have a good reason to live." She put her hands over his. "We have our whole lives ahead of us, Albert. We will see this war through and then we can start planning what we want next. I think we will have had enough of the fighting by then. We will find another path. I know we will."

"This war, Evie, this war. It's truly just begun. I don't think that it will be done any time soon."

"Hush," she said, putting her hand lightly over his lips. "Let's not worry about that now. Let's get to bed." She lifted the baby out of his arms and tucked her into the small crib they kept in one corner of their tent. Then she returned and took his hand, leading him over to their cot. They quickly stripped off their clothing and fell into the bed, naked and full of desire for one another. As exhausted as Albert felt, there was nothing that would stop him from having his fill of the woman he loved. Sleep would follow. For now, he just wanted to appreciate being alive.

. . .

The next morning, Evie was up before the sun. She gently got out of bed so that she didn't wake Albert and checked on Deborah who, thankfully was still sleeping, her tiny eyelashes fluttering against her cheeks. She was relieved that Albert was home, that he was safe, and after the story he had told her, still in one piece, but she felt unsettled. Even though she had told him the night before that they would figure out their future when their work in Rehovot was over, she had no true idea what that meant. She'd spent years working toward this moment, this drive for a free state for her people. She had no other plan, no life experience to guide her. She knew just one thing for sure: she didn't want to fight anymore. She didn't want to risk losing the love of her life in yet another dangerous mission.

She stepped outside into the cool morning air and allowed herself to daydream for a bit. Maybe they could truly learn to farm and work on a kibbutz that would produce crops to feed this emerging country of theirs. Or instead, they could both take positions in the government that was bound to form once the war was done. It was almost funny to think of Albert at a desk job–he was so good working with his hands–but anything was possible once they lived in an independent nation! Maybe she'd even take a page from her father's book and become a liaison between her country and the rest of the world…

Evie heard the baby stir in her crib from where she stood at the flap of their tent and rushed inside to pick her up before the child had the chance to wake her father, but it was too late. Albert already had Deborah in his arms, gently rocking her back and forth. Evie couldn't help but notice her daughter's gummy smile; she loved her father and he loved her back. For now, inside their small tent, all was right with Evie's world. She wanted to hold on to this precious moment and make it last forever, or at least for as long as she could.

AT THE SAME instant that Evie and Albert were enjoying some family time with their young child, Naomi and Judah were beginning to stir in their tent as well. They hadn't really spoken about the mission the night before. Once he had slipped into bed with her they hadn't made time for very many words at all. They were a tangle of lips and sensation, of two bodies twisted around one another in thanks for yet another dangerous assignment behind them. He was grateful to be home and she was warm and soft and willing; Naomi was everything he could ever ask for in a woman, and she was fully his. Judah knew that he had to tell her about the trip he'd just completed with Albert. He just wished he could say with all certainty that it was the last time he'd leave her. Even though Ari said that the lorry driver would take over the deliveries going forward, Judah was smart enough to know that there would always be exceptions and that he might be called upon again. He could continue to hope that he would serve out the rest of the war on the kibbutz but he had to remain realistic. Anything could happen. Just then he felt Naomi burrow into the warmth of his chest.

"*Motek,*" he began. "I need to tell you about what happened to Albert and me yesterday..." And he told her about the land mine. He felt her body tense as he explained the details, and he held her close to him. "But it all turned out fine," he added at the end of his story. "I'm here now and Albert is with Evie and Deborah. We won't be going out anytime soon."

Naomi was quiet for a bit, then said, "I don't know what

would happen if you were hurt while out on the road, Judah. I don't allow myself to think of those things. It's too scary."

"But, Naomi, I'm back home. You needn't worry." He wrapped his arms around her. "We have each other, we have right now. Let's make the most of our time together."

She rolled her body on top of his. "Promise me, Judah. Promise that you'll be careful, that you'll always come back to me."

"I can promise to be careful, Naomi, and I'd ask you to do the same. The rest of it is out of our hands."

She stared directly into his eyes. "I love you, Judah," she said simply.

"I love you, Naomi from New York," he replied before making love to her once more before the both of them needed to start their day.

As she became immersed in the small details of her tasks, Naomi was able to force herself not to dwell on what had happened to Judah and Albert on their way back to the kibbutz. But in the brief moments when she had a break, like right now as she stretched out her arms and legs in an effort to force some feeling back into her limbs after bending over the small packing boxes for hours on end, that was when she felt true terror. The life she once lived seemed so far distant to her now; the frivolous clothing, the parties, the endless gossip about who was dating which particular boy at what time, all of it was unimportant. All she cared about was winning this conflict, this war for the freedom of her people on this tiny piece of land, and finding a way to make a life with the man she loved. She tilted her head toward the sun and closed her eyes, feeling the welcoming warmth on her face.

When she allowed herself to daydream, Naomi wondered what would happen if she could convince Judah to come to New York with her. She'd love for her family to meet and get to know him as she had. It was more realistic to imagine that her relatives would make a pilgrimage here, to the Holy Land, instead. She would love the opportunity to play tour guide for them, to show them the marvels of Jerusalem, the innovative city of Tel Aviv, and of course, the kibbutz in Rehovot. She was sure that her parents would love her adopted home as much as she did. *If I could only dream that into existence,* she thought, *we'd all be sharing a meal right now!*

"Naomi!"

It took a while for Naomi to realize that Tamar was trying to get her attention. She turned in the direction of the woman's voice.

"Hmm? Yes? What do you need, Tamar?"

"Break is over. Time to head back in before the laundry workers return. C'mon."

Naomi scurried behind her coworker, rushed into the building, and made her way back down the steep steps to the factory. They had plenty of ammunition to pack and there was little time for thinking of anything other than the mission. Shaking her head in an effort to clear away any errant thoughts, she forced herself to focus, one bullet, one box at a time. There was no other way to get this massive job done.

wenty-Four

Rehovot

April 21,1947

NAOMI SAT SILENTLY in her tent in a rare moment of solitude. It was late in the evening, and as she waited for Judah to return from a meeting with Ari in the dining hall, she found some onionskin paper and a pen. She began to write:

DEAR MOM AND DAD,

I'm not really sure how much news gets through to you in the States, but let me fill you in on what's happening here. As you are well aware, this country is very much at war. We're pretty lucky to be isolated on a farm, but there have been bombings all over the country, both both the Arabs and by the Irgun, with multiple casualties and much destruction to property. Last winter, the British government called all the wives and children here in Palestine home to London. Evie was concerned about her mother, but she's since heard through the grapevine that her mom made it safely back to England. Her father is still here at his post in Tel Aviv, but Evie hopes that he will make it out soon as well. Although she's not in regular contact with them, she does get messages through every now and then. They've yet to meet their granddaughter, which is a shame because Deborah is such a pixie! Hopefully, when this conflict ends, Evie will bring her baby and her husband to London for a visit. That is, if her mother ever forgives her for leaving home in the first place!

. . .

I, for one, am glad that the American government has not called any of us back stateside. We're doing important work here, providing food for the soldiers and citizens of this country. I promise to stay clear of the danger. No need for you to worry about me!

NAOMI STOPPED, pen in midair. Telling this kind of white lie was necessary, but she truly wished, now more than ever, that she could share the truth with her parents. She reminded herself, though, that she didn't need to have them wringing their hands over the danger she was in daily. It was important that she keep up the ruse, not only to preserve the secret of their true mission in Rehovot, but to allow her family to sleep at night, not having to think about what might happen to her during this war. She went back to her letter.

HOW IS the fundraising going there? We can use all the dollars you can send. The Irgun keeps robbing banks to raise money. Can you believe that? Last month they stole over $100,000! I understand their motivation. I mean, we all want to be victorious, but they also bombed some British-owned oil tanks in Haifa and the fire that started destroyed a big piece of the waterfront. The damage was worth well over a $1,000,000 and the British government is claiming that the Jewish community here is responsible for making good on that loss! With all that is going on, we need more money than we can lay our hands on. Any help is greatly appreciated.

. . .

Now, for some answers to the questions of your last letter. Yes, I would say that my relationship with Judah is serious! He is very special and I think that after this war is won you should come here for a visit and meet him. I am happy to say that we are very much in love. I know that you will feel about him the same way that I do. No, we haven't figured out exactly what we will do after the war, but I can well imagine that Judah will have a post in the newly formed government. I think that I might try my hand at writing a book about my experiences as an ex-pat here. I'm not sure, but whatever it is that I do, I'm convinced that it will be great to be a part of this emerging nation.

Please, tell me. How is everyone at home? It's two years since the war in Europe ended. What's happening on the social scene there? Have you seen any new shows on Broadway? Gone somewhere fancy for dinner lately? Fill me in! I'm dying to hear some news from home!

Until the next letter, love to all of you,

Naomi

As she tucked the thin pages into the blue air mail envelope, Judah entered the tent. He had a scowl on his face.

"What's wrong?" she asked with concern.

"Hmm? Oh, nothing, really. Just had a talk with Ari. The Irgun has been busy, to say the least. They have to do what they have to do, I understand that, but…"

"But what? They don't affect our mission, do they?"

"Well, we're all at war, Naomi. They just tend to do things their own way, that's all."

"Right. But they keep stealing money that we're ultimately going to have to return. And all the bombings. It's frightening."

"Someone has to retaliate for what the British have done to us. They see that as a big part of their mission."

"I suppose." She stretched her arms up over her head. "I'm tired. I think I'm going to get ready for bed. Can I convince you to join me?"

Judah smiled. "I wish I could. I have to go back to finish up with Ari. I just needed to get some papers I left here on the desk." He shuffled a stack of files around until he found what he was looking for. Grabbing some maps, he said, "I'll be back soon. Go to sleep. I'll try not to wake you when I return."

"You can wake me," she said softly. "I won't mind."

His eyes widened. "Well, in that case…" He walked over to her and kissed her softly. "I'll hurry as fast as I can."

"I'll be right here," she replied.

Naomi watched as he left the tent, knowing that she would not sleep until he returned. Instead, she addressed her letter, put it on the desk to mail the following day and then undressed. She slipped into the cot and thought about all the places she'd like to touch on Judah's body once he came back to bed. But after a while, her day caught up with her and as much as she tried to fight it, sleep overwhelmed her, leaving her no option but to dream of him instead.

THE NEXT MORNING, Naomi woke with a start. Judah was not by her side and she wondered if he'd been there at all. She pushed the blanket off of her legs and swung them over the side of the cot, slipping her feet into her shoes and rising to gather her toiletries and clothing, placing them on top of her pillow in order to get her own day started. Once dressed, she went off to the bathhouse to wash up, then returned to the tent and found her lipstick. With a quick swipe of color, she looked in the small mirror she kept on the desk and smiled. She was ready to go find Judah.

As she walked down the path toward the dining hall, she inhaled the sweet scent of oranges from the grove near the railroad station. She had begun to associate this smell with her adoptive homeland; it made her feel centered and hopeful, and she smiled. While she could have never imagined this life for herself, it somehow felt right being a part of a collective whole, working toward a shared goal. Lost in her thoughts, she didn't hear Evie call out to her until she almost collided with her friend and her baby.

"You must have been thinking about something pretty special," Evie teased as she shifted Deborah onto her other hip. "I've been trying to get your attention for the last few minutes."

"Ha!" Naomi replied. "I wasn't really thinking at all. Just feeling happy, I guess."

"Oh. I see. Does that have anything to do with whatever you and Judah were doing last night?" Evie winked.

"Hardly. He wasn't with me last night. I think he was working with Ari. I was just about to go and look for him now." She leaned in and touched the baby on her soft cheek. "Isn't that right, Deborah? Shall we go look for Uncle Judah together?"

"Actually, can you take her for me? I'd love to squeeze a shower in, if I could. I promise not to be long. Albert should be in the dining hall as well. I'll be back before you have to go to work."

"Of course!" Naomi said, opening her arms to accept the baby. "I would love to have some time with my goddaughter."

"Thanks," Evie said, passing the child off to Naomi. "I'll hurry."

"No need. If I have to, I'll leave her with Albert. Go take a minute for yourself." Then turning to the tiny girl in her arms, she said, "Isn't that right, sweetie? Mommy needs a little breather." She continued down the path until she reached the dining hall and went inside. It was crowded with the camp's inhabitants filling up on their morning meal before work began. She searched the large room until she found Judah, still wearing his wrinkled clothing from the day before. Walking across the room, she came up behind him and tapped his shoulder. When he turned around, she watched his whole face light up when he realized it was her, and she immediately felt warm all over.

"Look who's here!" Judah said, taking the baby from her. "How are you, my darlings?" he asked them both.

"We're good, and one of us is hungry! Will you hold on to her while I gather up some breakfast?"

"Of course!"

"Can I bring you back anything?"

"Just a cup of tea, if you don't mind," he replied, turning his full attention back to the smiling baby on his lap.

Naomi hustled through the kitchen, gathering some cheese and warm pitas for them to share as well as two mugs of strong tea. Once back at Judah's table, she noticed the paperwork strewn haphazardly around the surface.

"Busy planning something, I see?" she inquired.

"Always," he replied. "Long night. Ari just left to get some sleep. I will do the same after you leave for work."

Naomi sat down and looked over at Deborah. The little girl was softly cooing, looking up at Judah's face. "You do have a way with women of all ages, I see," she teased.

"Well, this one is easy to please," he answered. "She enjoys being held."

"She's a smart cookie!" Naomi said, blowing on the hot liquid in her mug before taking a sip.

"Eat," he urged her. "You have a long day ahead."

"What about you? Aren't you hungry?"

He didn't answer, but instead just stared into her eyes, telling her everything she needed to know.

Naomi could feel herself blush. She stammered, "I mean for food."

Judah didn't have time to answer before Albert appeared before them.

"There's my daughter," he said gleefully, taking the baby from Judah's arms and lifting her up over his head. Deborah laughed.

"Evie went off for a shower," Naomi offered.

"That's great. She could use a break," Albert replied. "I can take the baby back to the children's house now. It's almost nap time."

"For her or for you?" Judah asked with a smile as he watched his protégé play with Deborah.

"Well, if you two don't mind, I'm going to head for work. There are a lot of bullets that need packing!" Naomi said. She took one last sip of her tea, picked up a pita to take with her to the laundry building and then turned to Judah. "Will I see you later?"

"Yes. I'll see you tonight."

"Good." She turned to plant a kiss on one of the baby's chubby cheeks. "Be a good girl for daddy, okay?" She had to tear herself away. "See you, Albert."

Naomi walked outside into the bright sunshine. She could see the laundry and the railway station behind it, the workers scurrying along to their appointed posts, everyone with a specific job to do. She heard the whistle of the daily north-bound train as it approached its destination. And then there was a deafening sound. An explosion, a crash, hot fire spraying everywhere. She was knocked off her feet as the ground shifted beneath her and when her head hit the dirt path hard, she felt nothing at all.

JUDAH HEARD the blast and jumped into action. He began shouting instructions to the workers still left in the dining hall, directing them to start the practiced fire and bomb protocols that had been drilled into each kibbutz member's head from day one. He tried to push aside his worry for Naomi and fervently hoped that she'd made it underground before this trouble began. He realized, however, that he wouldn't rest until he knew that she was safe.

As he pushed his way through the rubble outside, he saw the large crater left in the wake of the bombing. He counted five derailed train cars now resting in a heap to one side of the damaged tracks. Passengers were sitting, dazed and bleeding in the shade of some olive trees; kibbutz members were tending to their wounds. There were fires everywhere and he watched as a line of men and women, who had trained for a catastrophe like the one unfolding in front of him, passed buckets of water in a line from the well to douse the flames. A woman crying over the body of a little boy, now lifeless and limp in her arms, her clothing torn, her legs bloodied, sat off to one side of the chaos. British soldiers were everywhere, their guns poised for retaliation should they happen on the perpetrators of this gruesome event.

He scanned the landscape, relieved at first that he didn't see Naomi sitting among the injured. Then, off to one side of the path, under some low vegetation, a familiar fabric caught his eye. It was the blouse Naomi had been wearing moments ago, he was sure of it. Judah ran over to the thick cover of brush and found her there, a deep gash on her forehead, her knees and palms skinned badly. There was blood everywhere. He kneeled down next to her motionless body. *No!*

Judah carefully rolled Naomi onto her back and put his ear to her chest. *Her heart was beating!* He gingerly lifted her up into his arms and carried her to the hospital building, praying silently the entire distance. *She has to be okay. She has to be okay.* Right at the entrance, her eyes fluttered open.

"Judah," she rasped. "What…" She motioned to his shirt, stained a deep red. "Are you bleeding?"

"Shhh," he insisted. "No. I'm fine. Don't try to speak. You'll be alright. Let's have the doctor get a look at you."

He carried her into the clinic and one of the nurses cleared the way for him to put her down on a gurney.

"I'll find Dr. Weissbaum. Wait here," the nurse ordered as she pulled a privacy curtain behind her and hurried away.

Judah held on tightly to Naomi's hand for what seemed like an eternity until the doctor arrived.

"Step back, Judah," the physician commanded. "Let me examine her."

Judah watched as the other man gently turned Naomi's head, looking for further injury. He then checked her arms and legs, being careful not to brush against her cuts and bruises as he did.

"Naomi," he heard the doctor ask, "do you know where you are?"

"The hospital?" she asked.

"Yes. Good. Do you know what happened?"

"There was a bright light at the train station. A bomb?"

"It would seem so." The doctor stepped back, relief on his face. "You were very lucky, my dear. You've got some scrapes, a nasty cut on your forehead, and probably a concussion. But you're alive."

Naomi shifted on the gurney and made a weak attempt to sit up.

The doctor put a firm hand on her shoulder and said, "Now hold on a minute. You're not going anywhere. We have to clean up these wounds, and you may need a stitch or two on that forehead. Not to mention, I'd like to keep you overnight for observation."

"No, I'm okay, really," she replied. "Can't Judah take me back to our tent? I promise to rest."

Judah shook his head at her and said, "Listen to Dr. Weissbaum, Naomi. Spend some time here. When you are totally fine, I'll come and get you."

"I'm fine now," she said, but as she tried to sit up, a wave of dizziness threatened to overtake her.

"So it's settled then. You're staying," Dr. Weissbaum said as he wrote some orders down on a paper attached to a clipboard at the end of the gurney. "The nurse will come take care of you. I've got other injured patients to see." The doctor stepped outside of the curtained area, leaving Naomi and Judah alone.

"I'm so sorry, Judah. I was just heading to work. That's the last thing I remember."

"Don't be silly. There is no way you could have known that this was to happen. I am just so relieved that you weren't more badly hurt. I don't think I could have survived that." He pulled a chair from against the wall over to her gurney and sat down, carefully lifting her bloodied hand in his own. "I can't live without you, Naomi," he said softly.

Tears sprang into her eyes. "I feel the same way, Judah. I need to know that you'll always be with me."

"Of course I will. I love you." He gently kissed her lips.

"Promise me."

"For as much as it's in my power to do, I give you my word that we will always be together. Now rest and get better. I have big plans for you once this war is over."

"I'm going to hold you to that," she said, closing her eyes as the pain in her head began to intensify. Instead of focusing on what hurt, she chose to think about what might be if there was ever a time for peace in this infant country. As long as that future included Judah, it would all be good. Just then the nurse returned to dress her wounds. Suddenly exhausted, she closed her eyes and felt herself drift into sleep.

Twenty-Five

Naomi's hospital stay was much longer than she expected. It was a full three days before Dr. Weissbaum released her to bed rest in her tent and another week before Judah would even discuss her going back underground. She had grown restless, worried about the work that she wasn't doing, about the need for the bullets to reach the front lines and her part in that effort being delayed by her injuries. She, along with the other members of the kibbutz, mourned the loss of the young boy killed in the bombing. Another innocent life taken too soon.

The scrapes and cuts were well on their way to healing, but she still had a slight headache and a persistent ringing in her ears, a grim reminder of just how close she'd come to being a serious casualty of the bombing. The train tracks were more fortunate; they'd been repaired and operational a mere twenty-four hours after the blast. It was truly amazing to Naomi that despite being in the midst of a war, the railroad kept running and life continued to move forward. She was finally allowed to go outside again and although she was under strict orders to continue to rest, she was given permission for a visit from Evie and Deborah for an hour today, and she was looking forward to having the company. She was sitting outside in front of the tent when her friend arrived, her young daughter in tow.

"Hello, Naomi!" Evie exclaimed. "How are you?"

"Much better," she replied, "and so happy to see you both!"

"You gave us all quite a scare, Naomi. I am so happy to see you sitting up and out of bed."

"Me, too. I am getting very antsy, though. There is so much

more work to be done and I'm not doing my fair share at the moment."

"Don't be silly," her friend said as she sat down on the chair next to Naomi. "Do you think you're strong enough to hold your goddaughter for a bit?"

"Definitely!" Naomi replied. "That will make my day!"

Evie passed the squirming child over, settling her on her friend's lap.

"She's getting so big," Naomi said, bringing one chubby arm up to her lips and kissing it from elbow to fingers with an exaggerated smacking sound, causing the little girl to laugh.

"Isn't that the most wonderful sound?" Evie asked. "I love hearing it."

"She's a happy baby, that's for sure. You're doing something very right." She continued to make faces at Deborah, the little girl's face lighting up with glee.

"Oh, I don't know. I have no idea what it is I'm doing. I think she was just born this way. What I do know is that she makes every day brighter. When I look into her eyes, I swear that I can see the future. We're doing what we do here for her, for the children yet to be born into this country we're building."

"That is the goal, right?" Naomi asked as Deborah's fingers grasped her own. Then changing her tone, she said, "Tell me, Evie. What's the latest news from the factory? I feel like I've been gone from there for so long. I miss it."

"We've been working nonstop, as I'm sure you can imagine. The bullet production is on target and we've moved hundreds of thousands of rounds to the troops."

"I can't wait to get back to it!" Naomi exclaimed.

"Not so fast. You had a real trauma. It's best to be fully recovered before going back underground. As much as you want to work, what's best for you right now is fresh air and sunshine, the very two things you don't get in the factory."

Naomi lifted the baby up into the air. "Deborah," she said, speaking directly to the baby. "Please let Mommy know that I realize that I should enjoy this time off from work, but I can't. There's just too much at stake. We're trying to build a better world for you!"

The little girl opened her eyes wide and cooed, as if to agree with what Naomi had just said.

"You see, Evie! Even your daughter knows that I'm right. Besides, I'm not some withering little flower. I'm strong and I'm ready to work."

"You'll have to go through Judah, first. He hasn't been the same since your accident. I've never seen him so shaken by anything."

"Do you really think so?" Naomi asked worriedly.

"Are you kidding me? All he does is talk about retribution. He thinks Al-Jawrashi was behind the bombing of the train. He wants his head on a platter."

"What do you think?"

Evie sighed. "I don't really know. I mean, sure, the Arabs would like us all dead. But so would the British. And lots of other people as well. You understand that it could have been anyone, including the Irgun. We don't have enough information yet."

"I'm concerned that this whole incident made him think about Geula," Naomi said in a voice barely above a whisper.

Evie shifted her body closer and put her arm around her friend's shoulder. "It's very possible that it did. The similarity is striking, with one enormous exception. You're here, you're going to be fine. What happened with Geula was tragic, yes, but it was a long time ago."

"Can anyone ever truly get past that kind of loss?" Naomi looked into Evie's eyes. "I don't know if he'll be able to forget her, no matter how many years pass. She's the ghost that haunts the both of us."

"No, no she's not, Naomi. While Geula was Judah's first love, you are the woman he wants by his side. May she always live in blessed memory, but you are here, in the flesh. And it's you that Judah loves. I see it each and every time he looks at you."

Naomi could feel her eyes begin to fill with tears. "I love him so much it hurts, Evie. My feelings scare me." She shifted the now sleeping baby in her arms. "I can only pray for a safe future for all of us, a time when we're free to live and love in this crazy desert. When I can look ahead and not be terrified that there will be no tomorrow."

"That's how we all feel, Naomi. And now that you understand, you are truly one of us. No turning back."

Naomi nodded. "No turning back," she repeated. "No turning back."

THREE MONTHS LATER, Naomi had completely fallen back into her routine. Her accident was more than a memory, but it was no longer at the forefront of every conversation she had with Judah. As she sat in the dining hall with him after dinner, the mail was being distributed to the residents of the kibbutz. She looked forward to this particular event, as it didn't happen daily. They received sacks of mail twice a week, deposited at the train station, and on the nights when Ari parceled out the letters or packages, everyone tended to be in good spirits. At the same time that it was thrilling when letters arrived from far-flung family members like hers, it was also disheartening to know that some workers would never get anything because the war had claimed everyone they'd known and loved before arriving in Rehovot. Despite it all, when a package arrived bearing candies or foods from other countries, everyone shared in the bounty. They would receive a variety of goods. Honey from Greece, marzipan from Italy, licorice from England, and of course, tubes of M&Ms and Beeman's Teabury or Clove gum from her mom in the USA. The excitement in the room was palpable as Ari began calling out the names on envelopes and packages from around the world.

"I hope I have a letter with news of my family. The last one was a who's who of engagements and weddings," she joked with Judah.

"Does it make you homesick when you hear of these things?" he asked.

"Interestingly, no. You would think it should, but it doesn't. I like my life here better," she said, leaning in to kiss him chastely on one stubbled cheek.

He reached for her hand. "I'm glad," he replied.

Just then Ari called out her name and Naomi jumped up. "Ooh," she said to Judah, "let's see what Mom sent this time!" She scurried over to retrieve the brown paper-wrapped package, colorful, canceled air mail stamps strewn across the right top corner of the box. Once back at her seat, she carefully opened it, amused to find the "Gristedes" logo on the inside of the wrapper. Leave it to her mother to find an alternate use for a grocery bag. Despite her comfortable life, her mother had grown up in a time when one wasted nothing. She found a use for almost anything, from a solitary button to an empty coffee tin. It made Naomi smile to think of her mother putting this package together and walking to the post office with it. She could be sure that the postal worker got an earful about the destination of her mother's parcel.

Once she opened the box, she was delighted to see multiple tubes filled with M&M's, packages of gum and bars of Hershey's milk chocolate. The sweets had made the journey intact and she passed the candy over to the women sitting at the distribution table, who would portion it all out. Underneath the bounty of sweets, there was a newspaper clipping with a letter stapled to the top. It was an ad from the *New York Post* with a headline that read "We are out to raise millions for you." Naomi laid the paper out on the table before her and pulled the letter off and opened it. A bank check for ten thousand dollars fell into her lap! She began to read:

Dearest Naomi,

I thought you'd like to see this advertisement showing the world just how committed we are here in the States to a free Palestine. We've been working hard to send funds (see the check enclosed) to help the cause. Your father and I admire the passion you continue to display for a Jewish homeland and we pray for your continued safety and good health while you toil in the fields to feed your fellow countrymen.

Naomi couldn't help but feel a small pang of guilt at the thought that her parents didn't know her true mission, but she pushed it aside for now.

We will continue to contribute to the cause. I am chairing an Independence Day cocktail party for this purpose on July 4th at the club and will send the proceeds as soon as they are available. If we can be a free and democratic society here in the States, we need to rally and support the birth of a true democracy in Palestine...

. . .

THEN, of course, her mother had to fill her in on all the babies born to her classmates and cousins alike before ending the letter ever so sweetly.

WE MISS YOU, dear Naomi, each and every day, but we are heartened to know that you've met someone who makes you happy and that you are doing your best for your adopted homeland. When this war is over, your father and I will brave an ocean crossing to see you both. I pray that day is soon.

LOVE ALWAYS and please be careful!
Mom

HER EYES WELLED up with tears at the thought of seeing her parents again. She prayed it was sometime soon.

"What is it?" Judah asked. "Is your family okay?"

She handed him the letter and the check. "Look what they sent," was all she could say as she watched his eyes widen at the amount on the thin blue paper.

"That is a lot of money, and in dollars no less. Do you know how far this will take us?" He took her face in his hands and kissed her soundly on the mouth. "Naomi, you must write back immediately and thank them for all of their commitment and trust in us for what we are trying to do here."

"Maybe with this money the Irgun will stop robbing banks for a while? Do you think--"

"I don't know if it will stop them, but let's go share this with Ari."

She looked up to see the older man still handing out packages and letters to a joyous crowd. "Don't disturb him. Wait for him to finish. Good news can wait. It's the bad news that always seems to intrude, right?"

He squeezed her hand. "I suppose so. Shall we go get a drink? I have some really nice brandy that Ari got from one of the lorry drivers. It's back at our tent."

She smiled. "Judah, we both know that if we go there, we won't be returning here tonight."

"I like the way you think, Naomi. Besides, as you so perfectly put it, good news can wait."

With those words, Naomi felt herself begin to melt in the way only Judah could cause her to. "Well, if you think it can wait until the morning..."

He reached for her hand and pulled her onto her feet. "I know that it can. But I cannot..."

HOURS LATER, after the most passionate of lovemaking, Naomi felt content. As she lay awake in the tent, listening to the soothing sound of Judah's rhythmic breathing, she could not help but to think about their future. Would they live in Tel Aviv, or somewhere more south, like Beersheba? Would they have a role in the infant government that she knew would be formed, or would they farm the land? Would they eventually have a child of their own and live a quiet existence together?

Naomi knew the risks of war--she had almost paid the price with her own life--but she was beginning to allow herself the thought that they were close to the finish of this conflict, that they would come out of it and find a new life at the other end. Time would tell.

She closed her eyes and imagined her parents stepping off of a boat and onto the docks of Haifa, just as she had done. *Oh, what a day that will be!* she thought. She could not wait to show her mother and father all of the wonderful crevices and corners of this land. She knew that they would fall in love with it, just as she had. And she knew that they would love Judah, too. She rolled onto her side, placed her hand on his chest, and fell asleep to the gentle beating of his heart.

Twenty Six

Rehovot
April 11, 1948

ALBERT WAS EXHAUSTED. He'd just returned from a bullet run to Jerusalem, this time dressed as a pauper in rags, the bullets carried in a bundle on his back. Every muscle ached. While the lorry drivers still moved most of the ammunition to the front lines, he'd been charged with some smaller, more targeted drops. It was important work, he knew. But he also understood the risks. He hesitated to think about what might happen if on one of these trips, he didn't make it back. Evie and Deborah would be okay, he always told himself, in an attempt at reassurance. But he'd miss so much. Already, his daughter was walking and calling his name when she saw him at the end of the day. She was his joy, his light. He did not want to miss a thing as she grew. And then, of course, she and Evie were his world now. He'd long ago given up the dream that he'd see his father again. It helped to have his own family, his wife and daughter, to lean on whenever he thought about Paris and the life he'd left behind. He wanted to believe that his father was still alive somewhere, but he knew that it was a fantasy, that he probably didn't survive much past the day he was rounded up on the street outside of their home years before. Shaking off his maudlin thoughts, he went to gather his things in order to wash up before looking for his wife.

A short while later and somewhat revived from the shower,

he headed off for the dining hall, hoping to find Evie seated in her usual spot bent over a stack of reports and maps. He was disappointed to see that she wasn't there. Instead, he found Judah and Ari, cigarette smoke swirling around them, deep in discussion.

"Albert!" Judah exclaimed. "Good to see you back safely. How was your trip?"

"Fine," he answered. "And easier on the way back, without that heavy sack to carry."

"Good work, Albert," Ari added. "Unfortunately, there's more to do."

"Trouble getting lorry drivers?" Albert asked.

"Not exactly," Judah replied. "It's just that with all of the bombings, the curfews, and the robberies, at the banks and in the diamond district in Netanya and Tel Aviv, it's harder to get a large truck through to the front lines. We're going to have to be creative here."

It was true. In the past twelve months, the Irgun and the Stern gang had attacked banks, stealing hundreds of thousands of dollars, as well as the diamond market in an attempt to secure funds for the revolution. Their Arab neighbors continued the constant assault on the country's borders with bombings and shootings, killing many innocent farmers for which the Haganah would retaliate. It had become a vicious cycle of unrelenting violence, reminding all of the members of the kibbutz that they were at war and that the job they were doing was vital to the effort toward victory. And then, of course, whenever Albert went out on a mission, he had to be mindful of the land mines that Al-Jawrashi had set along the way; he'd not soon forgotten how Judah had saved him from a bloody fate. It was a dangerous business, and he took his role in it very seriously.

"So then, what's my next assignment?" he asked the other men.

"Rest. You'll have a plan in hand shortly," Ari said, rising. "Until then, enjoy your time on the kibbutz with your family." Turning to Judah, Ari said, "I will come find you later once I have all of the details of what we just discussed." He turned and walked out of the dining hall.

Albert sighed. "I had hoped to find Evie here. Have you seen her this morning?"

"I think she's in the factory today. You'll need to wait for lunchtime, I'm afraid."

Albert glanced up at the clock on the wall. It was after nine in the morning. "Well then. I think I will close my eyes for a while. I am tired from my overnight journey."

"Of course, of course. If I see Evie here at lunch, I'll tell her that you're still sleeping. I'm sure she'll come to find you."

"Thank you, Judah," he said as he stood. "Until later, then."

But Judah already had his head down, his mind busy with whatever was in the report he was reading in front of him, Albert's goodbye left unheard.

Albert made his to his tent, looking forward to the rest he knew he deserved. Once there, he slipped out of his boots and lay down, fully dressed. *The clothes are clean,* he told himself. *Evie won't mind.* Truthfully, he was too weary to remove them. He switched on the portable radio they kept on a small table next to the cot. The sound was static-filled and tinny, but he could hear the soft voice of Evie's favorite BBC news reporter. As he drifted off, he could have sworn he heard that a number of ancient biblical scrolls had been found by some Bedouin boys in caves near the Dead Sea in the West Bank. Albert struggled to listen, but the fatigue he felt was overwhelming. Before he knew it, he was dreaming of caves, winding, clear streams and warm, soft breezes.

When Albert awoke, he could tell that he'd slept most of the day away. He stretched his arms overhead and felt the strain of his overused muscles. Forcing himself to sit up, he slowly placed his feet on the ground and stood. No matter how sore he felt, he had the overwhelming need to go find his wife. He was grateful to be back in the camp in one piece; he knew that she would feel the same.

After lacing his boots back up, he went down the path toward the dining hall and went inside. As if they had a sixth sense about one another, he felt her presence before he saw her face. And once his gaze found her, she turned as if she knew he was there. When she looked at him, Albert felt warm all over. Evie was the sunshine he so desperately needed. He crossed the room quickly and drew her into his arms.

"It's so good to see you *ma chèrie*."

"Did you have a good sleep? I did stop by our tent at lunchtime but you were resting so peacefully I didn't have the heart to wake you."

"I was very tired, but I'm better now, with you."

"Was it a rough night?"

"They each have their own particular dangers. This time I just kept trying to watch my steps. I didn't want to step on a land mine in the dark."

"Of course," Evie said, holding him tighter.

"What keeps me going on these missions is my desire to come home to you, and to Deborah. That is what is most important to me."

She kissed him then, softly on the lips in the crowded dining hall.

"Hey, you two. Go somewhere more private for that!" she heard Naomi call out as she walked toward them, her teasing tone lighthearted. Once she reached them, she said more seriously, "Good to see you home safe, Albert."

"*Merci beaucoup,* Naomi. I am happy to be back as well."

"Shall we get some dinner, then? The sooner you eat, the quicker you can find the time to be alone."

"Naomi!" Evie said, her British sense of decorum apparent. "Hush now!"

"Okay, Evie," Naomi responded, rolling her eyes. "Whatever you say. But you know I speak the truth."

"Let's just all get something to eat," was Evie's response.

They moved through the canteen line together, filling their plates and returning to their favorite table. In between bites of warm pita dipped in hummus, Albert lifted his head from his food and asked, "Did you hear anything about some ancient scrolls being found in the West Bank?"

"As a matter of fact, yes," Naomi said, switching to journalism mode. "So interesting. It seems as if these young Bedouin farmer boys happened upon them in the Qumram caves. Absolute proof that the bible is a real and very ancient book."

"Whose bible, though?" Albert asked. "Moses? Or..."

"From what I could ascertain from the limited news I've heard, they are Jewish documents. If I get more information, I'll share it."

"So, to all those who question if this is meant to be the Jewish homeland, maybe, just maybe, they'll finally understand," Evie said plainly.

"That's very wishful thinking, *mon amour.* I go out of the

confines of this kibbutz often. I feel the hate for our people. It's from everyone, too, not just our closest neighbors."

"True. The British would be happy to be rid of us as well," Naomi added.

"Not just the British! The Americans too," Evie said, her voice shaking. "Did the US not place an embargo on critical arms shipments to us last year? And don't forget that your government turned away ships full of refugees from Nazi Europe during the war. The *Drottningholm* and the *St. Louis*. Your FDR was no saint." She shook her head then continued, "We have few friends in this world, Naomi. We must control our own fate."

"While that remains a fact, we do have the aid of so many American Jews. My very own father was almost arrested by the FBI this winter when he was suspected of involvement in the shipment of TNT to the Haganah. You and I both know that he raised funds for that mission. He was lucky to be cleared of all charges, despite the evidence against him."

Evie's face softened and her eyes filled with tears. She reached across the table to grab her friend's hand. "You're right, Naomi, and I am sorry for snapping at you. There are days when it all seems too much to bear."

In a gesture not lost on Albert, Naomi squeezed back as a sign of forgiveness. "I know, Evie. I do. But we must lean on each other. That's all we can offer."

Albert then put his arm around his wife and drew her in close to his side. "I'm glad to see that there are some cracks in that armor of yours, Evie. No one can remain strong all of the time. You are allowed to feel as you do."

"Most of the time I don't let things bother me, but for some reason the discovery of those scrolls makes me feel that our mission is even more important. We need to protect this land

and the history of the people that have come before us. There can be no more important work than that."

"Of course, Evie, of course. Now finish your dinner. I think we'll have time to see Deborah before her bedtime, don't you?" Their daughter was now old enough to sleep in the children's house. He felt her body relax next to his own at his suggestion.

"That would be lovely, Albert. It would be the perfect tonic for me, I suppose."

"Glad that's settled," Naomi interjected. "I was worried for a moment." She stood. I'm going to get some tea. Can I bring you each back a mugful?"

"That would be nice, Naomi, thank you," Albert responded.

When the other woman slipped out of sight, Evie said in a voice barely above a whisper, "Oh, Albert. I'm worried every moment. I guess that's the problem. The danger is unrelenting."

"But I think the end is near, *ma chèrie*. We will be victorious. I can feel it."

"I take comfort in your words, dearest. I really do."

He smiled at her, hoping that she didn't see the truth in his eyes. From his travels outside the safe walls of the kibbutz, he knew that this conflict was about to explode in almost unimaginable ways, and that victory, while desired, was never predestined. It would take a whole lot more than wishing it to make it happen.

AFTER EVIE HAD FINALLY FALLEN asleep, Albert found himself wide awake. It often took him a day or so after an overnight mission to get his body clock regulated again. Rather than toss and turn, taking a chance at waking his wife, he silently rose from the bed and got dressed. He knew that Ari and Judah were often still in the dining hall late into the night and went out to seek information about where he was to be sent next. As he walked down the path, he thought about Evie's anxiety and wished that she didn't suffer so. He knew there was little to be done about it; he just hoped that when this war was finally over, she'd be able to begin to relax again. There was great speculation in the camp about what was to become of their bullet-making tasks after the need for ammunition lessened, with the majority of the workers eager to begin their lives in their newly free, adopted country. He favored the idea of farming, but he knew that Evie had aspirations for them to work in the nascent government that was beginning to take shape. Whatever the future held, he knew it would be just fine, as long as he was with his family.

His family. Thinking about those very words brought a heaviness to his heart, knowing that he'd never see his father again. It was the not knowing that bothered him the most, the thought that he'd never find out the truth about what happened that day in Paris, all those years ago. For as much as he'd come to understand that his situation was not unique, it still left him with a piece of his heart missing. So many of the others on the kibbutz had had a similar experience, and it helped to talk about it with those who shared the same sadness. It just didn't take the ache away. *How my father would have delighted in knowing both Evie and Deborah!* He shook his head to clear his thoughts. Instead of wondering about the "what ifs" in his life, he'd be better off focusing on the positive work that still lay ahead of him. He opened the door to the dining hall, hoping to find the men who held the key to that exact plan.

As expected, Albert found them hunched over an open bottle of whiskey and some detailed maps of a delivery route at a table in the corner of the room. He made his way to them.

"Is this a private conversation, or can anyone join in?" he asked in a half-joking manner.

"Please, Albert. By all means, join us," Ari said, pulling another glass from a stack on the table and turning it upright. "Have a drink."

"Maybe a shot of whiskey will help you sleep," Judah added. "I'm guessing that's why you're here tonight?"

"You know that it's difficult turning nights back into days. It will be fine, though. And worth it."

"Of course," Judah began. "As a matter of fact, we have one more big job for you. But because I would never ask you to do something that I myself wouldn't do, I'm going to come along on this trip."

Albert could feel concern creep up his spine. "It must be an important mission, then."

"Aren't they all?" Ari asked to no one in particular.

"I suppose so. What does this trip entail?"

Judah leaned in and pulled out a map. "We'll need to stay out of sight entirely. We'll take the donkeys and load them up with packs. It will be too much to carry as you did this last time."

"I don't need a chaperone, Judah. I can go it alone. No need for you to come along."

"Believe me, tavern boy. I wish that were true. But the road will be paved with mines. It will take two sets of eyes to keep us safe."

Albert smiled at the reference to his old nickname. Knowing it was useless to argue, he said, "Well then, commander. I should look forward to the company. When do we go?"

"After the Sabbath. We'll leave at sundown on Saturday night."

"I'll be ready," Albert said, draining his glass.

"I have no doubt," was Judah's only response.

Twenty-Seven

IT WAS NEARLY a week later when Judah prepared himself for his mission. He knew that Naomi was not happy with his decision to go, but he could tell that she attempted to hide her feelings as best as she could. They spent the day of rest together, in their tent, peacefully napping and making love in a repetitive pattern. He could not get his fill of her, no matter how hard he tried.

"I have to ask just one more time. Is it really necessary for you to go?" she inquired. Her fingers made gentle patterns against his back as he held her in his arms.

"You know that it is, my love. I wish it were different, that this war was done. One more push and victory will be ours. I just know it."

"How long will you be gone?"

"We've been over this, Naomi. Two nights. Two nights and I'll be back."

"Do you promise?"

"I promise to do my best to make it home. Of course."

"But what if…"

"No, Naomi. No 'what if.'"

"But Judah…"

He stood then, starting to put on his clothes before he said, "Shh. Say no more. You understand the risks, as do I. But my plan is to get the ammunition to our relay point and return. Nothing else to discuss."

He watched her face as she fought back the emotion he knew she was feeling. Dread. Anxiety. Fear. He shared all of those same sentiments but he hid them well. He had to in order to do his job. He slipped his gun into the waistband at the back of his trousers and strapped his knife to his calf. It was time to go.

"When I return, we'll do something special together. How does a picnic in the fields sound to you?"

"Good," she replied in a voice barely above a whisper.

"Then I'm off." He kissed her briefly and quickly left the tent, knowing that if he didn't break away from her then, he would never leave at all. He looked up at the inky sky and drew in a deep breath. It was crowded with stars. Knowing that his ancestors navigated their way with those very constellations gave him the courage he needed in that moment. The sooner he left, he knew, the closer he came to the moment when he could return to Naomi, to the warmth of her embrace, to the love he had come so deeply to depend upon. He went off in search of Albert.

NAOMI WOKE THE NEXT MORNING, her arms wrapped tightly around Judah's pillow. It was no substitute, she realized, for the real thing, but it would have to do. She was happy to have her own work at the factory while he was away; it was the distraction she so desperately needed. She quickly dressed, washed, and walked down to the dining hall for breakfast. Grabbing a mug of tea and some yogurt, she looked around the room for Evie. It didn't take long to find her friend, sitting at a table, alone.

"How long have you been here?"

"A little bit. I couldn't sit still," Evie said.

"I understand. I feel the same way."

"You know, Albert has gone out on so many of these missions over the past few years and they've all been dangerous, some more so than others. I should be used to this feeling."

"Does anyone truly ever get used to it? I mean, it's scary."

"It's war, Naomi. It's all scary. It's just that when he needs to go off the main roads, it gets all the more complicated."

"I don't know how you've handled this for so long, Evie. You are the strongest woman I have ever met."

"What choice do we have, Naomi? We can't cry over the jobs we're assigned in a war. We just need to put our heads down and do them."

Naomi suddenly noticed the small pieces of torn paper on the table between them. Evie must have been sitting there for a long while, or at least longer than she'd admitted to, nervously shredding the now useless pages. "If you say so, Evie. I can try my best to work past my worry. I just don't know if I'll succeed."

"I have every faith that you will, dear friend." She looked at the watch on her wrist and then pushed back from the table. "I have to go. There was a problem with one of the machines yesterday. Ari sent a crew down early to fix it. I need to check in to be sure everything is operational."

"Can I come along? I just want to stay busy."

"Of course. Let's go."

Naomi drained what was left of her tea as they walked toward the exit. She deposited her plate and mug in the container left at the door for that purpose and rushed to keep up with her friend. She was used to having to catch up to Evie. When that woman was on a mission, she moved with incredible speed.

"Let's be sure that no one is in the laundry yet before we attempt to go underground. The repair team was here before dawn. We need to be very careful ourselves."

Naomi nodded, a bit too breathless to speak.

As they entered the building, it was soon apparent that they'd arrived before any of the workers. The machines were silent and there was no movement anywhere.

"We're good. Help me move the tub," Evie ordered.

Naomi did as she was told, sliding the big metal container to one side. Both women stepped down the staircase and stopped to pull the tub back over the opening before entering the factory. Once downstairs, Naomi could see three men and Ari hunched over one of the machines, parts and tools strewn nearby on the floor.

Evie immediately walked over to join them. "Did you fix the problem?" she asked.

Ari looked up from his work. "Almost. One of the parts of the *mohel* was completely worn away. Overuse, I suppose."

"And you had a spare?" Evie questioned.

"Not exactly," Ari responded, stepping back, leaving the others to their work.

"What does that mean?" Evie asked.

"It means that production will slow down some."

"Some? We can't allow that to happen." She shook her head in disbelief then asked, "How much will it slow us down?"

"We won't know until we start production, Evie," Ari replied. "We're doing our best with what we have. You forget that this equipment was old when it arrived. We refurbished it to the best of our ability, but it's never going to be perfect."

"I realize that, Ari, but we're at a critical point. We're going to have to add shifts if we slow down during the day. Perhaps an overnight crew can pick up the slack?"

"And run this machine for twenty-four hours at a time? We'll burn it out for sure!"

"We'll only know that if we try, Ari." Evie stood her ground.

"I suppose in the meantime I can have these men fashion a new piece from some spare metal parts they have in the shop. I can't promise that it will work. These are small and specific pieces. They aren't easy to make or to replace. We certainly can't buy them anywhere. It would raise too much suspicion."

"I understand, Ari. But let's compromise. We can add a shift after dinner. We won't run the machine all night. Let's see what can be manufactured in one more six hour shift."

Naomi watched Ari consider Naomi's suggestion, finally nodding his head in agreement.

"Alright. We'll give it a go. Assemble one more shift and send me the names. Volunteers, only. There are those who have families that expect them to be home at night. Let's not reveal ourselves now. We've come so far."

"Of course, Ari," Evie replied. "I'll assemble a list by lunchtime and I'll come and find you."

Ari nodded and went back over to speak with the men gathered at the broken machine.

Naomi put her arm on Evie's shoulder. "Let me be the first to volunteer. You'd be helping me. I don't sleep easily when Judah is away."

"He'll be home in two nights, you'll see. Then you won't want to be here at work." Evie smiled. "I won't either."

"Yes, but until then another pair of hands won't hurt. I insist."

"Well, if you're in, then so am I. Let's think of who else might be able to work at night. Help me make a list," Evie said.

"Come to my table," Naomi said, walking to her bullet packing station and clearing a space. "We can work there."

The two women put their heads together and ticked off the names of each factory worker, compiling a comprehensive inventory of their staff, noting which ones were likely to be able to get away with staying out until midnight, those who might not be missed. They finished just as the bullet makers began to descend into the workspace. When all were assembled, Evie gathered the group into a corner of the room and filled them in on the current status of the equipment.

"So you understand, what I need are a few volunteers. We've put together the names of those most likely to be able to join us for one more shift after dinner. But of course, it's an individual decision. You can say no."

"But we won't," one young man called out. "We want to win this war. We want to make our country free."

A murmur of agreement went around the group.

"I appreciate that, we all do. To that end, if your name is on this paper, we'll expect to see you here tonight. If you can't join us, just let me know so that we can find a replacement." She handed the paper to the woman on her right and it circulated around the room.

"And if my name isn't there, but I want to help?" came a shout from another worker.

"If we have enough volunteers, maybe we can rotate shifts, one night on, one night off. We will make that determination when the time comes."

"No worries, Evie. We're here to make this happen!" another voice cried out.

Naomi watched as her friend's eyes filled with tears.

"Thank you one and all," Evie said. "Now let's get to work."

LATER THAT EVENING the first group met at the factory, and when they were sure that the coast was clear, they moved the tub and went down the stairs. Generally, they used the laundry to cover the noise of the machines so that the British soldiers would not know about their bullet-making operation. But the September before, the British had pulled most of their troops from the area, making it easier for the kibbutz to operate without exposure. They remained alert, because the train station might attract an official or two still left in the country, but for the most part, they knew this operation would be a safe one. Besides, the trains ran infrequently once it was dark, making it more difficult for the driver to spot any new land mines Al-Jawrashi and his minions might have planted along the tracks.

By the time Naomi packed up her last bullet and secured and sealed it in its box, she was finally tired enough to rest. It was a relief to feel this full-body fatigue. She felt confident that when she got back to her tent she would be able to fall asleep. She waited for Evie to double-check that everyone was safely out of the factory before pulling the other woman up the stairs into the cool night air. There was a lovely breeze that swirled around them as they walked together toward their respective tents in silence. The camp was quiet and peaceful at this time of night and as Naomi walked arm in arm with her friend, she couldn't help but reflect on how far they'd both come since having first met. She'd been in awe of Evie then and still was, but now felt more like a peer, not a recruit. She stopped walking when they reached the low-burning campfire in the middle of the circle of tents in the camp.

"Did you ever think that we'd find ourselves such fast friends?" Naomi asked as they approached their tents. "That we'd work together like this?"

"I couldn't have known when we first met at your campus. I was too busy trying to find willing volunteers to come here, to help us build what we have, to do the job we've been able to do. It seems so long ago now, doesn't it?"

"Yes, I suppose. I don't even really know why I agreed to sign on. It was your approach, I think. You didn't push too hard, but you did make this all seem so intriguing."

"And now that we're here, now that you know everything, are you glad you joined us? Taking Judah out of the equation, that is." Evie smiled.

"I couldn't be more proud of what we've accomplished. It's not something I could have ever foreseen and I certainly didn't know what to expect--" Naomi stopped speaking, mid-thought.

"What is it?" Evie asked.

"It's just that sometimes you think you have a clear understanding of what your future will hold and then something so unexpected happens and everything you thought was important suddenly seems so trivial…"

"What do you mean?"

"I was set on getting my degree and traveling the world, writing adventure articles for a newspaper. It seemed like an exciting life. I had no idea just how sensational working on a farm in the middle of a desert could be. Truly."

"Is that sarcasm I detect in your voice?" Evie teased.

"It just might be, dear friend." Naomi laughed. "But I wouldn't trade the decision I made to join this mission for anything in the world."

"Neither would I, Naomi. Neither would I."

"We should go to sleep now, because tomorrow's sunrise isn't going to wait for us. And once dawn breaks, Judah and Albert will be closer to coming back home. I just wish they were here now," Naomi said.

"Of course, so do I. But the quicker we move ahead with what we need to do, the faster it will seem that time will pass, bringing them back. Go to sleep, Naomi. There's nothing more either of us can do tonight, and we both need the rest."

"Right, as always. Pleasant dreams."

"You, too," Evie said, turning to enter her tent, leaving Naomi alone by the dying light of the campfire.

Naomi lifted her face to the inky black sky. There were stars everywhere and it was still very dark, no trace yet of the dawn across the horizon. All she could do was pick one twinkly light winking at her and send a wish up for the safety of the two soldiers out on the road. She imagined that Judah was looking at the constellations at the same time that she was and felt some comfort at the thought. With a sigh, she turned toward her tent and prayed for a few hours of dreamless sleep.

Twenty-Eight

JUDAH WOKE WITH A START, disoriented for a moment. He was in the middle of an orange grove, the white blossoms fragrant with the promise of fruit, and for the briefest moment he couldn't figure out exactly what he was doing there. Then he remembered. The mission, with Albert. He looked around and found the younger man, eyes closed, head resting on his pack, softly breathing under the shade of a tree. The sun was beginning to set and it was almost time to rise and finish the journey that would take them back to the kibbutz.

He heard a donkey bray. He sat up quickly and looked around. It would be terrible to be captured now, so close to home. His trained eye sensed no movement other than their own pack animals, tied to one of the nearby trees. Sighing a breath of relief, he stood up and stretched his arms overhead. It was comforting to know that by the end of the approaching night he'd be in his cot next to Naomi. He wouldn't miss sleeping on the ground, nor would he mind not having to watch each and every footfall for a potential mine. It was grueling, mind-bending work, and he was glad to be almost done with it.

He and Albert had done a thorough scan of the area where they had stopped at daybreak before they allowed themselves to sleep, hidden among the trees in this grove. Confident of their safety while they rested, Judah knew that they needed to leave now if they had any hope of covering the distance to Rehovot before the next day dawned. He knelt in front of the younger man, placing a firm hand on Albert's shoulder, gently shaking him awake.

"Time to go," was all Judah had to say.

Albert grunted in understanding and gathered himself for a brief moment before standing.

"I'll get the donkeys untied and meet you back on the path," Judah said.

Albert nodded back and stepped around to the other side of the tree to quickly relieve himself before the arduous journey home. When he was finished, he carefully stepped onto the path to join Judah.

The donkeys moved a bit faster now, the heavy leather bags emptied of the precious bullets that they'd delivered to the courier on the outskirts of Jerusalem the night before. Judah was impressed with Albert's deep knowledge of the narrow paths and hidden roads that they traveled. He could not have imagined finding his own way to see this trip through without Albert as his guide. He had been right about the boy he'd met all those years ago. He was smart, he was bold, he was intuitive.

"You've truly mastered your job, Albert," he commented.

"*Merci,* Judah. Coming from you, those words mean so much to me."

"Have you given any thought to what you'd like to do after this war is done? Have you and Evie discussed it at all?"

"Ah, yes. We haven't agreed, but we've talked about it," he said with a smile.

"Do you have different goals in mind?" Judah asked.

"Well, yes. She'd like us to be involved in government, to have a further say in the future direction of this country. I'd be content farming for the rest of my life. I've had enough danger and intrigue to last me. I want our daughter to grow up with peace around her."

"For that to happen, Albert, you both may need to step into government roles. We need to have level heads, like yours and

Evie's, planning our policies and making solid decisions for our people."

Judah watched as Albert thought about what he'd just said and could tell that his companion was carefully crafting an answer before speaking.

"When I came here with you, Judah, my pockets were empty. I owe you a debt that I can hardly repay. You saved my life that night in the tavern in Prague. I left nothing behind and it is my wish to do all I can to contribute to this country, my adopted homeland, to put down roots and raise a family. But our people must eat, right? I can grow the food that supplies them with sustenance, no?"

"We have farmers, Albert. We need minds like yours to help mold this nation, with common sense laws and policies. Your passion for farming aside, don't you think our country would be better served if you sat in a position where you could make a larger, more positive impact for all?"

"You flatter me, Judah. I have no real education for something like that. Not like Evie. She's the one who you should talk to. She would give you the response you are looking for."

Just then one of the donkeys began to wander down an offshoot of the path. "I'll go get him. Keep going. I'll catch up."

Judah nodded, keeping an eye on the path before him, making sure the rest of the animals didn't stray. He saw the shiny object in front of him just a second too late, and was unable to stop the forward motion of his foot, left with the undeniable knowledge of what was to happen next. He thought of how distraught Naomi would be when she heard of the explosion. Then, after the flash, he thought of nothing at all.

. . .

Out of the corner of his eye, Albert saw the bright light before he heard the explosion. He turned to witness the gruesome scene, at first not believing what he knew to be true. Judah was gone.

Nevertheless, he pulled the lone donkey he'd gone after to the crater-sized hole in the ground that was still smoking from the explosion. He got on his hands and knees looking for something that would possibly prove that his mentor had not been on this spot but had run ahead before the worst could happen from treading on the lone landmine that blocked their way home. But instead, he found undeniable proof of the disaster that surrounded him. Scraps of fabric, bits of leather, and bloody remains were everywhere. The smell of burned hair was heavy and thick in the air. It was all Albert could do to keep the bile from rising from his throat. Tears burned as they poured from his eyes. He struggled to form a thought, to figure out what to do next as the night sky seemed to close in around him. He sat for longer than he knew he should, next to the hole in the ground, next to the place where one of the greatest men he had ever known was now one with the earth, indistinguishable from the land where he had been born.

Sometime later, Albert stood up. He had been trained on what to do if such a calamity occurred and those lessons pushed him forward. He had to return to Rehovot, to his wife, to his young daughter. He had to tell the story of Judah's bravery and the last trip with the mighty bullets that would make them all free. And he would have to tell Naomi. But it was time to go. He grabbed on to the lone surviving donkey, the one he'd gone off the trail to retrieve, and began to walk, trying his best to avoid the same fate as his friend. As he went, he kept his eyes to the ground, scanning for the mine that would kill him as well. Then, about one hundred meters from the explosion, he saw something shiny beside a cluster of rocks on the path. It would be odd for Al-Jawrashi's men to plant a mine so far off the main road, so he slowly and carefully stepped closer to get a better look. Judah's dog tag! The two halves had remained intact and had been blown far away from their owner. He picked them up, put the separate halves together, tucked the small metal pieces in his clenched fist, and made himself a solemn vow. He would find a way to soften this blow for not only Naomi, but for everyone else on the kibbutz. He would do good work for the rest of his life, take a noble path in Judah's memory. But he would never forget the evil he'd encountered: Hitler and his Nazi army, Al-Jawrashi and his trail of terror. He would make it his mission to continue to fight for as long as he had breath in his body, so help him. He would remain a soldier for as long as the army would have him. He'd let nothing get in his way of keeping his country safe. He put one foot slowly in front of the other, all the way back to the path, and began the walk home.

IT WAS WELL past dawn when Albert finally rounded the last turn before the entrance of the kibbutz. Feeling relief at the sight of that safe haven, he rested for a moment, gathering his thoughts, knowing that the news he carried would be met with both sorrow and anger. He had made it back alone and alive and the guilt he felt was starting to creep in. He'd been saved three times now. Once in Paris, once in Prague, and once on a lonely dark road in this forsaken desert. Why him, why was he so lucky when so many others were not? There had to be meaning and purpose in it, of that he was certain. He could only hope that one day he'd know what it was. With a large gulp of air to fill his weary body, he pushed forward. It was later than his usual arrival time and the camp was at work. He knew that he had a brief reprieve, that Evie and Naomi were underground, that the farmers were in the fields, the bakers baking, and the laundry attendants busy with the loads of dirty clothing the kibbutz members left for them daily. He returned the donkey to the stable himself, not wanting to explain to anyone why only one animal came back alive, and then quickly ran to shower off the dirt and blood that he had carried back on his own garments. When he was done and in a clean shirt and pair of pants, he went off in search of Ari. He wanted to tell him first; it seemed like the right thing to do. But as he stood with a hand on the door of the dining hall, he felt that the news he carried was so hard to share that he would not be able to find the right words to do so. He thought it through in French, then translated it over and over again in his brain. *Judah est meurt. Judah is dead.* He went inside.

Ari was sitting, as usual, at a table in the corner of the room, papers strewn all over the surface in front of him, his cigarette dangling from his fingers, the ash precariously long. When Albert stood there before him, Ari looked up and said, "You're late."

"I know, sir. There was an incident."

"Tell Judah to come and fill me in."

"Sir… He… He…" Albert hesitated for a moment then blurted out, "Judah is dead."

Albert saw Ari's eyes widen. The other man rose from his seat. "What? What do you mean, he's dead?"

"There was a land mine. It happened so quickly, I was sent to get the donkey and…"

"And you are certain that he didn't escape off the path in time?"

Albert put a hand in his pocket and pulled out the dog tag.

Holding it in his upturned palm, he responded, "Yes, sir. I am sorry to report that I am sure." Then he closed his hand and returned the metal pieces to his pocket.

"Oh, Albert. This is terrible news," Ari said, as he placed his hands over his eyes.

For a moment, Albert was concerned that he would see the older man cry. He did not. Instead, Ari asked, "Who else knows?"

"No one, sir."

"Okay. Let me think a moment." He sat back down. After a few silent seconds, he said, "We need to tell Evie and Naomi first. I think that would be the right thing to do. Come with me."

Albert waited for Ari to put his papers away and then followed him from the dining hall to the laundry building. It was an hour until the lunch bell was set to ring. They sat on the bench together in the shade, and Ari asked him to recount exactly what happened to Judah as they made their way home. Albert did his best to give a detailed report, however, he left out the most gruesome aspects: the smell, the bits, the pieces. He was fated to remember them; he didn't feel he had to share those.

Once he was finished, he turned to Ari. "Judah was the bravest man I have ever known. I will work hard to honor his memory for the rest of my life."

Ari nodded. "I know. And I have every confidence that you will succeed, Albert. Judah was very proud of you and your contributions here and so am I."

After that, they sat together in silence until the workers started to come out of the laundry. When Ari saw Evie, he stood up and called out to her. She turned and smiled seeing that Albert was standing there as well.

"Where's Naomi?" Ari asked.

"She should be up in a minute, why?" Evie asked, as she went over to Albert and put her arms around him in an embrace.

Albert locked eyes with Ari and the older man nodded. He held Evie tightly and whispered in her ear. She stepped back, put her hand over her mouth, and began to cry.

"Please, Evie. We need to be strong for Naomi," Ari said.

Albert moved close to his wife and wiped the tears from her cheeks. "We will all cry together. For now, let Ari talk to Naomi. Then we'll deal with whatever comes next."

When Naomi stepped into the sunshine of the afternoon, she smiled. The first thing she said to the three of them was, "So glad you're back, Albert! Where's Judah?"

Ari moved to her side, guiding her over to the bench and sitting her down. "Naomi. There was an accident. Judah..."

"Is he in the infirmary?" She attempted to stand, but Ari kept his hand on her arm, keeping her in place. She said urgently, "We need to go there. I must see him."

"No, Naomi, no." Ari drew in a breath. "He's gone."

"Gone? Gone where?" she asked before the true meaning of Ari's words sank in and she finally understood.

Evie rushed to her side, tears now freely flowing down her face, wetting her shirt. "Naomi. We are all are here for you. Whatever you need."

Naomi said nothing, just sat, perfectly still, on the bench.

Albert knelt down next to Evie. Reaching into his pocket, he gently lifted the dog tag out, opened Naomi's tightly clenched fist, and put it in her hand before reclosing her fingers around them. She didn't look at them at all or make any move to stand. She just sat, staring out at the horizon, as if she didn't believe a word of it, as if at any moment Judah would come walking around the corner and back into all of their lives.

"Naomi," Evie gently prodded. "Let's go see Dr. Weissbaum. He can give you something for your nerves."

Naomi just nodded, but made no effort to stand up.

Albert looked at Ari, and the two men helped the woman to her feet. Then each linked an arm through one of hers and they all made their way over to the infirmary. Once there, they told the doctor what had happened and he took Naomi over to a more private, partitioned off space to treat her. Evie stayed by her friend's side.

Ari turned to Albert. "Word will spread throughout the kibbutz quickly. We'll need to figure out what sort of memorial we want to have for Judah. I'd appreciate your thoughts. You were the last one of us to be with him while he was still alive."

"My thoughts?"

"Yes. What do you think we should do?"

Albert was stunned to be asked such a thing. He was good at taking orders but unaccustomed to being asked his opinion about other matters.

"All we can ever do. Say the traditional prayer of mourning. Remember him in our hearts. Continue to do our best work every day in his memory."

Ari put one hand on the younger man's shoulder. "Of course. We'll have the camp gather before dinner tonight and we'll say the mourner's prayer together."

"And after that, Ari, Judah would tell us to go back and finish what we started here."

"Yes, Albert. Yes, he would."

ALBERT FELT as if for the rest of the day he moved around in a fog. He knew that he should try to get some sleep as he always did after a mission, but realized that it would be fruitless to try.

Instead, he sat and thought about his moments with Judah: meeting in the tavern in Prague, all those months gathering goods in Haifa before coming to the kibbutz, learning how to be a soldier, to properly execute a mission, hours of practicing the proper way to fire a gun and care for the weapon. All of Albert's training, every lesson and each new task, had been taught to him by his mentor. Judah, Albert realized, had stepped into the role of his father. Judah had known before Albert allowed himself to accept the truth: his own father was long gone. Judah had tried to compensate for that cruel fact by teaching him everything he himself knew, things that Albert would need to know to stay safe as a soldier in this war. By understanding the risks, Judah had done his best to guarantee Albert a future.

So now it was certain. Albert knew that he had an enormous responsibility. The question remained–what would he do to make good on the promise that he'd repay this debt to Judah.? He owed him his life and more. He'd need an excellent and comprehensive plan. He put his head down and got to work.

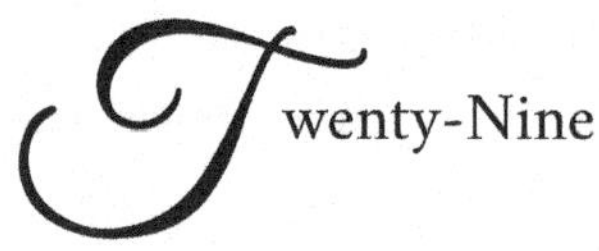

Twenty-Nine

Rehovot
May 14, 1948

NAOMI COULD HEAR the joyful sounds coming from the others outside of her tent. There was music playing and she was sure that the members of the camp were dancing as well. Independence had been declared; the state of Israel had been recognized as a free nation, a homeland for Jews everywhere. Their mission at the factory had been deemed a success. But she had no desire to join her campmates in celebration. Since Judah's death the month before, she'd only come out of her tent to go to work. She took little bits of food back with her, not wanting to talk to anyone, to interact at all. She remained devastated at the thought that he would not be a part of her future.

As she sat motionless on a chair and listened to the chatter on the other side of the thin canvas of her tent, Naomi thought about what she would do next. So much had changed. The dream she had once had was no longer possible and she knew that she had to alter her plans.

"Naomi," she heard Evie's voice call out to her. "Naomi. Are you in there? May I join you?"

Hanging her head for a moment, Naomi wanted to tell her friend to just leave her be, to let her wallow in her sorrow for a bit longer. But she knew Evie would not go away, so she rose and walked over to the flap of the tent and drew it open. The bright sunshine of the afternoon startled her.

"Come outside, Naomi. Join the living. Please."

Deborah was standing at her mother's side, a rapidly melting ice cream pop in her hand. When she saw Naomi, the child smiled, and it was all Naomi could do not to smile back. She stepped into the light.

"Thank you for coming by, Evie, but I'm not really up for a big party. I just can't face it.

"Then just come and eat dinner with us. Albert and I miss you."

"I don't know, Evie. I don't think I can."

"Well then, come with me to the bathhouse so I can wash this little one before her bedtime. She's been out much of the day playing with the other children and Ari saw fit to give them all a treat tonight. Hers is melting everywhere! What a mess!"

Naomi looked down at her goddaughter and smiled for the first time in what felt like forever. "Okay. But just to the bathhouse."

"Good!" Evie exclaimed, taking her daughter's free hand. "Let's be off, then."

They walked slowly as Deborah tried to finish her dessert before it melted away. Once at the bathhouse, Evie picked the little girl up and held her aloft. "Can you strip her down, please? She's covered in ice cream."

"Of course." Naomi quickly removed the child's shoes and socks before unbuttoning the back of her dress, leaving her dangling in her mother's arms clad in only her diaper.

"Thanks." Evie efficiently ran the water in a large sink, added some bath soap and then after unpinning the diaper, gently placed the naked little girl down in the warm, sudsy water. Content to play with the bubbles, Deborah sat splashing to her own delight.

"Well, we did it, Naomi. We've supplied the bullets to our soldiers and we're going to win this war."

"I suppose so, Evie. I suppose so."

"Naomi, I know that you miss Judah terribly. So do I. But he would not have wanted you to mourn him forever. He would have wanted you to move on, to do more good in this world."

"It's not that easy."

"Nothing worthwhile ever is," Evie responded.

"I don't think you understand," Naomi said. "It's not just that I am alone now. It's that everything I'd dreamed of died with Judah. The life I thought we'd share, the children I thought we might have. All of it, gone in an instant."

Evie turned and placed her wet hands on Naomi's shoulders, leaving two wet spots on Evie's blouse. "I do understand, Naomi. It doesn't alter anything. You need to accept what you can't change and move forward. You still have a future. You have to decide what it will be."

Naomi turned her head to watch Deborah play in the sink, her little hands grabbing for the bubbles in the water. She had no desire to make any decisions, to make a choice on how her next years might unfold. What she wanted, she could not have. Judah was not coming back to her, not even in her dreams. How she longed to see him again, but he had not made an appearance at all, which made her feel even more bereft. She thought of him constantly and prayed that in his last moments he felt no pain. She struggled with the whole thought that they could not even bury him, that his body was torn from her in the explosion of that rogue land mine as he made his way back to her.

"Naomi, it's time. Rejoin the living. Judah would have wanted that for you."

"I know he would, Evie. I'm just not ready."

"There's a very special dinner planned for tonight. Please come along, if only for a short while. We'll put Deborah to bed and go find Albert. You need to eat a real meal, Naomi. You're wasting away."

"I'm truly not hungry."

"Yes, but you need to eat. You'll get weak and then sick. We simply can't have that."

Naomi felt herself almost smile at her friend's British formality. "Okay, Evie, but only for a brief time. And I won't promise to eat. I don't find the thought appealing at all."

"Well then, we'll just have to see if there isn't anything that might tempt you. It's sure to be a grand feast." Evie turned her attention back to Deborah. "But we can't go until this little one is clean. I'll get to work."

Naomi watched as her friend poured some sudsy water over her daughter's head to wash her curls, then rinsed the soap away. "Would you pull that towel out from my bag please?" Evie asked.

Naomi did as she was asked and Evie deposited the dripping wet child into her arms. She felt solid and warm and the baby made Naomi feel grounded to the earth for the first time in days. She drew Deborah in close and gave her a tight hug. "I love you, little one," she whispered into the shell of the little girl's ear before handing her back over to her mother. Then to Evie she said, "I'm going to put on a dry dress. I'll meet you outside the dining hall in an hour?"

Evie smiled broadly. "That's perfect. I'll be there."

Naomi bent over and placed a kiss on Deborah's head and then left to go change her clothing. Once in her tent, she nearly backed out of Evie's invitation, but was sure that her friend would not take no for an answer tonight. This special dinner was the culmination of all of their hard work and even if she only made the briefest of appearances, it would be enough to quell Evie's insistence that she attend. Running a brush through her hair, she caught a glimpse of herself in the mirror on her desk. She had dark circles under her eyes and her face looked gaunt. She turned the mirror over so she didn't have to face the truth of what she saw there. Judah might be dead, but she was the ghost.

LAMB WAS BEING GRILLED outside of the dining hall when she arrived. As she waited for Evie and Albert, every member of the camp who passed by stopped to offer a kind word or share a brief story about Judah. Naomi was surprised at how much it helped to hear these things, at how much comfort she took from her coworkers and the farmers who lived on the kibbutz. She hadn't realized just how isolated she'd been for the past month. When her friends appeared they went inside, and Naomi looked around in awe. The room had been decorated with crepe streamers and a white flag that had two blue stripes going across it horizontally, one across the top and the other across the bottom, with the traditional Star of David in the middle. The atmosphere was festive. There were platters of dried fruits and nuts as well as bottles of wine on each table and mouthwatering smells coming from the kitchen. Just as they entered, the bakers arrived with large, warm challahs to be served with hummus and tehina, as well as baba ganoush and beet and vegetable salads. All of a sudden, she felt overwhelmingly sad that Judah was not there to see it all. He would have loved this celebration.

"Come, Naomi. Let's go sit with Ari," Evie said, bringing her back into the moment and steering her over to their familiar table.

"Naomi!" Ari stood and called her name. "I'm so happy you decided to join us. It's a momentous night!"

She nodded wordlessly.

"Any truth to the rumor that the new government will adopt that flag as the nation's symbol for the world to see?" Albert asked, pointing the one hanging across the room.

"It would be fitting, no?" Ari responded as he poured them each a glass of wine. It's based on the idea of the tallit. And the word 'Maccabee' under the star in the center says everything one needs to know of our people. We will fight on, we will never give up on our freedom."

"No matter the cost, right Ari?" Naomi said softly.

"Ah, Naomi," he said quietly. "We are all broken, we are all missing him. We honor him, though, with what comes next. We will build this nation and we will do it together." He raised his glass. "To our missing comrade, Judah. May his memory be for a blessing, always."

Around the table, all eyes were on Naomi. She knew what she had to do. "Amen," she said as she lifted the glass to her lips and took a sip. The others followed her lead. For the first time in weeks, as the sweet wine coursed through her bloodstream, Naomi felt herself begin to relax. Although Dr. Weissbaum had prescribed her some sedatives when she first went to the infirmary, she never took them. She hadn't wanted to dull the pain of Judah's death. But with her friends, and for tonight, the alcohol did help.

"Ari, what will you do now? Will you live in Jerusalem or Tel Aviv? Or maybe go farther north? Haifa, perhaps?" Albert asked.

Ari twisted the stem of his wine glass between two fingers. "It's not truly up to me. I will wait for my next assignment."

"So you'll continue to work in the government?" Evie asked, leaning in, waiting anxiously for his answer.

"Yes. I hope all of you will, too," Ari replied.

"That's music to my wife's ears," Albert said with a smile. "Right, *ma chèrie*?"

"It is where I'd like to dedicate my time. I think I'd be good at working through the new laws and regulations for this country, but I'd take any assignment. I'm ready to work."

"And you, Albert. What will you do?"

"I'll follow my wife. I had thought about farming, but more recently, well, let's just say that now I'd like to learn more about land mines and bombs. I'll leave it at that."

"Hmm," Ari said, nodding his head. "The military will find good use for a man with your skills."

Naomi listened to the conversation around her, willing them not to ask her of her future plans. They were newly formed and she realized just how unpopular they would be. Thankfully, she was spared, as just at that moment, dinner was served.

LATER THAT NIGHT, once she was back in her tent, Naomi began to pack. She'd quietly made arrangements to sail back to New York on a ship that would depart from of the port of Haifa in a week's time. It hadn't been an easy decision to make, but once she'd settled on it she knew it was the right choice for her. At dinner, she heard many of her coworkers talk about moving to a new kibbutz now that the one at Rehovot was to close. After all, they were never really there to farm the land; this camp had served its greater purpose and could now be shut down. Whether or not the truth about the factory would ever come to light was not really Naomi's concern. She would never speak of it to anyone, she knew that. Ari made it clear after dinner that the secret of the bullet-making and all the documents that went along with it would be permanently sealed for the foreseeable future.

She didn't have much to take back with her, just a few mementos of her time on the kibbutz. Her most precious possession, Judah's dog tag, was worn on the piece of fabric he'd fashioned for her around her neck. She could feel the metal resting between her breasts and knew that she would always carry his memory close to her heart. Leaving out the clothing she'd need for the time she had left here, she closed the suitcase and began to ready herself for bed. Naomi had planned to tell Evie tonight that she was to return to the States, but the festivities and good cheer during the evening made it difficult for her to bring up the topic. She would do it in the morning instead. She undressed and slipped into her night-gown, pulled back the blanket on her cot and folded her body into it, all the while craving the darkness that would shroud the tent once she turned off the gas lantern, which sat on the table at the side of her bed. She held on tightly to Judah's pillow, breathing in deep, rhythmic breaths, as if she could conjure him with each inhale. Only then, when no further tears fell and reality flooded in, when she knew for certain that he was no longer there, she finally was able to force herself into a dream-less sleep.

EXACTLY ONE WEEK LATER, Naomi and Evie stood at the foot of the stairs that led up to the ship that would take Naomi home. The friends had made the trip to Haifa together, with Evie claiming that she could use a break from the bustle of packing up at Rehovot. Albert was watching Deborah, and the two women had given themselves a little time together before Naomi was to sail.

"It was wonderful of you to escort me here, Evie. I loved spending the time alone with you. And at least this trip off of the kibbutz did not involve any smuggling or espionage!"

"Yes. It was lovely to window shop and eat dinner in a real café again. But I still can't believe that you're going."

"I think it's best. I will go back to my original plan, to travel and write about what I see. I feel as though it will keep me busy, keep my thoughts on new challenges."

"You can always come back here. Work with us. This will always be your home, too."

"I know that now, Evie. And how I will miss you, my friend." She drew the other woman into a long hug. "We've lived a thousand lives together already. You'll go on to greatness here. I am sure of it."

"Let's just hope that Albert can keep up!" Evie teased, as they stepped back from the embrace.

"You'll keep him on his toes. Please, bring back a kiss for him and one for Deborah as well."

Just then the ship's horn sounded a warning. All departing passengers were to be on board.

"That's my cue. I'll write as soon as I'm back in New York," Naomi promised, holding back her tears.

"You better," Evie ordered, her own tears freely running down her face. "Until we meet again, Naomi. Now go!"

At her friend's parting words, Naomi turned and climbed the ship's steps. She did not look back. There was no need. Her work here was done and there was no longer any reason to stay. With a deep breath, she went inside to find her stateroom and to find the strength to begin again.

Thirty

PARIS

June 1968

ALBERT TOOK his daughter's arm and crossed through the Cimètiere du Père Lachaise in the 11th arrondissement of the city where he'd been born.

"Remember what I told you, *chèrie*? About the last day I was in this place?"

"Of course I do, Papa. How you saw your own father rounded up by the Nazi soldiers, how you made your escape and came to Israel with my godfather Judah. I remember it all."

"Yes, I know you do. It's so important that you tell your own children about it someday."

"Papa, please! I just finished my army service. Let me get through university before I get married and have children."

"You know that your mother would be so proud of you, had she lived…"

Albert remembered that he had held his breath the entire time his daughter fought in the six day war, just the year before. He recognized that his small part of history, transporting bullets from the factory in Rehovot with Evie, Naomi, and Judah had led his country here, to fight and be victorious once more.

They walked in companionable silence for a bit, each lost in their own thoughts. They'd lost Evie the year before to a long fight with cancer. Albert missed her every single day but was so pleased to be with their daughter on this long awaited trip. A stop in Paris to see his old home for the first time in all the years since he'd fled from there, and then they would go to London for a visit with Deborah's grandmother. Evie's father had passed away when Deborah was a baby, not long after Israel's war of independence had ended, but her mother remained in her beloved town house in a very fashionable section of the city. To make the trip even better, Naomi had offered to meet them in England, having just completed a two-part interview with the British Prime Minister for *Newsweek* magazine. Albert could not wait to see their old friend.

After a bit he picked up the conversation. "So you see, Deborah, I had just come around this corner when I saw the soldiers." He stopped short. As they made the last turn onto his old street, he was overcome with emotion. There, mostly unchanged, were the large wooden doors that led to where he lived with his parents all those years ago. He could hardly believe it.

"Papa, is everything alright?"

Albert collected himself. "Yes, I just didn't expect it all to look the same, I suppose. I thought that the Nazis would have destroyed it, that I'd come back to find it all different."

"Do you want to get a closer look?" his daughter asked.

"Yes," he replied. "I think that I do."

They walked up to the doors and pushed them open. The familiar scent of lavender hung in the air, stripping away the years since he'd been gone. On the other side of the doors was a courtyard, a series of houses flanking both sides. Albert found his way to the entrance to his childhood home. To the left of it was a graceful Linden tree. He reached out and touched the bark.

"My father planted this tree. I'm sure of it. It was just a sapling when I saw it last, but look at it now!" Albert said with some amount of pride.

"And it survived the war, Papa! That's remarkable."

He looked at Deborah's sweet face and said, "Some things are meant to withstand man's evil."

"Do you want to see if anyone is home? Do you want to try and go inside, see your old house?"

Albert thought for a brief moment. Then he shook his head. "No. I think not. This was my home once, but not anymore. I think perhaps we'll go sit at a café for a while, have a nice glass of wine instead. What do you say?"

"I say, *oui, s'il vous plait.*"

She laughed, and in that instant, Albert could have sworn that he felt Evie's presence there with them both. "In that case, *allez!* Let's go."

TWO DAYS later they met Naomi in the lobby of their hotel in London. She was dressed elegantly in an emerald green wool skirt and white silk blouse, her red hair now streaked with grey and swept up in a graceful chignon. Despite the years that had come between them, Albert still held a deep affection for his wife's best friend. She had time tonight, before her flight to Morocco the next morning, and they had been enjoying each other's company and the chance to catch up.

"You know, Aunt Naomi. Israel is not so far from where you are headed. Why not stop on the way back to the United States? We'd love to have you come stay. Dad would enjoy the company and I know you won't believe what our little country looks like now. You won't recognize it!" Deborah said.

"I'm sure that you're right, sweetheart. But after Morocco

I'm due in India. I'm writing an entire series on the trend toward meditation as a way to control stress. I hear it's highly effective."

"Well, will you ever come visit us? Another time then?"

Albert glanced over at Naomi. He knew what her answer would be. It hadn't changed since the day she stepped foot on the ship that carried her away from them twenty years before.

"You know what, Deborah? I think that maybe it's time for us to return for another visit to the United States. We all had fun the last trip. Remember going to the Statue of Liberty?"

"Don't change the subject, Papa." Turning back to Naomi she said, "My mother told me once that your memories make it difficult for you to come to Tel Aviv. Just know that you are always welcome."

Naomi smiled at the young woman. "I appreciate that dear. I will keep that in mind. Now, for you." She pulled a brightly wrapped package out of her bag.

"What is it?" Deborah asked, a wide smile on her face.

"A university student needs a fine writing implement for her studies, don't you think?"

Albert watched as his daughter carefully unwrapped her gift. He was so proud of the woman he and Evie had raised. She was a strong-willed feminist, just like her mother.

Deborah opened the box to find a sterling silver pen with her initials engraved on its surface. "Aunt Naomi, it's beautiful. Thank you so much."

"You'll do great things in the future, Deborah. With the memory your mother as your role model, I just know you will. Look at all she accomplished, rising to the ranks of government leadership! Now, you need to study, and study hard. Perhaps you'll consider spending some of your college years in New York City? Lots of good schools there!"

"I think I'll stick with Tel Aviv University for now," Deborah said. "Besides, if I leave Papa alone for too long, who knows what he'll concoct in his workshop. He's always out there tinkering around with one thing or another."

"Well, all those years building better bombs for the Israeli army have most certainly refined his skills. What are you working on now, Albert?" Deborah asked.

"Nothing of consequence anymore. I'm retired from service, remember?"

"And I'm happy to hear it! No more war, please!" Naomi glanced down at the gold watch on her wrist. "I must go. But we'll meet again. I promise."

Albert stood and reached over to kiss his old friend on each cheek. "I'll hold you to that, Naomi."

Deborah jumped up and hugged the older woman. "See you soon, Aunt Naomi. Safe travels."

"For you both as well," she replied. And then she was gone.

"Now, Deborah. You have a date with your grandmother and I have theater tickets, so let's be off. I'll drop you by the house and we'll meet back right here at the hotel, later tonight?"

"Yes, Papa. But are you sure you don't want to have dinner with us?"

"*Non, mon chèrie*. You spend some time with your grandma alone. She loves to have you all for herself and I have been looking forward to this performance."

"As you wish, Papa."

They went outside and he hailed a taxi. Albert dropped his daughter off at Evie's mother's home and directed the driver to take him deeper into the city, but not to the theater district. He had one final mission to complete.

. . .

He had the cab leave him in a residential neighborhood. The homes were not lavish. They were just the opposite: quite ordinary. A person could blend in here easily, and if one lived a quiet life, no one would ever suspect a thing. Albert had it on good authority through back channels of Israeli intelligence that Al Jawrashi lived here. He had reviewed the reports, become acquainted with the killer's routine. Al Jawrashi had assumed a different identity years ago when he made a life for himself in London, but through his contacts in the Israeli intelligence community, Albert confirmed it was him. He waited long enough to see their old adversary return from work, park his car on the street and enter his home. Once inside, the devil stood in the light of his front room and Albert had a clear sight of the man for the first time ever. When he and Judah worked during the war effort, Al Jawrashi was just a shadowy figure, no true photos had ever surfaced. Since then, the Mossad had done an excellent job of tracking these villains who had done such destruction during the war, slowly bringing to justice each and every one. Now, standing across the street, Albert was sure this was the man for whom he'd hunted for what seemed like his entire lifetime. And it was finally time for this evil man to meet his fate.

From the pocket of his coat, he pulled out a small package wrapped in plain brown paper. Inside was an explosive device. It was spare and would do the job he needed done. He quietly walked across the street, checking right and then left to be sure he was not seen. He got to work, quickly setting a switch, then ringing the bell. He put the package down on the mat and disappeared quickly back across the street behind a thick set of bushes. When the door opened and Al Jawrashi bent down to pick up the package left on his doorstep, Albert depressed the remote button in his hand. There was a very bright light, a loud boom, and then nothing. Albert turned on his heel and quickly left the scene as within seconds, he heard the loud whining sound of police sirens in the distance. Satisfied that his debt to his old friend was paid, he went off to his hotel to raise a glass to all those he'd lost. Then, he'd meet his daughter as planned, knowing that he'd made the world a better place just by having lived in it.

NAOMI'S TRIP to Morocco had been delayed by the news that the terrorist, Al Jawrashi, had been killed in front of his home by a bomb left on his doorstep. Her editor asked that she stay on in London to cover the story, which she did, never letting on that she was sure she knew the perpetrator. The trip that brought Albert and Deborah to England at this precise moment wasn't a coincidence. Her years of working in the secret factory alongside Evie, Albert, Ari, and Judah had made her keenly aware that promises made were promises kept. Albert owed one final debt to Judah and he was always going to find a way to repay it.

As soon as she'd heard of the bombing, deep down she knew the truth. Albert had both the expertise and the motivation to complete this one, final mission. It had to have been his work left on that evil man's doorstep, a final salute to his friend and mentor, Judah.

Judah. He'd been the love of her life. Everything she'd done since leaving Rehovot, rising from her grief to fulfill her destiny as a journalist was for him, in his memory. He'd been gone for so long now and yet she still missed him terribly and would always feel his absence, but that pushed her forward, allowing her to achieve the well-deserved recognition in her chosen profession that she knew would make him proud.

There had been men, of course, but she'd never married or had children. Instead, she had dedicated her life to truth-telling. After years of keeping an important war secret, she wanted to find a way to tell impactful stories, and she traveled the world in search of them. Naomi had one hard and fast rule, though. The one place she vowed never to return to was Israel. The memories that lay buried there were just too painful to confront.

Naomi sat in a conference at Interpol headquarters and listened carefully as the press secretary reported that there were no known suspects in the killing of Al Jawrashi. Whoever left the bomb had to have been a munitions expert and had left no trace of himself behind. Quietly, Naomi let out a sigh of relief. She wanted her friend to be safe, for him to travel home to Tel Aviv with her goddaughter and disappear back into the landscape of that bustling city. Over the years she'd observed how much more modern it had become as she followed the stories and photos other journalists had posted in newspapers and magazines. She was proud of the people who had made that happen. The country was thriving and in her heart she would always carry the knowledge of her place in the history of its birth.

The conference ended and Naomi gathered her things, checking her watch, noting it was time for her to go to the airport. She took a moment to close her eyes briefly and say a silent prayer for the dead, Judah among them. She instinctively checked to be sure her necklace still sat tightly clasped around her neck. She'd replaced the frayed ribbon years before with a solid gold chain, but the dog tag remained, tucked between her breasts. She would never ever forget him. She would honor him always.

When Naomi opened her eyes, she watched her colleagues bustling out of the room, hurrying off to their next assignment. She pushed herself to stand. She had more stories to tell, and now, she was off to find yet another adventure.

ACKNOWLEDGMENTS

It takes a village.

Writing an historical saga was a challenge, but this is a personal and true story that I wanted to put out into the world for a variety of reasons. The seed of this story was planted in my brain in June of 2016, when I attended the wedding of a dear friend's daughter on a kibbutz outside of Tel Aviv. I had been to Israel many times prior to that trip, but had never had the opportunity to visit the Ayalon Institute in Rehovot before. It was there, at the wonderful museum on the site of the actual bullet factory, where I saw the machines that the young recruits used to produce the ammunition needed to win the War of Independence in 1948. If you have a chance to visit this incredible place, don't miss it. It's truly something to see.

I read and researched a large number of sources, all invaluable in my desire to get the facts of this heroic effort correct. The small book published by the museum, "The Ayalon Institute,

Kibbutzim Hill-Rehovot" by Eli Sa'adi, not only told the story of these volunteers, but captured the time with amazing photographs. "Letters from Jerusalem, 1947-1948" by Zipporah Porath, helped me conjure up what it was like for an American student to have lived through this time abroad. "Israel, A Concise History of a Nation Reborn" by Daniel Gordis put this complicated era into focus as did "Lioness, Golda Meir and the Nation of Israel" by Francine Klagsbrun. Newspaper articles and journals from the time filled in many details of life in the Middle East during that era.

More importantly, my dear friend Danny Feinstein shared his love of Israel with both me and my husband. We traveled there multiple times together with him and his wife, Meryll. It was their daughter whose wedding brought us to the museum that fateful afternoon. Danny sadly passed away before this novel was completed, but I am sure that he's cheering me on from above, as is my father, a Holocaust survivor who made me promise to never forget those who lost their lives during the atrocities of WWII. I haven't, and I hope that I've honored their memories with this novel.

To my writer's group: Ellen, Helen, Joan and Niki, who listened to the early drafts of this story and offered both invaluable support and critiques — I owe you all a debt that I can never repay. And to Niki, who edited this book within an inch of its life, thank you, thank you, thank you.

This novel has my heart at its core and took over four years for me to finish, but my cheerleading section at home never let me down. My husband Ken was my source of encouragement from word one. I know how lucky I am to have him in my corner.

My sons know my dad's story; now it's up to them to tell it to their own children someday.

Finally, while my characters are fictional, this book is based on true historical events. Any missteps or errors are purely my own.

ABOUT THE AUTHOR

Hilari T. Cohen is an award-winning editor who has worked and consulted in the publishing field for over twenty-five years. She built brands for Berkley, Harlequin and Zebra Books as well as edited many New York Times bestselling authors and titles in both fiction and nonfiction categories. However, she always harbored a secret ambition to write a novel of her own, and she did, successfully publishing *The Lyric of Memory, Adjusting the Rear View, Perfectly Polite* and the romance series, *The Gypsy Moth Chronicles.* She lives in suburban New York with her husband, loves to bake, drink red wine and read voraciously when she's not writing!

Photo by Leslie Magid Higgins

facebook.com/HilariCohenAuthor
twitter.com/hilaricohen
instagram.com/hilaricohenauthor

ALSO BY HILARI T. COHEN

The Lyric of Memory

Adjusting the Rear View

The Gypsy Moth Chronicle Series:

June

July

August

September

October

Quarantined By Love, a novella

Perfectly Polite

Find me on Amazon: https://www.amazon.com/Hilari-T-Cohen/e/B01CO92M4G/ref=dp_byline_cont_pop_ebooks_1